Praise for Bud

Accidental Pro

"To an age where Russian agents are now household names and dystopia is just a click away, comes a revelatory novel that seizes the reader's attention like the final stroke of the doomsday clock...The writing is masterful and sagacious from first to last."—Kyle Thomas Smith, author of *85A* and *Cockloft: Scenes From a Gay Marriage*

Somewhere Over Lorain Road

"Five stars. Highly recommended!"—*Gay Book Reviews*

"I was absolutely enthralled with the story from the opening paragraph until the final moments. Moving, gripping, and unforgettable."—*The Novel Approach Reviews*

"While the chapters in the present kept me riveted to the unfolding mystery, the chapters in the past damn near broke my heart. The writing is impeccable and the plot enthralling." —*Love Bytes Reviews*

"Every once in a while, a book comes along that grabs me in the first paragraph and does not let go even when I have finished reading it. I was totally mesmerized."—*Reviews by Amos Lassen*

"This book, with its tight narration and unexpected turn of events, kept me glued to its pages until the very last one. It's riveting—a page-turner, and masterfully written."—*My Fiction Nook*

By the Author

Butterfly Dream (co-written with Dave Lara)

Elf Gift

Somewhere Over Lorain Road

Accidental Prophet

Inherit the Lightning

INHERIT THE LIGHTNING

by

Bud Gundy

2022

INHERIT THE LIGHTNING

ISBN 13: 978-1-63679-199-9

THIS TRADE PAPERBACK ORIGINAL IS PUBLISHED BY
BOLD STROKES BOOKS, INC.
P.O. BOX 249
VALLEY FALLS, NY 12185

FIRST EDITION: MAY 2022

CREDITS
EDITORS: JERRY L. WHEELER AND STACIA SEAMAN
PRODUCTION DESIGN: STACIA SEAMAN
COVER DESIGN BY TAMMY SEIDICK

Acknowledgments

Thanks to everyone who made suggestions, edits, and offered advice, especially Scott Boswell, Barbara Brunetti, Christopher Calix, Shoshana Dembitz, Susan Domingos, Elaine Eichman, Pat Elmore, Laura Grodek, Gabriel Lampert, Tyler Patton, and Clint Seiter. I'm also grateful for the talented editor Jerry L. Wheeler, who was crucial in helping me iron out some very difficult scenes, and whose precision is amazing. And thanks again to the team at Bold Strokes Books for their dedication to publishing stories the world needs to hear.

Once more, for Chris

PROLOGUE

Collinwood, Ohio
March 4, 1908

Ingrid would always remember nearing the school that morning and seeing the smudges on the foreheads of the Catholic students. They called it Ash Wednesday, and it had something to do with Easter.

She would also remember how the morning was so cold she wrapped up in a muffler and gloves and ran off without waiting for her sister Maddy, who was one year older and in the fourth grade.

Collinwood's elementary school stood a block away, a stately red brick structure with dormers and a peaked roof. The first class started at nine o'clock and, with five minutes to go, students converged from every direction.

Ingrid passed under the brick arch of the entrance and through the front doors. Inside, the open stairs to the left led down to the basement and the restrooms. Using the stairs to the right, she hopped up to the first floor.

Large classrooms filled the corners, with an open hall in the center. She hung her wraps in the cloakroom and hurried to class, rubbing her arms. Just before she entered, she saw Maddy climbing to the second floor, chattering and laughing with a friend.

Several of Ingrid's classmates had kept their coats on, and their teacher Miss Fiske said with a pretty smile, "I'll allow it just this once, until Mr. Hirter gets the boilers going." She wore a long skirt and lacy blouse, her hair twisted into a swirl.

The first class was grammar, a difficult subject for the many students who spoke European languages at home. Miss Fiske often grew cross.

After a while, a class started singing upstairs. Ingrid glanced at the clock. It was nine thirty, almost time for math. She'd labored over yesterday's homework and was anxious to see her grade.

Bang! Bang! Bang!

The speed of the fire gong implied danger. Muted, fearful cries rippled across the room. Miss Fiske frowned and clapped. "I'll have order, if you please. Line up."

They'd rehearsed how the first row would file out, followed by the others. In the third row, Ingrid stood and waited.

Miss Fiske opened the door and drew back, eyes wide. Black smoked poured inside, rolling across the ceiling with a sharp, chemical smell.

Her voice went high. "Don't be frightened, children, but be brisk about it." She led the first row away. The second row followed but halted when a girl in the main hall shrieked.

Students near the front pushed their way out, the orderly line breaking apart. Others in the fourth row, which was supposed to leave last, bolted for the door, setting off a stampede.

Ingrid plopped back to her seat to let the others rush past. A handful of students remained in the room, sharing terrified looks as caustic smoke curled down the walls. Coughs filled the classroom.

Worried about Maddy, Ingrid rushed to see what was happening as a fearsome tumult erupted outside the door. Terrified, she looked out.

For the rest of her long life, Ingrid would say that no more than ninety seconds passed from hearing the fire gong to seeing the front staircase engulfed in flames. The demon blaze devoured the oiled wood, reaching out with blistering tendrils ravenous for more. Smoke roiled across the ceiling like a hellish upside-down river.

The daylight through the back doors looked like salvation, but Ingrid soon realized one of the vestibule doors had slammed shut, tripping the latch and blocking half the escape route. The stampede funneled to the last open door and overtook a young boy. He staggered and tripped. In seconds, students piled up at the only exit.

Children in the main hall fled to the back, sweeping up stragglers without mercy. They ignored a teacher imploring them to use the fire escape, which they'd never rehearsed. Students from upstairs thundered down.

All three floors converged on the stairs to the blocked vestibule. Delirious with panic, the children slammed into the mass struggling to move forward even an inch. In the crush, they squirmed and flailed, wedging themselves into an immovable tangle. Younger students slipped from view.

"Maddy!" Ingrid screamed.

"To the windows," cried a teacher.

Ingrid started to turn but froze when she saw Miss Fiske descending the back stairs. Her teacher had amazingly found a path through the blockage, a way to lead the children to safety.

A second later, Miss Fiske did something so unbelievable Ingrid wouldn't speak of it for decades. And then she did it again.

The sight transfixed Ingrid until the fire suddenly roared, filling the school with blinding, searing light. She felt her skin tighten and smelled her hair singe. She fell back into the classroom, squinting through the smoke. She glimpsed a boy pushing himself off a window ledge, into daylight.

Someone had slid a table in place to reach the high window. Ingrid scrambled up to the ledge, her legs dangling outside. She gasped with relief at the fresh breeze on her face but hesitated at the sheer drop to the ground.

From every direction, adults raced to the school, drawn by the smoke and screams. Mothers tore across the street and yard, their aprons whipping in the wind. Men installing telephone lines and workers at the nearby railway junction ran about, shouting orders. Shopkeepers grabbed anything that might help. The horror on their faces revealed the scale of the unfolding tragedy.

Someone behind Ingrid screamed for her to jump. She pushed off, landing with a burst of pain in her ankles but otherwise unhurt. She stood, momentarily elated.

She suddenly realized Maddy might have used the fire escape, which was just overhead. Ingrid stood back, frantically scanning the students scrambling down the metal stairs, Maddy nowhere in sight. Above, a towering column of dark smoke pumped into the ice-blue sky.

She ran to the back of the school. At the rear entrance, in a brick arch like in front, the occasional child ran off when set down by a line of men plucking children from the tangle.

The writhing, screaming mass inside flashed in her mind. The men would never rescue more than a few.

Maddy would never make it, she realized.

Over the next few days, newspaper accounts of the fire at the Collinwood elementary school would horrify people across the world. For Ingrid, it faded to black as she crumpled to the grass.

CHAPTER ONE

Tri-Lakes Region; Adirondacks Park; and Cleveland, Ohio
Present day

Every so often, Darcy O'Brien remembers he's in danger of being pulled over and arrested for stealing the white pickup truck. He checks the rearview mirror for flashing lights zooming up the empty road. He'd taken the keys and sneaked outside hours ago, driving away from New York City at three o'clock in the morning.

He's on the verge of solving a family mystery going back seventy years, cracking open an older secret nobody had ever imagined.

The road had started to climb uphill at dawn, lifting him from tree-lined corridors to this sleepy mountain highway. Gentle woodlands meander through flowering grasslands. On the horizon, jagged slopes bristle with towering conifer forests, and sunlight flashes off distant lakes.

He feels invincible. Immortal.

He sizzles with the thrill of a beautiful melody you feel rather than hear, like the siren's call during a sea storm. The sensation would have mystified him only recently, but now the mountains are filling him with the immensity of their music.

The GPS beeps. *In one mile, your destination will be on the right.*

He spots a fence and slows. Weathered grave monuments tilt to and fro. He pulls into the open gates of the small cemetery and crunches to a crawl on the narrow lane running alongside, parking in back.

With the mountain valley sweeping away, he feels like he's at the edge of eternity. He walks slowly among the rows, some old headstones dateless, anonymous.

His head pounds and his breath gets shallow. If he finds his great-grandfather's grave, everything will change. Hundreds of millions of dollars are at stake. Family lore will turn epic. Momentous changes wait to reorder his life.

Five days ago, Darcy knew almost nothing about his great-grandfather, who died decades before Darcy was born. Cooper Tiller had owned a coal mine and a fancy department store, both long gone. After he died, his wealth seemed to vanish, and he survived only in old photos, as voiceless and blank as the weathered gravestones.

Darcy's grandma Millie was born in 1922, the only child of Cooper and Elena Tiller. She died ten days ago at one hundred and two years of age.

❖

Three days after Grandma Millie's interment at the family mausoleum, Darcy finds a parking spot next to the mirrored downtown skyscraper where the lawyer has asked to see him about her will.

His brakes squeak and grind. The replacement expense hangs over his head, one more thing he can't afford.

Darcy loves Cleveland's older skyscrapers, rising in brick, concrete, and granite, muscular and stout no matter how tall. They proudly retain their hale and hearty industrial spirit, built like guardians to protect a city with clanging steel mills, ports swarming with crews from across the Great Lakes, and trains heaped with coal. That city is gone, but its guardians remain.

Darcy and his two sisters have always wondered what happened to the money supposedly amassed by their great-grandfather, first as a coal baron and then the owner of a fancy department store.

Grandma Millie lived in comfort with her husband in the lakeside mansion her father had built. She paid a small army of workers to keep the house and grounds maintained, she hosted dinner parties and family events, and she was always generous with birthdays and graduations. Yet she rarely splurged and didn't luxuriate in finery.

Grandma Millie gave birth to Darcy's mother, but his parents died hooked up to ventilators during that surreal first summer of COVID-19, and now his grandmother's inheritance will come directly to Darcy and his two sisters. Serena and Lydia had already left Cleveland after the services, returning to their homes in Indiana and Minnesota.

After his parents died, Darcy moved back to Cleveland from San Francisco to help his frail grandmother as well as to escape his dead-end life. Instead, he'd only delayed having to deal with his future.

Inside the office building, Darcy shows his ID to a security guard, a turnstile opens, and an elevator waits, programmed to take him to the twenty-third floor.

Upstairs, a printed sign at the empty reception desk leads him to a huge corner conference room with a table the size of a dance floor. Glass walls offer breathtaking views of downtown Cleveland and miles of Lake Erie shore.

Their lawyer, Trevor, sits alone at the table scattered with papers and folders. He's sleek and handsome, in a careful way that doesn't appeal to Darcy. Darcy figures him for thirty years old, which makes Trevor the latest responsible adult younger than Darcy, who is thirty-six.

Trevor says, "Will your sisters be calling in?"

"They had to take off work to attend the funeral, so they told me to call them later tonight."

"The situation is complicated, but I'll try to simplify it for you. Your direct inheritance from your grandmother, to be split three ways, is roughly one and a half million dollars, not including antiques or artwork that need appraisal."

Half a million for each of them is a welcome amount and seems about right. It fits Grandma's comfortable lifestyle and explains why his parents raised their kids in a typically suburban world.

"But her father, your great-grandfather Cooper Tiller, had *two* beneficiaries, and he ordered his estate to remain intact until one of them died. Even after all these years, your grandmother was the first, and the inheritance is close to five hundred million dollars."

Darcy can't grasp the amount before Trevor continues, "The majority comes from a six-story, mixed-use property in midtown Manhattan. It holds no historical or architectural significance, which means it's basically an empty lot in one of the world's most expensive real estate markets. If a bidding war breaks out, the value could skyrocket."

Trevor keeps speaking about investment accounts, stocks, bonds, all the usual securities. "Your great-grandfather added percentages for each child and grandchild. Apparently, the other beneficiary never had children, so the complicated math to resolve competing offspring won't be necessary."

Darcy's head spins. "What does that mean?"

"You and your sisters inherit roughly one hundred and twenty million dollars each, possibly much more." Trevor hands him an envelope. "Yesterday, I received this from the Byington Ellis law firm in New York, where Cooper Tiller filed his will. It gives a brief overview of the estate, but there's a catch. The second beneficiary's husband is claiming complete ownership of Cooper Tiller's estate."

"That can't be right. We don't have any other family. What's this person's name?"

"The husband's name is Charles Greene. Ring a bell?"

"No. How is the second beneficiary related to Cooper Tiller?"

"I don't know. I haven't seen the will yet. Byington Ellis was hit with a ransomware attack, so they're a bit disorganized, but it won't take long."

Darcy fills with sudden anger. "We have to fight this."

"We need to sit tight until we get our hands on the will."

"Not with that much money at stake."

"I know it's frustrating, but you can't do anything to speed the process. Don't do anything stupid like go looking for Charles Greene. I'm serious. Nothing good will come of that."

"I can't sit around. We've been wondering for decades what happened to Cooper Tiller's estate, and now I'm supposed to let a stranger take it from us?"

Darcy's rage cools. He has a purpose now. A goal. He's determined for the first time in years.

"It's just an opening gambit," Trevor says. "The world of inheritance law is full of games, and most of the time they come to nothing. Now, there's one more thing. We started getting our ducks in a row and had a hell of a time locating Cooper Tiller's death certificate. Thank God for the internet." He lifts a sheet of paper. "Do you have any idea why Cooper Tiller died in Franklin County, New York?"

"No. He's buried in Lake View Cemetery. Fifteen minutes from here."

"That may be where he's buried, but he died in the Adirondack mountains in 1960." Trevor straightens the papers and says he'll call

Darcy the moment he has the will in his hands. "Promise me you won't do anything rash about Charles Greene."

Darcy grumbles something like a promise, but no matter what Trevor says, he's resolved to learn Charles Greene's connection to his great-grandfather.

Outside, he heads for his car but stops and walks to the nearby Lake Erie shore.

He'd been broke and desperate when he moved back from San Francisco into Grandma Millie's lakeside mansion. He'd imagined lazy afternoons lakeside but had been up early to make all three meals for Grandma and her rotating nurses, doctors, cleaners, physical therapists, and even the nuns who came to pray with her.

Instead of a natural shoreline, downtown Cleveland offers a calming breakwater and concrete sloshed by small waves. Light undulates crazily on the surface, breaking and reforming. The mesmerizing movement takes him back to his years in San Francisco.

Realizing he was gay when he was twelve years old, Darcy longed to move out of suburban Cleveland and live openly. After high school, new, adult allures such as sex and romance drew him to the idea of living in a city filled with gay men. Only when he dropped out of community college and moved to San Francisco did he tell his parents and sisters he was one of the creatures he'd heard them scorn. They'd been regretful and asked him to come home.

Darcy never considered it, for within a few weeks he was working as a barback, which paid enough for a room in an apartment he shared with two other men, just a few blocks from the world's most famous gay neighborhood, the Castro. Within a month, he fell into a thrilling swirl of gorgeous men dancing in dark rooms pulsating with lights in the chemical scent of opaque fog machines.

His party nights would begin in one ratty apartment or another, lounging about with a group of his new friends who unabashedly discussed their sex lives. Soon he was invited to snort a line of white powder just before they left for a club. He insisted his friend take five dollars he could scarcely afford before lifting the straw as if he'd done it a hundred times. It burned his nose and afterward, he waited to feel something, but as they entered the warehouse dance club, he wondered if he was immune to cocaine.

He started dancing, and the colored lights filled the air with mystical creatures darting through the fog. The music thrummed in his chest as if recorded only for him, every pulse the force that pumped his blood. Virile men grinded against each other, fueling blistering desire and overwhelming joy.

He collected many sex partners, but he longed for the muscle guys who never gave him a glance. He found a no-fuss gym that charged a fraction of the others, located in the garage of a former small apartment building converted to offices. He enjoyed the rough atmosphere, the reek of dude sweat, and the challenge of lifting heavier weights.

A bartender at work quit suddenly, and Darcy's reliability got him the job. He quickly learned the popular mixed drinks and used a laminated guide under the bar for more complicated requests. His tips ballooned, and he started buying his own cocaine from his friend's dealer.

His friends went nose-up frosty when he discussed the gym. They never offered to pay when Darcy laid out some lines, and they gleefully gossiped about everyone who'd just left the room. He grew restless with them.

One year after moving to San Francisco, he got an especially potent packet of cocaine that he kept for himself, stretching it for multiple Friday and Saturday highs. The magic soared to new heights and one night the muscle guys gave him unmistakable looks. He danced over, and they welcomed him to San Francisco's gay Mt. Olympus.

Being an attractive, well-built young man gained him entry into sex parties in homes with raunchy, wealthy older men. They invited other rich men who whisked the young men away, sometimes for good.

A man named Kendall, scion of a hotel family, took an interest in Darcy but invariably spoke to him with a leer. Tall and thin, with limp, gray-streaked brown hair, Kendall invited him to his apartment in Paris.

"I don't have a passport," Darcy said.

"I have a place in Miami, then. I rarely go, but you'll love the beach."

After a lifetime of sunburns, Darcy had learned to accept his pale skin and wasn't keen on beaches, but he gladly accepted, enjoying the first-class flight and the town car that picked them up from the airport.

The sun shot through Kendall's high-rise Miami condo like a nuclear blast, intensified by a blinding glare off the ocean. The first morning, Darcy reluctantly agreed to join Kendall sunbathing naked on the balcony, with metal railings that showed everything to anyone who looked. Painfully aware of nearby buildings, he shifted uncomfortably for a few minutes before ducking back inside.

"What's wrong?" Kendall said, following.

"I don't want old ladies to see me naked."

Kendall gave a coarse laugh. "A young brute like you will make their dreams come true. I know how to loosen you up." He pulled a packet of cocaine from a drawer and laid out two lines, handing Darcy a ceramic tube. "Go on."

It was ten o'clock in the morning, but he was grateful for the escape and sniffed up both lines.

Darcy scanned the art in the spacious main room: a wall slashed with brilliant neon lights; a ghoulish bust of a melting head; and a dystopian cluster of rusty metal tubes. *Why buy all this expensive stuff for a place you rarely visit?*

The sudden understanding Darcy was just another piece of Kendall's art didn't upset him. Wealth made life easier, but it also led self-absorbed simpletons like Kendall to snazzy roadblocks like this pointless condo in the sky.

He drove off fear of such a hopeless life with a determination to never let money drag him to these depths. It felt instinctive and was so forceful it seemed rooted in experiences he couldn't remember. When he'd first moved to San Francisco, he'd recoiled from the extreme poverty of his friends, their moldy apartments in smelly buildings skittering with bugs, but they'd never seemed as desperate as Kendall.

Afterward, Darcy ignored Kendall's calls and texts, which quickly ended. He redoubled his efforts at his gym, which had only a small locker room where a toilet sat next to an open stall with two shower heads. By default, the clientele was mostly men, mostly straight, and during slow hours with no women around, guys often stripped to work out, glossy with sweat.

Darcy had felt freeze-dried when Kendall planted him nude on his balcony for the neighbors to envy. When the men at the gym got naked, the thick atmosphere made his urges lush and languid, radiating a rich warmth of unashamed male bonding. In private, men scratch their crotches and tug their penises, and Darcy learned naked gym brothers think of privacy as something they share. Darcy stripped to his jockstrap, too nervous about his desire becoming visible to take off everything, but it made him one of them and they were friendly.

Darcy understood the complaints of women who felt the sting of exclusion from such places, and he was pleased by how swiftly the men grabbed nearby clothes when someone shouted, "Hey, guys," from the entrance. They understood responsibility.

If forced to choose, he would gladly spend his life here among such men instead of a condo filled with expensive art nobody saw. He decided his happiness would never rely exclusively on money.

Rationalizing he wasn't remotely addicted to cocaine, he continued to buy a steady supply for nights dancing in the stratosphere. He enjoyed partying with San Francisco's elite gay studs, but as a popular bartender in the Castro, he became friends with people of all sorts.

He became day manager after three years slinging drinks, which required him to tend bar during the lazy afternoon hours while reconciling the previous day's books. He watched online videos about accounting and how to keep ledgers. After sorting the last manager's mess, he discovered an average twenty percent revenue dip whenever a handsome bartender named Luke worked, a man Darcy had always liked.

He pictured Luke with his dazzling smile and dark hair, and how men lined up at his station. Darcy fired him without hesitation, surprised to feel nothing.

His weeks fell into a fun pattern of partying Thursday night until early Monday morning. He could sleep for a few hours and after a couple of lines, put in a full day at work. Darcy knuckled down and did his job, getting a raise every year. The better-paying night manager position opened several times, but Darcy turned it down because the evening shift meant keeping a bar full of drunk people and shady bartenders under control. Darcy preferred obedient numbers.

Darcy's roommates circled in and out, and while they were friendly, he never became close to them. The apartment had direct access to a small backyard, with houses rising above, held in place by huge concrete retaining walls.

Every morning he took veggies and fruits to a patient group of possums and brush rabbits. The unhesitant rabbits hopped forward to munch, while the possums inspected and sniffed their food carefully, before pulverizing it with a few bites.

His job paid just enough to keep his life active with trips to Cleveland for family events, but he woke up the day after he turned thirty-two and called his dealer because he was running low. He was short of cash but had a neglected savings account with less than two hundred dollars, enough to get him to his next paycheck.

A jolt froze him. He was closer to forty years old than twenty, he had no investments, owned nothing, and his job had started to feel like a dead end.

He had also started using every morning.

Coke, he forced himself to acknowledge. *I use coke daily.*

By then, talk of a coronavirus was growing louder, and two weeks later, shelter-in-place destroyed his job when the bar closed.

Four years later at the lakeshore in downtown Cleveland, Darcy looks up from the hypnotic motion of light on water as questions about his family's inheritance dissolve his memories of San Francisco.

Why was his great-grandfather's death certificate filed so far from home? Who is the second beneficiary? Is it an unknown relative? How many family secrets remain hidden, and why didn't Grandma Millie say anything?

A sudden surge of grief at losing his grandma rises from his chest, yanking down a gasp. He misses her, recalling her kind, crinkled smile.

He sits on a bench to call his sisters but pauses when he takes out his phone. Both are still at work, and he suspects they won't answer. He can't possibly explain about the enormous fortune dangling out of reach. He leaves messages with half the truth: they are going to inherit half a million each from Grandma Millie, maybe more if some of the antiques are valuable.

He opens a search engine and types in the name Charles Greene, feeling defeated by the sheer number of hits. He narrows the scope with New York, but it hardly makes a dent.

He returns to his car and heads for the lakeside mansion built by his great-grandfather Cooper Tiller, his brakes trailing a shriek.

CHAPTER TWO

Asheville and Cleveland, Ohio
1880–1920

Coop had never seen cruelty like this. He never knew it existed until a man named Harold drove on to his farm in a cart that looked empty. But on that fateful afternoon, Harold put Coop on the road to wealth, while Coop set things in motion for Harold's murder.

Harold held the horse's reins, slumped in the top seat. His body looked like a gnarled switch underneath his loose, faded overalls. He raged at someone in the cart.

"…all that goddamned blubbering! I'll belt your hide clean off, and that's a promise!"

As Harold pulled into the barnyard, a woman and three children in the bed of the cart came into view, bouncing in unison. They wore plain clothes, stained and flapping in the wind. The round-faced woman held a baby, with a towheaded and pimpled boy to her right. Two little girls sat to her left, one sucking up tears. Coop recognized their dull expressions as helpless despair. All sat flat on their behinds like dolls on the floor, their legs straight out, covered by blankets.

Harold saw Coop and went quiet, and Coop saw how Harold sized him up as easy to push around. Coop felt steel rise in him.

Harold fixed Coop with a long stare, popping a cork from a clay jug and taking a swig. He wiped his mouth with the back of his hand.

Coop said, "I don't like all that swearing on my land." He wanted to order Harold away, but he was only fifteen and didn't quite dare.

Harold jumped off and walked over. Coop stood his ground. Harold's teeth were stained and crooked, his eyes the sickly greenish yellow of dandelion tea. Balding, gray, grungy, and sunburnt, he looked like a swamp legend.

His voice came in one flat note. "My name's Harold. I heard about an orphan boy struggling to keep his family farm going. I got an idea that will suit us both."

"Harold," his wife called. "We need to drink."

Harold scowled before giving Coop a sneering smile of commiseration. Coop didn't see why thirsty people deserve scorn, and he pointed to the well pump. "You can have as much as you like."

No one in the back of the cart moved. Harold grumbled as he walked over and tossed aside the blankets from his family's legs, barking orders.

In a flash, Coop saw how Harold had strapped them to the cart like hogs to the slaughter. A brace propped their backs upright while leather strips pinned their legs tight. An overpowering stench of human waste knocked Coop back.

Coop trembled to imagine God's punishment on a world that allowed a man like Harold to roam free.

Harold loosened a wrench under the cart, releasing their binds. His wife and children grunted and cried out as they climbed down, gasping in pain. Spotting big patches of filth on their backsides, Coop looked away.

Harold dropped his voice at Coop's disgust. "You ain't got no idea what it's like keeping them in line." Harold's family shuffled the walk of the hopeless, living every moment wilting under the rage in his eyes.

This was only the beginning. Coop had no inkling everything he knew and loved would be gone by sundown.

❖

Twenty-five years later, in his spartan room at the Admiral Perry Club in downtown Cleveland, Coop thought about Harold. It was 1920, and Coop was nearly forty years old. On the night before Coop's wedding, he still remembered Harold as the meanest man he'd ever met.

Coop's dark musings about Harold arrived like unwanted wedding guests. He thought he'd banished his secrets to a place deeper and lonelier than Harold's grave.

According to everyone, the holy blessings of matrimony soothe a man's soul. They discipline his restless thoughts and bolster his spirit against lust. He puts away childish things. God rewards him with wisdom and purpose in exchange for his oath.

As promised, Coop had felt sure-footed after proposing to the beautiful Elena Parks. He cut a spirited figure in a social whirl of congratulations, handshakes, and toasts.

All the while, in times of private stillness, he shivered when feeling his secrets rise from their trenches in his soul. They lived, and they waited.

He felt them stirring even now, on the eve of his wedding day.

He slapped his desk, shaking his head. Tomorrow he would marry Elena, who was half his age and held the promise of bearing many children. He would walk from the church and step confidently into the future because marriage changes a man. It changes everything. Everyone said so.

The Admiral Perry Club was no more than a minute's walk from the Rockefeller office tower. One of the world's wealthiest men, John D. Rockefeller, made his first fortune in Cleveland, built the regal tower, and decamped for New York.

The first two levels of the Perry housed spacious rooms called public, although entry was tightly regulated. Private rooms filled the top four floors, temporary housing for men whose business brought them to one of the most important ports on the Great Lakes. A handful of other residents lived at the club, but only Coop had no other home or family.

It was a man's world. Uniformed male attendants catered to an exclusively male clientele. He'd never seen a woman inside, not even cleaners or cooks.

Coop ate most of his meals in the dining room, where a seat was always open. Beautiful, polished wood gleamed in the billiard room and library, filled with precise rows of gilt books. Dimpled leather chairs and fine rugs softened the grumbled conversations in the smoking room and the bar, while the ceramic white tiles of the basement gymnasium echoed with brash, elevated spirits.

He'd lived at the Admiral Perry for fifteen years. Despite its swank reputation, the rooms offered uncomplicated living, with a bed, a desk, and a standing wardrobe, which Coop found more than suitable. He liked sitting at his desk, where he watched the steady glow from electric lights in tall buildings across downtown Cleveland, as he was doing the night before his wedding.

Curled on her soft bed of blankets on the floor, his dog, Dolly, gave a great heave of a breath but remained sleeping. She didn't have much longer.

A yellow snout sniffed into his thoughts, and Coop smiled at the memory of Target, one of his life's dearest friends. Target was the leader of a pack of feral yellow dogs that roamed the woodlands and fields of central Ohio. Coop was separating the cucumber harvest one day when Target walked up like a man with an opinion. Crisscrossed by old wounds and freshly bloodied in a scrape, Target ate two whole cukes, and their friendship was sealed.

Remembering the brave dog's affection, Coop drove off tears.

After twenty years of wealth, Coop could buy many things, but his only comfort came from memories of making others happy, or when they cared about his happiness.

Coop would pay any price to relive the day just after his fourteenth birthday, when Target gave Coop the idea that saved his family farm.

Coop would spend every penny to relive a night when he was nineteen years old, and he saw with his own eyes why the Tuscarawas Indians had named the hill where he was living Lightning Mountain.

Coop would hand over every dollar, the rest of his days, even his very soul to repeat a few moments of a buggy ride through the Appalachian foothills with Will. He'd only just met Will the night before, and they rode squished into a single small buggy seat with a chatty old hillbilly named Elmer. Somewhere on that bumpy road when they were little more than boys, Coop and Will fell in love.

From his window in his room at the Perry, Coop watched the electric lights of an office snap off in a building across the street. He looked at his pocket watch. Tomorrow afternoon, Elena would sweep down the aisle in her wedding dress, aglow with the joy of marrying one of the wealthiest men between New York and Chicago.

Until a few days ago, he'd been pleased with himself for bringing so much joy to Elena and her family. Now, he could barely face the shameful truth of his selfishness and self-pity. He wondered when deceit became the only thing that mattered to him.

❖

In the lowlands and till plains around Asheville, Ohio, corridors of lush green foliage trace rivers, streams, and creeks cutting through fields of wind-rippled beige and gold. Scraggly varieties of oaks and crabapples rise above buckeyes and box gum, in turn sheltering wild raspberries and willow shrubs. The greenbelts curve through pastures swaying with switchgrasses, wild sunflowers, goldenrod, and every kind of milkweed.

The soil is dark, fertile, and loamy enough to plow with a spoon, as Coop's dad was fond of saying. Farmers grow barley, oats, hay, and wheat, and all the vegetables of summer and winter.

Coop's dad, Clayton, grew up in southern Pennsylvania, but he inherited a farm in Ohio from a branch of the family that headed west and vanished long ago. Clayton married the girl next door named Petunia, and the young couple packed up for a new life.

Coop loved hearing the story about his parents' first glimpse of the farm, which they never tired of repeating to Coop and his brother Kenny, who was two years older.

None of the neighbors remembered who built the farmhouse or when. From the outside, black pitch sealed half-cut timber logs. The door opened to the kitchen, a sitting area, and two narrow bedrooms side by side. Plain-saw planks lined the walls and floors, with hand-cut ridges, natural warps, uneven shapes, and empty knot holes.

In cold weather, Coop's family spent most of their time gathered at the table in the main room. One small window looked out to the road, opposite another overlooking the barnyard. With the old cast-iron stove, they never missed having a fireplace.

Dad was thin and covered with tight muscles. His protruding forehead and chin made his profile look inverted, like a quarter moon. His dark eyes sank into wrinkles, and he slicked his hair straight back. He was mild and steady of temper, his anger as rare as April snow. Their wealthy neighbor, Mrs. Porter, said Dad's voice was as deep as a philosopher's.

"When your mother and I first laid eyes on this farm, it looked like nobody had tended the place since before Noah's flood. And I'm not lying when I say the spiderwebs in the barn loft were pulling down the roof all by themselves!"

"And that's not all," Mom would say. She was pretty and slender, her skin browned like the bread she baked on rare occasions. She twisted her dark, silver-streaked hair into a fuzzy bun at the nape of her neck. She angered faster than Dad but only for short spells. "The door to this house was swelled up like it was expecting. We busted inside where about a million field mice were having one of those gala soirees, living high on the hog and thank you very much."

"The crowning glory is the roof," Dad said. "Top quality shale, but it's a fortune to move. New York millionaires would be green with envy and give us whatever we asked!" Coop filled with awe as he imagined millionaires gathered in the barnyard, coveting their roof.

Kenny was born just after their parents' second harvest, when Dad tore down the old barn—"Hardly took more than a sneeze"—and pounded together a sturdier and bigger one using mill-planed and finished lumber.

Cooper came two years later, in 1880. By the time Coop was five years old and could fit the pieces of his life into a picture, all seemed fine on the Tiller farm.

Between the house and barn, chickens pecked at the ground and cooled themselves under bushes behind a woven stick fence. A cock strutted among them, jerking his red comb about like he disapproved of everything. He roosted in the tallest bush while the others gathered in the henhouse. Most hens were content to share a nesting box, but every so often Coop noted one who spent her days flapping in and out as she drove interlopers from her spot.

On one side of Dad's sturdy barn, a fenced-in pen held four ornery doe goats who trusted only each other. A horse and two donkeys who were the best of friends lived in the other pen. The mare, Daisy, was sweet-natured yet as vain as any horse, and she lived in mortal fear of the unexpected. Mom named the donkeys Mr. and Mrs. Bumphead for the affectionate way they greeted humans.

When Coop was eleven years old, the Bumpheads surprised everyone when the missus bloated into an expectant mother. After the long pregnancy of donkeys, Mrs. Bumphead was ready to drop her foal.

The horse watched the birthing sick with dread, but Coop would never forget how Daisy's eyes widened with amazement when she saw the newborn donkey glistening with silver slime. Transported by joy, she bobbed her head and clopped her hooves, nudging his mother aside to lick Baby Bumphead clean.

"I've never seen the like," Mom said when the new foal was a week old. They watched as Baby Bumphead finished feeding from his mother's nipples before toddling over to slump against the horse Daisy, who gave him a protective lick. "That horse took Baby for herself and turned his mother into a wet nurse for her own foal!" Mom laughed to the sky, but Mrs. Bumphead didn't seem to mind.

Coop had daily chores as soon as he could walk, starting with brushing the animals, clearing rocks, foraging walnuts and hazelnuts and drying them for weeks, along with the kindling he bundled with switchgrass. He also collected eggs with extreme care, bewildered by how their fragility seemed to undermine their importance. The skittish hens scattered and bit him a few times but before long, they clucked over to peck his boots.

By the time Coop was seven, he was responsible for the entire barnyard, feeding and watering the animals and keeping everything squared away. His friendly banter softened the cranky goats, and they stopped fussing when he milked.

He made cheese, weeded the crops, fetched endless pails of water, moved and carried and cleaned. He repeated his chores in the early evening, although the hens laid fewer precious eggs after noon.

One day, while he pumped water from the well, Mom emerged from the house. "We need a chicken for tonight." He started to argue but she cut him short. "Stop being such a prissy-missy. You gather the eggs, so you know best which hens have stopped laying. If you do it quick like we've all showed you, the hen doesn't know anything."

Coop gathered up an old chicken, petting and speaking tenderly as he carried her behind the barn because Dad was steadfast about hiding slaughter from the other animals, especially their own kind. Coop set the bird on a wooden block scored with countless axe blows dark with chicken blood. He trembled as he took the hand axe from the wall, but he went steady as he raised it. In one swift move he flattened the chicken and chopped its neck mid-squawk. He held it steady as it flapped and twitched, its blood shooting with fading spurts. He tied the legs and hung it to drain over a pit sprinkled with powdered lye to keep scavengers away, surprised to not feel much of anything.

The brothers shared the critical chore of making fertilizer. Coop shoveled the manure into a wooden bucket several times a day and dumped it in bins set back from the barn. Kenny mixed it with a bit of straw, always muttering about the stink.

Mom regularly pestered Dad for a new house. "You leveled the land years ago, so we're all set to start building."

"I want to get us settled in a nice place, too," Dad said. "But year after year, it's the same struggle with the crops and we need to save. A new farmhouse is never far from my mind."

"I'll be an old gray hag before I get a nice house."

"I'm doing my best."

A few weeks later they'd chase each other in the same circle.

One day without warning, when Coop was thirteen years old, two carts from the lumber mill arrived, laden with beautiful blond two-by-fours for the foundation and frame of a new farmhouse.

Mom cried with happiness and Dad gave her a hug. She looked nervous, happy, and worried all at once. "Are you sure, Clayton? You said we were living on a fine line."

"Never you mind. You deserve a nice house. Shouldn't take more than a year to move in."

It was June, and the crops were thick and green. Dad and Kenny got to work, sorting lumber and hammering. Coop begged to help but animals couldn't be left by themselves the way crops could, and Coop could only watch between chores.

The greenbelt of Slim's Creek marked their property line. On the other side, the wealthy and sociable Porter family owned a vast cattle farm. The widow Porter and her five sons oversaw every detail of their business and made the best neighbors anyone could want. When they heard about the Tillers' new farmhouse, four of the five brothers came to lend a hand for a day. The oldest brother, Warren, was absent and the youngest, Clyde, apologized.

"Warren's a bit under the weather," but Coop saw Clyde flush at the absurdity of the lie.

Warren was conceited and haughty. "All razzmatazz and lollapalooza," Coop's mom said more than once. "Learned that from his pop, who was the same way. But don't you go bad-mouthing old

Mr. Porter. It isn't neighborly, and lots of folks think a rich man has a right to be a cur."

"Why?"

"They plan to be rich themselves someday. Foolish gits. It gives them permission to play the part even if they don't have a pot to piss in."

Coop was too young to remember how Mr. Porter died, so his mom told him the story.

"He'd go storming across those pastures like a one-man locomotive, huffing until his face was red as a radish. The herd dogs dropped to their bellies soon as they saw him, wriggling like worms until he was gone. All those rough and randy cattlemen about did the same. The day he died, the men said he was off in the distance hollering as usual, too far away to make out a word. He went splat, like a manure plop. He gave his family the comfort of no need to mourn. You could tell how happy everyone was."

Despite Mr. Porter's foul nature, Coop felt desolate his death had cheered people. In desperate hope, he said, "Maybe Warren was sad."

"He was the happiest of them all. He thought he was gonna inherit and turn his mother and brothers into his vassals." She chuckled. "But it seems Mr. Porter had reservations about his first son, and he left it all to his wife. She was surprised as anyone. She put Warren in his place, and right quick. She raised her younger sons to be polite and helpful, but Warren was the oldest and had already picked up his pop's worst traits."

"Mrs. Porter's always nice to me."

"Don't go thinking she's your friend. You need to keep your place around rich folks. They're no better than you and me, but most of them think they are. Be smart about people and get folks to like you. It makes life easier."

Save for Warren, the Porters were a neighborly crew. The older brothers were tall and well-shaped, clean shaven and firm of feature, and widely regarded as the most handsome men around. Mom swooned over them, patting her heart, and making what Dad laughingly called "love eyes."

The youngest, Clyde, was husky with a round face and a warm smile beneath a cozy brown beard. He walked with a rocking gait, his arms wide, his forearms thick with hair. Just looking at Clyde often stirred something exuberant in Coop's heart. A grin from Clyde made him feel like he was flying, and Coop didn't understand why his mom or anyone else preferred the older brothers.

Over time, the abundance next door clarified the puny scale of life on the Tiller farm. The Porters owned vistas of land and enormous cattle herds. They paid an army of workers, wore nice clothes, and lived in a beautiful big home.

Every month, Mrs. Porter had her fattest heifer slaughtered and distributed the roasts, ribs, steaks, and ground meat to her neighbors, calling it her "watchful eye tax." She always sent a big slab to the Tiller farm where they drooled as Mom described her plans to cook it.

Mom thanked Mrs. Porter with a perfectly crafted crabapple pie every Christmas. Coop loved to watch as his mom gingerly opened tins of cinnamon, sugar, and nutmeg, allowing her husband and sons a deep sniff of each. She carefully peeled and cored the small crabapples and poached them in preserved lemon peel and sugar. "It takes the country out of the flesh." She added the coiled crabapple peels to the simmer, and they dried to a sweet crisp for their own family Christmas treat.

Mrs. Porter always sent a thank you note on pastel-colored paper, with graceful handwriting that could silence the whole family with its beauty. Mom saved the notes in her little kitchen drawer, delicately brushing her fingertips along the pretty colors when she didn't know anyone was watching.

The day the Porter brothers came to help with the new farmhouse, they brought two roasts, along with a bottle of wine and a sack of jerky. Mom served beer, and as they were saying their goodbyes, Clyde said, "Oh, Clayton, I noticed some of your turnip leaves looking brown and sickly. You know how much damage those underground bugs can cause."

"Was it that section nearest Slim's Creek?" Clyde said it was and Dad thanked him. "That patch got a little swamped after last week's storm. I dug a drain to the creek, but the leaves always take time to recover."

"Well, that sounds fine. Your corn and squash are looking mighty good. It's smart to plant in thirds."

Coop's dad had a well-known theory he was always willing to share: "Don't grow all vines, or all stalks, or all roots. One bug can wipe out everything. Plant in thirds."

As the brothers walked off, Clyde gave Coop a big smile and ruffled his hair. The touch of that meaty hand fired bolts down to Coop's feet.

Dad sent Kenny to check the turnips, and he returned with, "They're waterlogged, but there ain't no bugs." Scorn thickened his voice. "What does that goop Clyde Porter know about farming? All he knows is cattle because he's as big as a cow." He mocked Clyde's walk with an exaggerated sway like he was missing half a leg.

Coop yelled, "He's not a goop!"

Dad barked at them to knock it off and Coop shot his brother a look of contempt, but he was confused. Why was Kenny so mean when Clyde was so neighborly?

For the next week, Dad and Kenny built the frames of the new house walls and raised them just long enough to measure against the foundation. The whole family whooped and hollered at these skeletal glimpses of their future home, but Dad said they couldn't raise them permanently yet. "One big storm, and they'll go flying."

Mom's face sagged with disappointment. "I was gonna start making plans for the inside. You can't plan if you can't see it."

Dad put his hand on her shoulder. "I know you set store by it. We'll get them finished and next year, you'll see. The whole frame won't take more than a week."

Mom shook her head with deferred dreams in her eyes.

A few days later, Dad set out to check the crops. Coop did his barnyard chores and Kenny stomped about while mixing the straw and manure. Coop heard his brother fling open the wooden lids in a rage, but he didn't understand why Kenny hated it so much. After a while, you don't even notice the smell.

Coop heard a strange cry in the distance, but he grabbed the rope handle of a wooden bucket to water the animals. Behind the fence, Daisy stood next to Baby, inseparable as always. Their heads moved in unison, watching Coop's every move.

He heard it again, a voice bellowing, and the pitch sounded like Dad's. It faded long enough to hope it was his imagination, but it started again. He went to the edge of the barnyard where the cries grew louder and steadier.

Mom hurried from the house. They locked worried eyes before looking to the fields. The voice resolved. It was Dad. Kenny came running from behind the barn. They braced themselves as Dad got closer.

He burst from the corn. Even at a distance Coop saw the panic on his face. They raced to meet him. Dad screamed, "Get all the shovels and hoes! Drop everything, all of you! We're gonna lose the turnips!"

For hours they dug up slimy and desiccated turnips that stank a million times worse than manure. The rows with healthy leaves were a cruel illusion, for the pretty vegetables with purple fading to white were fissured and dripped with pus. The crop was wiped out, and all that remained was a burning pile.

Coop was horrified to see his family's panic in the storm-tossed soil of the former turnip crop.

"It's not a total loss," Mom said softly. "The corn is still healthy, and this will be our best squash crop yet."

Dad had planted the less valuable feed corn because it was heartier than the lucrative sweet corn. Squash was also so reliable it didn't bring a lot of money.

Stony, Dad said, "I can't afford the materials to finish the house. We need to protect the lumber, so we'd better store it properly."

Kenny choked and blubbered. "I'm sorry. The leaves looked waterlogged."

"It's not your fault," Dad said evenly. "Clyde Porter is a smart man. I should have dropped everything when he warned me."

Mom broke down, and Dad rested a hand on her shoulder. "It's my fault for being a one-horse husband. If I hadn't bought that lumber, we'd be fine." Mom started to object, but he talked on. "We won't starve, but we're on the edge. We need money."

"I can take the eggs to the market," Coop said. "I start school in September, and I'll go right past the grocer's every day."

Kenny said, "I could go work for the Porters." He'd wanted to work at the cattle farm for years, and everyone saw through his ruse.

Dad said, "You'll be needed at home more than ever."

Kenny crossed his arms and moped.

"I could take in some washing and mending," said Mom, sniffling.

"All put together that won't hardly make a difference," Dad said without emotion. "There's only one thing that will get us through this slump, and only by the skin of our teeth. I know someone who will give me a good price for that jack donkey."

Coop gasped. "But Daisy loves Baby!"

Dad told Kenny to start tearing apart the frames. "Lay out some tarp in the barn, and we'll stack the lumber there. I'll go see about selling that donkey."

He stalked off. Coop watched in disbelief. "Daisy loves Baby!" he yelled but his dad walked on.

Mom hugged Coop from behind. He tore away.

"He can't sell Baby! Daisy loves Baby more than life itself, and the Bumpheads will miss him, too!"

"I know, honey, but he has no choice."

"He can sell those mean goats!" Remorse pricked him because the goats were nice once they got used to you.

"Those does are near worthless at their age. Farm families can't afford to be sentimental. Your father warned me not to name any of them, and I wish I'd listened to him."

"You're just as mean as he is! It's your fault because you wanted a stupid house." He whirled on Kenny. "And you're so lazy and stupid you couldn't even tell the plants had bugs! I hate all of you! And I hate living here!"

He ran as far as he could. It felt like he'd never stop running.

Hours later and miles off, Coop sat creekside, looking out at the Porter cattle pastures. The sun had set, and the world was gray. In the distance, a large herd settled in for the night, big black shapes on the land.

He didn't hear Clyde until he spoke. "Coop?" Clyde held a horse by the reins. "What are you doing way out here?"

He stammered and stuttered until a thought burst in his head. "Can you give my dad some money to replace the turnips?"

"He lost the crop to bugs?"

Coop nodded, and his tears returned. "He has to sell our donkey, but our horse loves that donkey. It's like he's tearing apart our family. He said we have to stop working on our new house and we might lose the farm."

"Your dad wouldn't want me to know these things, and he won't take my charity. I know how attached we get to some of the animals but on the farm and everywhere else, you always lose everything you love."

The words hollowed Coop. "Why is life so sad?"

"If you live within your means and treat people fairly, you'll have happy times too. And you'll remember those more than the bad ones."

Two more of the Porter brothers came up behind, leading their horses. Even in the dim light, he recognized Timmy, followed by the foul Warren.

"Is that you, Coop?" said Timmy.

"You shouldn't be running around on our pastures," Warren snapped. "It's trespassing. Not to mention our dogs are likely to rip you to pieces."

Coop blinked in surprise.

"Those dogs know Coop better than they know you," Clyde barked. "Now, come on, Coop. Let's get you home."

Warren scoffed. "You're giving escort to a dirt-poor farm boy? Let him sniff his way back, like a hound tracking a bitch in heat."

Timmy clucked his tongue, and Clyde inhaled sharply. "Why you gotta be so disrespectful to hard-working folks?" Clyde said.

Warren made exaggerated gestures of contrition. "I'm so very sorry. I'm sure nobody else will think your interest in this mongrel seems a bit queer."

"Come on," Clyde said with gritted teeth, pulling Coop to his feet.

As Clyde dragged him away, Coop caught a glimpse of Warren's face, his eyes focused within, as if trying to remember when he wasn't so angry all the time.

A few minutes later, as he and Clyde walked along the green belt, Coop said, "What did Warren mean by queer?"

"I hope you never find out. But you should know my brother's not so flinty at home. He's getting married soon, and a wife and children will make him a better man."

The buzz and trills of bugs filled the darkness as they reached the border of the Tiller farm. Clyde said goodbye and Coop trudged off. The raw pain of losing Baby was overwhelming. He hopped the creek, and it felt like it took hours to walk the length of the corn crop.

As Coop passed the barn, the Bumpheads whimpered and snorted, and he knew Baby was already gone. Daisy whinnied with a despairing groan that hammered into Coop's chest like a spike.

In the following days, Coop went about his chores in silence, unable to bear looking at Daisy, who wailed as she begged Coop with tearful eyes to bring back Baby. He thought nothing could be more agonizing until she stopped looking at anything, alone in her pit of desolation.

The gloom didn't lift all summer. The feed corn and squash sold well, but everyone knew how tenuous their lives were, and all because of some stupid lumber and a partial crop failure.

In the fall, Coop started school. He walked half an hour to the single-room schoolhouse next to the church, selling the morning eggs to the grocer on the way. He knew most of the kids, but only a few seemed interested in learning. The teacher, Miss Everson, pulled her hair tight, making Coop feel her face was always rushing at him. Miss Everson seemed to care about her students, and Coop got some learning, but he attended erratically, like everyone else.

All the while, Coop couldn't forgive his family.

The scope of his rage and betrayal demanded a stoic, emotionless distance, with short answers, no questions, jokes, or casual words. It worked better than screaming or shouting ever could.

He came to understand how his sorrow over the loss of Baby only accounted for some of his bitterness. He'd worked without complaint his whole life, assuming he was earning as much respect as he gave. And the first time he'd demanded it, when it was most important to him, his parents had ignored him.

Mom blew up a few times and told him to stop sulking, but Coop didn't respond. Dad tried a nice approach, but even he gave up. As time passed, Coop found it easier to ignore their feelings as much as they'd ignored his, and he found satisfaction in their frustration.

The next planting approached. Wooden, he helped Dad and Kenny fill the wheelbarrow and buckets and set out to fertilize what they could with the meagre amount Kenny managed to make. They walked in silence until Dad suddenly froze, looking at the weedy field to the east of the farm. His mouth hung open.

"Holy Moses, Clayton Tiller," Dad said. "You stupid son-of-a-bitch."

Coop and Kenny shared a look of disbelief at this shocking violation of their parent's absolute ban on profanity.

Dad dropped the wheelbarrow and ran into the field. After a stunned moment, the boys followed. They found him staring in horror at a bunch of weeds on the ground.

Dad pointed. "That's an old well hole. It was plugged with paving stones when I inherited this place. Back then, I checked it every few months, but I've let at least seven or eight years slip by, and now the plug is gone. Probably tumbled right in. Who knows how long that hole's been waiting for somebody without a care to walk by and vanish forever?"

Kenny moved forward craning his neck, and Dad cried out and swept him back. Kenny tumbled into the weeds, his eyes widening as Dad bore down on him. "Don't you go near an abandoned well hole! You'll be lucky if the fall kills you instead of dying slow!"

Dad lifted him by his rope suspenders, and Kenny let out a cry of fear. With a quick shake of the head, Dad lowered him. Kenny's eyes flooded with humiliation, and his face twisted with rage. He ran off, and Coop's heart tore for his brother, the first time since last summer he felt anything for one of them.

Dad knelt, pulling and pushing the weeds, revealing an inky black hole that chilled Coop with its ruthless indifference. He'd run through this field countless times.

Dad dropped a rock inside. Coop felt the eventual faint splash in his stomach. Dad said, "We have to deal with this now. Fertilizing can wait."

They cleared the overgrowth and dug out the rim, unmasking a hole almost two feet wide. Kenny's absence went unremarked. As it grew dark, they returned to the farm to dump the fertilizer and use the wheelbarrow to cover the well overnight.

Kenny was lying on his straw mattress, wide awake when Coop returned.

"Dad didn't mean it," Coop whispered. "He's worried about this year's crop."

"They'll fail again."

"Shh. Why would you say that?"

"Coop, you don't see what I see. Those bitty little ears of corn. Scraggly green beans, looking like worms. Whatever we fertilize grows fine, but otherwise this land is cursed. We've never had a single good harvest. Why do you think it took him ten years to get the first load of house lumber? Most of what we grow is sold as cattle feed. That ought to cheer you up since you hate Mom and Dad so much."

"I don't hate them," Coop said, startled. He never meant anyone to think he hated them.

"You do a death-on imitation, giving them the silent treatment. But I hope the crops fail, too. I don't hate them, but I hate farm work, and I hate making fertilizer more than anything. I don't think it's fair to have kids just because you need more hands for your farm."

The next day, Kenny, Coop, and their dad returned to the abandoned well with a tree log and boards. They pounded together a panel twice the size of the hole and shaped the log into a plug. After nailing the parts together, they turned the whole thing upside down, burying the overlapping edges to keep it secure.

Coop asked, "Why not bury it all the way, so nobody will ever see it?"

Dad's nostrils flared. "You have to think long-term, Coop. That wood will rot underground, and in a hundred years the dirt won't hold a field mouse. If we disguise an abandoned well and a child falls in, God will yank us from heaven and toss us to hell." He deflated. "Years ago, I tried filling it with rocks but after one wheelbarrow, I realized it was a year's worth of work. It's on county land and it's their responsibility. I reported it till I was blue in the face."

Dad painted *warning–well* in red paint. Coop started walking away when his dad put a hand on his shoulder. "Promise you'll keep your eye on that well after I'm gone. It's important."

Dad's eyes filled with sorrow and terror so stark it melted Coop's resentment in an instant.

A day and a half after they set out, Coop, Kenny, and their dad spread the fertilizer as thin as window fog over a pitiful quarter of the field. Dad said, "You did a real good job with that fertilizer, Kenny. Every little bit helps."

Kenny stalked off. Coop caught up with him. "He was trying to make up for being mean yesterday."

"It's too late, Coop. I'm going to follow your example and treat them like I hate them. Maybe they'll kick me out." He snorted. "When I grow up, I'll shoot the man who asks me to work with stinking fertilizer. That's all I learned from this farm. How much I hate the stench of fertilizer."

Coop wondered how long before they woke up to find Kenny gone. Everyone knew the stories about siblings, fathers, even mothers walking off into the night.

Coop wandered over to look at the six empty fertilizer bins Dad built long ago. Even a year's worth of barnyard manure never filled more than two.

Dad walked up quietly. "I'm sorry I wasn't able to save this farm without separating that donkey from that horse. It made my heart feel bigger to see how much they loved each other. Your mother's, too. I can't really explain, but it made us happy seeing love in such an unexpected way."

Coop couldn't think of a reply.

"A boy is supposed to worship his father as a wise provider, but when I was your age, I knew my father was an alarmingly stupid man. I swore I'd never be like him, but then I inherited this farm. They said it had a farmhouse and a barn and I thought, oh, look at that lucky son-of-a-gun Clayton Tiller, a regular champagne Charlie. And then we got here, and you boys came, and nothing ever seemed to go how I planned."

"I don't think you're stupid, and I don't hate you."

Dad coughed like something was caught in his throat. "I'm grateful for that, but your brother thinks I'm witless. He's sixteen, which means I can't stop him when he gets it in his mind to leave, and he will. But you and I can make a real go of it. If we get a good harvest, we'll pull through."

"Just one good harvest is all it will take?"

"We'd be fine if I hadn't ordered that lumber. It was a credit plan where you send payments and if you miss one, you lose it all. I was squeezed like a baby with seven aunts. Everything comes down to this year, and you already know we spread the fertilizer too thin. I can't rely on Kenny. We need more fertilizer. A lot more. We need to fill all six of those bins and fertilize before we seed. That gives us five weeks."

Although it seemed impossible, Coop felt a surge of determination.

Dad went on. "People say you can enrich manure by mixing it with other things, things with nutrients. You have a mind, Coop. It would be a big help if you could figure it out."

Coop thrilled to the challenge. "What about all the cattle manure next door?"

"The Porters sell it by the barrelful as a side business. It's premium, just like their cows, and we can't afford it."

"What if we offer to pay them back?"

"No!" Dad dropped his head. "I don't mean to shout but agreeing to terms is the worst decision I made in my born days. Can you go around and find some things? Anything rotting? They're full of nutrients."

Coop nodded. "But let's only plant sweet corn this time. It'll bring the most money."

"If it works, we'll be in the pink. But one wrong turn, and we'll be wiped out for good."

Once again, Coop wondered why the breakable things are the most valuable. "We've never had trouble growing corn."

Dad nodded. "All right. Might as well go whole hog. Even knowing you're willing to help makes this pressure easier to bear."

Coop felt as if the missing purpose in his life had returned. He hurried to the barn for fresh manure. He scraped the droppings from the hen house, which would add little in volume but must be rich in nutrients.

He dug through the compost pile for likely additions, avoiding Mom's potato patch. He realized the whole mess of soiled hay, dried corn stalks, squash leaves and more might be perfect as it was. Washed clean by rain, the compost smelled earthy with a rich vein at the bottom like dark soil. He filled three bins, halfway in just a week.

He scoured the woods and the banks of rivers and streams. He picked blackberries and raspberries and wild strawberries, enjoying a few but throwing most in a sack. He noticed how butterflies and bees skimming the fields like they were drunk always landed on goldenrod, and he plucked piles of the tight yellow flowers.

He put it all through a meat grinder and it came out a thick, sticky paste that smelled like every fruit and flower all at once. He mixed it with chopped straw until it crumbled. It looked like the best fertilizer anyone ever made, but it wasn't near enough.

Late one afternoon, Coop was searching for inspiration at the empty bins when he heard a growl ending with an inquisitive whine.

A pack of wild dogs that roamed the grasslands and forests paced anxiously at the edge of the field. With the same short yellow fur and boxy heads, they were as indistinguishable as birds of a flock.

Their leader stood in front like a hero's statue, wagging his tail calmly. He bore the long-healed wounds of a warrior, including a floppy ear ripped in two and hairless scars that crossed on his crown like a target.

"Target," Coop called, and the dog sprang forward, whipping his tail. The others held back and erupted with anguish, whining, wriggling, and circling like they were going down a drain.

Target visited Coop about once a month from spring through fall, his pack following. They survived deep winter somewhere, but as soon as the weather warmed it never took long for Target to say hello. Coop always sensed his arrivals a day or two beforehand. Target treated him as an equal, and Coop understood the weight of the compliment.

Target bounded up and planted his paws on Coop's shoulders, panting.

"You banged-up old mutt." Coop scratched his furry cheeks and removed burrs tangled in his fur. "Are you behaving or making trouble?"

Target crumpled belly up and Coop squatted to rub. Target moaned blissfully, his paws limp, his eyes slits. Coop wished he knew how to fill up with good feelings the way animals do, but he liked knowing a wild pack dog lived a happier life than a president or a king. On the other hand, Daisy was still in deep mourning for Baby, and Target's pack were worrying themselves to death at the edge of the field.

Coop smelled something and grabbed a crusty paw. "That's cow manure, Target. You stay out of Mrs. Porter's pastures. She says wild dogs are dumber than a box of rocks and should be shot on sight. She thinks you'll take down a cow, but it'll be so big you won't know what to do with it. She said, 'We'll have to shoot the cow and those dumb dogs won't even get a bite.' So that's where you stand with her."

He stood, reaching into his pocket. Target went serious, flipping to his feet and planting his butt, intent as Coop unfolded a scrap of old fabric. It held a chunk of cooked chicken Coop slid from his plate two nights before, stealthy as a thief so his parents wouldn't see. He always got something ready when he sensed Target coming. Coop gave it a sniff and figured Target wouldn't mind the mild reek.

Target wolfed it down and rubbed Coop's legs. Coop scratched and petted. "Remember what I said. Hunt rabbits and possums, or better yet, gophers. But don't mess with a big ol' cow, unless you want to see Mrs. Porter in her nightdress coming at you with a rifle."

Target licked Coop's face, shot off and tore past the others like greased lightning before leaping into the weeds. They scrambled to follow. Target never stayed long, busy with keeping his pack fed and sheltered. Coop understood.

He yelled another warning to stay away from the cows. "And don't step in cow manure!" An idea came to him like a bash to the head.

❖

A group of men in the hallway of the Perry passed his door, rousting him from his thoughts with thick, bass laughter. Coop knew it well. Whether it came from a group of miners or men of business, earthy appreciation sounds the same. The topic could be lewd, profane, or scatological, preferably a combination.

Coop enjoyed masculine company of every sort, but bull sessions made him uneasy for their likelihood to charge into dangerous topics. Still, he was proud of the way he'd learned to melt into such scenes. Nobody could match him for an earthy chuckle.

Another burst of laughter came from the group, now far down the hallway. His mind drifted back to his boyhood.

The manure on Target's paw filled Coop with an exciting idea, and he ran for the Porter Cattle Company on the other side of Slim's Creek. He slowed as he reached the greenbelt, where the land dipped to the water running fast and clear with recent rain.

He peered through the foliage to a square, deep pond across the way, dug by Porter cattle workers as a swimming hole where they ran around buck naked on hot days, hollering and laughing. He'd watch from behind a bush or tree, pounding out a quick jack when he couldn't help it.

The wide variety in men intrigued him, from skinny to hefty, hairy to smooth. And although he found all their penises mesmerizing, the variety boggled him. Thick, thin, tapered, hooked, curved, or irregular as a tree branch, the majority hung down a bit and swayed, while others looked like buttons in a tangle of pubic hair. He noticed how the men silently evaluated other penises, casual and unconcerned, but never commenting.

Now and then, a worker removed his pants and the huge pendulum between his legs demanded widespread acknowledgment, usually with good-natured mockery. The owner nearly always responded with gyrations that sent his slab spinning or slapping from leg to leg, drawing uproarious laughter and applause.

Sometimes the workers saw him and waved cheerfully, yelling

that he should strip and jump in. One day, he hoped to find the courage to join them.

On the day Target gave him the idea, the pond was empty, the surface still.

Disappointed, he hopped across the creek and up a small hill. At the top, cattle pastures stretched like biblical lands under the sun, washed in greens and golds. Dozens of narrow, flat cattle barns stretched across the western horizon. Far ahead stood the big Porter house, dazzling white in the afternoon sun.

The Porters protected their enormous pastures from poachers and trespassers with a vigilant system of riflemen and specially trained dogs. When a herd reached woodland borders, armed men patrolled the greenery night and day, and they rode a high saddle when the cattle were on the move. A bushy-haired Australian breed of dog kept the pastures organized and sensed intruders with the intensity of the sun through a magnifying glass. Dad said the Porters should be put in charge of Fort Knox.

He ran for the house, smiling when herding dogs appeared out of nowhere in three directions, tracking to intercept him at the closest point. They'd recognize him soon, but keep chasing for fun, barking their heads off. When he stopped, they'd greet him with butts wiggling like fish on the dock.

They converged at the back of the house, the dogs panting happily but trained to not jump. They sniffed Target on him and suddenly nothing else mattered. They growled with incredulity and anger.

"What's all the commotion?" Mrs. Porter said, her form just visible on the other side of a door made of expensive wire cloth painted white. Most people used cheesecloth doors to keep bugs and birds outside on hot days, or just let the pests come inside like Coop's family, but if something better came along, the Porters would have it first.

The house rose three stories in segments that sharpened to high peaks. Fancy large windows rose and fell as smoothly as ice, and Coop could just make out the high dome in front that capped an amazing round tower wrapping one corner all the way down. His dad once pointed out how the windows in the tower curved with the wall, even the glass, leaving Coop speechless.

Coop delighted at seeing Mrs. Porter at church, fairs, and traveling circuses, when crowds parted with deferential nods. She always dressed fancy in public, and people whispered about her trips to Paris to buy the latest fashions. Coop asked his mom if the neighbor lady took such grand journeys, and she'd ticked her tongue. "She goes to Paris to buy clothes like I go to Japan for Japanese apples."

Mrs. Porter pushed open the screen door and emerged in a plain dress. Her frown didn't conceal a happy crinkle. She was always nice to him.

"Young Mr. Tiller, why are you working those dogs into a state right at my back door? They're crawling with fleas and ticks, and I don't like them near the house."

He apologized, and the highly disciplined dogs obeyed his order to leave at once. "I need to make more fertilizer for our farm, and I thought about how much cow manure you have."

She pulled a large straw hat with intricate, decorative weaves from the inside wall and anchored it firmly over her hair. His mom said the light brown color came from a dye. "No woman has nice hair at her age. She's as gray as storm clouds underneath."

Mrs. Porter leveled a serious gaze. "The manure is my most profitable side business. I pay men to do nothing but fill barrels every day that fetch a pretty penny." She fiddled with a charm hanging from a delicate necklace. "Would you ask for my gold jewelry at the same time?"

His face went hot. "No, ma'am. I'm sorry. I was wondering if I'd have your permission to take the pats from the ground."

"We never collect the pasture pats. It's too much work for too little reward."

"I don't mind the work to help my family. And I won't get in the way. Everyone here knows me, even the dogs."

"Because you're our neighbor and you asked respectfully, I will allow you to have whatever you can scoop off the land. I'll tell my sons and workers to let you be, but no matter what you say, those dogs will hound you to death. They're good herders, but like all dogs they're as dumb as posts."

He struggled to express the scope of his gratitude, but she didn't wait for him to finish. "It takes no time at all for a hot sun to bake those cow pats to bricks or dry them to powder. So, you take my advice and follow the herds. How are you planning to carry them?"

"I can use a wheelbarrow."

"Larry!" she called to a group of men outside a smokehouse. Her high voice pierced the day and brought everyone within hearing to a halt. A worker banged on the door of the smokehouse and men spilled out. From every direction, people came running, Larry presumably among them.

The crowd gathered, and she announced Coop had her permission to scavenge. "Give him some of the burlap sacks the chicory chips come in." She waved everyone away. "Now get your sacks and be on your way, young Mr. Tiller. And tell your parents you'll always have a job waiting for you here. But not your brother Kenny until he learns to stop brooding for ten minutes at a time." She turned away. "Like a sultan without a throne, that Kenny."

Elated and staggering under a pile of ripped burlap sacks, Coop set off for home. He scanned the ground. Just as Mrs. Porter said, the pats were dry and crumbly, but he could mix in a little water.

He was raring to go, but he needed a trowel and shovel as well as a method of carrying the sacks without struggling to keep the wheelbarrow balanced. Absorbed, he walked down the slope to the swimming hole, where a movement drew his attention.

Even from behind, he recognized Clyde, who was naked, hairy as an ape, and facing the other way. He was so close Coop couldn't believe he didn't see him until now.

The same bushy brown hair of his head and forearms swirled over his body and knit a thick mat on his butt. Clyde tipped his head back, his eyes closed and his mouth open. One hand was clamped to his hip and the other moved rapidly back and forth as he jacked.

Many people said Clyde looked like a circus fat man. Like Kenny, they mocked his voice and his walk, implying he was a lumbering idiot. They said the older Porter brothers were ashamed of him and his mother refused to look at him.

They were lies. Coop never saw Clyde's family treat him poorly.

Coop crept forward, going still at seeing Clyde's penis stretched full, straight as a corn stalk. Frozen with fear yet hypnotized, Coop couldn't think clearly. He realized he should have backed away silently and now he was practically at Clyde's elbow.

Wonder rooted him to the spot. His heart hammered in his head. Heat filled his face, and the air sparkled in his throat. He couldn't imagine a finer sight.

Seeing Clyde's grip around his swollen penis filled Coop with a joy that made him grateful for life. Everything had led him to this moment. He felt his own penis twitch and grow. Only a second too late did he feel a bunch of sacks slip from his shoulder. They landed with a soft thump.

❖

In his room at the Admiral Perry Club, Coop caught his breath at the memory of Clyde Porter jacking next to the swimming hole. For the rest of his life, he'd regret he let the sacks slip and didn't get to watch Clyde finish.

When the sacks hit the ground, Clyde spasmed and whipped around. "Cooper Tiller!" he bellowed, his face going scarlet. "You never interrupt a man when he's—" He bit off the rest, smashing his inflated penis against his abdomen. His clothes were nearly thirty feet away. He shook his head in surrender and didn't hide anything as he walked over in his usual way, arms wide.

Clyde was firm and packed solid, Coop saw. The lumbering strides balanced his bulk perfectly when seen naked. Clyde's penis deflated rapidly, the bounces sagging to flops.

"I'm sorry," Coop said. "I didn't know you were here."

Clyde waved it off as he turned away and dressed. "I know you didn't, Coop, and I'm sorry I barked at you." He chuckled as he slipped on his trousers and shoved himself inside, fastening up tight.

Coop said, "Your mom said I could collect cow pats from your pastures for fertilizer. She gave me the burlap sacks from the smoke house."

Clyde turned about, smiling, his face faded to pink. "That sounds like a good idea, Coop. I'm glad we can help. I know your family works hard to make that stingy land grow anything."

"I better get going." He stooped for the sacks.

"Hey, Coop."

He looked up.

Clyde chuckled. "You caught me with more than just my boots off, that's for sure, and it makes it easier to say this. Even when I was a loose-legged calf, I knew people called me a big stupid oaf. It hurt my feelings when I was younger and forced me to consider how I treat people. I realized I wasn't so awful, and all those bad feelings left, just like school was out. But it's a different thing when people tell a true tale of a man making a spectacle of himself with his bare ass hanging out. In front of a kid. My mom would feel ashamed of me, Coop. Sometimes being neighborly, being a man, means keeping things to yourself."

Coop glowed with the thrill of sharing an intimate secret with Clyde. "Yep. I'll never tell, I swear. We're good neighbors."

When Coop returned to the barn, he ducked into the corner where he usually jacked. Picturing Clyde, it took no time at all to finish.

For the next three weeks, Coop scoured the pastures for wet pats, dry pats, and everything in between. After a few days, the herd dogs stopped coming over to see what he was doing. Coop filled sack after sack, balancing them on a strong branch across his shoulders. He filled the fourth fertilizer bin and most of the fifth.

He felt hopeful, but he had no time to waste. One Saturday morning, he rushed through his chores and was leaving for the pastures when Miss Everson arrived. The teacher glided as if on wheels under her skirt. "Cooper Tiller, please come with me as I call upon your mother."

Mom was respectful but confused as she invited Miss Everson to sit. Seeing the women across from each other, Coop was thunderstruck. Sometime over the last year, Mom's nose had sharpened. Crinkled gray hair stuck out from her bun, her dark natural shade gone. Her skin was pale, pitted and creased, and her arms were like dead twigs. She wore the same apron and raggedy dress she always wore, stained permanently.

If Miss Everson noticed her sickly appearance, she said nothing. "Mrs. Tiller, I'll come to the point. Within his first month of school last fall, Cooper impressed me as one of the most promising students I've ever had. I was deeply disappointed when he stopped his lessons. I understand he's needed on the farm, so I'm offering to tutor him in his hours with no chores. Saturday evenings are restful on a farm, are they not? I don't make this offer lightly, for I value my solitude. We can have our lessons in Pastor Birmingham's parlor."

Dad entered, curious about their visitor. The stress was also taking a toll on his father. His elbows were sharp, his knuckles swollen, and his fingers misshapen.

Mom happily repeated Miss Everson's words to Dad. His parents looked so proud, Coop was sorry to drop his eyes and say, "Thank you, Miss Everson, but for the next few weeks, I have too much work here."

She touched her forehead. "Of course, for planting. And after that?"

Mom said, "Our older son wasn't cut out for books, but Coop's always had such an inquisitive mind. We gladly accept your offer."

They worked out the details and Miss Everson left. Coop started to argue, but Dad said, "There's not one farm boy in ten million that will get a private education in his spare time. You have potential, Coop. I'll not let you miss an opportunity like this."

Coop saw how much they needed to feel they were giving him a future with promise, something beyond the toil of a middling farm. Despite his misgivings, he was pleased to see them so happy.

For the next week, he scoured the pastures and piled the manure next to the bins. Shoveling back and forth, he mixed thoroughly to create an even look and texture that filled all six bins.

Dad pulsed with hope. "You pulled it off, Coop. Let's spread this and start planting."

With no time to waste, Coop and Kenny fertilized a few steps in front of Dad, who commanded the plow. Daisy plodded along, still forlorn but used to this annual ritual. Coop and Kenny finished far ahead. Wasting no time, Dad and Kenny started planting while Coop took over the plow, encouraging the horse with gentle words. In three days, they fertilized, plowed, and planted the farm.

Dad said the dark, rich expanse was the best-looking planting he could remember. They held their breaths and waited for the sprouts. It usually took two weeks but as the sun set on the fourteenth day, the field remained empty.

Coop wondered if he'd made a stupid mistake like mixing in a poisonous flower or berry, tainting the entire field. Nobody said anything. Nobody looked at each other. He filled with a worry so turbulent he felt sick.

In the morning, corn shoots blanketed the farm, their leaves opening like arms excited to see the world. Weeks later, a forest of light green baby stalks filled the field. By mid-June, the healthy, dark green corn looked like life itself.

In disbelief, they watched as shanks started growing halfway down every stalk with a daughter ear, usually a feed crop. Coop couldn't help imagining the fortune they'd make from two sweet ears from each stalk.

Coop watched in wonder as the wind rustled the roughly textured leaves. His parents and brother did the same, staring endlessly because all they had was the bounty of the here and now, and they needed it to go on for one more minute, and then another, until the hours piled up.

They didn't dare commit the scene to memory. They already knew recalling a season of plenty brought no comfort in want. Desperate people block sorrow by living every moment without thought of the past or future. It flattens the gaze and leaches emotion from the face. For the rest of his life, Coop could spot despair at a glance.

Coop spent Saturday nights with Miss Everson in the pastor's parlor, decorated with thick fringe, tassels, and doilies. Miss Everson was nicer and more patient in private. She taught history, art, and literature, and she gave him books to read at home.

He enjoyed the lessons and the books, especially *Robinson Crusoe*. "But this is only fun. Can't we learn something more useful?"

She loosened her hair at home. She was pretty and younger than he thought. "Think of it as fertilizer for your mind. Feed crops are fine, but if you want summer vegetables bursting with sweetness, you need the humanities."

Coop started sleeping outside. It was silly, but he wanted to be near if the crops needed him. He read Miss Everson's books by camp light. When the fire sputtered, he curled up and listened as the nodes popped free of their stalks, soft as a cork from a bottle. At times they came as steadily as musical beats and he created melodies in his mind.

Every dawn, the hearty stalks topped with flowing tassels reminded him of the drawing of a Roman army in Miss Everson's history book.

By August, a golden harvest was weeks away. Coop, Kenny, and Dad stalked the fields in silence, examining the leaves for pests they crushed one at a time. Coop returned home late one evening and stood silently at the door until he had their attention. "I saw the first silk."

Dad nodded. "Harvest in twenty days." His voice caught, and Mom put a hand to her mouth as a tear ran down her cheek.

The green-gold silk went amber, deepening to the clumped brown of ripeness. Mom picked four of the daughter ears. "Let's see if we'll get two sweet cobs from each stalk." She ripped away the husk, revealing perfect rows of plump, sunny kernels. She boiled them and handed the first to Coop. His heart thundered as he took a crisp bite.

In an instant, he knew they'd saved the farm. The kernels popped in his mouth, releasing the rich and satisfying flavor of the finest sweet corn. He closed his eyes and chewed, savoring the richness. The others bit into theirs. They cried and laughed as corn juice dripped from their chins.

It was their best harvest ever, and when the last cart piled high with ears pulled away, Dad said, "Coop, you saved your father's bacon. That's a hell of a thing for a fourteen-year-old boy to do. I don't know what I've done to deserve a son like you."

The next morning, Mom walked off without a word. A few hours later, Coop spotted her returning in the distance, leading Baby with a rope.

Elated, Coop rushed to the pen where Daisy sprawled in barn shade, leaving the uncomplaining Bumpheads to share a tiny sliver of cool gray. "Come on, girl!" Daisy blinked with surprise and pushed up. She followed him to the barnyard with a touch of alarm while the Bumpheads dutifully shuffled behind.

Coop stroked Daisy's cheeks and nose, his excitement rising as Mom led Baby onto the farm. He pushed Daisy's head in their direction. "Look who's back."

Affronted at being manhandled, Daisy flicked her head. Suddenly, she froze. With a grunt, her body swelled, her eyes as large as pail lids.

Behind Mom, Baby caught sight of Daisy and slowed uncertainly.

Daisy reared and pawed with a thrilling ferocity. She issued a high-pitched whinny that pumped across the land, her eyes enflamed. In one graceful move, she tipped into a swift gallop.

Baby braced and stretched, belting a toothy, screeching bray. He sprang into a donkey's dainty trot.

Daisy overran Baby and skidded, circling back to rise on her hind legs, furiously paddling the air while Baby turned about. They reunited in a clumsy, twisting dance, desperate to rub their cheeks together. They bobbed and adjusted for better aim, but more often they missed or knocked heads.

The Bumpheads rushed past Coop to join them. Even the goats bucked and kicked across their pen. Mom and Coop fell into a tight hug, sobbing as the air filled with a joyous chorus of brays, neighs, and bleats, one of the happiest sounds of his life.

Baby's return restored the farm's spirit. Dad triumphantly pulled the tarps from the lumber. "We'll build this danged house yet!"

A few weeks later, Coop was in the barn when he overheard Dad tell Kenny he wanted to test the frames on the foundation. "But let's be quick about it so the others don't see and get their hopes up too soon."

Coop led a doe up the ramp to the milking platform while another rested her snout on his thigh. He pinched the swollen nipples, squeezing and stripping as he heard Kenny's urgent warning, followed by Dad's terrified bellow.

Coop froze. At a loud snap, Dad went silent before shrieking in the highest pitch a man can reach.

Later, Kenny said, "He was running up and down that ladder like he was twenty years younger. He just slipped, that's all there is to say."

Dad landed perpendicular on a two-by four and broke his back. Coop and Kenny used his straw mattress to move him inside as he wailed. Mom babbled nonsensically, soggy with tears and snot. That night, the doctor said there was nothing he could do, and Dad would never walk again. He left two big bottles of laudanum.

Mom abandoned everything to tend Dad, rarely leaving his side. Black shadows formed under her eyes, and she hobbled with a stoop. She developed a relentless cough that made Coop and Kenny wince. Sometimes, Coop heard her hacking inside the house from as far away as Slim's Creek.

Coop had plans to grow winter wheat and oats, but Kenny had other ideas. He started disappearing for days at a time and always returned with jugs of something clear and sharp-scented that he drank all day. When Coop asked where he went, Kenny smiled and said, "Making plans."

"Are you gonna leave me here?"

"It's not like that. I need to start my own life."

"Work for the Porters, like you always wanted."

Kenny went dark. "I wanted to ride with the herds or be an overseer in the barns. But that old prune Mrs. Porter said I had to start at the bottom, shoveling cow shit for fertilizer. I wanted to spit in her face."

With no one to help him, Coop let the winter planting season pass. A storm howled into central Ohio, the worst freeze anyone remembered. Coop threw extra tarps over the huddled animals in the barn and Daisy thanked him with a look. The land froze for two bitter days. When it warmed, Mr. and Mrs. Bumphead and three of the does were dead. The rooster strutted out of the henhouse, wobbling like he'd been on a bender. Coop found most of the chickens frozen except for a few at the bottom of feathery piles. Coop had a good long cry and moved the remaining goat into the pen with Daisy and Baby, who welcomed her without question.

As soon as it was warm enough for outside work, Coop started getting the plow ready. He was in the barn sharpening the blades when Kenny approached carrying his blanket, tied into a sack over his shoulder.

Coop stood, feeling like the earth was breaking under his feet. "If you leave, I got no chance."

"No chance for what?"

"No chance for anything. How am I supposed to fertilize, plow, plant, and harvest all by myself? And all the while, take care of Mom and Dad?"

"They're gonna die in that stinky room no matter what."

"We're all they have. Who else will look after them?"

They cringed when they heard her cough.

"They weren't good parents," Kenny snarled. "I don't fault them for failing, but it's not our job to fix what they broke. There's no future here."

"There is if we work together."

Kenny's face brightened. "That's a sound plan, Coop. Why don't you come with me? I'd be glad for your company."

Kenny seemed sincere, baffling Coop, given everything he'd just said.

"I'm heading to New York to work on the steamships. They say you can cross the Atlantic to Europe and get work on ship after ship until you end up sailing across the Pacific to California. Imagine you and me, sailing all the way around the world! The wages are a regular inheritance, as they say. When we get to California, we could get an orange or lemon farm and never trouble with ice storms again." Kenny gripped his shoulder. "What do you say? I'll be glad to wait while you pack up."

For as long as a flint spark, Coop felt a surge of freedom and joy. He pictured himself beside his brother on the deck of a ship slicing through crashing waves. He longed to see an ocean, a mountain, a desert. All of it was waiting for him, and he felt an invisible hand plunge inside, grip his heart and fling him skyward, soaring to a new life.

Mom's cough brought him crashing to earth.

"You're staying?" Kenny said.

Coop nodded, hoping his determination would sway him.

"Then I guess this is goodbye, Coop. And I'll never trouble you about this farm. You take my half with all my blessings. Come look for me if you're ever in California. Or New York. I'll write if I can." He held out his hand. After one shake, Kenny swung the bundle over his shoulder and headed for the field.

Coop followed. "Kenny," he called.

Kenny walked on. Coop started to trot. "Kenny."

His brother didn't respond. The weeds snapped back in his wake.

"Kenny," Coop said with broken breath, sinking to his knees.

Two weeks later, Mom roused herself from her gloom. "I can't remember the last time I saw Kenny. Where is he?"

"He left. To get a job in New York."

Her mouth hung open. "When?"

"A few weeks ago."

She closed her eyes and dropped her head. "Well, look at this fine mother, not knowing where her own son is."

"Dad needs all your time."

Mom's body looked like it was sucking in on itself. She said, "How are you going to manage on your own?"

Coop waited out a coughing fit. "I can plow and plant in shifts. I'll harvest one crop at time." He'd been dreading sharing his other plan, but now was the time. "And I'll sell that lumber."

She looked as if she'd forgotten about the new farmhouse. She took a deep breath and wilted. "You have it all figured out. We always knew you were smart."

She pushed to her feet and limped back to Dad's side. He was either incoherent with pain or dull with laudanum. The house stank of feces and urine, and Coop would have slept outdoors if it wasn't so cold.

Clyde came over one day, carrying a wooden box. "Our mom is worried about you, and she sends this with her regards."

It smelled wonderful, and Coop kept his head down so Clyde wouldn't see his tears of gratitude and shame.

Clyde's soft voice felt soothing. "Coop, the doctor's been talking about your situation. We can't let a good neighbor go on like this. It's time you came to work for us."

"I have to take care of them."

"They need proper nursing from people who know how to tend to infirmities. My mom won't let them have anything but good care. She said you can live right in our house." Clyde's voice faded to a near whisper. "They're gonna die soon, Coop."

He looked up sharply, wondering why people say things that destroy their intent. "That's why I can't leave most of all, Clyde. If I don't provide for them, what good is having a family to begin with?"

Clyde's eyes went wet. "Okay, Coop. You're a good son. In the meantime, if you need anything at all, we're just across that creek."

By starting a month ahead of schedule, Coop plowed the whole field and still had a full week before planting.

He'd seen the doctor leaving earlier that day and knew he'd left bottles of fresh laudanum that roused Dad's spirits for a while.

Coop heard his parents talking as soon as he entered the house. He sat to listen. Maybe he was extra quiet or maybe his parents' regrets were extra loud, but they didn't know he was there, or they wouldn't have spoken so plainly.

"Oh, Clayton, who knew we'd have such a hard life?" Mom said, anguished. "I remember growing up and some families just seemed cursed. You never think it'll be you."

Dad's voice trembled. "I never told you, but the first time I laid eyes on this farm, I heard a voice tell me to turn right around and never look back. I wish I'd listened. I never provided a good home."

"You did your best, and that's all a wife can ask. What matters is we failed our boys." She stopped for a coughing jag.

"Kenny will be all right. A boy like Kenny needs booze in his belly and enough money for the cathouse, and the world is his oyster. But Coop's got too much heart for this world. He'll either get torn to pieces or be a millionaire. When it's one of those two, being tore up is the sure bet."

"I can't count how many times the Porters said they wanted

him." She sounded proud. "The old lady told me she'd start him as an overseer. Imagine how high he'd climb."

"Coop isn't cut out to be a cattle man. If old lady Porter asks him to pick out the heifer for the 'watchful eye tax,' he'll be stuck. One moo with those big wet eyes, and that cow will be sleeping in his room. He loves animals, and they love him, like that mongrel pack leader."

"That's the scariest dog I ever saw."

"Looks fearless enough to take on a bear. And many are the times I watched that dog fall at Coop's feet for a belly rub."

Mom took heavy breaths to suppress a coughing fit. "It's a good sign he tamed that dog. He'll need that kind of strength. He'll never be tempted by the cathouse."

Coop held his breath.

"I don't take your meaning," Dad said.

"You're not that simple. You know what I mean."

"He's a late bloomer, is all."

"Well, could be. But I don't think Coop will let anyone pull him apart, so I guess our son will be a millionaire." Her voice broke with sudden sobs and went sharp. "I just hope he doesn't hate us for this."

"When he's older, he'll understand we were thinking of him."

They went quiet, and Coop wondered if they were planning to move.

He stood to ask what they meant, but changed his mind when he heard their tight, breathy squeaks of torment, the kind of sorrow that forces you to bend and gasp. It was unnatural for children to see parents laid so low. He sank to the bench, helpless and desolate. How does one gain the wisdom to ease such pain?

"Come on," Mom managed. "Let's get this over with."

"I love you, my pretty Petunia."

"I love you, too, Clayton. See you in heaven."

When Coop figured out what they meant, he leaped to his feet.

The first shot exploded like a cannon. The shock and horror blasted him back. He scrambled, but the second shot came while he was still on the floor.

He watched as a curl of gun smoke drifted through the light of oil lamps. The sharp scent of gunpowder overwhelmed the usual stink, followed by the thick smell of metal billowing off a seeping pool of blood that fanned out from their room.

He forced himself to stand and walk, shaking furiously. They were his parents. He had to make sure.

He sidestepped the blood and gripped the doorframe.

In a flash, the scene stamped permanently on his mind.

Red canyons in flayed faces. Mom on the floor in her stained dress. Dad was on the bed because who else could it be? On the wall behind Dad, a million red lines traced down from a spray. Dark rain dripped from the ceiling, along with heavier things that plinked and plopped to the floor. Something large went splat and he pushed back in revulsion.

He flailed for balance on the blood-slick floor. His legs whisked free, and he fell. He tried to push up, but his hands slipped, and he crashed on his stomach. Every attempt to stand collapsed in a tangle of skidding feet and slippery hands. Frantic, he rolled to a dry patch and rose. His moans sharpened to hoots and whistles. He crashed outside, where he found his footing in the cool air and ran.

Coop watched the windows in another downtown Cleveland office go dark. The world was locking up. Soon only the morning would stand between him and marriage, between him and a wife.

He forced himself past the bloodiest memories.

He'd banged on the Porters' back door. Mrs. Porter, along with her four sons who still lived in the house, were soon crowding about. Coop jabbered and howled. They caught the gist. Mrs. Porter sent two of the boys to the Tiller farm and told Timmy to fetch the sheriff and Clyde the doctor.

She wore a flannel nightdress under an open, colorful wrap that brushed the floor. Even in his dazed state, Coop admired how she'd made herself more presentable.

He'd never seen her hair so frizzy, kinky with age. Her skin looked different. Shiny.

She pulled him into her clean white kitchen and made him sit. "Stay there and I'll make you a nice cup of hot chocolate, young Mr. Tiller." Her voice quaked. "And you've earned a shot of brandy, I dare say."

She was working at the stove as a disheveled young maid named Elsie arrived and looked curiously at Coop. Elsie's eyes flew open, and she cupped her mouth, muffling a scream.

The metallic smell hit him the moment he saw all the blood on his clothes and skin. He cried out, jumping to his feet.

"Elsie," Mrs. Porter said, rushing to grip Coop's arm. "Search the chest in my sewing room and find a set of clean trousers and a shirt that will fit." Elsie fled, trailing a muted shriek.

Mrs. Porter held firm while Coop staggered aimlessly. He saw his faint bloody trail across the white tile floor and drew back, pulling in a breath, filling with shame. He must have looked like a demon come raging from hell when the Porters opened the door.

Mrs. Porter steered him back to the table. "I got more boys' clothes than Carter's got pills, so sit and don't disobey me again, young Mr. Tiller. I run a cattle farm, and it takes more than a little blood to get me at sixes and sevens."

She returned to the stove and stirred, the scrape of metal on metal. It intensified the bloody smell until it thickened in his throat. A gag became a sudden urge to puke. He fought it with loud and painful convulsions.

Mrs. Porter slammed over and dragged him to the sink. He aimed and let loose a violent spray of acidic yellow bile that felt like fire in his throat. "You're doing a good job," she said softly. "See, it's going right down the drain. Elsie will be grateful, and believe you me, she's never grateful for anything, so you're doing me a real favor here."

When he was finished, she wiped his mouth with a towel and told him to sit again. A moment later, she set a saucer holding a steaming cup of hot chocolate on the table. He gave it a cautious look. She slid it closer. "Go on. I promise you'll feel fortified."

He took a sip. The brandy overpowered the chocolate. His body demanded more, and he ignored the scalding heat to gulp the rest. The alcohol felt cleansing, burning away all the sick and rot inside.

Mrs. Porter brought a bottle of amber liquid and a small glass to the table. She poured a splash and took a tiny sip. She brushed his hair from his forehead. "Poor young Mr. Tiller. How old are you now?"

"I just turned fifteen."

"You're growing into a handsome devil." She smiled sadly and clipped his chin. "I dare say none of my sons were as fanciable at your age, and they were no motley crew, so that's saying something."

She took another sip and chuckled at the way he eyed the drink. "I suppose it's no time to join the Temperance League." She gave him the glass, and he drained it with a gulp. The liquid seared his chest and cleared his nose. He wanted more.

Her voice went serious as she held up a finger. "Now, you listen to me, hear? Folks make their own decisions, and we aren't responsible. I've got two hundred men working for me and I can't get a-one of them to keep their boot strips hooked and tied."

"They do everything you say."

"Only when I'm watching. If I'm not, they stomp around until their feet get tangled and they go down smack on their faces, usually into a cow pat."

He wasn't sure if he was supposed to laugh.

"One day you'll wonder what you could have said or done." She brought his hands together and squeezed, not bothering about the blood. "The answer is, not a plug thing."

He whispered, "I heard them talking about it. If I'd figured it out just a few seconds sooner…"

She pressed a finger to his lips, shaking her head. "Not a plug thing. They were determined, and it wasn't in your hands." Kenny's departing back flashed in his mind, the way the weeds snapped back, and how his brother paid no mind to Coop's calls. "So, don't you go shouldering burdens that aren't yours." She gathered up the things on the table and returned to the stove. "I'll let you have one more shot of brandy but not a straight finger. I'll make another hot chocolate."

A set of fresh clothes flew into the kitchen and scattered softly across the floor. Elsie's footsteps pounded upstairs. Mrs. Porter sighed. "I guess I can't fault the girl."

Coop gathered the clothes and stood. "Thanks kindly for these. I have to go home, to figure out what I'm going to do next."

"You're going to work here, and that's my final word. I need a reliable overseer and you'll be crack dandy, I'm sure. I'm used to getting my way, so don't you go making plans out of turn, Mr. Tiller." Despite everything, he felt proud she'd left off "young" for the first time.

Coop said, "Everyone's afraid of you, but you've been kinder to me than just about anybody. You must be the nicest lady in the whole state, but I gotta decide some things for myself." He thought of her husband's wretched memory. "Just like you did." He shook his head. "I'm not saying it properly. What I mean…"

"I know what you mean," she said, eyes agleam. "I've seen my share of troubles, it's true. A body needs to set a spell after a shock, specially one so big as you've had this night. But no fiddle-faddle, hear? No fallow fields and animals starving in pens, not while I live next door." Swiftly, she swiped her eyes. "You have a mind, there's no denying. So, get on home and find your feet. Plant this year's crops, but you'll be working here by harvest, so plan accordingly." She shook her head. "Who'd have believed it? A poor farm boy next door."

He wanted to give her a hug, but it would be too familiar. He was at the door when she said, "Coop."

She'd never called him Coop. Amazed, he turned. She walked over, holding out the brandy. "For when you need a shot of courage."

It took weeks to plant the whole farm. From a shady spot next to the barn, he watched the first green shoots rise. The goat was lying next to him. He'd named her Petunia, and he scratched her head from time to time.

Coop hadn't been inside the house since the night of rifle shots and blood. He took to sleeping in the barn, up front, like he was watching over the animals as they slept. He left the stalls and pens open to let them wander wherever they liked. Daisy took Baby on little walks in the field, and Petunia sometimes scurried alongside, but they always came back.

One late spring day, he saw Daisy's head bobbing above the weeds. He could just make out the brown hump of Baby's head alongside. Petunia looked content at Coop's side.

Over by the henhouse, little yellow chicks ran about. Coop let the rooster and hens do as they liked, and while he took a few eggs to scramble on a cook fire, many hatched. He kept the chickens fenced to protect them from a squawking, feathery massacre by coyotes and raccoons. Hell, Target and his pack could annihilate them in moments.

About a week before, Clyde had arrived carrying a sealed tub. "Coop," he said, setting it down, "Where's the deed to this farm?"

Coop shook his head, not understanding. Clyde went into the house and came out coughing and shaking his head, holding a small leather folder.

"That place needs to be burned," he said angrily, retching, his face aflame. "It stinks to high heaven. Flies and maggots everywhere. You can't let that much blood just sit like that. Are you living in those conditions?"

"I sleep in the barn. I haven't been inside since that night. Matter of fact, I've been thinking of setting it to flame. Nobody in this world will miss that shack."

Clyde's anger evaporated. He gave Coop the folder. "I found this in your parents' room, and how I found the moxie to step foot in there I'll never know. But this proves you own this farm, so keep it safe. My mom wants to know how your plans are coming along?"

"I want to tend this crop. That's as far as I can think, Clyde."

"It doesn't make sense to me." Clyde pointed to the container. "That tub is full of our best jerky. My mom's worried you're not getting enough to eat. It's expensive, so don't go giving it to animals."

Coop feasted on the delicious jerky for days, and it seemed the tub would never go empty. With Petunia at his side, he ripped another strip with his teeth and chewed. At a growl and a whine, Coop sat up happily. Target was at the end of the barn.

"I knew you were coming! Here, Target."

Target ran over while his pack fell about with overwrought despair. Petunia looked nervous until Target gave her a friendly sniff.

Coop held up a jerky strip and Target went solemn, licking his chops. Coop tossed it gently, Target leaped, and it vanished with a swallow. The dog sniffed around, mad for more.

"Let's get some for your pack. There's plenty for everyone!"

Target followed him to the barn where Coop opened the tub and grabbed a fistful. He approached the pack slowly. They went rigid with alarm but seeing their leader happily jumping at Coop's side set off a chorus of confused whines, like a hundred squeaky pulleys.

Coop gave Target another piece before carefully tearing and tossing several strips to the pack. They recoiled and skittered, growling uncertainly until they caught the scent of the jerky and sniffed furiously. One brave dog found the courage to creep forward and crane his neck to delicately pluck a strip with his front teeth. He trotted a few feet and slumped, gnawing and swallowing. Another dog stepped forward tentatively.

Coop held back, feeding Target from his own hand and gently tossing the rest. Soon, the whole pack was gorging and grunting with pleasure.

Coop smiled, happier than he'd been in a long time.

An angry bellow shattered the moment. The dogs crouched as one while a cart came in from the road, driven by a hollering man.

Target's fur rose in a line down his back. He growled, baring his teeth, his lips trembling. Coop didn't want this angry man to see the pack, and he threw the jerky into the weeds. "Go on, Target," he said, pointing. "This is a human problem. Get your jerky."

Target jumped in the weeds and the rest followed.

Coop walked over. A line of people rode in quiet submission in the back of the cart, seated strangely with their legs straight out.

It was Harold and his family. With a drooping face and uncombed hair, Harold gave Coop an appraising look. His wife timidly asked for water and Coop watched in horror as Harold unstrapped them from the cart.

As his family limped for the well pump, Harold said, "I'm not one for social talk." This close, his face looked like the mess Daisy sometimes puked up. "I have some land up north. It's hill country with good fishing, but you can't farm it and I got mouths to feed."

Coop saw how Harold wove truth and lies effortlessly. He probably did own a hill, but he only mentioned providing for his family for sympathy. Coop wondered if Harold had any idea how easy it was to see what he really meant.

"I got the deed right here," Harold said, going back to the cart and removing a sack from under the bench. "If you got your deed, you just need to write the details of the trade on the back of yours and mine. Then each of us sign both right here and now."

Coop was suspicious. "Why do I need to write the details of the trade for both of us?"

"Can't read or write," Harold said without hesitation. "'Cept for my name. They call my hill Lightning Mountain. That's what the Tuscarawas called it, but it ain't no mountain. It's a big hill, though. Folks say there's coal around, but I never had the chance to look."

He was lying about the coal in some way. "Where up north?"

"In Harrison County, not far from Pennsylvania. Take about a week on foot. It's even got a cabin, right by a fishing lake. Everything you need."

Coop struggled to keep Harold from seeing his sudden, explosive need to leave. He'd have a good life with the Porters, but this farm, capricious and uncaring, would always be just across Slim's Creek for the rest of his life. The place that killed his parents and drove his brother away would taunt him, so close he could hear the leaves rustling in the wind.

He suddenly understood why he'd delayed moving into Mrs. Porter's fancy house. When he left this farm, he would leave for good. Moving in with the neighbors was no way to make a clean escape.

"You interested?" Harold said.

"Show me on a map."

Harold pulled a map from the sack and snapped it open, pointing to a spot using a cracked and filthy nail. Coop knew the general region from Miss Everson's maps.

Harold was looking around. "Hang on. This farm ain't got no animals other than those chickens?"

"No," Coop said, suddenly realizing his responsibility to keep Daisy, Baby, and Petunia safe from this man.

Harold sneered. "If you got no other animals, is that your girlfriend?"

Petunia stood at the edge of the field, looking back nervously. When Harold's eyes fell on her, she plunked into the weeds.

"She belongs to the neighbors, who let her run free."

Harold snorted. "That old doe would be stew if she came on my land. Finders, keepers."

Coop thought of the infrequent times a Porter cow crossed to this side of the creek. One time, he found a heifer slumped in the shade of the barn, ignoring Daisy, Baby, and the Bumpheads, who were trying to welcome her with their noses through the fence. Harold would learn a quick lesson in humility if he went up against the Porters.

Harold scanned the healthy crops, nodding. "And that old shack is the farmhouse?"

"Yep."

"I don't know. Far as I can tell, you ain't even greased your dong for me. I think I may rescind my offer, as the ladies say." His eyes fell on the open door of the barn. "Now, hang on, what's this?"

He walked over to throw aside the tarp from the beautiful, golden two-by-fours. He ran his hand along a surface, whistling. "This is mighty good lumber. Mill-cut and finished." A beat passed. "Let's fix a flint on this here deal."

"How do I know you're telling me the truth?"

Harold acted offended. "Are you doubting my word?" A laugh escaped Coop and Harold snarled. "I've slipped plenty in my pocket and went on my merry way, but how can I do that with a farm? If I ain't telling the truth, you come back with a notice from Harrison County and the sheriff will drive me off your land."

It made sense. Disturbed by his casual confession of thievery, Coop wrote the details of the trade on both deeds before they signed. As they exchanged the papers, Coop was amazed how easily land changed hands.

Harold clapped loudly to get his family's attention. "Get a move on. Home sweet home. You," Harold shouted at his son. "Get a look in that barn and tell me what you find. And keep the rifle handy. I saw a pack of wild dogs when we pulled up. The leader had a bunch of scars on his head. We kill him. and the rest will run off with their tails between their legs, so don't miss." When Harold wasn't looking, his son glared at his father with hatred.

Coop felt frantic to get Daisy, Baby, and Petunia away, but his mind was blank. Thankfully, they seemed to be on one of their longer walks.

Harold pointed at the little girls. "Get on over to that henhouse. See if there are any afternoon eggs and tell me how many chickens we got."

Harold's wife walked with a limp like Kenny's parody of Clyde, holding the baby tight with both hands. Harold told her to get the house in order, and she hobbled off.

Harold took another swig from the jug and acted surprised to see Coop. "Be on your way, now. This is my farm."

Coop was out of time for a clever way to save the animals. He raced around the barn and nearly cried out. Daisy had come to see what all the commotion was about, Baby and Petunia on her heels.

Quickly, he led them back into the weeds. They followed dutifully, and he took them a good distance away before cutting over to the creek. Daisy and Baby picked across without trouble, but Petunia was terrified of the water, so Coop carried her.

On the clear cattle pastures, Coop started to trot. Daisy and Baby kept up but shrank back when the herd dogs charged. Coop cut them off and ordered them away. By the time he reached the smokehouse behind the main house, Clyde had seen them and was marching up. "Coop, what are you doing?"

"I traded my farm for some land up north. But he's a mean man, nasty, and I can't leave my animals with him."

"What do you mean you traded your land?"

Coop explained and showed him the deed.

Clyde said, "I don't like this. I think this man is taking advantage of you. And you're supposed to live here and work for us. My mother is counting on you."

"I really like your mom, Clyde. She's been real good to me. I like your whole family, but I need to leave. I guess the best way to explain it is that even though you're the nicest people I can think of, and I'm so grateful I could burst, I still gotta leave. It's that strong."

Clyde looked sorrowful and respectful at the same time. Dully, he said, "What am I gonna do with these animals? We got no use for them."

"You got a million pens, Clyde. Just put them in one that's big enough for all three. They love each other and just want to be together." When Clyde hesitated, Coop said, "We're friends, and friends look out for each other. I never told a soul what I saw out by the swimming hole because we're friends. I'm asking you as a friend to do this for me."

After a moment, Clyde smiled. "You got me, Coop. I'll take care of your animals, but I don't like this trading land business. I think I'll go have a talk with this mean man."

Clyde would despise Harold and cancel the trade. "Clyde, I need to get away. For a while, at least. Did you ever read *Robinson Crusoe*? I need to see new things for once. While I'm still young."

They went back and forth a few more times until Clyde nodded reluctantly. "I'm gonna miss you. We all will. You better write, or you'll hurt my mama's feelings."

Happiness and sorrow squeezed Coop's throat at the same time. "I'll write when I get a feel for the place. Tell everyone I said goodbye and how grateful I am. And tell your mom I feel like she's my own mom in some way."

He held out his hand and Clyde took it and pulled him in for a hug. "You're a good boy, Coop."

Coop raced off before he started crying. He glanced back to see Clyde leading Daisy, Baby, and Petunia away. Daisy strained to see where Coop was going. He ran harder, pounding his feet to drive off the sorrow before it swamped him.

Back at the farm, Harold had taken off his overalls and was marching barefoot in a pair of flimsy drawers while bellowing orders. The kids rushed about in plain linens, too. Coop didn't see the wife, so she must have been in the house.

One of the girls spotted a piece of pink paper blowing across the yard, one of Mrs. Porter's thank you notes to Mom. Harold or his wife must have thrown them to the wind. Enchanted, the girl raced after it. Behind her, the rest of Mrs. Porter's notes sailed off in a colorful spiral.

"You!" Harold came roaring at Coop. "Why didn't you tell me the house was full of blood and brains?"

"I haven't been inside since my parents died in there. I didn't know what it was like."

"You get off my land."

There was enough jerky to feed him on a trip around the world, and he couldn't leave without it. "I have to get a few things."

"If you're not off my farm in one minute, I'll take a shot at you."

Harold gave him a glare so dark Coop knew the threat was real. Harold wouldn't think twice about killing and burying Coop on the farm. Now that he'd told Clyde he was leaving, no one would know he was missing. Harold would get away with it.

A daring idea that would even give him a measure of revenge popped into Coop's mind. "I'll make a deal with you. Let me get the rest of my stuff, and I'll tell you how you can eat as much beef as you want. Me and my dad worked out a system. Must be something like ten thousand head of cattle right across the creek. You wanna know how to get some, you gotta let me get my stuff."

A lucrative swindle could distract a man like Harold from his anger, but only for a little while. That was all the time Coop needed, and he quickly spread out his wool blanket. He tossed his pillow inside, along with *Robinson Crusoe* and a few other things. His hands shook as he followed with fistfuls of jerky, hoping the sweat pouring from his forehead and trickling down his neck wasn't obvious. Harold would pounce on fear without mercy.

"My farm, my jerky!" Harold shouted.

Coop smothered the urge to run. He decided to confuse Harold by not complying but also not complaining. "You'll have a right smart chance at a whole cow before long. Maybe tonight, but you gotta know the secret."

Harold bristled with suspicion, but he hesitated. It gave Coop the courage for another casual indignity, and he emptied the tub of jerky into his blanket. Harold stiffened. Coop didn't say a word as he tied it together, popped it on his rifle stock and flipped it over his shoulder.

Harold's eyes burned with something deeper than hatred, an emotion Coop couldn't name. Or maybe it was no emotion at all. "You better be careful, boy. I'm a meat axe, I am. I've killed men for being all gum and women for disrespect. I won't take none of that from no pissant farm boy."

"I'm not all gum. All you need to know is that the cattlemen hate the family, all possessed like. Don't take more than a dollar to make them look the other way while you walk off with a heifer. One cow will feed your family for months or more. Get two, and you can slaughter the other and sell it for a prince's price."

"A dollar?" Harold looked concerned, and Coop realized it was easier to catch a weasel asleep than for Harold to save a whole dollar.

"But those herd dogs are blind and deaf. If you don't let the guards see you, you won't even need a greenback." To make it seem more real, he added, "But they'll want their money if they catch you."

Coop worried Harold would spot all the weak spots in his tale, like why was Coop so poor if it was so easy? Relief washed over Coop as Harold's eyes filled with plans to spend his imminent beef fortune. Harold believed every word because stealing from neighbors was part of life, as far as he was concerned. It was all visible on his face.

Coop wished he could watch Harold offer a bribe to the loyal

Porter workers or see the vigilant dogs descend on him, snapping with rage. It capped the climax to imagine Harold's face when he realized Coop got the upper hand, until Coop realized Harold's wife and children would pay.

"Now get," Harold snarled. "I'll plant you in that field if you ain't gone next time I look." He saw one of his daughters doing something to rage about and marched off.

Coop went around the barn, almost tripping over Harold's son crouched against the wall. The boy clenched his teeth, looking anguished as his father's words filled the air like wasps. He aimed his fury and humiliation at Coop.

"You don't got the brains of a headless turkey," the boy spat. "We left the Lightning eight months ago when the roof caved in on the cabin. It's a heap of splinters by now."

"You've been on the road for months with him?"

The boy looked uncertain about commiserating but went hard again. "And we did look for coal on the Lightning but never found shit. There ain't nothing but trees and rocks and big cliffs." His voice went high with a sneer. "My dad won that hill in a hand of poker. You traded farmland for a worthless hill, you stupid twat."

"What's your name?"

"I'm a meat axe, is who I am."

Harold's voice came relentlessly, and the boy's anger melted into resignation. He reminded Coop of Kenny after Dad pushed him into the weeds. "Why don't you come with me?"

Hope momentarily infused the boy. "I can't leave my mom and sisters with him."

Coop understood. "I want to tell you one thing about this farm. If you go halfway from here to the creek and into the field thirty paces, you'll find an old well we plugged up. My dad painted a warning on top. You'll see it. If anyone goes in, they'll never be found."

The boy snarled. "Let 'em fall in there and die. It don't trouble me."

"They don't have to be alive when they go in." Coop gave a meaningful look to the barnyard where Harold was still shouting. "Dead or alive, nobody will ever find him."

The kid looked at his dad as if seeing something for the first time.

As Coop left, he gave the farm a final look, remembering how his father, just before he killed himself, confessed his regrets for not turning around when he'd arrived.

"I'm leaving, Dad. I'm doing it for you."

❖

Twenty-six years later, in his room at the Admiral Perry Club, Coop recalled the farm shack the last time he saw it. He was surprised how badly it was listing, almost as if a good push might bring it down.

On his desk in front of him were the drawings he'd commissioned for the new mansion he would build for Elena and the family they planned on having. The home would rise cliffside above Lake Erie.

Their top-flight architect hated Coop's idea for a rounded tower with curved window glass. He was also scornful of Elena's shy request for a lacy version of carpenter gothic trim that would drip like year-round icicles.

The architect also fumed at Coop's insistence that all the materials had to come from Ohio, the state that made Coop rich.

The bricks would be fired from the fine-grained, silky pink clay deposited in vast sweeps under the eastern half of Ohio. Limestone and sandstone quarried down south would create a sturdy foundation and line the basement. Since Ohio had no lumber industry to speak of, he would buy from private woodlands: oak and pine for structural elements, American beech and black cherry to fill rooms with a glow as rich as mahogany.

Coop thought back to that last day on the farm, how the shack was leaning, and forced himself to remember the hardest part.

After planting parricide in the mind of Harold's son, in the field just off the farm, Coop called for Target until it seemed pointless. Just then, one of Target's pack members peeked above the weeds with comical caution, before it took off running.

Coop followed, leaping through the weeds, calling out until Target raised his head. They had a brief reunion, and Coop gave him a piece of jerky as the pack looked on in sorrow.

"Come on, boy. You want to come with me to hill country?"

Wagging, Target gamely took a spot at Coop's side. The pack slunk along well behind, all droopy heads and tucked tails.

Coop talked a stream, about his life, and how much he wanted to see his new home. Target walked as surely as any confident man. Now and then, both checked to make sure the pack was following.

It was growing dark when Coop and Target emerged from the weeds onto a narrow pasture. On the other side ran a length of woods stretching from north to south as far as he could see.

"If this is where I think it is, the road isn't too far on the other side of these woods. Come on, let's find a spot to camp."

Coop had nearly reached the forest when the moment he'd dreaded arrived at last. He heard a distant whine.

In the darkening light, Target stood back, halfway across the field. Far off, his pack was running for a place they seemed to know.

"Come on, Target."

The dog stayed put no matter how many times Coop called. He let out a breath. "I understand. You have your pack to think of. It was sure nice knowing you, Target."

Target whipped around halfway as if to run but stopped and doubled back to stare at Coop expectantly. Coop was mystified. Target did it again.

"I don't know what you're trying to…"

With Target's third false start, Coop understood. Target was inviting Coop to come with him, to join his pack.

Coop staggered back with a torrent of feelings, but unworthiness took him to the ground. His soul split, opening a grief deeper than the deepest abandoned well. He doubted he'd feel anything but the aching, sudden silence of loss for the rest of his life.

Target waited in the last of the lingering light.

Coop wiped his eyes. He shook his head. "I wish I could, but I can't." He waved and Target slumped when he understood it was time to leave. "You stay away from that farm, Target. Harold will kill you. You understand?"

Target trundled over to lick Coop's face. Coop pulled him close and kissed the target at the top of his head. "Thanks for being such a good friend."

Target looked into his eyes before racing into the night, a bouncing yellow patch that quickly dimmed. Coop strained to see the last flash of color before everything he knew became the charcoal sketches of memory.

CHAPTER THREE

Bay Village, Ohio
Present day

Scrolled black iron gates hang from river stone posts, blocking the driveway to the mansion Cooper Tiller built along a still-fashionable stretch of Lake Erie coastline in the upscale suburb of Bay Village. Lush summer trees and bushes shield most of the house from street view. A spiked fence encloses the property on three sides, while a cliff falling ten feet to a narrow rocky beach protects the back.

Darcy clicks the gates open and drives slowly up the long driveway, the screech from his brakes echoing off a small grove of evergreens. The house slides into view, rising three stories in red brick, a study in confident yet restrained splendor.

Darcy has many memories of the suburban home where his parents raised him and his sisters. And yet, this house provides the magnificent setting for his most pivotal moments.

The house is famous for its turrets, cupolas, dormers, gothic trim, and a magnificent tower along the left side. He remembers his amazement when his mother pointed out how the window glass curved with the rounded wall.

A wide porch pools into a large gazebo on the right, and Darcy remembers summer family lunches under the canopy. He can hear the creak of the wicker chairs, the muted clatter of plates and cutlery on the plastic tablecloth. He remembers the exhilarating abundance of fried chicken, hamburger patties and hot dogs, buns, chopped lettuce and onions, macaroni salad, pickles, potato chips. Maids in blue uniforms brought the food and whisked away the remnants.

The lunches ended with a sprawl of sweet ingredients for banana splits and strawberry shortcake. "Or both," Grandma Millie would say with a twinkle.

The huge house was meant to accommodate the many children Cooper and Elena Tiller must have been planning, but their only child Mildred, Darcy's future Grandma Millie, arrived just as the house was completed.

Darcy parks in front of the detached brick garage. His brakes mercifully go quiet. Grabbing a handful of crackers he keeps in the glove compartment, he calls, "Albie," as he walks the meandering, paving stone path to the house. "Wake up, Albie." He squats at the edge of the porch, pushing bushy branches aside.

As he'd hoped, he'd woken the albino raccoon who's been living under Grandma Millie's porch for months. Darcy thinks of her as a girl, and when their eyes meet, Albie wriggles with happiness, pure white except for a quivering pink nose. She looks like a fluffy little bear, and she almost seems to smile. "Hey there, pretty girl," he says. She squeaks and hums with joy as he piles the crackers next to her. She gives them a sniff and rolls on her back to demonstrate her trust, her way of calling him a friend. She falls asleep.

Darcy stands and approaches the house, looking closely for the first time in years, admiring the artistry of the millworkers, the precision of the bricklayers, and the accuracy of the carpenters.

The path curves to the porch, but Darcy stops to look at the spot on the lawn where he'd found Grandpa Bob.

Darcy was six years old, and his family had dressed up for a special dinner at Grandma Millie's. Grandma was waiting on the porch. As Darcy climbed from the car after his sisters, he saw a pair of feet lying on the grass beyond the tower, half-obscured by a bush.

His mother took his hand as his family walked up the stone path. Nobody else noticed the strange sight on the lawn.

"I don't know where your father is," Grandma Millie said to Mom. "He was going to do some gardening, and I've been calling and calling." In the hugging and kissing chaos of a family greeting, Darcy slipped away to investigate.

Along the side of the house, next to a small tarp piled with wilting weeds, Grandpa Bob lay on his back with his arms awkwardly spread, his head angled up sharply and his mouth open as if taking a gulp of air.

His eyes were half-closed and milky gray. With a start, Darcy noticed Grandpa had peed his shorts.

When he returned to the porch, everyone but Grandma had gone inside. "I found Grandpa," he said, and she followed him, looking worried. She turned the corner and inhaled sharply, her hands flying to her mouth. After several deep breaths, she patted her chest and forced another look.

With a gasp, Grandma snapped the tarp clean and draped it across Grandpa's lap to hide the pee stain. Tears sparkled in her eyes, and Darcy thought she'd never looked more beautiful.

Tenderly, she said, "He was a very brave man. We got married in 1949, and he agreed to move into this house with my parents. Most men at the time considered it shameful for the wife to provide the family home, but he put my wishes first."

She smiled, wiping her eyes. "You were very dignified, Darcy, not making a commotion. Your Grandpa Bob would be proud of you. Come along now. We'd better tell the others."

The sad memory fades and Darcy walks up the steps to the front double doors, framed by etched glass panels: a dog and a fox run side by side, herd dogs corral cows, stalks of corn hold a second cob halfway down.

An exuberant barnyard scene crowds the transom. A horse on its hind legs seems at battle with a donkey, although opinions have always differed if the scene is meant as a fight. On either side, a warrior dog with crossed scars on his head shares stature with another dog scattered with light and dark spots.

Darcy unlocks the doors and gives a gentle push. They open to a wide hallway paneled in dark wood, ending with a gleaming staircase rising into the ceiling. Memories crowd his mind.

He remembers his father, stocky and solid in jeans and a tight polo shirt, sliding down this hall in white socks, while Darcy's sisters, Serena and Lydia, wore stockings. They'd laugh and run back to the bottom of the stairs where Dad would clap and shout, "You have to run to get some real momentum!"

Dad often patted his stomach, voicing his pride that he was as fit as when he was in the Navy. He let his hair grow a bit shaggier than his work buddies at the electrical company, enjoying a veteran's indulgence.

The middle of five brothers from an Irish family in Chicago, Dad was on a training exercise with sea cadets on the Great Lakes when he met Mom. "I became a Clevelander the second she told me she'd never move."

"The second you saw the house where I lived," Mom would say with good-natured ribbing. They'd share a smile, and Darcy knew they loved each other.

Darcy noted the differences between the families as a child. Mom grew up in the leafy, refined world of comfortable living and small families. She enjoyed quiet pastimes and, along with Grandma Millie, took Darcy and his sisters to museum exhibits, music recitals, and book readings. Holidays and special occasions meant dining at Grandma's Chippendale table, served by smiling women in uniforms. The conversation flowed naturally, and the laughter was soft and appreciative. Dad always seemed to have a good time.

Dad's brothers lived in the Chicago suburbs, raising sprawling broods in crowded, cluttered houses. Family dinners were backyard events with card tables groaning with crockpots and platters covered with cellophane, and kegs of beer with towering piles of red plastic cups. Darcy's many cousins shrieked and ran and conspired, while Dad and his brothers razzed each other and joked at the tops of their lungs. The wives usually formed a loud circle Mom joined with ease.

Darcy grew up straddling the worlds. When he was a teenager, he'd asked his mom if marrying into such a different family had been difficult.

She'd laughed. "No, it was easy blending our families because we were both Catholic. It's old-fashioned to use religion to bridge class divides, but it works. You understand each other perfectly."

All wasn't perfect, Darcy knew, for he'd seen Grandma Millie tighten her lips and leave the room when Dad told a bawdy joke. And he'd heard Uncle Paddy ask Dad how he could stand living so close to "that wrinkled old snob." At first disorienting, incidents like these led Darcy to realize how a frictionless life was both impossible and unnecessary.

Everyone tried, that was the important thing, and Darcy smiles remembering Grandma Millie cheering on her son-in-law and grandchildren as they slid down the big front hall in their stocking feet.

Just inside the house, to the left, is a red salon with big chairs and couches upholstered in plush ruby fabric. Matching wallpaper features tight regal patterns in velveteen, slick with age.

Above a fireplace mantel cluttered with family pictures hangs a large sepia-toned photo portrait of his great-grandparents on their wedding day, a full-length view to show their outfits. They stand at a slight angle to each other, a hand clasped high between them. An engraved brass plate at the bottom reads *1920*.

Cooper Tiller is enormously handsome in a formal, high-collared suit, his face a study in firm symmetry. A prominent brow gives his eyes a thoughtful intensity. Shadows subtly reveal his sculpted cheeks and the hint of a cleft chin. People always said Darcy is his spitting image.

The much younger Elena is beautiful in a straight-lined, drop-waist gown. Yards of lace flow from an elaborately embroidered cap, exuberant with all the flounces the dress lacks. Ribbons tumble from her bouquet.

They look dutiful and joyless, reflecting the stiff formality of period photos but also empty of affection. They gaze flatly in different directions, as if trying to remember how they came to this point.

He scans the framed photos on the mantel, black-and-white or pastel snapshots stuffed with happy relatives. Most come from Great-grandma Elena's side of the family, with intricate lineages Grandma Millie could detail by heart, even in later years when the different branches grew into remote mist.

"As for my father's family," he remembers Grandma saying, "my dad mentioned an older brother Kenny now and then. They had a falling-out as teenagers, something about Kenny not pulling his weight on the farm. Apparently, Kenny came to their wedding, but as far as I know, that was the last anyone heard of him."

In an instant, Darcy's certain his great-grandfather's brother is the link to Charles Greene, and the source of the mystery.

A door leads to Cooper Tiller's home office. Filled with heavy furniture and brass fittings, the room reeks of wealthy industrialist seriousness. The wood-paneled walls glow, and a huge standing globe looks well-consulted, the ink worn by fingers tracing distribution routes that streak away from Cleveland and Lake Erie.

The next door leads to Grandma Millie's study, handed down from her mother Elena, the bride in the photo. Dainty furniture and fixtures look as carefully arranged as the masculine fittings next door, with cheerful blue wainscoting and flowery wallpaper.

He steps into the main hallway. The staircase on the left leads to the bedrooms. He wanders across to the afternoon salon, where everyone gathered countless times.

The dining room is adjacent, with a wall of windows overlooking the back porch and lawn. The polished, expansive table reflects the cloudy light as a wooly gray splash, surrounded by twelve shapely chairs pushed in close.

The rooms on this side of the house feel airier, more welcoming. Bright wallpaper covers the walls from top to bottom, with no fussy wainscoting. The scattered chairs, love seats, and sofas offer pretty but functional upholstery. Even the wood is lighter.

Darcy told his parents and sisters over the phone that he was gay, but he'd wanted to tell Grandma Millie in person, alone.

They'd sat in this room, in the stuffed chairs along the far wall with a small table between them. He squirmed and fussed until she said, "Whatever it is, just spit it out. I'm an old lady, and I've heard everything."

"Grandma, do you know what a homosexual is?"

"For heaven's sake, I've known gay people."

"You have?"

"Yes, and I guess you're about to tell me I know another one?" She'd smiled and reached for his hand.

Darcy walks into the music room through the open archway. A grand piano fills a corner, black-lacquered to a mirroring brilliance. Leather snap cases hold a cello and violins balanced on wood supports, alongside brass music stands.

Mom played the piano at almost every gathering, creating a magnificent flurry of notes as her fingers raced along the keyboard. She had a beautiful soprano voice, so pure it left first-time hearers breathless and carried her to a sublime, private summit. She always played "O Mio Babbino Caro" because it was Darcy's favorite, and when the final vibrato would fill the house, the world seemed to stop.

Darcy was a teenager when his mom astonished everyone by saying, "Mom, we haven't done our duet in years. What do you say?"

Grandma's reluctance crumbled under the insistence of the whole room. They sat side by side and sang "The Flower Duet" from *Lakmé*.

Their voices flitted along the sawtooth scales of the pretty tune, and while Grandma had a pleasant voice, Darcy thought Mom carried them both. The room erupted with cheers.

After every performance, Mom would run her fingers wistfully across the piano's fall board and say, "I always wanted to be a concert pianist," prompting Grandma Millie to set the record straight with, "I always encouraged you."

"The Navy came to town and that was that," Mom would say, smiling as she took Dad's hand. "There's just something about a sailor."

"It's that Navy chow," Dad would say. "Turns boys into men."

Darcy walks to the front room where hundreds of books line the walls. He brushes his fingers along the spines but freezes when hearing the hearty engine of the gardener's truck. The white pickup parks beside his car, and Jake unloads his lawnmower and gardening tools.

Darcy saw Grandma's new gardener on the back porch at her annual neighborhood Fourth of July party, when Darcy was visiting from San Francisco the summer before the pandemic that killed his parents. With curly brown hair and deep green eyes, Jake blinked at Darcy and his mouth dropped. Darcy's heart fluttered and a growl rumbled in his throat. Like gravity, their mutual attraction spun and accelerated, feeling unbreakable.

Jake had been wearing cargo shorts, well-used for manual labor and not as a fashion statement. He wore a plain blue T-shirt and work boots over white socks, and their expressions communicated raging lust.

Everyone congregated in Grandma's backyard for her peerless view of the local fireworks. Jake left during the show. Darcy wondered how he could have misread Jake's interest, but he was heading back to San Francisco the next day.

When he moved back to Cleveland, Jake was still tending Grandma's lawn and tidy little gardens, but Darcy did little more than smile and nod, unwilling to repeat his mistake.

Jake is still unloading his truck when Darcy fills with a propulsive desire, an affirmation of his life and instincts. He's certain Jake gave him a look of desire that first time. Maybe he's nervous and wants Darcy to take control. He steps outside and heads for the garage. Jake looks up and smiles.

If possible, Jake is even more handsome. The natural waves in his light brown hair frame his face. His shoulders and chest fill out his grungy T-shirt. Raw lust pulses through Darcy and crashes in his brain. His skin tingles at the thick fur on Jake's muscular forearms and legs.

Jake says, "I'm sorry about your grandmother. She was a nice lady and always treated me with respect. You took real good care of her."

"Thanks. Did someone ask you to keep looking after the lawn?"

"She always prepaid me for the season, so it seems only fair to keep coming until someone tells me to stop." Jake lifts a rake from the truck and starts pushing the lawn mower. "I'd better get to work."

"Are you hungry? I can make lunch."

Jake gives a crooked grin. "It's three o'clock. That's a late lunch."

"Then how about an early dinner?"

Jake goes red with embarrassment and Darcy realizes he was right. Jake *was* waiting for Darcy to make the first move. "Yeah, that would be great. This is my last job of the day, and I don't have plans tonight. But it's gonna take a few hours to get this lawn squared away."

Inside the huge but old-fashioned kitchen, Darcy decides to make his grandmother's fancy but easy favorite, pork chops in mushroom cream sauce. He'll throw together a salad, but the fresh bread dough is frozen and won't thaw in time. Grinning, he puts a loaf in the refrigerator for the morning.

He fries the chops, makes the rich sauce, tucks it all together, and sets the burner to low. He starts setting the small kitchen table before moving everything to the elegant dining room, only to move it all again to the wicker table on the porch.

Darcy sees Jake in the distance on the big lawn, shirtless and sweaty. He's always admired the furry carpet of Jake's chest and stomach, feathering onto his back. An erotic charge shoots through him, fueling his determination to correct his fumble from the long-ago Fourth of July party. Hot with anticipation, he frosts two mugs for the beer he's seen Jake drink after a hot day.

As Jake piles his equipment in his truck, Darcy brings the food and beer to the table. Jake slips on his T-shirt as he nears the porch. Darcy wishes he would leave it off but says, "You don't have to get dressed up for me."

Jake chuckles, reacting with amazement at the "pork chops and gravy." He raves with every bite.

They discuss their families and after Darcy tells him about his parents and his two older sisters, Jake says, "I have a younger brother and sister. My oldest sister died of a heroin overdose a few years back." His face crinkles with distaste. "I hate drugs. They turn people into monsters."

Darcy thinks of the lines of white powder he used for waking up and dancing. After resisting a sudden urge to reveal the worst, he says, "Do you want another beer?"

"It's tempting, but I have to drive home."

"Or you could have another and stay for a while."

"How long is a while?"

"Spend the night. I can make some French toast in the morning."

Jake blushes again. "Where will I sleep?"

"There's room in my bed."

A bashful chuckle. "Yeah?"

"Yeah."

"Well," Jake shakes his head, like he's about to decline, "I'd like that, actually."

CHAPTER FOUR

Central Ohio and Appalachian Foothills
Spring 1894

Coop headed north on the road outside Asheville, on the lookout for an eastern fork leading to coal country and his new home, Lightning Mountain. On the first afternoon he came upon a boulder by the side of the road. He'd never seen such a huge rock, and he gawked as he walked past.

It felt like a sign that his life was changing, and he thrummed in anticipation for his first glimpse of the Appalachian foothills.

Over the next week, two roads broke west. The east fork and the rising threshold of coal country remained a promise over the horizon.

Few people passed, and none on foot. High in their carts or carriages, they gave a friendly nod and grudgingly slowed their horses when Coop asked about the eastern fork. They always pointed north.

His dad used to say farmers know more about patience than any saint, but the unchanging scenery of gently rolling land brought Coop to the edge of his endurance. He rose at dawn and walked until sunset, but every day the horizon churned up more of the same flat landscape. At night he shot his rage at the uncaring stars.

He ate the last strip of beef jerky, gloomy as he fantasized punching his own stupid face. He'd brought his rifle from the farm, but no bullets. He could picture the pile of many slingshots on a barn shelf. Next to that, he'd stuffed a cubbyhole with dozens of water skins, next to another with a sealed tin holding hundreds of dry matches. The farm offered work knives and tools, axes and buckets, things to ease a new start. He'd left it all behind, dumb as dirt.

The next day, he woke with a grumbly stomach, scanning fields of clover and wild grass that offered desperation meals. He wasn't above picking a vegetable or two from the many farms along the way, but nothing was ripe enough. He set off for another day on the road, wondering what lessons hunger would teach. He'd already been jolted to realize clean water wasn't always on hand.

He stopped for the night and the next morning his stomach demanded food with nausea and bolts of pain that faded as he moved about. He set off again, into a horizon with no mountains or hills.

Hours later in mid-afternoon, hunger threatened to bend Coop at the waist when a horse and vehicle appeared in the distance. As it got closer, Coop could make out a heavy old hillbilly atop an itty little buggy. The man cheerfully stopped his horse and invited Coop for a "pic-a-nic." Coop nearly buckled with relief.

The man had a wide, plain face, and his nose went unexpectedly crooked twice as it drooped to his mouth. His hair looked unnatural too, coal black on a man of his years. He wore a baggy suit of good quality with a clutch of colorful paper flowers pinned to his vest. He reminded Coop of a half-deflated air balloon he saw at a carnival once, the bunting and swags hanging like rags. His name was Elmer, and he said he cut his teeth in Kin-tucky.

"Let's pull well away from the road so we don't bother nobody," Elmer said.

They moved the horse and buggy behind wild, bushy greenery and Elmer rummaged in the cart for "lunch fixins."

"It's nice to meet a new friend on the road," Elmer said. "With folks on the railways, you hardly see a body anymore. My work takes me from place to place, but it's gotten lonely out here."

"What's your work?"

"I travel from house to house." He threw aside a wool blanket, revealing a beautiful wooden chest with gleaming brass fittings inlaid with swirling initials. He grimaced and covered it quickly, as if revealing it was an accident. Coop felt uneasy.

In a little while they were sitting on the ground, sharing a jug of cider. The first sip improved Coop's spirits, and his strength returned as he followed Elmer's example and used his fingers to scoop from a honey pot. They cracked roasted peanuts Elmer called goobers. A big tin offered dry fruit "varietals" with exotic flavors. A little chewy orange fruit was so tasty he dug for another.

Elmer beamed. "That's an ape-ee-cot, come all the way from Calee-fornya, where the sun never sets and you can stuff your pockets with gold nuggets sitting in plain sight, pretty as you please. But God don't permit lives so sweet, not after the Fall. You can't ever enjoy yourself because the earth gets quaking, the land cracks open and buries you before you die. Happens all the time. That's why I'll never leave our little corner of the world."

Elmer fired bits of spit as he banged from story to story about the Bluegrass state, the most beautiful land since Eden. His kinfolk lived in the hollers and hills, "descended from the gypsies" with pious hearts but helpless to resist an escapade. Elmer would finish a tale and dart to the next, weaving such a spell Coop didn't mind dodging his spit.

His hunger sated, Coop tingled with ghoulish glee as Elmer described drunken tomfoolery that left Kentucky littered with body parts you can lose without dying, like limbs, eyes, and fingers. Grisly murders and rollicking mishaps mesmerized Coop and made him laugh in turn.

Coop was shocked when the sun started to fall. For dinner, Elmer sliced a summer sausage and a hunk of smooth cow cheese, and with a flourish, he set down a pot of marmalade with crackers. When he lifted a fresh jug of cider from the back of the buggy, Coop understood how deeply true gratitude runs.

Elmer jabbered like a tireless Virginia Reel. Coop went fuzzy, and the names and places melted together. Even Elmer's kinfolk mixed into a giant tenderfoot goofball, wobbly with moonshine, shedding body parts across the hills like a trail of breadcrumbs.

By twilight, Coop let the spit smack him as it would. He never knew some people talked so much, and he worried Elmer might spin yarns until dawn.

With the stars sparkling above, Coop let his head drop for just a minute, and it felt so restful he closed his eyes. Sleep cradled him gently, just about to carry him off.

Elmer gave a raucous laugh that made both Coop and the horse jump. "I got the gift of gab from my grandpappy, and a finer Irishman or stouter drinker never lived. But I'll rest a spell to hear your tales."

Coop pleaded exhaustion, but Elmer insisted Coop talk about his kith and kin. "Telling your tale is about the finest thing there is. You'll perk up like a daisy once you get going."

It felt rude to refuse, so Coop droned a bit about his family's struggles on the farm, leaving out almost everything that counted. He said his brother went to New York and his parents died and left it there.

Elmer shook his head. "That's a mighty tale of woe. Where you headed now?"

"Harrison County."

"Harrison County? God must have sent me to put you on the right path. You're going the wrong way."

Struck with fear, Coop said, "I started on this road south of Columbus and I've never left. I'm looking for the eastern fork, but it sure is taking its time."

Elmer slapped his knee. "You passed the fork on the first or second day, no doubt about it. There's no need for shame, for it hides in a small woodland, skittish as a kitchen mouse. It's opposite a boulder that looks like it dropped from the sky."

The clear memory of the boulder flashed in Coop's mind. "I passed that boulder a week ago. I need to get to Harrison County. I own a hill there called Lightning Mountain. It's all I have!"

"Now there's a tale I'll be glad to tell, an orphaned farm boy that owns a hill all to himself. I know Harrison County, and you'll find only good souls and fine forests and lakes, but you've never been farther away from there than you are right now."

Coop lashed himself with fury. "I've wasted days. I've been going crazy wondering why the Appalachian foothills were taking so long to show themselves. It was like I could hear them just over the horizon."

Elmer whistled in wonderment. "It's a rare soul that sings harmony with the mountains. And not every mountain range, mind. One time, my business took me across Kansas as far as the border of Colorado. Nothing but endless flatlands until one day I saw the Rocky Mountain ridge in yonder distance, a jagged line filled with ocean blue running clear across the earth. It looked like a saw, ready to slash the sky open. It gave me such a feeling, I swore I'd go no closer."

Elmer went reverent. "But the Appalachians on the horizon is the most comforting sight in the world, mild as moss. It's like God tossed His softest pillows to earth, so you can rest untroubled. You best pay heed when land beckons you, Coop. Only a soul with a charmed destiny can hear the mountains sing."

"I just want to get to my hill."

"Don't fret so. I'm on my way to Pittsburgh, which takes us along Harrison County's southern frontier. We'll set off top of the morning and the heel of the evening, so rest your eyes."

Elmer was a guardian angel, crooked nose and all.

Coop woke when something cold and wet blasted his ear. He leaped up, and in the light of dawn, Elmer's horse, Jemma, huffed good morning. Coop laughed and patted her nose, pleased to note the gentle disposition of a horse with a kind owner. She pushed her snout into his chest, accepting him as family.

Elmer stood at the edge of the road with his back to Coop, scanning the horizon with worry. He turned, saw Coop, and his face went jovial in an instant. It gave Coop pause, and he remembered Elmer's guilty look when he accidentally revealed the beautiful chest.

"Something wrong?" Coop said.

"Just checking the weather." He'd been watching the road.

After a breakfast of apples and pickled eggs, Coop helped attach Jemma to the buggy and tie everything down before climbing into the seat. Elmer circled below, securing the bonnet to the cart and tugging knots they'd already tightened. He shot quick, nervous glances in both directions.

He pulled aboard with unrestrained grunts, his face red with effort. He plopped down and took the reins as the seat bounced and squeaked. With a flick, they were off, retracing Coop's wasted days. Jemma settled into an easy clip, and they made good time on the dry road.

Elmer started with his stories again but with the jangles, bangs, clops, and other noise of the road, Coop didn't need to respond. He nodded and reacted when it seemed necessary, but otherwise wondered if Elmer was a thief or a highway robber. All the pieces fit.

They stopped only to let Jemma drink and rest, while Elmer searched the distance.

Hours passed, and Coop kept his questions to himself. He owed Elmer so much already, and everyone has a right to secrets. He'd proven his worth as a friend to Clyde, for being silent about what he saw at the swimming hole, and Elmer deserved no less.

Elmer was telling a story about a filly, which Coop learned

yesterday meant a young girl. Elmer said she was in a family way, dropping his voice to imply it was bad. The girl's father appeared, and the story filled with flying fists and broken bottles.

When Elmer took a breath, Coop blurted, "I had a friend with a secret, and I never told."

A slow smile spread under Elmer's crooked nose. "You did the right thing. A true friend knows to keep a secret."

They bumped along until Elmer started on his stories again.

Just as the day started to fade, Coop saw a rotting wagon wheel off in the weeds and gasped. "I remember that wheel. It feels like twenty years ago when I slept right next to it."

It was more like four days, and he was jubilant they'd covered so much territory in just one day.

Once more, Elmer insisted they camp clear of the road, behind towering evergreens. As they ate salami and cheese on crackers, Coop said, "Are you in some kind of trouble?"

"What makes you ask?"

"You keep looking, for danger or something. If you tell me what it is, I can lie for you if the time comes."

Elmer drew back. "You'd do that for me?"

Coop nodded and Elmer sighed. "That is just about the nicest thing I've ever heard, but I'll never ask you to lie for my sake."

"But if you need me to, I will."

"I don't, but I thank you from the bottom of my heart."

Coop didn't believe him. Elmer was only trying to set a proper example, and he would lie for Elmer when needed.

The light was fading when they settled in for sleep. Coop made a fuss so Elmer and Jemma could see him stretch out in the long grass in one spot. Quietly, he crawled to another place closer to the buggy, where neither Elmer nor Jemma would find him. He was nodding off when he heard someone swishing secretively along. He rose to a crouch and saw Elmer remove the beautiful chest from the cart, wrapping it in a blanket to carry back to his sleeping spot.

Coop lay down, certain he wouldn't sleep.

At dawn, Jemma licked him awake again. "How'd you find me?" he muttered with a smile. He rubbed her snout, looking around until he saw Elmer scanning the road back and forth. Coop stole his way to the buggy. Elmer had returned the chest to the cart.

On their second afternoon on the road, Coop was stunned when they cleared a wooded area and the road dipped, beyond which central Ohio stretched to the horizon. The boulder sat at the bottom. In a day and a half, they'd covered the ground it took a week to traverse on foot.

They neared the crest of the lengthy, gentle slope. The distant boulder stood like a swashbuckling visitor in this mild landscape. Just across was the eastern fork he'd missed, made obvious from above by a wide apron slipping into lightly scattered trees.

Elmer checked in every direction.

"Oh, for Pete's sake, Elmer. Who's after you?"

"After the life I've lived, could be the legions of hell."

"You keep driving, and I'll keep watch. Deal?"

"Deal."

Only minutes later, when they were halfway down the slope, Coop saw a man on a horse come trotting from the woods they'd just cleared. The man sat up with recognition before leaning in. His horse burst into a gallop.

"I think we may need to speed up."

"What?" Elmer said, trying to turn.

The horseman flew down the incline.

"Go!" Coop screamed.

The man waved his arm back and forth, shouting.

"Heeya!" Elmer flicked the reins. Jemma straightened with alarm before breaking into a run.

The horseman swiftly gained on them.

"Faster!" Coop yelled.

Coop's cry caused Jemma to bolt. In the cart, something crashed and barreled off. The seat bounced and screeched. Coop gripped the bar and held Elmer steady around his chest, pushing this way and that to keep from flying off.

The horseman was at their back.

Wild with fear, Jemma tore along, aiming for the east fork. Coop knew she wanted to hide, but they'd surely crash into a tree.

"No!" Coop screamed. Elmer pulled the reins to keep her straight. The frantic horse ignored him and charged into the turn. The immovable shafts hitched to the buggy strained against the axles and hinges.

Jemma's massive weight twisted the rigid shafts out of alignment, lifting the left wheels. They screeched against their bearings and the buggy careened, sliding into a skid. Coop felt the angle nearing the point of no return.

Elmer dropped the reins. They could only hold on.

In a moment, the buggy would tip and hurl them away. They'd be aloft as the vehicle crashed to the hard earth, shattering with every bounce. *If we survive*, Coop thought, *we'll wish we hadn't*. All seemed hopeless.

Suddenly, the horseman charged up the left side. He reached for Jemma's harness. With a lunge, he gripped and pulled.

Jemma slowed. The left wheels dropped, and the buggy tipped back to the ground, upright. The horseman brought Jemma to a stop as Coop and Elmer bounced, safe.

"Bluegrass!" the horseman cried. He jumped from his horse in a fury. He was a young man with a thick blond mustache, wearing dungarees, a button shirt, and a holster weighted down by a six-shooter. Coop didn't see a badge. "Bluegrass!"

Perfectly steady, Elmer said, "You stay here, Coop. These are my affairs." He climbed down.

Watching the horseman descend on Elmer, Coop's heart pounded, and he gulped for air. He remembered the way the Porter cattlemen called across the pastures with deep voices that rolled like barrels of rocks. If Coop could give his voice that much authority, this man might think twice and be on his way.

After an enormous inhale, Coop cried, "Ain't no Bluegrass here!" It came out a high screech. He flushed and cupped his mouth. Elmer gave him an amused but grateful smile.

The horseman squinted, his hand on his gun grip. "I been riding four days from Chicago!" he said to Elmer. "What do you mean by giving me chase? I coulda died getting control of your pea-brain horse. Now you got some pipsqueak shrieking at me like a banshee."

Elmer crossed his palms on his chest. "Doesn't take much for a mind to fill empty roads with dangers. Now, you have something for me?"

The man ranted a blue streak as he flipped up a wool blanket protecting a double pouch slung over his horse's hindquarters. "Dang blasted thing when I'm just doing my job!" He removed a small package wrapped in brown paper and tied with twine. "Think a hillbilly would be grateful for work that don't involve rattlers!" He shoved the package at Elmer and pointed at Coop. "You shriek at your parents that way?"

"My young friend is recently orphaned," Elmer said.

"They probably died while he was at the reins."

Elmer dropped his face to hide his smile, but Coop didn't mind because he nearly laughed himself.

"Get that package to Pittsburgh," the rider said. "There's more deliveries waiting for you there. Why you don't use the railways like a normal person I'll never understand."

"Reliable couriers would have saved every fallen empire you can name. Go on, name one that couldn't have been spared from destruction if they'd been able to count on faithful deliveries."

The man mounted his horse. "If they'd had trains, they'd still be empires." He raced back the way he'd come.

Elmer and Coop checked the cart and buggy parts to make sure everything was still attached. "We lost the dried fruit varietals but nothing else," Elmer said. They climbed aboard and Jemma pulled them into the wood. At last, Coop was on the east fork.

They talked about Elmer's life as a private courier. "It's mighty good pay," Elmer said. "Started as a young buck and made a reputation for myself. Every city you can name in these parts has rich men who need to send things to other rich men. They don't trust the post office because it means letting the messages slip from their hands. No telling who might decide to take a gander."

"Why not take the trains?"

"I won't ride those iron dragons no matter how many men want faster deliveries, but I've not lost one customer. I've earned the trust of all the wealthiest families in these parts. Noodle on it. What's a few more days if you have confidence in discretion and reliability?"

"Why'd you act like a thief, like you didn't want to be caught?"

"I didn't want to be *found*. I charge by the length of delivery, see. This man in Chicago always sends one of his men to find me on the road. Since he's already paying his own worker, he saves half, even though he's rich as Croesus and getting richer all the time. Never trust a wealthy man who picks the pockets of his workers. But I must grin and bear it. A bad reputation will spread faster than a rumor in church."

Before long, Elmer started again with the antics of the Kentucky yokels Coop was beginning to hate. They pulled to the side of the road as it went dark.

As they climbed down, Elmer said, "Now *that's* a scent from the home hollers! That's a rabbit if I'm a day. Close by."

Coop smelled it, too, spotting a faint glow edging a nearby bush. "Hello?" he called. "We don't mean no harm."

Nobody answered. Coop's mouth watered at the smell of cooking meat. He swallowed. "Maybe we should offer to share some of your stores."

"I do savor a juicy bite of rabbit."

Coop called again as he headed for the light. Behind a cluster of short bushes, they found a cook fire with low flames glazing hot embers. A skinned rabbit sizzled above, skewered to a spit balanced on twig braces.

"Roasted to a turn," Elmer said softly.

"That rabbit didn't cook itself. Someone heard us and hid."

Fat dripped, teasing a high flame.

"We're not bandits," Coop called. "We want to trade."

A boy snarled from the dark. "What if I say no?"

"Then we'll let you be."

"Then get!"

Elmer put a hand on Coop's shoulder. "Come, Coop. Let the lad enjoy his meal in peace."

Inexplicably crushed, Coop turned away.

"I'll trade two legs for some water. Or all four if you have cider."

A boy who looked the same age as Coop walked into the faint fire light, wearing a buttoned shirt, his thumbs jammed into trousers belted with rope. His dark hair hung to his shoulders in long waves. He looked nervous, braced to flee.

Coop had an urge to take him into his arms and comfort him.

"We'll take the cider trade," Elmer said.

Coop fetched a jug, a packet of crackers, and the honey pot. The boy waited until he saw the jug before sliding the rabbit to a board and slicing the legs. He grabbed the cider with both hands and guzzled.

Suddenly ravenous for hot food, Coop took one of the larger legs. The lean flesh was firm and tasted of the wild. He gnawed the bones clean and took a smaller leg, finishing his portion in moments. He sucked and licked his fingers, eyeing the rest.

The boy's name was Will. He was fifteen, and he'd been on the road since his father, a trapper, died a few months before. "I can skin a fox or a rabbit in less than a minute. We sold the pelts for fancy coats."

"What happened to your pappy?" Elmer said.

"Half a tree fell on him." His voice went pained. "I saw it happen. Looked like that tree planned it all along. The biggest branch cracked off and conked his head. Didn't take hardly a second."

Will looked lonely and sad. Coop clenched his arms tight, fighting a powerful urge to pull Will close and pat his hair.

"My parents died, too," Coop said.

"Didn't say my mom died," Will said in protest, puffing up. "She's from a prosperous family in New York. She'd tie a blanket around her waist and show everyone how a lady walks wearing long dresses. She showed me how she curtseyed, and she always drank with her pinkie out. You shoulda seen how nice she moved." He shrugged. "Sometimes she'd cry for days and days."

"Where is she?" Elmer said.

Will hesitated. "She always said if she went away, she'd be waiting for me in New York, where she grew up. So that's where I'm going."

"City or state?" Coop said.

Will froze. "How's that?"

"Does your mother's family live in New York City or somewhere else in the state of New York?"

Eyes wide, Will didn't answer.

Coop was confused until Elmer gave him a soft, secret pinch. He understood, and a wave of pity washed over him.

Elmer spoke like all was fine. "You can ride with me as far as Pittsburgh. Coop will leave us soon, in Harrison County. He owns a spot called Lightning Mountain."

Will looked awed. "You own a mountain?"

"It's a hill called Lightning Mountain."

"They don't call a hill no mountain," Will sneered. "That's illegal."

His dismissive tone angered Coop, and Elmer said, "It's perfectly legal to call a thing something it's not. Like the packaged loaves they sell in stores as country bread, unless country folks use sawdust. And doesn't that bring to my mind a story about a family in a holler with an outdoor oven..."

The next morning, when the sun was high and they were leaving, Will climbed into the cart in back.

"Come sit beside Coop," Elmer said.

"You only got the one seat, and there's barely room for you two. We'll be squished."

"Better than being rattled apart down there. You'll be like bones in a poke before long. Our seat is small, but it has springs that keep you comfy. I'm not moving until you get up here."

As Will climbed up, Coop jammed against Elmer, leaving a narrow strip that didn't look wide enough for a dog. Will wedged his butt inside.

"Ouch!" Coop cried, exaggerating the pain. "It's like a wrench!"

As they set off, Coop and Will squirmed and wriggled, bickering.

"It's too tight," Will said. "Feels like I'm gonna pop straight up."

Coop struggled, no longer pretending. "Elmer, he's right. It's hard to breathe. This seat isn't big enough."

"Ain't you got more room over there?" Will snapped.

"I gave you as much room as I could," Coop shouted.

"For the love of Tammy Troutbreath," Elmer said, sounding exasperated, "can't you find a way to accommodate each other?"

Tammy Troutbreath's name soon had the boys giggling. "Wait," Coop said, pushing up to release the tension. He raised his left leg high. Will slid his right leg under, and they hooked at the knees. They adjusted until they clamped together comfortably, Coop halfway in Will's lap, his arm slung across Will's shoulders.

Elmer started on his stories, and it faded to a buzz. Tight against Will, Coop felt wonderful. Pleasant tingles skittered across his skin.

The cart joggled, and their heads bumped lightly. Without thinking, Coop wriggled closer. He froze when realizing what he'd done but felt a cleansing desire when Will nudged in, too.

Coop grew exquisitely sensitive to where their bodies met. He felt Will's arm trapped along his leg, Will's crotch beneath his thigh, Will's shoulder under his hand. His own crotch was on full display for Will. His pants stretched unmistakably, and he felt an intoxicating rush because he was helpless to hide it. Soon, he didn't want to.

Heat tightened his face. With a slight turn, he was free to inhale the thick smell of Will's hair and admire the strands in countless shades of brown and black.

As Coop moved his head, Will's long hair brushed the tender skin on his neck. The delicate touch exploded into surging waves of pleasure, and goose bumps rolled by the thousands. Coop repeated the move, and his eyes leaked with passion. Once more, and his lust snorted and thrashed to run wild. He dropped his face and closed his eyes, the blissful sensation almost paralyzing. He gripped Will's shoulder. Under his thigh, he felt Will become steel.

Elmer talked a blue streak just above their heads, his words distant and meaningless.

Coop nearly cried out when Will gently brushed their cheeks together. Coop licked the edge of Will's ear and thrilled when Will tensed with a gasp. Will pulsed harder under his thigh.

Coop's passion billowed with immense pressure impossible to hold. Just then, Will slipped his fingers under Coop's shirt and brushed the skin on his lower back. It released the unstoppable surge, when nothing else mattered. Coop pulled Will tight, smashing his lips against his ear.

He burst. He closed his eyes with a mighty effort to contain his cries of ecstasy to tight grunts and concentrated gasps. He pumped into his pants and went dizzy knowing Will could watch the wet spot grow. Coop thought it the perfect way to express his gratitude for the bliss of every convulsion.

Will's eyes went primitive as he watched the stain in Coop's pants. He closed his eyes and burrowed into Coop's neck. He gripped Coop's head and grunted with a rising pitch until his breath burst with rhythmic gasps. Coop felt him pump under his thigh, soaking through his pants until it slicked his skin.

Elmer's voice seemed to hit them as one and they shot up, woozy and bleary-eyed. They adjusted and panted, eyes wide at what they'd done in the top seat of open buggy on a public road, smashed up against an old hillbilly.

Elmer gave no indication he saw or heard anything. They bounced along while Elmer spoke and the boys sprawled, numb and confused.

The land started to rise, and the road curved between gentle hills. Elmer said he wanted to make tracks, so they rode until it was too dark to drive safely.

Will made a fire even though there was nothing to cook. They gathered around to eat crackers and sardines and Elmer said, "You boys looked like two tadpoles sharing an egg."

Will shot Coop a panicked look.

"Seeing you squished together put me in mind of New York City," Elmer went on. "Did you ever kick an anthill and watch all them ants scrambling into and over each other? That's what it's like in New York City, except with angry humans instead of ants."

"My brother went to New York City," Coop said.

"And you never heard from him again," Elmer said in triumph. "That's because everyone gets lost in those crowds if they stay too long." Elmer yawned and said he was tired. "I better get some shut-eye." He walked over and bedded next to the buggy.

Coop and Will sat on the ground, the fire going faint between them. Coop was content to watch Will's face reflect the red embers. The shadows revealed the imminent emergence of a square jaw, a firm nose, a high brow, handsome as a man can be. Will caught his eyes a few times, and Coop didn't look away.

"How can ol' snaggle snout pretend he didn't see us?" Will grumbled.

"You know how he gets when he's telling a story. A gypsy jamboree could go by, and he wouldn't notice."

"He musta seen."

"If he did, that means he doesn't think we did anything wrong. Matter of fact, I think it was the best thing ever. We didn't even have to, you know, jack to get to the end."

Will picked at the fire with a stick. "My dad said my mom was touched, going from happy to sad and back again. All the same, he loved her, and he just about died from grief when she left. Not a word to either one of us." He shrugged. "I know she didn't grow up with a rich family in fancy land. She's not waiting for me, but I'm going to New York anyway. Might be lots of people, but that means lots of work."

"What kind of work?"

"My dad said we could make a fortune trapping rats in rich people's houses. But he said he couldn't live in the city."

Eventually, Coop lay next to the dying fire for the night. Will chose a spot some distance away. Coop worked up the courage to go over and sit next to him. Will opened his eyes, his face expressionless. Soft moonlight rode his hair in silver waves.

Coop combed Will's hair with his fingers. Will didn't react until Coop leaned in, aiming for his lips. Will shook his head, raised a palm, and said firmly, "No kissing. Never." He closed his eyes, but after a moment cupped Coop's hand in his.

Their hands looked good together, Coop thought. Will's skin was darker. Coop wove their fingers together, clenching tight. Will squeezed back. Coop stretched out and lay down. They went to sleep with their fingers entwined.

In the morning, Elmer shook them awake. "There's something to see," he said.

They'd let go of each other in the middle of the night, but Coop lost every thought when he stood. Will pushed up beside him.

The land stretched into the distance. Shredded clouds floated above the spreading burnt orange glow where the sun was ready to burst. Giant slashes of red molded to the textured surfaces of clouds, while orange and pink streaked the puffy canyons and fissures. The crisp blue sky made a vivid backdrop, dotted with the precision brilliance of the few brightest stars.

The gentle Appalachian foothills rolled across the earth in purple shades that grew lighter in the distance. A deeper shade of violet outlined every hill, too many to count. Coop scarcely believed this view had been here his whole life, waiting.

"This is only the foothills, but do you hear their music?" Elmer said, hushed.

Coop didn't hear anything, but he said yes. To his surprise, so did Will.

On the road again, their progress slowed as they wended through the undulating landscape that felt emptier and more isolated.

Elmer said they were nearing a good spot to send Coop to his destiny. Will sank into himself.

At the bottom of a hill, they passed a small river onto a wide meadow swaying with life. In the bright sun, insects swirled, bees flitted, and birds skimmed along. Above, gentle hills rolled, one a bit higher than the rest.

In the flat lowland, a line of half posts emerged from a wood and ran clear across the meadow. Elmer stopped the buggy, and they wondered about their purpose.

"It marks the new railway," said a young man standing next to a small girl at the tree line. He was tall and thin with a scruffy brown beard. He gave a friendly smile, dressed in ill-fitting clothes while carrying a dripping sack. The girl held a fishing pole twice her size, straight up like she was leading a church processional. She smiled shyly as the fisherman went on. "This branch will go to Cleveland. It breaks up back there a bit and you can ride all the way from Columbus to New York City."

Elmer groaned. "They're going to shatter the tranquility of this land with those iron demons?"

The fisherman looked puzzled. "It'll move coal to the steel mills and factories. It don't do any good in the ground."

"Ever hear of Lightning Mountain?" Coop said.

The man pointed to the highest hill. "That's the Lightning. That's how local folks call it, the Lightning." He gave a friendly wave. "Hope to see you folks in these parts again." They melted into the woods.

Coop's desolation rose in equal measure to his excitement. For the second time in weeks, he was saying goodbye to everything he knew.

"Well, Coop," Elmer said jauntily. "We've had some adventures, and that's the mark of a fine friendship. I always leave my itinerary at major banks along my routes, and I always get my messages but sometimes it takes a while. Just ask for Elmer Bluegrass. I hope to hear from you some day." They shook hands.

Will wouldn't give Coop so much as a glance.

Coop jumped down and rummaged in the cart for his rifle and pack, thinking about Miss Everson's history lessons. When he had his things, he said, "Elmer, is it really true all the old empires fell because they didn't have couriers?"

Elmer smiled. "I asked the man to name an empire that disproved my statement. It's a crafty way to land a point, seeing how most folks can't name even one ancient empire." Elmer's wide face and crooked nose bobbed with a chuckle, and Coop laughed.

On the other side of the buggy, Will faced away, his arms crossed tightly.

Coop rubbed Jemma's nose and kissed her scratchy fur. She bumped his chest with her snout.

Will still refused to meet his eyes. Coop circled around and stood below him.

"Come on," Coop said.

Startled, Will looked.

"Get now," Elmer said with an elbow nudge. "This is where you belong."

Coop's heart jumped when Will hopped off and removed his belongings.

"See you boys!" Elmer shouted, driving away.

The Lightning rose high and proud, bristling with trees.

"I'm gonna kiss you up there," Coop said with a smile. "You'll kiss me back. You'll see."

Will flushed and grinned. "Maybe not. Maybe so."

Side by side, they set off across the meadow.

CHAPTER FIVE

Cleveland, Ohio
Present day

A soft snore wakes Darcy in his bed. He raises himself to his elbows to look at Jake, facing the other way. A crack of morning sun through the drapes illuminates a glittering slanted line on his back hair.

Memories flash in Darcy's mind: drunkenly pulling off their clothes; grunts of approval as they explored each other's bodies; dirty promises; a kiss that grew deeper and transformed the moment into a passionate embrace of desire.

Darcy grins, remembering how he'd gone to sleep wondering if he'd ever enjoyed himself so much with another man.

Suddenly, he recalls Jake's comment about drugs. His spirits sink and he gets out of bed, taking his phone as he pads naked to the hallway, closing the bedroom door behind him. In the bathroom, he slips on flannel pajama bottoms and heads downstairs to the kitchen.

After starting the coffee maker, he opens a cupboard and removes a mug.

Kaaa. Kaaa. Cuh, cuh, cuh, cuh.

The calls come from just outside the kitchen window. The coffee drips, filling the room with its scent. Suddenly remembering the bread dough, Darcy opens the refrigerator and finds it thawed. He butters a tin, starts the oven, and pops it inside.

KAAA!! KAAA!!

"Give me a break," he mutters, removing two slices of packaged whole wheat bread from the refrigerator.

The cries escalate as he fills a mug with coffee. After adding some milk, he grabs the bread and heads out back, hearing a final excited *kaaa!*

Outside, clouds shadow the land and water. The smell of coming rain thickens the air. Bristled spring tree limbs dance and sway.

Click the squirrel comes racing around the corner from his morning sentry duty at the kitchen window, his claws clicking. Gray and white with a tail so puffy it looks styled, Click halts in a flash, standing on his hind legs.

Darcy sets his mug on a table. Squatting, he rips the bread and piles the pieces on the porch. Click waits until he's done to scamper forward and shove bread in his mouth, chewing so fast it looks like a heart beating.

"Where's Gramps?"

Click keeps eating, his paws finding the bread without looking.

Gramps pops his head up from the top step. He glares in silence until Darcy prepares his breakfast. He jumps up to eat, thin and scraggly and unawed by humans.

Click shoves the bread into his mouth, no longer chewing. With bulging cheeks, he gives Darcy a look before skittering away.

Gramps eats, stuffs, and limps off without so much as a glance, leaving half of the pile the little black starlings will devour when Darcy leaves. He hears them in the trees, twittering anxiously. One lands on the porch railing, pretending Darcy isn't there. Two more arrive and hop about, peeping angrily as they swivel their heads from the bread to Darcy and back again.

A starling blasts an angry warning and hops down to pick at the crumbs. The others find their courage and do the same, scurrying aside at Darcy's slightest move.

He sips his coffee and checks his phone, startled to see six missed calls. His sisters. He reads the voicemail messages he'd ignored last night. He sends texts to both saying Trevor can explain the details better than he can.

"Hey. The coffee's for the taking, right?" Jake's behind the screen door, wearing Darcy's rattiest robe. The starlings jump and peep but keep eating.

"Help yourself."

A minute later, Jake steps outside, the frayed terrycloth belt unraveling, giving a peek of swinging skin and hair. They sit at the table.

"Smells like rain," Jake says. "Gonna have to cancel my clients today. What do you have planned?"

"Maybe I'll drive to New York City."

"What?"

Darcy gives a brief explanation of the complicated inheritance, leaving out the huge dollar amounts.

"Do you get this house?"

"Yes. My grandmother left it to us. It's my great-grandfather's estate that's hanging in the balance."

"How is going to New York going to help?"

Darcy shrugs. "I want to find out who's claiming our inheritance. I searched the name Charles Greene online, but there were too many hits to narrow it down."

"How will you find him?"

"I have an address in New York City for a building my great-grandfather owned. I can start there." He sighs. "But I really should get my brakes fixed first."

"My brakes are fine."

"Right," Darcy says with a laugh.

"I'm serious. I've been gardening for five years and haven't missed a single appointment. I have a right to an emergency now and then."

Adrenaline pounds in Darcy's ears. "Is this an emergency?"

Jake blushes. "A handsome man I've had my eye on for years needs my help."

Darcy disguises a catch of breath with a cough. He pictures sitting beside Jake in the pickup for hours, days, and the possibilities roar in his mind. "If you're sure it's okay."

Jake guzzles the last of his coffee. "Let me run back home and throw a few things together. I'll be back in an hour."

Soon after Jake leaves, Darcy remembers the bread in the oven and races inside. He saves it just in time, and while he forgot his plan to make fancy French toast to impress Jake, he leaves it to cool and take for the road.

After he showers and packs a small bag, he looks up the address of the building in New York, on a one-way street between Fifth Avenue and Park Avenue. Despite knowing nothing about New York City, he recognizes the high-status location. It's an old, green, utilitarian structure of six stories with huge windows. On the ground floor, a posh designer and an architectural firm sit on either side of the arched main door. The five floors above look like old-fashioned warehouse space but seem to be apartments, with plants and other personal items visible through the windows.

Why did Cooper Tiller own this building but apparently no others? Does it have something to do with why he died in upstate New York?

Darcy suddenly realizes how he can get some answers this morning.

Jake returns, and Darcy climbs into the truck. "I need to make a quick stop at Lake View Cemetery. It's on our way, over by Little Italy." He explains about Cooper Tiller dying far away. "I just want to see when he was buried."

"Okay. I know exactly where it is. My aunt is buried there."

They take the freeway past downtown. After about ten minutes, Jake exits and drives to the main entrance of Cleveland's Lake View Cemetery. It opened in the second half of the nineteenth century and was instantly acclaimed as one of the finest examples of the new Victorian fashion for garden-style graveyards. Ohio's elite quickly made it their favored burial ground, including the country's twentieth president, James Garfield.

The administrative offices are just inside the gate, and Darcy jumps out. "I shouldn't be long." Inside a comfy front office, he asks an older woman at a desk about the date of his great-grandfather's burial.

She looks up the mausoleum in a computer and squints. "Who are you looking for?"

"Cooper Tiller."

She shakes her head. "Nope. I have Elena Tiller, interred in 1950, Robert Kohl in 1993, and Mildred Kohl just a few weeks ago."

"There's a plaque on my great-grandfather's crypt. He was born in 1880 and died in 1960."

"Our families demand the best, and we keep excellent records. If Cooper Tiller was here, we'd know." Darcy's too shocked to respond, and she seems to take pity on him. "There's as much secrecy in death as there is in life. It wouldn't be the only empty crypt on earth."

Reeling, Darcy goes outside. Jake stands in the first grassy patch of graves, in front of a peaked slab of polished red granite atop a concrete base. A green copper relief is embedded in the stone, featuring an angel comforting a group of frightened, sorrowful children. Beneath, a carved message reads *In memory of the teachers and children who lost their lives in the Collinwood school fire.*

"What's this?" Darcy says.

Jake startles and laughs. "I didn't hear you." He puts his hand on the granite. "This is where my Aunt Maddy is buried. She died in the Collinwood school fire."

"The what?"

"It happened in 1908, and nobody knows about it any longer. I'll explain when we're back on the road, but Maddy was one of nineteen children whose bodies were burned so badly they were never identified. They buried them all here in a mass grave. Just back there," he says, pointing to scattered headstones in tree shade, "are some of the other victims, the ones who were identified."

"Your aunt died in 1908?"

"She was our great-great-aunt, but that takes too long to say."

"They got a prime spot right at the entrance."

"It was a pretty big deal when it happened." He leads Darcy around the monument, where nineteen children are listed on a copper plate. He points to his aunt's name. "When I was little, we used to come here on the anniversary of the fire every year." Jake goes somber before asking, "Did you find out when your great-grandfather was buried?"

"They say he's not here." He suddenly has an idea. "Do you mind if we make another stop? It's near the Pennsylvania border and shouldn't take us more than a few hours out of our way."

"Sure. What is it?"

"Cooper Tiller owned a coal mine. It's near a town called Cadiz in Harrison County."

Jake looks intrigued. "I've never seen a coal mine."

"I don't know what there is to see. It was destroyed in 1950."

"I've never seen a destroyed coal mine, either. Let's do it."

Darcy's unexpectedly thrilled to share this part of his family history with Jake. *I used coke every day to wake up*, he thinks and tightens his mouth.

CHAPTER SIX

The Lightning, Harrison County, Ohio
1894–1899

Coop gawked at the scale of Lightning Mountain. A legion of trees climbed to the summit, and if each were a dollar, he'd be a millionaire.

Will knew how to find his way through a forest, and he led their exploration across the gentle east slope, where Coop's excitement soon ebbed. The rocky, crenellated land and overgrown forest offered few obvious ways to make a living.

The woods tangled impenetrably in places that forced them to backtrack. Rocks and small boulders studded the earth. They clambered through large cracks in the land, filled with rocky soil, roots, and rotting trunks. Streams trickled to a lake at the bottom they could glimpse through the trees. The placid water shone like a giant mirror, shaped like a tilted sandglass with a distorted lower bulb twice as big as the other.

The rugged western slope was too steep for anything but falling. Recent landslides had left deep scars and treacherous formations at precarious heights, where trees dangled like they were struggling for balance.

Coop was grateful for Will, who stepped through passageways normal people wouldn't see. He doubled back sharply when he spotted fur stuck to thorns and twigs. He squatted to examine animal droppings and studied faint tracks on his hands and knees, his face low to the ground. He said little, repeatedly hooking his long dark hair behind his ears.

Coop winced when remembering Harold's son calling Coop a

twat for trading farmland for this hill, so worthless Harold had won it at poker.

Hot with shame, Coop wondered if Will would spend a single night here. He expected Will to stalk off in disgust any minute and leave Coop to figure out life on the Lightning for himself.

The sun was setting when they reached a flat overlook holding a stand of tall evergreens near the summit, the ground lumpy with boulders. Will suggested they stop for the night and search for the lakeshore cabin in the morning.

"If there *is* a cabin," Coop said. "Harold probably lied about that."

Will didn't reply, transfixed. "Now, there's a sight," he said with wonder.

They were on the highest spot for miles. The view skimmed hilltops in every direction, a carpet of trees undulating to the horizon. Despite Coop's sour mood, he felt a burst of exhilaration.

The evergreen platform faced north, at the edge of a cliff that fell halfway down the hill. A vertical forest of ferns softened the sheer drop.

"A landslide left this cliff behind," Will said. "Probably happened before ol' Christopher Columbus sailed the ocean blue. See those big piles of earth down below? That's what's left of the landslide."

Will pointed out how new soil had accumulated over the cliffside scar, where the ferns grew like a swaying green curtain.

"This hill is falling apart," Coop said glumly. "I'm sorry to pull you into my troubles. I should've minded my own concerns and let you go with Elmer. There's no way to make a living here."

Will smiled. "A tangled forest means there ain't no deer making paths and eating bushes. It means bears probably lived here, back when bears lived in these parts. They scared away the big game, so there was nothing to hunt. That means the small animals made a home on this hill, and they have the best pelts."

Coop looked on in disbelief.

"It's got red and silver fox, pine marten, white rabbit. I even found American mink, which everyone says doesn't live this far south, but people catch them all the time." Will waved about. "'Course, it has all the rest, coons, badgers, squirrels, skunks. You can make a nice living from just those. I'll bet I find some beavers down by that lake, too. Soon as I teach you how to trap, we'll make a fortune."

Coop felt better, and they spent the night holding each other among the evergreens, squirming to find a comfortable position.

The next morning, they descended to the lake. "It's bigger than it looks," Will said, gazing across the water. "It'll take five minutes to row from end to end and another five minutes from side to side. That's big enough for an army of catfish. They love these hill lakes."

"Depends on how the owner of the lake feels about us fishing here."

They found the cabin hunched in the woods thirty feet from the shore, looking more miserable than the old farm shack. Just as Harold's son had said, part of the roof was caved in.

Will circled the building and sounded hopeful about fixing it. "It's late spring, so we can finish by winter. Easy."

Will showed Coop how to set deadfall traps, balancing huge rocks on sticks in the thick undergrowth, cautioning Coop not to be discouraged if they didn't catch anything right away.

The next morning, they found two American minks, a silver fox, and a white spotted bobcat, lifeless and floppy under the rocks. Will demonstrated how to skin an animal with one slice along the belly, folding back the skin to keep most of the legs intact. They scraped, washed, and hung the pelts. Will said, "That bobcat hide will look nice on our wall after we're done with the cabin. Let's keep it for ourselves."

They whittled fishing poles in no time. Will had hooks and line, and they caught a carp and a largemouth bass, enough to fill their bellies with some left over for trap bait.

Over the next few weeks, they woke early to fish, and even from the shore they managed to hook a catfish now and then. After cooking up the fillets, they set out to check their traps.

Uphill, Coop dug and covered trapping pits while Will set complicated snares. They caught more American mink and silver fox, along with beavers, white rabbits, skunks, and raccoons. Will showed Coop how to build trap cages from sticks, and soon they'd set so many traps they each took responsibility for memorizing half the locations.

The evergreen overlook near the summit became their regular spot for a grapple and tug, but despite doing everything else, Will still refused to kiss.

Often in the early morning at the lake, they saw a Black man fishing on a rowboat near the far eastern shore. He always vanished into an unseen channel to the right, where they later noticed columns of dark smoke.

Weeks later, as they tended a shoreside cook fire, a bristly old coot appeared through the narrow channel in the lake's sandglass neck, rowing furiously.

"Ya been here a whole month," he raged as he came near, his voice screechy. "It's one thing to travel through, but it's another to squat on my land."

"I own Lightning Mountain," Coop yelled.

The man rowed to shore, wisely ignoring the decrepit dock that looked likely to crumble underfoot. Coop offered his hand, but the man angrily waved it away. He used a hefty stick for balance as he teetered ashore in the shallow water. Coop stayed close, ready to catch the old guy if he fell.

The man held his tattered shirt together with pins, all the buttons gone. His raggedy pants hung loose from snap suspenders, and his boots flopped without hooks. Gray bristles roughened his wrinkled face. His lips twisted at strange angles, revealing stumpy, scattered teeth as he demanded Coop prove ownership.

Coop showed him the deed, explaining about his trade with Harold. The man's anger seeped away. "Well, I guess you own it after all. You gotta file this deed in Cadiz Township, the county seat. You'll find a flat road just past those trees. Head north. It ain't far."

"We're just cooking up some meat," Will said. "Rabbit and squirrel. Coop here grew up farming and knows plants real good. He found wild garlic and onions to make it savory. There's plenty."

Saliva leaked from the man's mouth. "You don't have badger in there?" he said, swallowing hard. "Badger's about the foulest meat there ever was."

"No badger," Coop promised, and the old man sat on a weathered trunk, sighing and groaning.

"Pinky's the name," he said when they introduced themselves. "I guess I had some other name when I was just a slug, but that's all anyone ever called me." He said he hadn't set foot outside the county line in seventy-two years. "Don't see any reason to leave when everything's right here." Will handed him a wooden bowl of meat and Pinky's eyes went wide. He picked with his fingers, chewing gently. "That's mighty good. When you planning to file that deed?"

Coop said, "Any day now."

"Just so's you know, they made a mistake on the new survey maps. Look over yonder where the land pinches the lake nearly in half. I own everything on the other side. Everyone will swear to the truth of it. I'm planning to get the maps changed back the right way, to show half of Nightwater Lake belongs to me."

"It's called Nightwater Lake?" Coop said.

"That's what I said. The water gets inky about a fathom down. That's from coal, I always said. You find it here and there."

"Coal comes in seams," Coop said. "If you find some, there's a lot more around."

"Then there's more around because I've been finding it for years. Maybe it's right under the lake."

"Who owns this side of the lake?" Coop said.

"The owner of the Lightning, that's who, and that means you own it. But only this side, mind."

Coop and Will shared a surprised look while Pinky went on. "You also own the flatlands for a quarter mile south. You got some squatters over there, a Black man and his two kids. They've been good to me, and I'd hate for you to send them packing."

Pinky finished his bowl and wiped his mouth with his sleeve. He refused their first offer to take some meat, but Will insisted. Pinky kept a battered pail on his boat, rowing off once Will had emptied the food inside.

"Coal," Coop said. "Harold's son said they looked for coal and never found any. Just to be sure, we should get the deed filed in my name. If there is coal around here, we don't want disputes."

In the morning, they set out for Cadiz Township, each carrying a stack of pelts on their shoulders. They followed Pinky's directions to the flat road that curved around the hills.

It was still morning when they saw a distant town clinging to lazy rolls of land. Hazy dirt layers kicked up from bustling streets floated gracefully above the rooftops and steeples. A departing train hooted as it sped eastward, while another chugged in from the west. Gray coal smoke pumped from the main funnels and unspooled to ashen mist stretching across the sky.

The sights and sounds of Cadiz Township overwhelmed Coop. The main street rose gently, topped by a building with glowing red bricks and a majestic staircase sweeping to the street. A construction site sat diagonal, a huge foundation for a massive building that would rise with four pediment corners.

They gawked, imagining the size of the building. A lady stopped and proudly declared, "That's the new courthouse. It'll be the grandest building in the whole state."

Ramshackle wooden buildings ran along one side of the street, with stately brick and timber structures along the other. The nicer buildings sported colorful, scalloped awnings shading large display windows jumbled with goods. Coop saw signs for banks, two newspapers, hotels, and a variety of merchants.

They walked on the wide dirt road among groups of high-spirited young men in work clothes dodging traffic. Black men drove most of the carts and wagons, carefully steering horses while politely calling, "Make way, coming on through, watch the wheels, now." Maids in plain dresses and aprons hurried arm in arm, carrying baskets and pails. A scraggly trio of sunburnt men, chained and shackled, shot as many insults as they got, to the amusement of two deputies with rifles sauntering behind. What looked from afar like small, walking grain bins resolved into a huddled group of Chinese men in woven round hats, wearing loose outfits the color of cornflowers.

Better-off people clacked on the sidewalk planks. Ladies wore frilly jackets and matching skirts, cinched at the waist so tightly another yank might pop their eyeballs. They held lace hankies over their noses, under enormous hats bouncing with feathers and ribbons. Men in trim suits and hats walked alongside, upright and aloof. At their feet, boys in knickers and girls with masses of curls under giant silk bows played and ran.

Euphoric, Coop said, "I went to the state fair in Columbus once. It's a bigger city, but you didn't see half as much."

"Pa took me to lots of crossroad trading towns. You get the best money for your pelts from town traders." Will slapped Coop's back. "I don't mean to brag. I'm just saying to stick with me, and I'll keep you safe."

Stick with me. Coop liked the sound of that. "Safe from what?"

"Well, for instance…" Will looked about until he nodded knowingly. He pulled Coop into his spot, pointing. "Look sharp down that alley, at the doorway at the end."

The passing hordes allowed only brief glimpses of the closed door. Soon, two men in railway uniforms stepped inside. A moment later, a wealthy man left, putting on his hat. The next glimpse left Coop thunderstruck, a woman leaning in the open doorway, arms crossed, naked as Eve eyeing an apple.

"Is that a cathouse?"

"It's nowhere you belong."

Soon, Will found a trading post. In a loud, cluttered room where men haggled, Will showed the pelts to a big, round man in a striped suit sprawling behind a desk. The man looked bored, sinking a finger into his fleshy cheek as he flipped through the pelts. At last, he made a half-hearted offer.

Will looked stunned. "It's worth four times as much."

"I set fur prices in this town. You got some nice silver fox and white rabbit and beaver, but otherwise it's just coons, skunks, and weasels."

"Weasels? They're American mink."

The man flushed with surprise and alarm. "American mink don't live this far south."

"Every trapper knows you get them sometimes. Every trader, too. You never saw any?"

"The educated men say they don't live south of Canada."

"Maybe they were visiting some furry kinfolk," Will said curtly. He turned to Coop. "Come on. If he's the only fur trader in town, we should hang a shingle. Every trapper will come to us."

"Listen, boy. Just 'cause you got some peach fuzz on your balls don't mean you know about trade."

They piled the pelts on their shoulders. Speaking loudly enough for the man to hear, Will said, "There's always traders at the rail stations. We'll get more for the mink alone as he's offering for everything. Come on."

"Hold your horses," the man said with a touch of desperation. "Let's try this another way. You make the offer, and I'll see if it's worth my trouble."

They left with a bit more than four times the original price. Coop cast secret glances at Will, proud to be at his side among all these other people.

At a general store, Will ordered tools and supplies for repairing the cabin. He dictated specifics as the clerk scribbled. They worked out deliveries with the help of a map, and they left with as many supplies as they could carry.

In the small county building, they presented the deed at a counter in a cramped and busy hallway. After Harold's signature was verified, they were sent to another counter. A bespectacled man in a perfect suit looked at the paper. "Which of you is Cooper Tiller?"

"That's me," Coop said. Will stepped away.

His pen poised, the clerk asked for his full name.

"Cooper Clayton Tiller." He glanced at Will, who was reading proclamations on the far wall. Coop leaned in and said quietly, "And Will Herrington."

"Is that his full name?"

Flustered, Coop said, "Can't you just write it down like that?"

"What is your full name?" the clerk said loudly.

Will whipped about and the clerk asked again. Dutifully, he replied, "Rex William Herrington." The man wrote.

"Why does he want my name?" Will said. Coop hemmed and hawed until realization dawned on Will's face. "Hang on. I don't own that land, he does."

The clerk made a sour face. "I already inscribed both names."

"Just cross mine out."

The man took off his spectacles for a reproachful glare. "Our records are embossed sequentially on the finest ivory stock, as is fitting for a town with three newspapers and just as many banks." He enunciated crisply. "We don't scribble on them. You may change ownership terms when you receive the new deed in a few weeks." He returned the spectacles to his nose and asked Coop, "Are you partners?"

Coop didn't reply. The man spoke like he was talking to a rock. "You have different surnames, so I assume you are business partners?"

Relieved, Coop nodded. "Yeah. That's it."

The man wrote on several sheets before banging three stamps across the pages. Coop signed as the lead owner. The clerk said, "Next time, be sure of your intentions before the ink is applied."

Coop's heart raced. "We're business partners," he said firmly. "It makes perfect sense."

In the joyful beam from Coop's face, Will's cross expression became a smile.

Their last stop was at a counter with the survey maps. They flipped through an oversized portfolio until Coop recognized the shape of Nightwater Lake. They leaned close to study the spare, precise markings. The plot line wrapped the west slope of Lightning Mountain and ran out the other side in generous diagonals, encompassing all of the lake and the surrounding flat land. A corresponding grid measured two hundred and twenty acres.

Will snickered. "I guess it's no surprise that Pinky's a squatter."

Coop could hardly speak. The unexpected size and grandeur of his land felt dangerous, like he couldn't hold it tightly enough and it would slip from his hands. "Harold told me it was just the hill." He lowered his voice and leaned in. "I think they made a mistake."

"It's the same plot number that's on the deed. Didn't you say Harold was illiterate? Maybe he didn't know."

"He won it at poker." Coop swept a hand over the map. "Who would bet two hundred and twenty acres on a game of cards? Plus, a fishing lake? Something's not right."

"I know what's wrong. You expect people to be sensible, but they ain't. I'll bet the very day that man gambled his land away, a hundred other people in Ohio did something dumber. It's your land now. Don't go looking at a gift like it's a horse's mouth."

Coop had always heard the saying differently and wondered if Will's version was the correct one. It made more sense.

Back outside, Will asked if Coop wanted to try restaurant food. "I saw a sign that promised home cooking."

The same sign had intrigued Coop. He'd never been in a restaurant, but he was anxious to get back and watch for surveyors arriving to draw new maps. He also wanted to be alone with Will, far from the cathouse.

"I like how we cook," he said. To his relief, Will agreed. They made it home before sunset.

With their new tools, they started on the cabin in earnest. His whole life, Coop had chopped wood, banged nails, and carted things, but Will had learned about proper building from his father. "Pa was always trying to make things fancy for Ma. She wanted a nice house, so we were always fixing it up with new things. People thought we were crazy, but Pa wanted to give her anything he could."

They replaced the wall beams, repaired the roof, put in most of a new floor, and rebuilt the fireplace. What they couldn't make from the wood and rocks on the Lightning arrived from the general store. It was exhausting but rewarding.

Many mornings when they went to fish, the Black man was floating in his rowboat near the east shore. He always paddled off in a hurry, veering south where he splashed out of sight, either not hearing or ignoring their shouts. Coop and Will talked about paying him a visit, but always got too busy. After two months, Coop said, "He's our neighbor. It's crazy we haven't met."

"Pinky said he has kids. He's probably afraid you'll send them packing."

"All the more reason to say hello and ease his worries. Let's pay him a visit right now." Will wanted to check a new snare and told Coop he'd meet him later.

They hadn't explored the southern acreage yet, the flat land between the lake and the next hill, running a quarter of a mile. Behind the lakefront woods, he found a long, weedy meadow stretching the length of the water, ending at the woodland beside the eastern shore.

Coop saw his getaway spot, a narrow but surprisingly long channel tunneling under a canopy of trees. The small bay ended in front of a well-made rustic cabin sheltering in the shade. A stovepipe poked out from the side and rose above the roof, streaked with dark black soot. The round-bottom rowboat tilted on land.

Behind the cabin, an open workshop with shelves and a bench sat beside a shed. Nearby were a huge firepit and two enormous, flat metal pots, each big enough to stew a whole cow. A sizeable vegetable garden flourished in the meadow's sunlight, protected by a sturdy fence of woven sticks, like the one back at the farm that penned the hens and rooster.

Coop was about to call out when the soot on the stovepipe suddenly demanded his attention. After a minute lost in the deep blackness of the streaks, he yelled, "Hello?" He heard a faint creak inside. "I own this land, and I'm here as a friend. I see your boat, so I know you're inside."

The Black man emerged warily, wearing plain clothes with suspenders. Built beefy like Clyde, he had thick arms and a round head, and his short black hair was shot through with gray. He took a big breath and lifted his chin. "My name is Thomas Whitney," he said with a deep voice. "My daughter is Emma, and she's twelve. My son Linus is seventeen. My wife passed on a few years back, and I'm raising them myself. We're quiet folks, and we're good Christians. If you don't want me fishing on your lake, I'll stop."

"You can keep fishing."

Thomas nodded, still cautious. "I appreciate that. Pinky told us there was a new owner. We've been trying to keep it so as you don't even see us most times, and to clear out if you do. Linus works on the land crew for the new railway. I make him walk twice as far there and back, so as not to pass your hill and disturb you. I sincerely pray you don't ask us to move on. It's a good spot, and we fixed it up nice, just as you see. Linus is earning cash wages, and he's saving every penny for his future. We're not likely to find another situation as pleasant as this one."

Coop walked up and they shook hands. "I came to tell you I appreciate having watchful eyes around. You're welcome to stay, and Linus can walk by whenever he likes. But your stovepipe reminds me of something. I've seen your smoke columns. That's coal smoke, right?"

Thomas nodded. "I found a little deposit. I didn't think anyone would mind. It's just yonder, but I'll dig it up for you instead, Mr. Tiller, if you want."

"My name is Coop. I only let Mrs. Porter call me Mr. Tiller, and you don't look a thing like her. You can have as much coal as you need, but I'd like to see where it is."

Thomas led Coop halfway across the meadow. "I found it when I ripped out a young oak by the roots. You can see it's a small deposit because I found the edges on every side. I never saw nothing like it." Thomas flipped aside a tarp on the ground.

With one look, Coop grasped the importance of the discovery.

A glossy black hole eight feet across sank into the earth, chipped into irregular layers by Thomas. The sunlight smeared across the smooth surfaces and rode the ridges in sharp white streaks, precise as the lines on the surveying maps.

"See how it shines?" Thomas said. "It's bituminous coal, and it's one of the most valuable kind because it burns so hot. One little chunk keeps my family warm all day in the winter, and another does the job all night."

Mesmerized, Coop knelt and ran his hands along the textured surface, like touching midnight itself. It left streaks on his skin. "Have you seen more around here?"

"No, but they say if you find some coal, there's a motherlode close by. You might be sitting on a fortune, Coop, but it could take years to find the seam, even with an army searching. 'Course," Thomas waved to the neighboring hill, "could be on someone else's land."

"You'll let me know if you find more?"

"'Course I will."

Coop's heart thumped. He found Will high uphill and rushed through the details of Thomas's family before telling him about the coal.

"It's not a few pebbles on the ground or in a stream, like how most people find coal. It's a deposit. It means there's more nearby."

"Mineral surveyors have been crawling over every inch of these parts for the better part of a hundred years," Will said.

"It's hiding underground. Thomas found it by ripping up a small oak."

"It can take a year of summer Sundays to find a seam. I'm not saying there's no coal, but unless it starts singing 'Oh! Susanna,' it's gonna take a miracle to find it." He squinted at a snare tie on a small tree, trying to work out tension and weight.

Coop trotted downhill on one of the new paths they'd cleared with daily use. He knew finding a coal seam usually meant blasting or tunneling, both impossibly expensive. They might never find it unless the coal decided to show itself. Suddenly, he was certain it would, and before long.

A gentle but shattering thrum in his soul stopped him. His mind flashed to the morning he saw the foothills for the first time, when Elmer asked if he heard the Appalachians singing. He'd lied to please the sweet old hillbilly, but the mountains had been silent and still.

The memory revealed the rumble inside of him as the song of the coal, but nothing like "Oh! Susanna." The plaintive notes entwined into an ancient melody of longing. A delicious pierce of sweet pain tightened his throat and brought tears to his eyes, until he sensed a power lurking under the music. It felt feeble yet omnipotent, too weak to bend a weed, while commanding the fate of every living thing. Like sunlight.

The next morning, in the muggy Ohio summer heat, Coop stripped off his clothes for a swim when a young Black man walked by a little way off.

Linus was shorter than his dad and smaller in build, but Coop put it down to his age and sensed Linus would grow to be just as big as Thomas. Linus glanced his way and gave an embarrassed grin at Coop's nudity. With no way to hide himself without looking ridiculously bashful, Coop smiled as they exchanged a wave.

Later, Coop was building trap cages on the north slope under the cliff of hanging ferns. He heard what sounded like a girl calling by the lake and headed down.

At the shore, a young Black girl sat on a stump. Dressed in a straw hat and a plain blue dress, she held on her lap the open *Robinson Crusoe*, which Coop had been reading to Will at night.

She saw him and stood, carefully returning the book to the bedding, giving the cover a pat. She was pretty, with dark skin, almond eyes, and a small nose and mouth. She smiled mischievously, pinched up her skirt, and did a little bob, saying with a smooth and melodic voice, "I'm pleased to make your acquaintance, Coop."

"You're Emma."

"Yes, I am," she said, her smile brighter. "Pa told me to call you Mr. Tiller, but I heard you say only a lady named Mrs. Porter calls you like that, so that's why I was a bit informal just now. I do hope you'll pardon me if I gave offense."

"You didn't."

She lifted something covered with a gingham towel. She folded back the cloth with evident glee and handed him a beautiful, golden pie. The tin was warm, and it smelled delicious, with thick purple syrup bubbling through slits in the crust.

"It's blueberry. I made it for my family, but Pa said I should give it to you to express his gratitude for your hospitality and friendship."

"That's neighborly of you and your pa."

"It's common to make lattice crust for blueberry pie, but everyone says my crust is the best they ever had, so I covered the top. I was so looking forward to a taste, but I'm delighted to present it to such a kind neighbor. Can you spare me a thought and save just a little of the crust?" Her eyes danced joyfully. "Just leave the crumbs in the tin and don't bother with cleaning it out. I can pinch them together for a bite, and that will be enough for me."

"My goodness, Emma, you'll have more than crumbs. I'll have a piece right now, and so will you."

She went rigid and her face fell. He turned as Will stepped from the woods. Emma gave a quick, reflexive curtsey and Will stopped to stare, open-mouthed.

Coop made introductions and Emma dipped another silent curtsey, eyes downcast. Her face sank deeper under Will's gaze.

Coop tried to revive the friendly mood. "Emma brought us a blueberry pie. She's known far and wide for her crust. We were just about to dig in. Let's have ourselves a blueberry pie party."

Will knelt to pull tin plates, forks, and a knife from his bag. His mood was grave.

A hard thought hit Coop as Will took a deep breath with his eyes closed. Will might dislike Black people, although he never gave a hint.

Coop's parents raised him to think it was the height of foolishness to distrust and hate someone because they were different. His mom had said, "I knew former slaves when I was a girl, and they never made trouble. But hear me true, nobody makes more trouble than a bigoted person." From an early age, he resolved to never make friends with a bigoted person.

Emma clasped her hands tightly, frozen, eyes firmly down. She looked tiny, her fear chaining her bright spirit.

Coop had always taken note when people used scornful words about others with different-colored skin or strange religious practices. A few times, he'd known and liked the person saying such things, and their stupidity crushed him.

He wished he could tell the world about Daisy and her devotion to Baby. Animals know friends don't always look the same, and love makes everything else meaningless. When did people lose the basic wisdom God gave barnyard critters?

Will towered in front of Emma with the plates and utensils clinking in his hands. "Emma, you surprised me with your curtsey. I never saw a lady curtsey besides my ma, and you brought her to my mind. Your curtsey was even prettier than hers. I relish a bite of your blueberry pie."

Her face snapped up, joyous.

It didn't take Emma long to prove she would vanquish Elmer in a chattering contest.

Emma told them how her parents were born slaves, but they'd been too young to remember. They'd been traveling from Georgia to Chicago for five years, "But I feel like we're the Swiss Family Robinson and keep getting stranded by storms. We had to stop in West Virginia for two whole years while Ma died. We got to the shores of Nightwater Lake about six months ago and decided to fix up our own little manor. Pa thought it was public land and when he learned we were squatters, I thought he might have an apoplectic fit. He was so happy after your visit, Coop. He was like Oliver Twist when he's adopted by Mr. Brownlow. Have you ever read Charles Dickens?"

She loved books. "Just about every new one I read becomes my favorite. Right now, it's *The Picture of Dorian Gray*. I never knew men are obsessed with being beautiful."

Although her voice was sweet and enjoyable, Coop got nervous. Their daily chores didn't allow long visits.

She stopped talking only to eat small bites of blueberry pie. Coop and Will had finished theirs long ago, complimenting her on the crust. When she finished at last, she scraped every morsel from the tin plate and sucked it from the fork.

Coop said they'd enjoyed having her over and they hoped to see her again, but now they needed to get back to work.

Emma set off but ran back for her towel. "And remember not to bother about cleaning the tin. I can manage."

Thinking of the way she scraped the plate, Coop said, "Take the rest for your pa and Linus. Your one pie can be a friendship gesture twice over."

She squealed happily and after thanking him for the best idea she'd ever heard, she left in a bright mood. When she was out of earshot, Coop said, "She's a sweet girl, but we'll never get anything done if she gets it in her head to visit every day."

Will looked curious. "Coop, she's a little girl with only her pa and her brother for company. She's happy, so they don't treat her poorly, but they probably haven't asked her a question in years, and she has nobody to talk to. I don't mind if she tells us about books. My ma loved books. You're supposed to be the kind one." He winked and headed uphill.

Coop watched Will's back as he left, feeling joyful in a way he couldn't name.

As autumn nudged aside summer and the yellow days went golden, they worked feverishly to finish the cabin. Coop was ashamed

Will needed to demonstrate everything for him. Coop didn't let on he'd never seen a sheet of plywood, and his first sight of the perfectly flat, square wood left him speechless. Even a simple task like mixing plaster was a challenge because if he measured wrong, he'd ruin the whole, expensive bag. He hammered more half-moons than nails. Small humiliations piled up.

Emma's visits became enjoyable when Coop suggested she read to them while they worked. She started with *All Around the Moon* by Jules Verne, which they loved so much she followed up with an even better adventure called *20,000 Leagues Under the Sea*. Next came a dull tale called *The English Governess at the Siamese Court*. After the second chapter, Coop asked for another Jules Verne, but Emma said the lady who lent her books didn't have any more.

Concerned, Emma hurried off, returning the next day with *Barchester Towers*, a funny tale of witless English clergymen and the schemers who hover around, plotting.

One day in October, they finished the walls with trim and paint. Hours later, after shaping and smoothing a large rock for the hearthstone, they completed the floor.

Emma's father had learned the Amish craftwork of making rustic hickory furniture, steaming thick, sanded branches in the huge flat pots on the fire pit behind his cabin. When they were soft and pliable, he shaped and nailed them into everything a home needed. Coop and Will traded a heap of pelts for tables, rocking chairs, and cots. They paid Emma to stitch pelt blankets and bought two down mattresses from the general store.

Will unrolled the white, spotted bobcat hide from their first trapping. He hung it at an angle on the wall. Coop thought the old cabin was fine enough to be a room in the Porter house.

Six months after they'd arrived, on a cold fall morning, Coop used a hammer and chisel to finish shaping two big rocks they jammed under the threshold, creating steps to the door. They immediately set out to collect more rocks to finish a new fire pit out front, until the sun started to fall and even moving rocks couldn't keep them warm.

Inside, they lit a fire as they discussed how to clear the woodland to the edge of the lake. Felling most of the trees by spring would give them enough wood to repair the battered old dock and build a boat. The biggest catfish lived in the deepest water in the middle of the lake, and selling a fresh catch along with the pelts might double their income in Cadiz.

With the night growing bitter, they closed and locked the inside shutters. Soon, the fireplace toasted the air. Orange and red shadows flickered on the clean beige walls and bobcat hide. The rocking chairs creaked softly. The conversation faded to a comfortable silence.

At an amazing realization, Coop bolted upright.

"We're done with the cabin," he said. "The threshold was the last thing. We've been so busy with the rest of our plans we didn't even notice."

Will didn't reply and soon words weren't necessary. They settled back and started rocking again, the creaks as soothing as a familiar voice.

The logs burned to fiery embers that settled into a hot, intense glow. Coop got sweaty and stood to take off his clothes. Will grunted agreement and did the same. They caught each other's eyes and grinned, turning the moment into a strip show. Will tossed aside his trousers and ran a hand over his chest hair. His olive skin reflected the orange light, and he looked like he'd blazed to life from inside the sunset.

Coop often thought about what his life would be like without Will. If he'd spent the last six months alone on the Lightning, he'd be here in this cabin but shivering on the floor. When he woke in the morning, there'd be no traps to check, no trees to chop. He'd have no plan. No goal. Will had given him a life.

He felt the unnamable joy again, a warm and golden sense of gratitude, pride, and galloping, charging lust.

He'd die without Will.

Suddenly, he could name his joy. He shook his head with happy disbelief because he was helplessly in love.

Their bedfellows twitched to life, and it was a race of swift, determined pulses. They reached full stretch at about the same time. Will growled and reached across, but Coop grabbed Will's hand and shook his head. It was time. It was past time.

"We've done that plenty," Coop said. "There's one thing we still haven't tried."

Will still resisted kissing. Even when they were as close and connected as two males can be, Will would turn away and scrunch his eyes. Coop told himself to be patient, thankful Will was so comfortable with all the rest, and that he'd never mentioned the cathouse again.

A pinprick of anger blazed in Coop's heart, roused by the fear in Will's eyes. Every part of their bodies had touched every other part, except for their lips. What was so frightening?

Not a damn thing.

Coop took a step and Will leaned back, twisting away, clenching his arms across his chest like a shield. Coop wrapped his arms around Will's waist and smashed their erections together, a solid sensation they both enjoyed.

Will blocked Coop with his arms, stopping him from leaning into a kiss. He clamped his eyes tight and turned away, leaving his neck and one side of his face exposed. Coop knew he could make Will buck with passion if he licked and bit gently. Instead, he used his nose to nudge Will's hair aside and kissed the side of his neck.

Will shivered, and Coop did it again, a bit higher. He felt Will's arms loosen. Fighting an urge to overpower Will, he kissed a line up to his ear. Will's hands slipped, and Coop knocked them away and pulled their torsos tight. With Will's mouth now in reach, he planted a long, slow line of kisses from Will's ear to his chin. He aimed to brush their lips at the corner.

Coop felt Will's heart pumping, while his own banged in his head. Their breath came in quick, frantic puffs. Coop stole a glance at Will's face. His eyes were closed but no longer scrunched, his face slack with desire's stupor. Coop felt Will's hands on his back, pulling him closer.

Will opened his eyes, and they were empty of fear. Coop felt a triumphant surge and gripped Will's head from behind. He leaned in, landing on Will's open mouth.

Coop never felt anything so intimate. Their tongues explored each other's mouths, their lips moving in effortless synchronicity. They moaned and hugged and gripped until they sank to the floor.

When it was over, Coop didn't care if he ever met another person, so long as he could spend his life with Will in their cabin.

❖

Even after five years, Coop thought dawn on the Lightning must be the most beautiful in the world, especially in the spring. Will was still sleeping when Coop stepped outside. The sun was rising behind the hills across Nightwater Lake, where curls of fog crept on the water like curious ghosts peering into the depths.

It was the first clear morning after days of torrential rain. The land, trees, and plants glistened with fullness and life. In the distance, he heard a boulder break free of the rain-softened soil and crash down the slope. It was a common hazard of living on a rocky hill after storms blew through.

Coop walked under a shower of soft red and orange shafts slanting through the rising remains of night mist. Their dog Butterfeet ran ahead, shaggy and spotted, walking with the prance that inspired her name. Close behind, their fox Girly made sharp sounds of happiness reminiscent of a little girl's cries, even though he was a boy.

Coop had found Butterfeet in the weeds a few years before, a puppy atremble with fear, her huge eyes glinting with hope. He picked her up, spoke softly, and she sank with relief against his neck. A year later, they found Girly as a tiny kit locked in a cage trap, frightened out of his mind until Butterfeet licked him and instantaneously took over as his mother.

They'd been inseparable ever since, and they reached the water and waited for Coop, panting happily.

Coop picked a handful of worms from the dirt bin and carried the wriggling bundle to the flat-bottom oar boat he and Will had made four years before. They'd repaired the busted old dock at the same time, and it looked sturdy enough to hold a steamer.

Butterfeet was afraid of jumping on or off the dock, so Coop moored the boat to the rusty eye socket of a leaning tie-off piling log he'd been meaning to straighten. He took off his sandals and splashed to the boat. After piling the worms on the bench, he lifted the dog and fox inside before climbing aboard.

Coop had cut and shaped the oars himself and used one to push off. He rowed for the last wisp of seamark fog that revealed the lake's deepest spot. He reached it and set the hooks and worms on both poles, clamping them in place. He sat back while Butterfeet and Girly curled together to sleep.

Streams of sunlight pierced the lake a meter deep, streaking through the mossy tinted, crystalline top water. He shadowed his face with his hat and closed his eyes, resting his feet on the hull to avoid disturbing the sleeping animals. The boat bobbed gently. Water lapped the hull like delicate kisses.

He'd never imagined such an untroubled life. As far as he and Will were concerned, they would spend their lives on the Lightning. They made far more money than they spent, and they'd saved enough to buy politeness from the men at their bank in Cadiz.

Coop found coal pebbles here and there, mostly around the lake shore. The deposit in the meadow was now so deep Thomas climbed down a ladder to split off huge blocks. He hoisted them up with a pulley, where he broke them into smaller chunks.

Coop came to understand the immense significance of the way the coal broke as blocks.

Three years before, in the general store, he was passing the book table when his eyes fell on a plain brown cover with the title *Innovations in Coal Mining*. Coop read it until he'd almost memorized the pages.

He was excited to learn that a new surface mine might be quarried for years before expensive pits were needed. If mined correctly, the coal could finance equipment like the new cutting machines that had replaced dynamite for underground tunnels.

Over the years, as Coop lived out the chores and leisure of his life, he formed a plan in his mind to leap into action when he found the coal. He knew what tools he'd need and where to buy them. He could snap up horses and wagons practically overnight. Hiring laborers was no trouble, at least while his operation was small enough to escape the notice of the United Mine Workers of America. If his workers eventually unionized, he figured he wouldn't mind because it would mean his strike was notable.

A year ago, he left a message for Elmer Bluegrass at the bank in Cadiz, where the clerks said the old hillbilly stopped now and again. Six weeks later, Elmer left a cheerful reply, saying he'd be back in less than a month, "on May twentieth for exactitude, and I'll rest overnight."

On the day, Coop had waited on a bench in front of the huge, ornate courthouse that had been under construction when he and Will first arrived, kitty-corner from the bank. The streets were busier and louder than ever, and the courthouse's central clock tower had just boomed eleven times when Elmer arrived, driving the same buggy. Elmer tied his horse to the hitching post, and Coop was sorry it wasn't Jemma.

Elmer, crooked nose and all, looked every day of the four years gone by. After a spirited reunion, full of compliments that cost Elmer some breath, Coop led him to the town's fanciest hotel, where he'd already paid for Elmer's room overnight. Elmer poured out his gratitude, but as soon as they took a table in the hotel's restaurant, Coop got down to business.

"Do you know any rich men who buy coal?"

"Most certainly I do." He gave a curious look. "Did you find coal on your land?"

"Might be."

"This is bituminous country. Prices on bituminous coal move like a turtle in mud."

"But every year, people want more and more. The more you sell, the more you make. Quantity is what counts."

Elmer smiled. "The first time I saw you on the road, you looked like a sneeze would blow you back to yesterday, but you had fire in your eyes. I felt the same ambition when I was all knees and elbows. It brings to mind the tale about..."

"Before we get to jawboning, can you ask one of these men if I might have a good word with him? What kind of service does he want from a coal field, how does he like it delivered? Catch on?"

"This a spanking prime case of serendipity, it is. Arriving by train tomorrow is Mr. Claude Decker, vice president of the Cleveland Forge Steel Company. He's journeying to his summer home in Rhode Island. I'll take possession of a package here in Cadiz and deliver it to his sister in Indianapolis."

Another piece of Coop's plan clicked into place. Nobody needed coal more than steel companies.

Elmer leaned in. "But it needs to be spoken, rich men appreciate a trustworthy servant with an incurious nature. Half my fee comes from not asking questions. I suggest you watch me take the package from him, and then make an introduction, you yourself."

Coop was surprised. "Rich people aren't scary, Elmer. They're no smarter or dumber than the rest of us. My family was poor as dirt, and we had rich neighbors. Not all of them were kind, and they liked having their way, but every family I've met is the same."

"But they're used to getting things how they like, when they like. It makes 'em different."

"Different is nothing to fear, Elmer."

"I live on their good graces, Coop. I'll become a stranger right quick if I ask for favors."

Coop grinned but he was shocked a man as old as Elmer let childish fears hold his tongue. Coop wouldn't push him. He wasn't afraid to introduce himself. "Then how about some food, hooch, and a few of your stories?"

Elmer grinned. "It's a fine thing to see you so prosperous. And tell me, how is Will?"

They talked long into the night, and Coop took a room at the same hotel.

In the morning, Coop and Elmer met for breakfast before walking to the station for the ten o'clock train. On the platform, Coop watched a uniformed Linus hard at work as a porter. He'd moved into town a while back. His little sister Emma was proud he'd made a name for himself at the railway station. Linus was so busy, so polite, and so efficient at helping passengers, he never noticed Coop, even when he was close enough Coop might tap his shoulder.

They heard the train in the distance and waited to say their goodbyes until it huffed and screeched to a stop at the platform. As the doors of the first-class cars opened, Elmer said, "Be quick about your business. They're stopping just long enough to get people on and off. And here's the man himself."

A handsome man with streaks of gray in his hair stepped to the platform in an overcoat, carrying a large, flat box. He nodded as Elmer approached and handed it over. After a few words, Elmer walked off, giving Coop a sharp look that urged him to hurry.

Coop trotted over and said, "Mr. Decker."

The steel executive turned back, startled.

"I'm Cooper Tiller, and I'm an independent collier. I want to know how to get my coal to Cleveland Steel Forge Company just how you like and with the service you expect."

Mr. Decker gave him a look of muted admiration. "You have a bituminous seam?"

"I believe so. The truth is, I haven't come across the seam just yet, but it won't be long, and I want to be ready."

He looked skeptical. "Bituminous coal must be processed into coke for steel production. There are several coke furnaces nearby. That will be your first step."

Coop already knew the procedure but thanked Mr. Decker. "I have reason to believe my coal is block bituminous, which is rare but was recently discovered near Youngstown."

Mr. Decker raised his eyebrows. "You're fortunate, for block coal works in a blast furnace the same as coke. It sells for the same price but without the extra effort and money, so you'll enjoy a bigger margin."

Steam burst from the train.

"Must I sell my coal to you before I ship, or do you buy it when it arrives?"

Mr. Decker grabbed the hoist bar. "Buyers will always be waiting at the railway station in Cleveland, ready to purchase at a fair price. Everyone needs coal."

"And what can I do to stand above the other colliers?"

He looked straight into Coop's eyes. At that moment, Coop knew he'd learn to navigate the world of business as well as any man.

"A businessman must be on hand while making an initial sale. Nameless, faceless men make worrisome partners, and you mustn't allow an unscrupulous seller to stain your reputation. Accompany your first few shipments to your buyers. You'll make a firm impression." A banging bell issued a final warning and he pulled himself up.

"I'm grateful for your time. Enjoy your summer in Rhode Island."

Mr. Decker gave a sly smile. "But how did you know?"

"A new man must know as much as he can. And I will accompany my first shipments right to your forge to learn how I can be your best supplier."

Mr. Decker looked pleased, intrigued. "Use my name with my buyers. I'll keep my ears open for yours."

Coop grinned. "You've forgotten my name already, but I'll remember yours."

Mr. Decker laughed. "You have the swagger of wisdom or tomfoolery. Perhaps both. Goodbye, Mr. Cooper Tiller."

Coop laughed as Mr. Decker ducked inside and the train whistle hooted, drowning out everything else.

More than a year had gone by, and he doubted Mr. Decker would remember his name after so long. Coop often thought of the trusting look that passed between them.

Drifting on the boat waiting for the first catfish to bite, he wondered if he was asking too much of the world. He had more than he could have dreamed when he lived on the farm and knew nothing of desire, or bonds of affection. Instead of discovering the totality of his feelings while, say, working for the Porters, they came unbidden and unexpected with the other man already in place. It was a wonder how it all came together without a plan.

He smelled fire and opened his eyes. Smoke rose from the rock firepit. Will was awake but nowhere in sight.

A fishing pole jerked, and he lunged and yanked.

He caught four big catfish and maneuvered them wriggling into a sack. Butterfeet and Girly sniffed but knew to let them be. Coop started rowing back, looking up when he heard a whooping war cry.

Butterfeet planted her paws on the rim of the boat and barked with joy, while Girly cackled his cry. Will pounded across the dock, his long hair flying, naked as the day he was born.

At twenty years old, his dark hair carpeted his muscles from his shoulders down to his feet. It covered his chest in thick swirls, draining to a line down his abdomen, fanning out in a thick tangle at his crotch. His male parts flopped about, pale against his hairy thighs.

Will grew more handsome by the day, and Coop smiled with pride and appreciation as he charged across the dock and leaped, grabbing a shin and plunging into the water with a splash that made the biggest waves ever seen on Nightwater Lake. A moment later, he burst with a force that lifted him to his butt. Coop grinned, knowing it was intentional because he loved Will's hairy ass more than anything, and Will loved showing it to him.

Will swam to the boat grinning, and Butterfeet and Girly hung over the side in welcome. "Hurry up and jump in. Feels like being reborn."

Coop powered to the shore and put the animals on land. He rushed through securing the boat, slapping the catfish to a board, and slicing eight filets that he hung high in a pouch dangling from a branch. He scooped up the fishy remains and tossed them into the water.

He stripped and jumped from the sturdy dock, tensing when he hit the cold April water. Soon, he felt Will's arms around him. The buoyancy felt like they were flying up. Coop tried to push away, but Will wouldn't let him. They broke the surface in a tight embrace.

Coop pushed away angrily, checking to see that nobody was watching. Will shrugged and lay back to float.

Coop returned to shore, trying to control his anger. He grabbed a towel from a peg beside the cabin door and dried off. He slipped on pants and a shirt and started cooking up the catfish at the firepit.

Will emerged from the water, walked by without a word, dried and dressed, and arrived when breakfast was almost ready. He set down two wooden bowls of cornmeal and oats. Butterfeet and Girly paced anxiously, sniffing.

Will said, "It doesn't feel so good to have you push me away like that."

Coop cringed with shame. "I told you how Linus saw us," he spat. "He was running like he'd seen the devil himself."

"He won't tell anybody."

"How are you so sure? One night he gets drinking, tells one person, and it's all over Cadiz."

Will sighed. "You brought me along to where I am now. How come it's you who's so afraid anyone knows?"

The catfish were cooked. Coop scooped three filets to each plate and shredded the rest to mix with the cornmeal and oats. As he set them down, Butterfeet and Girly descended with relish.

Will was chewing as Coop picked up his plate, reviewing the moment two weeks ago one more time: They were naked, kissing and groping. They'd just pulled apart when Coop saw a movement behind Will. Linus must have been visiting his family on his day off from the railway station. Maybe he'd come to pay his respects and instead got an eyeful of naked men embracing. He was tearing downhill, pushing off trees to get away as fast as he could.

Will swallowed a piece of catfish and said, "If people don't understand how we feel, it's their trouble, not ours. How many times did you say that to me before it finally got it through my skull?"

Coop loved Will so much he felt like he'd split in two if they were apart. Usually, they set the cots aside and slept on the floor, taking turns holding each other tight. Coop slept fitfully when business kept them apart at night, sitting up with panic when he reached for Will and he wasn't there.

Coop comprehended his luck in finding a man who shared his feelings, a man who appreciated another man's gait, his voice, shape, laugh, smell, and demeanor. Will's smile filled him with happiness, and Coop admired Will's reasoning and sense. They seemed made for each other.

Coop felt he could survive any torment ever devised simply by knowing a man like Will valued him above everyone else in the world. The joy never felt stale or familiar, but the freshness came at the price of certainty. The terror always lurked that Will would see Coop's faults all too clearly one day and leave.

He watched as Will used his fork to separate a creamy piece of catfish. Coop knew it was too big, but as usual Will shoved it in his mouth and chewed fast to make it manageable. He swallowed and gulped ale from a tumbler. He wiped his lips with the back of his hand and belched with his mouth closed. The delicious purity of the moment pierced Coop's soul like a golden needle.

When they were intimate, it felt so natural and perfect, he couldn't understand how any man felt differently. No artist had ever painted anything as beautiful. He wanted to charge to the summit of Lightning Mountain and yell for the whole world to hear, *Let Linus run! Let everyone run! If you knew the joy of it, you'd know we're the lucky ones!*

With a soft voice, Coop said, "I couldn't live without you, Will. I'd die, I swear it. But you gotta admit it was easier when we were younger. You know how it is when we go into Cadiz now. Mothers pushing their daughters in our path. Girls giving us pretty smiles at every turn. All those men who assume we use the cathouse as much as they do. How long can we keep smiling and nodding?"

"We could pretend we're deaf. Or witless." Will's face was serious, but his eyes laughed.

Coop gave a reluctant smile. "I've seen some of the men at the trading post giving us looks."

Will scoffed. "The men at the trading post are a grubby lot of cons and cheats. They're too skinflint for the cathouse, so they probably take turns with a ewe in back."

"They might talk to respectable people."

"They talk all the time, and nobody listens. And for the official account, I think we're mighty respectable."

Loud booms came from high up the hill. The screech of fresh wood tearing knifed the air, followed by a rolling crash. Distant birds squawked and screamed.

"Another tree falling," Will said, setting aside his empty plate. "Someday a rain's gonna come along and strip this hill clean. I'll see if it knocked out any traps."

"Take the saw. I'll get started on tilling the vegetable patch, and it's time to straighten that piling log."

Will leaned in without warning and smacked a kiss on his lips. "There, worrywart, nothing happened."

Coop pretended to find it funny, but as soon as Will turned, he glanced about to make sure all was clear. He grimaced at his cowardice, and a voice in his head badgered him yet again with its constant taunt: *Will deserves better than you.*

From far off, a train's hooting whistle soared above the chug of its engine. The railway was completed four years before, along the line of markers running across the meadow they'd seen from Elmer's buggy that first day.

He filled a bucket with water from an overflowing rain barrel, threw in some sudsy powder, and cleaned the plates and bowls. Emma arrived just as he finished, Butterfeet and Girly bouncing at her feet.

The chattering, pretty girl had grown into a beautiful young woman with an unmatched vocabulary.

The previous week in Cadiz, Coop had stumbled across a gift so perfect for Emma he hadn't checked the price, which he paid even after the shop owner stunned him by asking for a princely five dollars.

Excited, he told her to wait and ran to the cabin. He pulled the present from his knapsack and decided to let her remove the shop wrapping of brown paper and twine.

Back outside, he beamed at her delight when she saw plainly it was a book. "I saw it in the general store. I knew right then it belonged to only one person in Harrison County."

Carefully, she unknotted and cinched the twine into a bundle that she slipped in her pocket. She unfolded the book, smoothing the brown paper to save for later. Her pensive mood lifted as daintily as a ladybug rises from a leaf.

The title glowed with golden gilt, applied with precision to the fine tooled leather. "*Pride and Prejudice*," she said, closing her eyes and holding it to her breast.

"I know it's your favorite novel. It has drawings, and look at the sides."

Hand-painted, idyllic rural scenes ran along the three paper edges. Each showed ladies and gentlemen wearing beautiful clothes as they strolled in front of houses bigger than even the new courthouse.

She examined the edges and flipped through the pages, stopping to admire a few drawings. "This is lovely, Coop."

"I inscribed it and all. Nothing fancy, just to you, from me."

"I'm sure I'll never own a book more special than this one. It was so thoughtful of you, and I'm very grateful." Concern glazed her eyes.

"Is something wrong, Emma?"

"I am troubled by something Linus told me, and I'd like to ask you about it. I'm afraid it's not a pleasant subject."

His heart broke into a gallop. He braced, willing himself to be still no matter what she said.

"Yesterday afternoon, I took two loaves of fresh bread to that shantytown bachelor rooming house where Linus has been living. Allow me to observe as an aside, beer and ale keep bachelors alive. Men need women more than they know."

Here was a chance to risk truth, and he could think of no one safer than Emma. "A woman is not the solution for every man, Emma. Some men do well with other men."

"I'll allow that many men do. In the military, at sea, on dangerous expeditions." She gestured. "You and Will. But the men in that rooming house need a woman. Linus certainly does. In any case, that was merely the prelude to my question, which I fear might upset you."

"Ask away, Emma."

She took a deep breath. "Linus has been working at the railway station for four years. He's the best porter, finding, helping, fetching. He does what he can to improve the journey for weary passengers. Not a day goes by without the station manager hearing a compliment for his dedication. The old head porter died not long ago, and Linus asked for the position with every expectation of being rewarded. Yesterday, he learned they gave it to a white man who doesn't even live here." Her voice went high. "He's coming from Pittsburgh. Do you agree that is cruelty?"

"It *is* cruel."

"Linus is twenty-two now, an age when an intelligent and ambitious man should be rising in the world. When will he get another chance?"

"If I was in charge, Emma, I'd change the world in so many ways."

Unsmiling, she said, "Well, I won't detain you. I just came over to say that Linus saw some metal cage traps in the window of the trading post, and he thought you'd like to know."

A goodwill gesture from Linus. Perhaps a promise to stay quiet. "That's good of Linus. Please thank him for me."

"Pa also said to tell you he'll burn Pinky's cabin in the next few weeks. He wants to let it dry after all that rain."

They'd found Pinky dead two weeks before, floating aimlessly in his boat. His cabin was decrepit beyond repair.

"And thank you again for the book. It really is special, Coop, and I appreciate your thoughtfulness."

As she left, he wondered how many people walked the earth straining to find sense in things without reason, stung by unearned scorn.

She was right to worry about Linus's prospects. If a man without money is to gain stature, he must make good impressions early. Linus had dutifully followed the required path, his faithfulness rewarded by being knocked aside at the last moment by a white man. How many times can a man start young? The betrayal must be bitter.

In a sudden rage he didn't fully understand, he grabbed a sledgehammer and splashed to the leaning mooring log. He swung, and the force of the blow vibrated to his feet. It sheared a wedge of wood from the top that sailed away and splashed far off, leaving a surprisingly fresh scar on the weathered old log. He hammered until it stood straight.

His rage burned hotter. He grabbed the shovel and descended on the vegetable garden, where spring weeds were on the march and the rains had turned the soil to a backbreaking wet clay. He slashed and sliced, turning the earth inside out, not stopping until he was done. He leaned on the shovel, covered in mud and slick with sweat, his breath whistling on each pant. Even the satisfying sight of a garden ready for planting didn't slake his anger.

When he was a boy, two confirmed bachelors owned a nearby farm, sharing the toil, the earnings, and a farmhouse. In town, two spinsters had lived in a cottage, tending chickens and flower beds. Everyone accepted these friendships, as far as Coop knew, but those childhood neighbors had aged out of the marriage market when God was a boy.

He and Will wouldn't reach that stage for many years. For all the praise of piety and chastity, the world revels in randy young men. Young men of a different disposition earn a steady and chilly disapproval, as if they are too soft.

Exhausted, he limped to the water tank behind the cabin. He twisted the spigot and crouched to gulp right from the tap, before letting the blissfully cool water run over his head.

His anger still churned, making him wild for more heavy work. He spotted two boulders next to the cook fire pit. They'd rolled them downhill last fall, meaning to break them apart for a grill, but they'd never found time. Coop grabbed the sledgehammer, and sparks flew as he reduced one boulder to a pile of rocks before fatigue claimed him at last.

He stumbled to lean against the cabin, dizzy from panting.

Suddenly, his mind blazed with understanding. He wasn't angry at Will, or the world, or the hypocritical demands on young men. He was angry with himself for not accepting that his life was as good as it could be, which was better than most people could hope for.

Butterfeet barked happily, and Girly issued his staccato cries. They ran to greet Will, who carried a log on his shoulder that he dropped near the firewood pile next to their tool shed. He stooped to greet their pets.

Coop pushed to his feet, willing himself past his fatigue.

Will saw him coming and looked him up and down, smiling at his sweaty, muddy, raggedy appearance.

"We got some landslides on the way," Will said as Coop approached. Will's face broke with an appreciative, raunchy smile. "You look like you corralled a wild stallion and fought a battle as well."

They were high up on land they'd cleared of trees years ago, visible for at least a mile to the southeast.

Coop's rage became a wave of passion. He grabbed Will and

kissed him on the mouth. Will froze with surprise before joining with equal relish. Neither cared they were visible to anyone who might look up, although Coop told himself an observer was unlikely.

Coop took Will's hand and marched him back to the cabin, shutting the door before ripping off his clothes and falling on him.

It was dark when Butterfeet and Girly grew tired of waiting and started scratching the door.

"I'll let them in," Will said, rising. He stopped, confused.

"What's wrong?"

"Can't you hear it?"

In seconds, a faint rumble intensified to a mighty roar, like a train just outside the door. The cabin shuddered, and Coop imagined the entire hill crashing down to bury them alive.

Will threw open the door, and Butterfeet and Girly rushed in, yipping in fright. Coop followed Will outside. In the open air, the cacophony was easy to locate along the northern slope. Booms and crashes echoed across the land.

"I'll bet it's that fern cliff," Will said.

They slipped on boots and raced off buck naked. A full moon lighted the way, but by now both could guide the moonbeams around the Lightning.

Coop smelled the landslide ahead, the rich scent of turned dirt, the smooth cleanliness of broken wood, an undercurrent of shredded foliage.

They reached a scene from biblical times, a huge tide of dirt rippling with quivering fronds, tipping and flattening the trees at the edge of the forest.

Will said, "That's a mighty sight."

Coop looked up to the new cliff, wondering if Lightning Mountain would ever settle.

It took a moment to believe what he was seeing. His breath caught and his jaw dropped. He whispered, "Will. Will."

"How's that?"

Coop pointed. "Look."

Will raised his eyes and gasped.

The new cliff scar was as inky as pitch. The coal had decided to show itself at last.

Moonlight rode a zagged ridge with brilliant intensity in the center of the seam. The line cracked, and two forks flashed to the bottom. It looked like a lightning bolt hurled by an ancient god, frozen for eternity in mid-strike.

Coop said, "It's what the Tuscarawas saw. The ridges of a coal seam shaped like lightning. We're the first to see this in hundreds of years." His voice dropped to a whisper. "The Lightning."

CHAPTER SEVEN

Harrison County, Ohio
Present day

Welcome to Cadiz Township
Birthplace of Clark Gable

"Clark Gable?" Darcy says from the passenger seat of Jake's pickup.

"He was an actor, wasn't he?"

"He played Rhett Butler in *Gone with the Wind.*"

"My mom and sister must have watched that movie about a hundred times, but all those ladies running around in poofy dresses talking about love and marriage...I'm more of a *Star Wars* guy."

Darcy chuckles. "I'm right with you."

They drive on, past trailers with sturdy vinyl siding and single-family homes. Bright plastic toys scatter across spacious lawns, carved from woodlands pressing in on every side. They pass a row of enormous old houses, gracious living for the local gentry of a previous age, now chopped into multi-unit dwellings, judging by the number of vehicles.

Ahead, magnificent towers rise over a small downtown. At the main intersection, they stop at a red traffic light.

Lining the streets on all sides, pristine older buildings evoke a frontier spirit. The brick and wood command respect and promise safety, fairness, and fidelity. It looks like a movie set, except for signs promising discount prices and dollar values. The streets are lazy with scattered traffic and no pedestrians beyond an old lady walking a small dog. Yet the echoes of long-ago endless bustle and noise still reverberate.

Jake points. "I think that's our courthouse."

The lawn of a square rises to a summit holding an enormous building sheathed in pale stone. Jake parks in front, and they pause to admire the courthouse's riotous combination of classical symmetry gussied up with gothic and Victorian flourishes. A central clock tower rises highest. Arched windows parade along the top floor, announcing the noble work within, while square windows below suggest no-nonsense bureaucracy. A staircase sweeps up to a Greek portico sheltering the main entrance.

On the wide lawn, the statue of a passionate man makes a crucial point with a raised arm, the kind of politician who understood his obligation to live up to the standards of such a stately structure. Or at least they used to pretend they understood.

Inside, the main corridor features mosaic floor patterns and idealized wall paintings of local landmarks. It smells of old paper and dust, perhaps accounting for the hushed reverence of a library. They soon reach the recorder's office, with county deeds and titles.

A beautiful Black woman works behind the counter, curls bouncing past her shoulders. Her smart outfit is molded to her voluptuous hourglass figure. She gives an old white guy at the counter a skeptical smile. "I told you, Mr. Griff. I'm too liberal to get elected to Congress from this district. First thing I'd do is raise your taxes."

Beaming, Mr. Griff waves off her concerns. "Your family's been living in these parts for as long as mine. Who better to put the screws to you but old neighbors?"

She laughs as Darcy and Jake walk up. "How can I help you gentlemen?"

Mr. Griff turns their way with tiny shuffles. "Say, fellas, what do you think? Doesn't she have a face for Congress?"

Jake cocks his head. "I'd say more like the White House." Darcy's impressed he carried the joke without missing a beat.

"Hey! This fella has the right idea! Her name is Betsy Battlehurst. Battlehurst! Can't you just see it on a campaign sign or the ballot?"

"How about you plan my campaign while I help these two?"

"Now, fellas, that's what you call the ol' heave-ho." In good humor, he scuffs off. She looks at his back with exasperation and grudging affection.

"I'm trying to find property records for my great-grandfather," Darcy says. "He owned a coal mine somewhere around here. His name was Cooper Tiller."

She draws back, her eyes huge. Her voice echoes in the marble room, "You mean Tiller as in Tiller Coal?"

He nods.

"Well, that's a how-do-you-do. I curated an exhibition about the seventieth anniversary of the mine's destruction. I can look up any records you like, but I studied the history of the mine, and the land was jointly owned by Cooper Clayton Tiller and Rex William Herrington."

"Rex William Herrington?"

"He helped run the mine in the early years. Nobody's sure where he came from or where he went."

"Who owns the land now?"

She types. "Mildred Kohl, but there's a death notification. Looks like someone has started an audit of the estate."

Darcy's impressed by Trevor's efficiency. "I must be listed. Darcy O'Brien? And my sisters, Lydia and Serena?"

"They're all there."

"Anyone else?"

"Nope."

"Believe it or not, I've never seen that coal mine. Can you tell me where it is?"

"It's easy. Just take a left at the main intersection going south. It's a twenty-minute drive, tops. Park off street, but choose carefully because that twisty old road is dangerous."

"How will I recognize it?"

"You can't miss it. It's fenced off and closed to the public." She scrunches her mouth. "I'd better call the sheriff's department in case someone reports you as trespassers."

Mr. Griff returns as she lifts the receiver. "Did I hear you say your great-grandfather was Cooper Tiller?"

Darcy nods, struck by the awed look on the old man's face.

"My daddy worked at the coal mine, and his daddy before him, and my great-granddaddy, too. I planned to do the same, like most boys around here before the disaster. I was a kid, but I remember the day the mine collapsed like it was yesterday. It was like the world was ending. Your great-granddaddy saved a lot of men's lives."

"I know there was some sort of accident that closed the mine in 1950, but I don't know much about it."

The old man blinks, as if he must have misunderstood. "Now what's your name?" Darcy introduces himself and Mr. Griff extends his hand. "Your great granddaddy was a hero around here. They should've built him a statue, but with the mine closed, nobody could afford much of anything. If you got a few minutes, I'll tell you what happened. I might be the last living witness to see it with my own eyes."

Darcy's eager to hear the story, and he's grateful when Jake says they have plenty of time.

Betsy hangs up. "I notified the sheriff. Most of the deputies are my relatives, so you shouldn't have any trouble." She suddenly notices the change in tone, Mr. Griff's intensity, Darcy's amazement.

"This young man doesn't know about his great-granddaddy," Mr. Griff says to Betsy, "or what happened to the mine." He waves Darcy and Jake to one of the large, wide tables scattered across the room. The three men sit.

"Well, now." Mr. Griff taps a finger, his eyes distant. "Tiller Coal supported thousands of families in south Harrison County. That mine would last forever, is how it felt. They said the coal went so deep you could dig until you came out on the other side of the world. Cooper Tiller was the wealthiest man anyone ever saw in the flesh. 'Course, he moved to Cleveland way back when, but he was a generous local patron, built fire stations and schools, libraries, you name it, the way rich men used to do. He paid good wages, and he treated men fairly. It was always an event when he came to town."

His thin lips tremble. "I'll never forget how it started. One night, my daddy came home, saying one of the crews heard a gusher of water burst behind the tunnel wall and run like rapids. It drained away soon enough, but they could hear it trickling for days. Soon, distant pops like rifle shots started ricocheting through tunnels. Rumbles and vibrations shook everything, and cracks opened and spread, like they were looking for something. Showers of pebbles fell without warning.

"Back then, most miners never wore anything besides boots and the skin they were born in. Rocks came flying out of the dark, and men started coming out of the pits looking like ringside boxers. My daddy had the angriest bruise you've ever seen on his thigh and right across his," he looks for Betsy, who is nowhere in sight, and he whispers, "his male parts." He grins. "Daddy and his friends started telling us boys it was common for a miner to get injured right there."

Darcy and Jake chuckle.

Griff gets serious again. "Underground, you hear strange moaning and creaking, and little things you can't name. You get small cave-ins. Nothing to worry about, except when they happen all at once. The younger men were getting spooked. My granddaddy yelled and hollered, calling them yellow. I can still see him shouting, 'until a tunnel collapses, quit bellyaching,' is what he said." His face goes sour. "I never liked that angry old man. Nobody did."

He folds his arms on the table. "Most of the Appalachian miners came over from Europe, and they brought the old folk tales with them. The Welsh had tommyknockers, Scandinavians had trolls, Germans the kobolds, piskies from Cornwall, the Slavic Shubin. The kindly creatures keep the miners safe, while the mischievous ones hide their tools." His face goes dark. "But the evil ones want blood. They hate humans for plundering their riches. Nobody believed those old superstitions, but as the incidents went on, nobody could talk about anything else."

Betsy suddenly arrives and sits, setting a thick envelope on the table.

"All the women went digging through old family boxes, following their grandmas' recipes for saffron cakes, nut rolls, and vanilla bread. The fancier the better. They let bills pile up to buy those expensive ingredients and did nothing but bake all day, and nobody took one bite. The men hid the sweets in the tunnels as peace offerings. I guess that's all you can do when you're up against the earth herself.

"About six months after that first gusher, when the morning crew arrived, the access road was shattered like a concrete jigsaw puzzle. The supervisor phoned your great-granddaddy all the way in Cleveland, long before the sun came up. Mr. Tiller told him to close the mine until inspectors had a look. He gave the men one week off at full pay. That was on top of their regular vacation."

He leans in, entwining his fingers. "The next day at around noon, all the men and their families had a cookout, celebrating like it was a holiday, every one of us a fool. We were in a meadow by the old rail line, and you could see the top of the hill, even the headframe building and the hoist house. And everyone's eating and playing baseball when this sound came. It was like a buried monster dug his way up and let out a roar…" He fumbles with words and stops.

Betsy says softly, "Even this far away, people here in town heard the roar and felt the ground shake. Pictures fell off walls, silverware rattled. Fishermen and boaters said ripples raced from all directions across every lake in the area."

His eyes down, Griff says, "The explosions started. They sounded a million miles away, but they were strong enough to punch you in the gut. All those big trees started whipping in unison, like they were made of paper. Show me a person who thinks mankind controls nature, and I'll show you an idiot." He lifts his hands. "All of a sudden, this crazy smoke starts rising everywhere. It looked like the whole world was caving in until we realized it was birds taking wing. Must have been millions. You'd never think there were that many."

He describes how a chasm opened, and the forest tumbled inward as the hill sank out of sight. "That hill was called the Lightning for some reason nobody ever knew. It was the highest hill around for miles, and not ninety seconds later, it was no more than a mound.

"South county never recovered. Families left. Young people went off to find work and never came back. Those of us who stayed got older and poorer." He shakes his head. "My family stayed because my daddy got a job closing up Tiller Coal. They plugged the mine with concrete and cleared away all the dangerous equipment. It took years. Daddy said he felt like he was preparing his own grave. Sure enough, it killed him. He died on the job."

Darcy can't think of anything to say, and Griff nods like he understands. "On a normal day, that mine would have been bustling like an anthill. Nobody would have survived. But Cooper Tiller put his workers ahead of his profit, and not one man died. He came to town soon after and walked through the ruins. It was like the Pope was visiting, not a sound for miles. Afterward, he handed a final pay packet to the men with a little extra. People were sobbing as they thanked him for their lives, and the money."

Betsy says, "Family legend says my ancestors knew him even before he got rich." She slides the envelope across to Darcy. Her name is written on front in block letters, all caps: BETSY BATTLEHURST. "We have a ton of archival photos of the mine, and I ordered reprints for the exhibit. They accidentally made an extra set. I didn't want to throw them away, but I didn't know what to do with them, either. I'd love for you to have them." She smiles. "He was a very handsome man. You're his spitting image." She returns to her spot behind the counter.

Darcy picks up the envelope as Griff says, "We had a department store and a bowling alley and a pool. A real community. They tore it all down."

Jake pats Darcy on the back and motions for them to leave. Darcy doesn't dare interrupt Griff's grief by saying goodbye. He gets up quietly and follows Jake out, giving Betsy a nod. She smiles, tight-lipped and perfunctory, tears in her eyes.

"Hell of a story," Jake says as he pulls out of the parking spot and does a U-turn. He turns left at the light. In a few miles, the smooth town road narrows with cracks, splits, and potholes as it curves along the base of the hills.

"How you feeling?" Jake says.

"I'm not sure." He remembers his teenage dismissal of his great-grandfather as a greedy industrialist unconcerned with the little people. He realizes he'd invented that persona from the sparest details.

Coal? Cooper Tiller didn't know how toxic it was. He was wealthy? Darcy's known poor people he wouldn't trust to hold a handful of air.

Jake says, "You want my opinion, Cooper Tiller sounds like one in a million."

Darcy watches hill country go by. How much happiness did Cooper Tiller bring to the people in Harrison County? How much security, peace, hope? Coal was woven into the local community like religion, patriotism, weddings, and holidays. Coal was prosperity, survival, the future itself. They were wrong about all of that, but almost nobody on earth knew it at the time.

Soon after he moved back to Cleveland to live with Grandma Millie, he indulged one of his periodic attempts to learn more about his mysterious great-grandfather. Like his previous tries, he found mentions of Tiller Coal on languid regional message boards. Only a handful of newer postings had been added since his last online search years before. Aside from the occasional mention as the mine's owner, Cooper Tiller seemed entirely forgotten.

Darcy had clicked around a bit and found himself quite unexpectedly fascinated by the story of Ohio's bituminous coal.

In a distant epoch, before even flowers had appeared on earth, the land that became Ohio sweltered in the heat and humidity at the equator. A sea covered the western half of the future state. Runoff from the new Appalachian ridge, rising in the east to become the mightiest mountain range in earth's history, fanned into enormous deltas across the eastern shore, blanketed by a vast tropical canopy soaking up the sun's energy.

Plants thrive in part from absorbing and storing the energy of sunlight. When a plant dies, unused energy disperses in many ways. Under rare conditions of low oxygen, the dead plant withers to fibers that retain the sun's power.

On the eastern shore of the ancient sea, the plants at the surface sank into a tangle of billions of vines, stems, and leaves. They slowly descended to the swamp waters in the low-oxygen bog. The mass above pressed them into stringy layers of peat, dense with sun energy. The cycle repeated for tens of millions of years.

The land inched north to colder climes and the western sea drained away, leaving behind thousands of square miles of thick swamp peat. New seas washed in with sediments that hardened to rock, eventually compressing the peat into dense black veins of coal.

Over hundreds of millions of years, the earth's crust jumbled the rocky layers. Vast, irregular blocks of coal broke off, and many returned to the surface.

Ten thousand years ago, massive Arctic glaciers flowed south and plowed Ohio's northern topsoil into hills, crunching to a stop at the outermost edge of the Appalachian ridge. By then, the mountains were ancient beyond any human's understanding, smoothed by eons of wind and rain.

The mile-high glaciers melted, releasing debris trapped in distant lands, including boulders that settled on the ground far from home, looking shockingly out-of-place. The surging meltwater carved valleys and meadowlands.

Over the next several thousand years, in outcrops and stream beds, people in the Appalachian regions found a shiny black rock that burned much hotter than wood or grasses. No one understood that firing a nugget of coal releases centuries of sun energy.

Across the ocean, a man in England made an emergency water pump in a desperate attempt to clear a flooding mine. He improvised a mechanism powered by coal, the only abundant fuel on hand. Its speed and power amazed onlookers, and the humble water pump kicked off the Industrial Revolution.

The world went mad for coal and men amassed fortunes when finding a deposit. They didn't know how coal formed, or why it burned so hot, or how it returned to the surface to be discovered.

In Ohio, they didn't know about one huge seam from the ancient swamp that had snapped off under a topsoil hill in Harrison County. Like a spear, it pushed up on a vertical slant. Small landslides gave brief glimpses of the leading edge, but that was long before coal was valuable, and the few people who noticed gave it little thought. It was near to breaking the surface when Cooper Tiller arrived in 1894. In a few years he was wealthier than he'd ever dreamed.

Darcy's ripped from his thoughts when Jake brakes suddenly to round a sharp corner in the road. A tall chain-link fence blocks the land to the left. Old metal signs dimpled with pellet shots warn *Danger Debris* and *Private Property.*

A sweeping mound of tossed, uneven land jumbles on the other side of the fence and runs into the distance, thick with native plants.

An unexpected sense of wonder lifts his spirits and frightens him at the same time. He feels a primal connection to this land.

Jake pulls off the road in a weedy spot to the right. Sticks screech against the metal underfoot, but Jake looks unconcerned as he parks. "Someone clipped that fence at some point. Let's go find out where."

They're across the street when Darcy realizes he's still holding the envelope with Betsy's exhibition photos. Jake's already exploring the fence perimeter, so Darcy decides to hold on to them instead of returning to the truck.

They step carefully into the tangle until they can't see the road. After a few minutes, Jake says, "Here we go." The fence curls back from an old slice through the links. They ease past the rusty spikes left by wire clippers.

With a huge smile, Jake says, "It's pretty cool. Be a fun place to camp."

Darcy's definitely interested in camping with Jake.

"Do you feel at home?" Jake says, walking with happy bounces, straining to see, looking more handsome than ever. "This would be a good place for a little cabin. Bet there's plenty of flathead catfish nearby, and grilled catfish is just about the best thing ever. Hey! Used to be a lake here."

In a shallow marsh, grasses and horsetail sticks break the surface of still, mirroring water, edged with thick stands of cattails and trembling white thimbleweed flowers. Swamp milkweed and marsh stars preen with ravishing pink and purple petals. Bees and butterflies pick across the colorful bounty by the thousands.

Jake stoops to snap the green leaf of an ordinary plant with a pale seed pod. "This is sweet flag." He smells the break before handing it to Darcy. It has a distinctive sugary scent. "Sweet flag doesn't look like much, but it's one of the oldest plants in the world. And those horsetails in the water go back to before earth had animals."

Darcy realizes he's standing on the very spot where the ancient swamp became the coal field that made his great-grandfather rich. He takes another sniff of the leaf. He's never smelled anything so sweet.

Jake snaps another leaf to chew. "Doesn't take much to fill these little hill lakes, probably the slurry runoff from the coal mine. I bet this was a great fishing spot in the old days." He points to an ancient log lying in the weeds, one end chopped to a point. "Yep, I was right. That's an old tie-off piling log. You drive the sharp end into the lake bottom and tie off your boat."

"Looks like a nice spot to look at some photos," Darcy says, sitting next to a wedge-shaped break at the top of the log.

He slips a stack of at least fifty glossy, black-and-white photos from the envelope. With a single glance at the top picture, Darcy draws in a sharp breath. *They were lovers.*

He's never seen his great-grandfather so young, standing next to another man in a forest. In trousers and a loose shirt, his hair combed to one side but still messy, Cooper Tiller radiates virility. Next to him, a handsome man with chiseled features and wavy dark hair falling to his shoulders looks a bit more rustic. They're holding each other at the waist with their other hands clasped in front.

Darcy knows men of the past were comfortable displaying and expressing intimacy with other men, and holding each other tight doesn't mean they were gay. Everyone has seen the old pictures, but this is different.

His great-grandfather and the man who must be Rex William Herrington are smiling at each other, not the photographer. Cooper Tiller's face has all the ease, comfort, and love his wedding portrait lacks. The man with long hair looks even more enamored.

Jake sits next to him. "Let's see that."

He gives Jake the photo. The next picture shows the men hooking their elbows around the other's neck with their foreheads touching. They're laughing, their eyes meeting playfully.

"You look exactly like your great-grandfather," Jake says. "And these two guys look…"

"They look like they're in love. Here, you get the same vibe from this one."

In the next photo, the men pose happily in front of a cabin, one sitting on a stump, the other kneeling on the ground. They lean together, clamped at the shoulders, holding the spotted hide of a small animal between them. On the back, someone has written *Cooper Tiller and Will Herrington, 1900.*

He flips through the rest quickly, a high-pitched buzz in his head. The pictures give way to both men amidst small crowds of rugged miners posing next to a cart piled high with blocks of coal on a small track; the next shows them in a bank office, shaking hands with men in suits. In later photos, the easy camaraderie between Cooper Tiller and Will Herrington becomes formal frowns as they stand far apart. In several, one looks across the divide to the other, as if searching for something.

More people crowd the photos, large groups of miners with a United Mine Workers of America banner. Notably, a Black man stands out in several photos, posed in front of the workers wearing an official uniform designating a higher rank. As the photos become more elaborate, and the activity of the mine increases, Will vanishes.

"Is it possible they were lovers?" Darcy says.

"I guess we'll never know."

Darcy stands and blows out a breath. Jake rises next to him, silent, before he gasps. Darcy watches this complicated, sexy man lift something from the weeds and hold it up for view.

A hunk of coal. "This seems like the perfect souvenir for you," Jake says, his smile guileless.

He hands it to Darcy. The coal shines and glints. "Thanks," Darcy says. The black rock streaks his hand.

"You ready to hit the road?" Jake says.

"Let's go."

Looking around, Jake says, "It would be great to camp here sometime, though. Think that's in the cards?"

Jake's eyes are speckled green and brown, and in this light, he has a noticeable dimple when he smiles.

"Yeah," Darcy says, feeling both elated and terrified. He nearly spills his coke secret but forces it away.

CHAPTER EIGHT

Harrison County, Ohio
1905–1906

Coop and Linus crouched at a spot halfway down the Lightning's east slope, where diggers had recently finished a new shaft. The opening was just wide enough for a wooden chute with a burlap conveyer that brought coal to the surface, replacing the mules that hauled trams up the main shaft.

Linus had designed the new system months before and persuaded Coop to give it a chance. It promised a massive increase in coal yield, as well as an efficient way to remove the smaller backfill. But from the start, coal nuggets spilled over the sides and piled into heaps, jamming the contraption. The difficult work of clearing the narrow tunnel took hours, and the backlog idled everything.

Linus designed a better, taller chute he swore would stop the spills, but it required a pricey and time-consuming enlargement of the tunnel. Coop snapped that he couldn't manage another investment in an unproven system, and he ordered Linus to be quick about finding an affordable solution.

Secretly, Coop hoped Linus would fail, for he missed the homey, hard-working mules, intelligent and gentle. They'd filled the emptiness since the fox Girly and the dog Butterfeet disappeared several years ago, at around the time people spotted a puma skulking in the nearby hills.

In the world of miners, a mule was dull witted and deserved harsh treatment. Coop knew the animals were deliberate, not stupid, and they were desperate to please their raging taskmasters. Coop demonstrated for all three shifts how the animals eagerly responded to gentle words, adding, "If I hear about cruel treatment, that man can find new work. And that includes all men who see it and don't intervene. Harming a mule is harming my property, and the union won't protect you." Some men shared looks of disgust, as if it were beneath them to treat mules with dignity.

If Linus's latest innovation failed, it would give Coop the excuse he needed to bring mules back.

"Now you watch, Mr. Tiller," Linus said. "The improvements will come after the first two hundred feet or thereabouts. You'll see the difference right away." He waved his cap to a man at the foot of the hill, who cranked a motor that started with a puff of dark smoke.

Instantly, small chains sewn into the edges dragged the burlap through the chute to huge, open railway carts. Like always, the coal tumbled and bounced like popcorn, plinking to the ground or flying off.

"Now you'll see," Linus yelled.

Suddenly, a stately line of blocks and piles emerged from the hill, gliding with purpose. In a flash, he knew Linus had succeeded, and he couldn't bring the mules back.

Coop stood above the chute as a river of coal sailed smoothly along. The yield was an astonishing increase. "How did you do it?"

Linus waved for the man to kill the motor. "Here," Linus said, moving coal aside to show a curved metal brace attached to the chains every few feet. "That's all it takes, one bent piece of metal to keep things steady."

"That's a sound investment, Linus. We'll extract more coal than a mine twice our size. Order what you need to make the repairs." He gave Linus a respectful nod. "Of course, you'll be well rewarded for this."

Linus beamed. "I already ordered everything. I figured you'd see the sense of it." He looked down, and his face fell. Someone had purposely propped a line of coal blocks carved into bullet shapes.

Coop plucked one to examine. The details took a moment to resolve as veins and a head emerging from foreskin. He snickered. The miners treated him respectfully as Mr. Tiller, without any idea of his humble upbringing, and Coop was tickled by this evidence of bawdy spirits.

Linus looked uncomfortable. "Those have been appearing lately."

"Don't let this push your nose out of joint, Linus. Save your fire for important matters."

"Don't you see?" Linus dropped his voice. "It's a black penis. It's meant to mock me."

"Coal is the only material on hand."

"There's no mistaking the disrespect, Coop."

Coop looked about. "Come into my office." He tossed the coal penis into the conveyer.

In a few steps, they were inside a large but rustic room with simple furniture and tall windows. Coop sat at his desk. "I don't mean to sound high and mighty, but I've explained why you can't call me Coop. Miners see only contrast. Good and bad. Respectable and coarse. Night and day."

"Black and white," Linus said.

"I've told you I'm opening offices in either Columbus or Cleveland. You can work behind a desk, wearing a suit, with educated people about. That's the best I can do."

"I need to fire that Welsh woolyback Terrence Griff. He's conniving, lazy, and disrespectful."

Griff was one of the men who'd resented Coop's order to treat the mules well. "As a shift manager, you have the power to run your crews as you see fit, but you need to record violations, or we'll have a revolt. The miners in Pennsylvania called themselves the Molly Maguires and killed both managers and owners."

Linus looked exasperated. "How do I record his violations? Do I follow him all day, watch his every move?"

"If need be."

Linus went quiet until he said softly, "Emma wants you to know she's expecting."

Coop sat up happily. "Well, that's a fine thing to hear! Now that your Paw is gone, it's the perfect time. How is she adjusting to the name Battlehurst?"

He smiled, his brotherly pride radiating through his foul mood. "Well enough. I'll give her your best regards, Mr. Tiller. Her husband Henry is still looking for work, but he'll find something."

Confused, Coop said, "I told Henry we'd hire him here."

"Going to work down in the dark with men like Terrence Griff isn't a tempting offer to Black men. Which is why it's so difficult to document violations."

Growing frustrated, Coop said, "You and I had to learn how to lead men at almost the same time. You must find solutions to problems, like you did with that conveyor. If the leader doesn't find an answer, nobody will."

"I have. I realized the other men had their necks on the line and don't want a dangerous miner on their crews. Nor would their wives. I have ten confirmed violations."

"There you are. The contract says you need only ten."

"A Black manager needs twice as many to be safe. The union will find a misdated page or the wrong tunnel listed, and it goes right in the trash pail. If that happens with just one of those ten, Griff will be the cat that ate the canary, and I'll never get rid of him."

Coop couldn't argue. "What if…"

Linus raised a palm. "I don't need you to cut the food on my plate, or to file my complaint. I found ten violations in six months, and the next ten won't go any faster. I'll have to put up with his attitude for another good long stretch, but I've put up with worse. I'm going to shove off a bit early, if you don't mind. My apologies for addressing you improperly, Mr. Tiller."

Alone, Coop leaned back. He could move Griff to another crew, but that wasn't permanent enough. The fluid movement between shift crews meant you couldn't predict who'd be needed where, or when.

Coop considered putting Griff on swing shift or graveyard, where the managers would relish taking the piss out of an overbearing prick nobody liked, but Griff would never go meekly to the hated graveyard shift. He'd raise a right rowdydow of a dustup with the union, and they might well take his side in a racial dispute. Coop decided to set things right by being extra generous with Linus's financial reward.

Coop flashed on Linus running downhill after spotting him and Will as they embraced and kissed, naked as skinned rabbits. It seemed like a million years ago, but it was just before the landslide that revealed the coal. As far as Coop knew, Linus never said a word to anyone.

On the spot, he decided to pad Linus's financial reward with a five percent note of ownership. Surely Linus would understand how such an immense amount was Coop's gratitude for much more than the conveyer.

The four o'clock bells clanged, announcing the end of day shift. He bolted to catch the first cart back to Cadiz. Outside, a crowd of men covered in coal dust walked from the main portal, wearing boots and not much else. They looked like shadows that sprang up from the ground, grumbling, laughing, or sharing plans for high-spirited adventures.

They trudged downhill to the washing trenches, at the edge of the meadow that used to lead to the long-gone cabin where Thomas had raised Linus and Emma. A shower house for the men was rising in the same spot, built from the lumber of the felled woods. Coop earned bonus points when the boiler room started going up, and the men realized they'd have hot showers.

Nightwater Lake was shrinking into a slurry bog, and the fish must have died out long ago. All around, many of the trees were cleared, and nothing remained of that idyllic life, save for the cabin where Coop and Will had never been happier. Today, it provided sleeping quarters for men working short turnarounds, filled with bunk and trundle beds.

"Mr. Tiller, sir, a word with you."

The choppy Welsh accent made every sentence sound like a question. Terrance Griff, whom Linus wanted to fire, reminded Coop of Harold, who'd traded away the riches of the Lightning for miserly farmland. Griff even looked gnarled and twisted like Harold. The whites of his eyes floated in his coal-dust face.

Several other men stood back, shuffling nervously.

Griff said, "We've been talking about how it ain't right to put the Black man over the white. It's one thing to work with 'em. It's another to see them ordering proud white men about."

Coop gave a flinty stare. "Linus is the best mine manager in the state."

Griff spluttered. "'Twould be proper for him to run a crew of his own kind. That's what we was wanting you to consider."

"You're free to work elsewhere."

Griff creaked out a smile. "We got our union."

"I pay ten cents more per ton than the union contract requires, and I provide three days of vacation a year above it as well. I never pay in company scrip, and I have no company store." Coop's contempt rose with Griff's panic. "Perhaps I can cut the pay and time off for your fellow shift workers?" He raised his voice to the others. "What say you? How many agree you're free to question how I run my mine?"

Sweat streaked the coal dust like zebra stripes on the naked men. A chorus of support for Coop arose. Three men rushed to pull Griff away, one saying, "No man here disrespects you, Mr. Tiller."

"You'd best not!" Coop roared. Wielding authority had come more easily than he'd expected. "And if I hear of one more coal penis, there will be hell to pay."

He stalked off as the men shoved Griff downhill.

The early summer afternoon was clear and warm. Coop trotted down a wooden staircase to the road where horse carts delivered the men to Cadiz or more rural environs. Coop had seen the coal towns of Appalachia built next to the mines. It looked sensible to live so close, but families were forced to rent from the owners and pay higher prices at company stores with chits that held no value elsewhere. It was little more than enslavement, so Coop decided to provide transportation instead.

While the miners washed, the men who worked above ground in offices left for home first, and their cart was just about to depart. Coop jogged up, and the man on top with the driver stood to offer him the best spot. Coop waved him off and hopped into the back just as the cart started to move.

The men in suits shifted with delight to have the owner riding with them. Coop shared the good news about the conveyer and asked if they had anything to discuss. They assured him all was well.

Someone asked about his evening plans, and Coop said, "I have very special guests arriving soon and staying the night. I've ordered seven courses."

The regal size of the meal raised eyebrows. "Are you entertaining a young lady and her parents?" asked Ervin, a handsome accountant.

Suggestive chuckles rose. Coop shook his head. "Old friends from where I was born. A lady named Mrs. Porter and her son Clyde. They own the Porter Cattle Ranch."

Years before, Coop was pleased to learn Porter beef was famous. The men in the cart shared approving looks, and Coop knew they were wondering what it was like to grow up rich and socialize with other wealthy families. They had no idea.

"It's nice to visit with home friends," Ervin said.

"I haven't seen them since I moved to Harrison County. Mrs. Porter is heading south to live with her sister for a year or two, some fine place by the seashore. It fills my heart to think of seeing them again."

Such polite talk flowed until the cart stopped next to the looming courthouse. Coop wished the men a good evening as they hopped off and headed in different directions.

Cadiz had grown busier since Coop and Will had walked these streets for the first time, the money from their first pelts in their pockets. Eleven years later, Coop could buy almost everything he saw. Men tipped their hats to him, women nodded and smiled, and children went wide-eyed.

The dirt streets in the city center were paved now, and motorcars sometimes puttered along. He'd thought of buying one, but it made little sense given the pockmarked dirt roads everywhere else.

He turned left at the main intersection, and a toddler running at top speed promptly crashed into his leg and plonked on his rear end. With dark hair and eyes, his ears looked like they could lift him in a strong wind. The boy grinned at Coop as if they were playing a game.

"Oh, Mr. Tiller, please excuse him," said a woman who rushed up and wagged a finger in the boy's face while pulling him to his feet. "William Clark Gable, you must apologize to Mr. Tiller. He's a very important man."

The boy grinned impishly. "I'm very sorry, Mr. Tiller."

"Do you promise not to run in crowds?"

"I promise, sir."

"Then all is forgiven, Mr. Gable." With a smile for the woman, he went on his way.

After a long block, the busy commercial street became a pleasant, tree-shaded residential lane with sweeping lawns. Judges, bank presidents, hoteliers, and other wealthy men lived with their families in mansions with elaborate gingerbread or expensive brickwork, even full-sized Greek pillars.

He hurried past the mansion with the glass terrarium where the mayor lived, who was eager to have Coop or Will marry one of his daughters. He often raced outside when seeing either man pass, but Coop made it to the other side safely.

Coop and Will had bought their three-story home two years before. They learned the architectural style was called Georgian, and it was built from pale river stones with a peaked roof punctuated with dormers. The clean lines and perfect symmetry struck them as the ideal stately home for two men masquerading as eligible bachelors.

Inside, whitewashed hallways opened to rooms agleam with finely grained dark woods. The scent of seasoned chicken filled the house, along with other delicious flavors and spices. He checked the dining room and was pleased to see the table looking so impressive, with good china, silver flatware, flowers, and candles. According to Clyde, Mrs. Porter could no longer climb stairs, so Coop had ordered a drawing room just across the hall be made up as her bedroom. He checked, and a tidy bed was waiting. He noted a little silver bell on the table alongside.

In the massive kitchen, young girls hurried about, overseen by the sharp eyes of Kendra, an older woman who never missed a detail.

Coop and Will had asked Emma to cook for them when they first moved in, but she was busy with her ailing father those days, and she suggested her friend, Kendra, instead. Kendra gradually took on other chores until she ran the household, arriving every morning around eight o'clock. She brought in cleaners when needed, dealt with the laundry and gardeners, and everything else a big house demanded, even if little used.

Kendra was inspecting the preparations when she saw him and clapped, bringing the kitchen to a halt. "Good afternoon, Mr. Tiller," she said loudly, which the others repeated with less gusto.

"I trust you have everything well under control?" Coop said, casting a smile across the room.

"Perfectly under control, Mr. Tiller. Have you seen the table?"

"Indeed I have. You've made it as extravagant as any table could be."

She smiled proudly. "And your dinner will be just as fine."

"And have you," he felt himself blush and dropped his voice, "settled those other things?"

When Coop had told Kendra one of their guests was an elderly lady who couldn't climb stairs, she'd said, "I don't wish to be indelicate, but that lady will need help with other things."

Coop had been mystified. "What things?"

"The water closet," she'd whispered. "I'll have two girls ready to assist her at any time. They'll also sleep just outside her door, and I'll put out a bell. And I'd best get the handyman to build a ramp for the front stairs."

Thunderstruck by how much he didn't know, he'd told Kendra to spend whatever was needed to make the visit pleasant for all.

In the kitchen shortly before the Porters were expected, Kendra nodded knowingly. "All is ready."

Grateful for Kendra's foresight, he bounded upstairs. A long hallway ran the length of the house, with his bedroom at one end, Will's at the other, and a private office adjacent to each.

He heard Will in his office and headed down the hall. The previous week, when Clyde had confirmed the day of the visit, Coop shot off a telegram to Will, begging him to return from Denver immediately. He wanted Will to meet the Porters, and he longed for Will to love them as much as he did. Will had returned the day before without grumbling, which was cause enough for gratitude.

He remembered their first months in this house before they'd hired Kendra, the exhilaration of sliding across the floors wearingly only stockings, and the erotic animal thrill of having sex wherever they liked. They never worried about which bed was unmade in the morning and gave no mind to furnishing the house properly.

When the novelty began to fade, Coop took to wandering the house, trying to recall why they'd moved here. Becoming rich and buying a mansion had seemed to flow like a leaf riding a stream, but he couldn't remember why.

Will had never taken to working at the mine. He'd done as much as any partner could that first year when it was only the two of them, but he announced new plans as soon as they began hiring.

"You want us to be known for our attention to customers," Will pointed out at the time. "Someone must travel to speak to them, as well as arrange meetings with new clients."

Coop had agreed without realizing Will's trips would sometimes stretch for months. The briefer journeys came with such frequency Will spent only a few days at home in between.

Coop reminded himself to be grateful Will had rushed back in time to meet the Porters. Outside of Will's office, he felt the warm breeze from the open window on his face. He took a deep breath and stepped inside.

Will was at his desk writing. He gave an unsmiling nod. "How are things at the mine?"

"Linus fixed that contraption of his. We'll see a huge increase in yield."

"How much?" As a businessman now, Will kept his hair close-cropped. Coop missed the way it fanned across his pillow, not that he saw much of Will's pillow lately.

"We can transport four or five times the current yield to the surface, but don't count our chickens yet. The issue of capacity is still outstanding. I'll have a better idea when I can concentrate on it. Right now, I'm just looking forward to seeing the Porters again."

"What time do they arrive?"

"They'll be on the five o'clock train from Columbus. I'm glad the weather won't delay their arrival."

"And remind me of the plans again."

Coop sat in a chair against the wall, next to a small table where Kendra collected and dropped mail. "They've hired their own car with security, so they'll leave their luggage aboard and bring only overnight bags. Kendra will have drinks and appetizers ready in the front parlor at six o'clock, dinner at eight. In the morning, we'll have breakfast, and they'll be off by ten for the train to Philadelphia."

"I see."

"We'll have a full house tonight. Kendra wants the girls to clear and wash up dinner, and prepare for breakfast early, so they'll be using the servant rooms overhead."

Will nodded and started writing again.

"Linus says Emma is expecting."

Will looked happy for the first time since arriving home the day before. "That's wonderful news, except that it will mean a new young Battlehurst in this world." He shook his head. "I suppose you don't choose or reject a husband for his name, but Battlehurst must inspire extra caution."

Coop wondered when had their conversations shrank to utilitarian exchanges. When had they last talked of their feelings, or celebrated, or planned the future?

A large, sloppy pile of sealed envelopes sat in the dish. Coop scooped them up to arrange with the addresses right side up and facing out. He glanced at the names and lofty titles of men who worked at steel mills and factories. As he shuffled, he saw the word "personal" on a letter addressed to someone named Seamus Healey in Pittsburgh. He stared at the envelope before looking at Will, who didn't yet know Coop had seen it.

Coop feared creating a sour mood just before the Porters arrived, but he couldn't restrain himself. "Seamus Healey," he said.

Will looked up sharply. He saw the letter in Coop's hand, and he went defiant. "He's a friend of George and Phil's. I met him at a dinner party at their house."

❖

Two years before, Will returned after a month-long trip along the East Coast. He crackled with excitement, telling Coop about a male couple he'd met in Pittsburgh.

"They're named George and Phil, and they're the center of social life for the homosexual men in the region," Will enthused. "They are anxious to meet you, and I'm anxious for you to meet them. We will all be mighty friends!"

Coop felt a surge of excitement at such unbelievable possibilities, which he easily suppressed with a corresponding jealous chill. He saw hope in Will's eyes and felt a vicious need to crush it. "I would like to meet them someday," Coop said so blandly Will's face fell. Coop wished he could retract his words.

Will started leaving enough room in his schedule for an overnight stay with his new friends whenever he traveled east.

George and Phil invited them to spend a summertime holiday at their cabin on South Saranac Lake, a remote spot at the edge of the High Peaks Wilderness in New York's Adirondack range.

Coop was excited by the invitation, but hesitant because he'd never met them. Will insisted all was fine. "They surround themselves with men like us, and they are all unmet friends. We are building connections and communities now that the railways permit easy travel."

"Why do we need communities?" Even as he spoke, many reasons came to him.

"Coop, there are no other cabins nearby. We can be ourselves, without fear of what anyone says or sees. They will invite others as well, and there'll be swimming and barbecues and parties. We can stay as long as we like."

Coop had never dared to imagine any kind of summer holiday, let alone one where they would laze away the days with other men who understood their feelings and shared their secrets.

By the time they left for the lake, Coop was just as giddy as Will but felt a need to disguise it.

After two days on slow trains, they rented horses and set out on a surprisingly well-maintained road with mountain vistas in the distance. They passed several carts filled with huddled patients, coughing softly, desperate to reach the village of Saranac Lake where the famous writer Robert Louis Stevenson had been cured of tuberculosis.

The sun was setting when Coop and Will reached the lower basin of the lake. They guided the horses down a gentle bluff to a promontory where Coop was surprised to see a large house. He would never have described it as a cabin.

It was a month of magic, with guests coming and going, but no less than four male couples at a time. Mornings began with hearty mountain breezes that washed the lake with sparkling sunlight ripples. In the swelter of still summer afternoons, the men lounged naked at the water's edge, glazed with sweat, woozy from the endless Gin Rickeys, Grasshoppers, and Jack Roses that appeared at lunch.

At night, especially when a thunderstorm blew past, the men passed pipes around and wandered in a haze from room to room. Even among grunting men running their hands everywhere, Coop knew he would never surrender to such abandon if he hadn't inhaled the sometimes pungent, sometimes scentless smoke. He found he didn't care, even when waking in the morning to a room filled with snoring naked men, everyone tangled every which way.

Coop soon realized the experience was much more important than he could have imagined. Being close with Will, holding his hand and kissing without fear, refueled a love gone stale in routine.

George and Phil knew all the places in Pittsburgh and Philadelphia where men went to meet other men, which restaurants to patronize, which bars to have drinks. Other friends came and shared insights into their own cities, including a good-looking man named Jerry from Cleveland.

Coop was excited to talk to Jerry. "Our first client was the Cleveland Forge Steel Company. I arranged for it, which is why I go to Cleveland when necessary, while Will oversees the rest of the country."

"Where do you stay when you come to town?" Jerry said. He was muscular, with the rare and attractive combination of pale skin and dark hair. Coop hit it off with him from the start.

"I'm a member of the Admiral Perry Club downtown, so a room is always waiting."

Jerry looked impressed. "How posh. There's a walking-about area for men downtown, but from what I've heard of the Perry, you don't need to go anywhere."

Confused, Coop asked what he meant. He listened with his mouth open.

Everyone collected names and addresses and promised to meet again next summer. On a train heading back home, Coop said, "I'm glad we did that."

Will had grinned. "Why don't we sell everything and get a cabin of our own? We can live there year-round. We don't need more money, and Cadiz has never really felt like home to either of us."

"Let's hold on to the mine for a few more years and see what happens."

"Why?"

"I don't know."

Will huffed. "It's because sharing a home with your business partner isn't usual, but it's not suspicious. What I'm suggesting is sharing a life, and you're afraid to do that without the business to hide behind."

Will was right, but Coop wouldn't budge.

The following year, Coop was bitterly disappointed when George canceled the holiday. His mother was dying and needed tending. The group shared letters and promises about next year's adventures.

Will saw George and Phil regularly and had become accustomed to sleeping in their guest room. The men often threw dinner parties for him, which Coop longed to attend. Pittsburgh was only a few hours by rail, and he could return to Cadiz the next morning, but Will never invited him and, hurt by Will's thoughtlessness, Coop never suggested it.

❖

"Is Seamus Healey a single man?" Coop said. He returned the envelopes to the plate.

"Why does that concern you?"

"You can't think of a reason?"

Will lifted his chin. "Seamus is single, and he's my friend. I meet many people and make many friends on my travels."

A distant train hooted.

Will glanced at a clock on his desk. "That must be the train bringing the Porters. We should confirm all is ready."

Later in the front parlor, Mrs. Porter wore a deep purple, modern dress that showed her ankles. It hung from her shoulders over a filmy blouse with purple flowers. Coop had seen young women in such outfits, but older ladies mostly wore the frilly, full-length skirts and huge hats of the last century.

"It's a mite too glamorous for me," she said, "but it was so pretty I had to try it."

Clyde laughed, a deep rumble. "She's been fussing about this outfit for weeks. She wanted something fancy in case she gets invited to society events with her sister. I told her to wear it tonight and see what folks said."

Will said, "It's a perfect choice that announces your individuality."

She raised her eyebrows playfully. "You speak very fancy for a boy who was raised a trapper."

"I speak to educated men all the time, so I hired a tutor for vocabulary and grammar. He accompanied me for a year on my travels."

Will had told Coop he studied on the train, but he'd never mentioned a tutor. He couldn't bring it up now.

Mrs. Porter looked a bit older, but if not for her wheelchair Coop would have said she'd hardly aged at all.

Clyde still stole his breath. He was even more handsome. Streaks of gray in the brown hair on his head and in his beard gave him a sexually charged maturity, a man who knew what to do. Maybe he was heavier, but it didn't matter. Coop recalled seeing him naked by the swimming hole, hair swirling over his body. He tried to imagine how it looked with silver streaks. His heart pounded, and he banished the image before his crotch came to life.

"All and sundry will attest to this," Mrs. Porter was telling Will. She was more animated than he'd ever seen. "When I heard Coop had left, I said when a perspicacious boy like Coop sets out to find his fortune, fortune sets out to find him halfway. And how right I was!"

"Everyone said Coop had the most nimble-witted mind around," Clyde added.

"Considerate, too," said Mrs. Porter. "He wrote regularly, just like he promised. He told us how you taught him to trap, the coal, the mine, all of it." She looked about. "But not once did Coop let on that he was so much in the chips."

"You were lucky to meet such a business partner when you were both young," Clyde said.

Will started to speak, but Coop went first. "We were both lucky. If not for Will, I'd have starved on Lightning Mountain. Because of him, we had money right away."

"Men need to be around other men for a good start in life," Mrs. Porter announced with authority. "It helps them grow a head for business and learn the value of hard work, and competition. But now it's time for both of you to get busy courting some of the local girls."

"Mama," Clyde groaned. "After all the years of pushing your own boys to the altar, you gotta start branching out?"

"Button up your shirt. What's all this for, if not to add a wife and children? Especially with well-favored bucks." She winked and smiled. "But you'll have to stop sharing expenses with one house. Wouldn't that be awkward for one of you to marry and bring your wife home while the other still lives here!"

Will laughed. "Awkward indeed."

She went on, deeply serious. "Don't wait too much longer, or you'll end up like Clyde. He preferred the fizzy-headed girls who don't have the smarts to snag a man properly, and now there's nothing left for him." She gave her son a tender look. "And what good is a confirmed bachelor to anybody but his mother?"

Kendra knocked, entering with a formal smile. She'd changed from her kitchen wear into a shimmering pale green dress with a high collar, long sleeves, and an embroidered lacy overskirt. "Dinner is ready whenever you like."

"Thank you, Kendra," Coop said. "We'll be there directly."

After she left, Mrs. Porter said, "First thing, a wife would work out that a maid who can afford that dress is being paid too much."

"She's not a maid," Will said. "She's the housekeeper. This place needs a constant watch."

"Hear that, Mama?" Clyde said in good humor as he grabbed the wheelchair handles. "The farm boy next door now has the deep pockets to keep a housekeeper better dressed than your daughters-in-law. And you think having a bachelor son is your worst problem."

She gave an affectionate laugh.

The dining room sparkled with candlelight, along with a dim gas fixture falling from the ceiling with frosted glass the color of roses. The two girls assigned to help Mrs. Porter waited next to her chair, wearing traditional maid outfits of black dresses with frilly white aprons and caps. Working together, they swiftly moved Mrs. Porter to a dining chair.

Mrs. Porter and Clyde had been happy and amazed to learn the two girls would be looking after her. "My sister sent a maid to meet us in Philadelphia tomorrow," Mrs. Porter said. "It was up to Clyde to help me until then. A ranching family isn't squeamish about practical matters, but it's a delight you're still so thoughtful, Coop."

The servant girls bustled in with the first course and bottles of wine, and dinner was under way.

Conversation never stopped, except when a new course arrived, and they took the first taste to see if it was as delicious as the last. Will didn't offer many comments but seemed to enjoy listening.

Coop waited in vain for the Porters to mention Harold and his family. He lost his patience and pretended it had just come to mind. "Say. You never told me what happened with the family that took over our farm."

Clyde and Mrs. Porter shared a fleeting look. She said, "Harold Plunkett was an evil man. Things happened over there I don't care to discuss."

Clyde said, "Not even a year after they arrived, Harold up and abandoned his family, and good riddance. His son, Oscar, tried to grow up fast and take up farming, but that old cart horse was nothing but a bag of bones. It pulled that plow for ten feet and keeled over. I saw Oscar out there with a hoe, a little kid trying to cut furrows all the way across that field. Just about broke my heart."

"His mother was no help at all," Mrs. Porter added, hard with disgust. "Scared of her own shadow and hardly spoke a word. No matter what, if a mother has children to feed, she'd best find her footing."

Will said, "How old was Oscar?"

"My age," Coop said. "Fourteen or fifteen."

Clyde shook his head. "No, Oscar was a big fella, but he was only twelve when they arrived. After the horse died, he asked if he could work for us to support his family, but we had to say no."

Coop was stunned by the lack of charity.

Will said, "Why wouldn't you help a desperate boy looking after his family?"

"They hadn't been there three days when we caught Oscar trying to take a heifer in the middle of the night."

Coop's stomach curdled. "Clyde, his father must have forced him."

"I know, but it doesn't matter. We learned a bitter lesson several times at the ranch. Hire a criminal, he'll commit crimes."

Mrs. Porter said, "It sounds harsh, but the blood of Christ redeems the lost soul, not Porter Cattle. But you couldn't help but pity the lad."

Coop's guilt was so overpowering, he couldn't contain it. "It was my fault." He told them how he'd lied to Harold about the ease of stealing cattle from the Porter ranch.

Will said, "Why did you do that? Didn't you know he'd involve his son in his dirty business?"

Coop recalled how he'd disregarded those concerns. He felt sick at the judgment in Will's eyes. "I only wanted the herd dogs to take a bite out of him. I didn't imagine anything worse."

Lies, hissed a voice in his head. *You told Oscar about the empty well.*

Horror pulsed in his chest. The sinister scope of his words that day registered at last. He'd encouraged a boy of twelve years to murder his own father.

And suddenly, Coop thought of that poor old horse. It must have been the same sad creature that dragged Harold's family into the barnyard that fateful day. Coop pictured that horse trying to pull the plow and falling over dead. The implications came to him as terror gripped his soul.

"It's long over now," Mrs. Porter said, "The mother died, and Oscar dropped off his little family at our back door and left, just like his paw. What could we do but give them a meal and send them to the orphanage?"

The conversation slowed until the last course was whisked away.

Coop felt short of breath and feared everyone could hear his hammering heart.

Will excused himself by saying he had to finish some correspondence. Mrs. Porter wanted to get ready for bed, and the girls rolled her away.

The servants cleared the table of everything but the flowers and candles. Clyde asked for an ashtray, and Kendra brought it herself, along with two small glasses and a large bottle of port. She said good night and went upstairs.

Coop and Clyde were alone.

Clyde offered Coop a cigar, and they lighted them with candles. Coop's hands trembled. They puffed until the enormous scent of cigar smoke filled the room.

Clyde took a curious sip of port and tried to hide a disgusted contortion. "Coop, don't blame yourself for Oscar. His father put him on the path to failure, not you." Clyde couldn't meet his eyes. "You're too polite to admit you've heard the stories about my paw, but I know people talk. He was a beast from hell most of the time. He didn't teach us to steal because we had money, and that's the only reason we never strayed."

"I deserve the truth from you, Clyde. Your story doesn't line up, especially about that horse."

Clyde squinted with confusion. "Matter of fact, I saw it with my own eyes. I was bringing over a roast, like we used to do with you. That horse wobbled and tipped over. Why would I make that up?"

"You're telling me Harold left the horse behind for his family's sake? The only reason that horse was working in the field after Harold disappeared is because Harold never left. He's at the bottom of that well, right where I told Oscar to leave him, and you know it."

"Damn, Coop." Clyde retrieved a bottle of whisky and two shot glasses from a sideboard. "You want some?"

Coop nodded. Clyde poured, and they clinked glasses, which struck Coop as ridiculous in the moment.

"Good whisky. I got the truth out of Oscar in two questions. He shot Harold in the back of his head when they were hunting rabbits. When I heard where he put him, I was thankful to you, Coop. He'll never be found, and Oscar didn't deserve punishment for killing the man who terrorized his family. I nearly did the same to my paw."

They puffed in silence for a while and did another shot of whisky. Coop wondered about Clyde's moral beliefs, in which trying to steal a cow was unforgivable, but killing your no-good father was fine.

"That empty well came in handy for me once, to be honest," Clyde said.

Coop drew in a breath.

"It was a few years after all of that business. He was one of our men who rode with the herds, as good a man as we'd ever had, and I had my eye on him as an overseer. Lots of fellas liked him, but you heard talk."

"About what?"

"You're a man of the world now, Coop. You've heard of sodomites? Buggery?"

Coop managed a tight nod.

"His name was Albert, and I thought the world of him. I didn't listen to any of the talk until a fella named Denny said Albert grabbed him by the nuts while they were keeping overnight watch in the greenbelt. He said Albert made unnatural suggestions and wouldn't let up until he had no choice but to knock him back with a spike hammer."

Coop gasped. "A hammer…"

"Denny is a third-generation Porter ranch hand." Clyde sounded defensive. "He rode to the house before dawn. Me and my mama listened to his story, and I could only think of one solution. Denny and I took care of it before the sun rose."

Images raced in Coop's mind. "How many hammer blows does it take to kill a man?"

Clyde leaned on his hand, hiding his eyes. "Denny said he only swung once, but Albert was beat up pretty bad. I didn't like it, but Denny's family gave us fifty years of honest work, all told. On the other side was a deviant. Nothing else for us to do. Took that rotting smell months to go away. That's when I sent a crew to plug it with rocks and dirt. Only three people know Albert is down there. Me, Denny, and my mom."

"And now with Coop, it's four," Mrs. Porter said, wearing a nightdress as she rolled herself to the table. "A few years ago, Albert's twin sister turned up on our doorstep. She came all the way from Florida because she knew something was wrong when he stopped writing. Poor dear was frantic. She talked of nothing else but his kindness and generosity. I about bit my tongue in half to keep from spilling the truth." She motioned to Clyde, who got another glass. She poured a shot of whisky, and Coop remembered her kindness that night when he needed it the most.

She tipped the drink back. "My, that's some smooth whisky." She looked at Coop. "You look right queer, Coop."

He shrugged, not trusting his voice.

"In the end it was his own fault. I don't understand how such men can carry on. I could respect a pervert who ended things for himself, but let's stop talking about it, when it's troubling Coop."

Coop's breath went shallow. Bangs and thumps echoed inside, like ten out-of-tune marching bands. This conversation both frightened and angered him.

Coop thought back to the previous summer at Lower Saranac Lake, every man intelligent, thoughtful, and considerate.

Clyde said, "I'd hate for you to think poorly of us, Coop. But imagine how you'd feel finding out one of your most reliable miners was depraved. No matter how much you depended on him, he could never make up for it."

"You'd never forgive him," Mrs. Porter insisted. "You know we're right."

Coop eked out a thin smile. "I suppose."

Clyde and Mrs. Porter nodded.

Two days later, Coop and Will were standing just inside the front door when Coop revealed his conversation with the Porters. Kendra had already left for the day, and Will was on his way to the train station, his luggage and satchel at his feet.

Will's eyes burned with disbelief. "And that's your plan? To do and say nothing?"

Coop drew back. "Do and say what? To whom? They're my oldest friends."

"And what if it was me at the bottom of that well? Would you still call them friends?"

"It isn't you. We never met him, and according to Clyde's story, he was indiscreet."

"You're defending the murder of an innocent man?"

"My friends didn't kill him."

"They covered up for the murderer."

"Those are as different as they can be," Coop snapped. "And I didn't tell you about this to give you an excuse to find another fault in me."

"You told me because you wanted my approval for your plan to neglect justice." Will was icy as he picked up his things. "I'm not giving it to you."

Coop searched Will's face for a glint of an emotion he could trust. He saw nothing and opened the door. "Maybe I told you because I'm used to sharing all my deepest secrets with you. Looks like we're both done with that."

Will lifted his chin. "You realize what you've just said?"

Coop nodded and after a pause, Will left.

"Give my regards to Seamus," Coop called, and although he knew Will heard, he didn't react.

❖

A month later, in the muggy heat of August, Coop came home and found Kendra waiting for him in the hall. She looked agitated and said, "Something odd happened today. As is usual, you'd already left when I arrived at eight. Not half an hour passed before I heard a knock on the front door. It was a hackney with four and a crew."

Four horses? "Who would send such a large cart?"

"The man in charge had precise instructions for packing and shipping items from Will's room and office. It was much less than they expected, and they were gone by midday. He gave me this."

He recognized Will's handwriting on the envelope that read, "Coop."

Waves of heat and cold pulsed on his skin. His heart quickened and his throat tightened. He took the envelope and stared at the familiar hand. These would be the last words Will ever wrote to him. He felt an excruciating pain inside, tearing his heart in two.

"Is there anything I can do?" Kendra said. "I have nothing in particular waiting for me at home. I'll be glad to spend the night if you're in need of company."

Her eyes were watery. She'd known the truth all along.

He sniffled and shook his head. Tears spilled down his cheeks. In a broken voice he said, "I'd prefer to be alone."

She squeezed his arm, picked up her handbag, and left.

He slumped to a hall bench, ripping open the envelope. The top page contained a short note with a signature, the rest were legal documents. Evidently, Will didn't have much to say.

In his first two paragraphs, Will explained his intention to withdraw from the company. He also left instructions for how a new man could pick up his responsibilities in short order. Coop read the rest in the hope of finding an expression of love, or loss:

> *Against legal advice and the entreaties of many friends, I believe my years of toil are generously compensated by the substantial funds already in my accounts. You are the rightful owner of Lightning Mountain, Tiller Coal, and all the subsequent land purchases. In recognition of these facts, I relinquish all claims to real and intellectual properties, and acknowledge no outstanding debt between us. The following pages confirm these details.*
>
> *If you wish to send communication to me, our friends in Pittsburgh with the lakeside cabin will always know my whereabouts.*
>
> *I am grateful for our years of partnership and friendship. We can rightly take pride in our worthy deeds. You may rest assured of my regard and affection.*

"Yours very truly," Coop muttered.

He read it again and whispered his thoughts aloud, as if Will might hear. "Our friends with the cabin. How easily you wriggle free of raising questions by naming two men."

He went to the dining room, where he poured a splash of whisky and read the note many times, his outrage rising. Words like "partnership" and "friendship" infuriated him. Will had sneered at Coop's discomfort with letting sunlight shine on their relationship, only to insult their love and passion by referring to them as "regard" and "affection." The words were the common, cheap waxy cakes of romance. He snorted with disgust.

His rage fueled months of backbreaking work at the mine. The miners needed the extra income above their salaries only coal provided, so Coop gratefully took the hated lower-status tasks. He relished the mind-cleansing and exhausting days, clearing backfill rocks ranging in size from pebbles to boulders. He hauled lumber, carved new ventilation shafts, and hacked away errant pieces of rocky footwall, which was supposed to rest at the coal's base but rode vertical with the seam.

He demanded his shift managers and crew leaders treat him as any other man, although they never berated him, even when he knew he'd made a mistake. He arranged to never be in Linus's crew, and thereby never work with Griff and find himself in the middle of their disagreements.

Coop followed the miners' routine, stripping with the others in the dry house and trooping naked underground. At the end of a long shift in the swelter of underground tunnels reeking of sweat, the coal dust felt glued to his skin and hair. He was in the first group of men to use the new shower house, and he shared the appreciation for the luxury of standing in a cleansing spray of hot water.

Coop rarely felt lustful in the mine, where exhaustion overwhelmed desire, but it could roar in his head without warning and soon he'd feel the unmistakable reaction in his crotch. The thick smell of naked men would overwhelm him, forcing him to turn away or head into the dark for a moment to get control.

At first, the other men in his crew worked in silence, unsure how to behave alongside the rich owner, even if he was buck naked and busting rocks. The change started after about a week, when a miner broke his finger and the manager sent for a replacement mid-shift.

Unaware the owner was among them, the new man arrived. With a German accent, he introduced himself as Rolf and said, "I have a glad thing to say for all of you. It makes me happy to tell you beer farts do not smell."

Objections nearly drowned out the ripping sound Rolf sent echoing down the tunnel. When it was over, only Rolf laughed.

The rancid smell hit Coop. "Well, I guess that wasn't a beer fart."

The explosive laughter hit as a physical force. It washed over him, as cleansing as a hot shower. Hands slapped his shoulders and back as the masculine appreciation for earthy humor rolled like underground thunder. He grinned with happiness for being welcomed into this tight fraternity, among men whose trust was hard to earn, and whose good opinion he'd always craved.

Some of the crew asked him to join them for a Saturday night of drinking. They named a saloon in the alley by the cathouse, in the run-down part of town known as Mudlane.

In all his years in Harrison County, he'd never set foot in Mudlane. It was already dark as he turned off the main road, feeling all eyes on his back, as they were for any man who ventured toward the cathouse. The sensation made him giddy, and he stuck out his chest. Why should he hide what he desired?

You don't desire it. Your real desires would disgust your new friends.

From street view, the alley appeared to end at the cathouse, but a narrower alley angled off to the right, and another curved out of sight to the left.

It was an undiscovered world of shabby warrens surely teeming with vermin; leaning wooden buildings awash in mold; low brick structures with flat roofs and windows caked with grime; and tin and tarpaper shacks hammered together without strategy. His eyes stung with the heavy smell of urine and feces on top of a powerful base of wet, irreversible decay.

The muddy lanes were busy, and Coop soon realized the alleys led to the shantytown crammed into the field behind the main street frontage. The Blacks of shantytown lived crowded together, but Coop knew they would never permit this filth.

Four women sat smoking in glum heaps on the cathouse steps. They looked exhausted, with limp hair and faraway eyes. One girl absently scratched a puppy's head while its little gray face lolled in the crook of her arm.

One of the girls said, "If it isn't Cooper Tiller, the most eligible bachelor in town."

From a distance, the cathouse girls looked glamorous in their velvets and feathers and heels. Up close, he was surprised by their rags of stained silk, moth-eaten lace, and shredded ribbons.

He smiled. "Have we met?"

She rolled her eyes. "Everyone knows who you are, Mr. Tiller."

He felt a grip of alarm when the girl's pudgy nose and rounded cheeks revealed a young teenager.

"Are you looking for a little comfort?"

"I'm meeting friends." Across the alley, a group of men shout-talked and stumbled outside a lighted doorway. "Just there."

Surprised, she said, "You drink at the blood bucket?"

"No, I'm looking for the Spit and Sawdust. Is it near?"

"The blood bucket's sort of the unofficial name."

"I see." It felt impossible to leave the girl. "Are you from Ohio?"

"Toledo. I'm a good singer, and they need singers on Broadway. Only I didn't have enough for a ticket to New York City, so I decided to go as far as I could afford, get off, and earn enough to get me to the next town."

"That's a clever plan."

She gave a faint smile.

He was cracking through to her, he thought. "How many stops did it take to reach Cadiz?"

"It's the first. It's taking longer to save than I planned. Been here a year now."

He removed his wallet. "How much do you need to get to New York?"

She sat up straight, wide-eyed. "Three dollars."

He gave her a ten dollar bill. "That's a gift. I expect nothing in return."

She held the money with gingerly disbelief. Someone had left bruises on her arm. She folded the bill and removed a stained red satin shoe to slip the money inside. Coop noted bruises on her legs. She pretended to casually look around, checking if the others saw her hiding spot. They had. All of them.

To Coop's surprise, she hurried off without a glance. The other girls jerked to life and followed angrily, as if she owed them money. The puppy rushed to the edge of the stoop, trying to keep its girl in sight. It sought a place to jump on the crowded lane, bobbing about until it leaped and disappeared among many moving feet.

Coop headed for the saloon and recognized three of the men drinking outside as the youngest bucking broncos in his shift crew. Two of them gave him uninhibited, admiring grins. The third looked distressed.

"Looks like you're strolling for a strum, Mr. Tiller," said Tommy in a voice thick with leering approval. "We saw you pay for some time with that dolly at the cathouse."

Max nudged him with his shoulder. "We had you pegged as a randy goat. Her name's Sandra, and they say she's a healthy ride."

The third man gave a strangled cry.

Tommy and Max laughed. "Frank here thinks he's in love in with Sandra."

"I'm mad in love. Sick with love." Frank spoke with the desperate sincerity of drunks. "And she loves me back. Did you see how she gave me a smile just now?"

"You got rocks in your head," said Max.

"She did smile at me, didn't she, Mr. Tiller? For a full minute, at least."

Coop shrugged. "Even if she did, her mind was a million miles away."

Tommy and Max hooted derisively. "Her mind was just down the alleyway," said Max. "She can't stay away from that man."

Coop gripped Max's arm. "She's gone off to meet the man who hits her?"

"Ask Frank about those bruises."

Coop demanded Frank tell him who was battering Sandra. "She can't be a day past sixteen."

"She's fourteen," Frank said with a soft wail. "It's that chemist down the alley. He has opium and heroin, and that's all she cares for."

"They thin the blood," Max said with authority. "A whap with a feather turns you black and blue."

From inside the saloon, a lusty cheer roared to life. Coop leaned in, where two men with angry purple faces threw sloppy fists.

A desperate man rushed out with a hand clamped to his mouth, knocking Coop aside. He charged to a shallow ditch and puked.

From the shadows, adolescent boys erupted with outrage and tore down the alley leading to shantytown. Tommy explained, "Black folks aren't allowed here after dark, and those white boys don't dare set foot in shantytown. All night long, one side baits the other with a foot over the line. Usually nobody gets hurt."

"Sometimes the boys get their hands on a flamer," Max said. "They come around later, when it's quiet, looking for bums and buggery. Those boys make quick work of them. Just like we did when we were their age." Max and Tommy clinked mugs.

Coop said, "I just stopped to say hello. I'll be off home now."

"You're fibbing, Mr. Tiller," Frank cried. "You've already paid Sandra, and now you're going to collect."

"I gave her train fare to New York." Coop put a hand on Frank's shoulder. "Don't pine for an opium fiend. They lose sight of everything else."

Tommy laughed. "We keep telling him Sandra will be his forever if he puts heroin on his little man."

Frank raised his fists and tried to rush Tommy, but Coop easily held him back with one hand. "You boys should take him home."

Coop left as Frank collapsed into a maudlin pile.

This was not his life. It felt like visiting a foreign place where nobody speaks your language, and you make others angry and suspicious because you don't understand the customs.

His crew mates unknowingly made ominous threats against him. The Porters had unintentionally revealed their hatred for him. Boys waited in the shadows for a chance to club him to death, a crime that would bother few people.

What was left for him?

He couldn't fix the world, but he could improve his little spot, if only he knew how.

On the way out, his eyes landed on the shaking, gray-coated puppy, huddled in the miserable shelter of an empty drainpipe recess. Coop knew the girl had already forgotten about it, and the little dog was frantic to understand the chaos, scanning the crowd for clues. In a flash, it sensed Coop watching and locked eyes. Its trembles intensified.

He stooped, and the dog flattened its ears and hunched. With a sweet voice, he said, "You're coming home with me." He tapped his thigh. "Come, now."

The puppy crawled to him, still shaking. He lifted and cradled it like a baby. "You're a little girl." He scratched her cheek, and she wriggled and squeaked with hope. "My friends call a pretty girl a dolly. You're so pretty, it must be your name." In Dolly's expressive eyes, he watched her fall in love with him.

He declined other invitations to go drinking with the crew, but they remained chummy, and he worked in the mine as fall and winter rolled past overhead. There are no seasons underground, and the weather never changes. He started to appreciate the devotion many miners feel for life in the tropical heat of the tunnels, such a rare human existence it sometimes felt religious, not unlike those hazy nights at Lower Saranac Lake.

In early spring, on a day when warm, misty rain fell, Coop heard a ruckus as he stepped from the main portal at the end of the day shift.

Linus wore clean dungarees and a work shirt, and he looked like the boss of the world with his legs wide and his arms folded. In front of him, Terrence Griff sparked and crackled like a live electric wire as two friends held him by his arms.

Coop walked over. "What's all this?"

"Go wash your dirty naked ass, Hercules," shouted one of Griff's friends, directly into Coop's face.

Coop drew back at such open disrespect. He didn't recognize the man, who must be new to the mine. Coop understood how a new miner could make such a mistake, but he'd have to take him down a peg in front of everyone, and soon.

Griff shook free and charged at Coop, stopping just short. "You give the likes of him the right to fire a white man?"

Linus sauntered over. "I have a list of twenty safety violations, Mr. Tiller."

Griff screamed. "You ain't been in the tunnels for months!"

Linus addressed Coop. "I have witnesses. It's all verified."

Griff growled in a low voice, "You're the owner. You can overrule him. Think about what me and my boy might do."

"Your boy?"

Linus said, "His son works graveyard."

"Are you threatening sabotage?"

"Don't test us."

Coop raised his voice for all to hear. "Linus is not just a shift manager. He owns five percent of the mine." A ripple traveled through the crowd. Coop leaned into Griff's face. "And even if you didn't have one violation, I'd fire you for disrespect and fight the union with everything I have."

Griff lifted a finger. "Now you listen…"

Coop batted it from his face. "Get your clothes and go!" He looked at Griff's friends, and the one who'd snapped at him was properly terrified. Coop pointed. "I'm docking you two days' wages to teach you to respect your brother miners. But both of you are responsible for making sure he gets his clothes and leaves the premises without disruption. Do it!" They sprang to life.

Coop turned. Every miner from day shift was watching, around twenty-five men. They looked like melting candles as the light rain collected coal dust that dripped down their skin.

"I'm not firing his son, nor that man who yelled at me without knowing I'm the owner. I'm a fair boss who pays well and who doesn't think of himself as above you. Ask any man on my crew." Grouped together, his crewmates nodded. He dropped his voice. "Now go shower, men. It's time to refresh."

The crowd walked off as Linus approached. "That didn't go how I wanted."

"Looks like we both made an enemy for life, but it couldn't be helped."

Linus cleared his throat. "Five percent owner?"

Coop smiled. "It was going to be part of your compensation for the conveyor, but then you proposed to Gladys, and I thought it would make a better wedding present. So, that's my gift, two weeks early."

"Five percent." Linus swept a gaze slowly over the mine, an operation that grew by the week. "Five percent," he repeated.

Back home, Kendra had left the door open so Dolly could stay dry as she watched for him. When he came into view, she cleared the steps with a leap and came racing. Black and white spots had emerged on her pure gray fur as she grew, and she weighed nearly thirty pounds. They greeted each other for a minute until Kendra called from the door.

Dolly ran ahead, shook off the misty rain, and let Kendra towel her off.

"Today's the day I told you about," Kendra said. "We're having a little bridal celebration for Gladys tonight, just the neighborhood ladies, and I need to leave a bit early."

"Of course. Please give my regards to Gladys and tell her I'm looking forward to meeting her."

Kendra always left his dinner on a plate in the kitchen, and today it was meat hash and pearly onions. He shoveled it down, saving the last bits for Dolly, who knew to wait patiently.

He left the plate in the sink and walked through the dining room, reaching to turn off the gas when he saw his reflection in a glass-fronted china cabinet.

Hercules.

He smiled and shed his clothes, feeling foolish until he caught a full-length view of himself. He knew he'd grown muscular working in the mine but didn't know how much until that moment. His shoulders flowed to enormous biceps and thick forearms. From his chest down to his feet, he looked more powerful than a circus strongman he'd seen in Columbus as a boy. He felt an erotic charge at his own form and practiced smiling while naked.

Dolly watched intently, trying to work out this new ritual.

He burst out laughing and rubbed her head. Dressing, he went to the front parlor, the only room he used any longer. He closed the door behind him, which made it easier to forget the yawning emptiness beyond.

With Dolly at his feet, he flipped through the mail, most of which was still addressed to Will after almost a year. He separated the letters into piles he would drop off at the office on Monday, scribbling instructions when he could.

Dolly whined. Coop let her outside and waited in the open front door. Down the street, the mayor's house was ablaze with lights, music, and laughter. He vaguely remembered Kendra pointing out the invitation weeks ago, but he couldn't remember the occasion. Even after years of never appearing, he was rich enough to always be invited.

Life went on in multiple rooms in mansions up and down the street. Shapes and shadows moved behind the windows. He looked up at his house, brooding and dark, with one lonely room in use on the first floor.

Dolly returned and headed straight for the parlor, ignoring the rest of the vast and empty building because she knew they only used the one room. At night, he slept on the daybed while she curled on a heavy blanket on the floor.

It would depress him if he thought about it too long, but his labor at the mine put him to sleep early.

The noise exploded in his head and Coop awoke with a startled cry. Dolly yelped and growled. Coop dashed to the parlor door but stopped to steady himself and let his mind focus. It was the middle of the night. Someone was banging on his front door and screaming his name.

Dolly raced ahead, full of fury to protect the house. She barked with unrestrained menace, until she caught an unmistakable note of Kendra's voice.

Coop unlocked and threw open the door. Kendra had her keys in hand, but couldn't aim properly.

She rushed inside and Dolly jumped and hopped, confused to find her friend causing the fearsome commotion.

"Mr. Tiller! It's Linus!"

"What about Linus?"

"A group of white men broke down his door and dragged him from his bed! They had rope!"

Coop had gone to sleep in his work clothes and had only to pull on his boots. He told Kendra to stay put and raced down the street. Worried people who'd heard the screams were gathering on porches. He yelled, "Lynching!" as he passed the open-mouthed, well-dressed mayor and his wife, along with a few remaining guests. The word caused a spasm on the porch, but he didn't stop.

He reached the main intersection. The shantytown was to the left. All was quiet. There was no sign of Linus, and no clue where he might be. Coop tried to listen, but his ears were filled with his thumping heart and labored breaths.

Dolly was at his side, growling angrily, her eyes fixed just to right of the enormous courthouse on top of the small hill. She bolted straight for the spot, and in a flash had crested the summit. Coop followed until a hellish sight stopped him.

Downhill on the other side of the square, a crowd of anguished people gathered beneath a lift hoist sticking out several feet from a warehouse roof. It held a hooded body, hanging limp and unmoving. Dead. Linus was dead.

Men climbed the balcony supports and drainpipes to cut him down, as others tried to comfort women who shrieked and wailed and prayed. Coop spotted Emma, convulsed by sobs as she clung tightly to another woman who was most likely Linus's fiancée, moaning with indescribable pain.

Coop shook with rage.

Dolly stood back from the crowd, whipping about to check on

Coop. A sound or a movement got her attention and she urgently fixed on something to the right.

Coop looked. A small group of men were creeping along a row of dark wooden warehouses, trying to hide their faces. "It's Mr. Tiller!" someone said, and they broke into a run.

"Come," he yelled to Dolly, who charged as he raced after them. Men in the crowd joined the chase as soon as they heard and saw what was happening.

The killers had a big head start, fleet of foot and with a desperate motive to escape. They turned the corner, heading for a red brick church, and the slower men started to fall back. In last place was a gangly, uncoordinated oaf who was almost certainly Griff.

They were getting away.

Coop charged and gained on the last man. He was nearly upon him when the man turned and jumped aside. It was Griff. He wore a miner's belt and carried a small pick hammer. Griff swung his arm in a high arch, aiming the tapered end at Coop's head.

Coop saw Griff's terror, for he could never return to a time before murdering a manager and aiming a hammer at the mine owner's head. Coop blocked Griff's arm and twisted away, but his feet skidded. He fell on his hip and cried out.

Griff towered over him, a spark of hope in his eyes, reasoning he might still escape by killing Coop. With a delirious look, the wiry miner raised the pick hammer with both hands. Coop's feet slid uselessly on gravel, and he tried to kick away as Griff brought the pick hammer down.

Coop raised an arm to shield his face just as Dolly leaped and sank her teeth into Griff's neck. The pick hammer wheeled into the dark. Griff screamed and fell. Dolly attacked from all sides, clamping and shaking her head as she growled with rage. Griff shrieked and kicked and flailed, but Dolly had gone primitive, a ruthless hunter.

The others got away.

Coop pulled Dolly back, her mouth and teeth stained with gore. Griff howled, covered in torn flesh and blood. He started to rise just as the other men from the crowd arrived. They knocked him back to the ground, showering him with abuse and threats so relentlessly, he was sobbing and incoherent when the sheriff arrived.

Chapter Nine

New York City
Present day

The leading orange wedge of dawn rises, giving Darcy and Jake their spellbinding first looks at Manhattan from across the Hudson River in New Jersey. Scattered stars shine like brilliant pinpoints on dark blue velvet, above an expanse of silhouetted skyscrapers. The view spears Darcy with an exquisite pain of longing for something he can't grasp.

"Gosh," says Jake.

Darcy hides a smile. "How much longer?"

"GPS says twenty minutes."

Darcy and Jake would have arrived in New York hours ago, but they stopped in rural Pennsylvania early last night to grab a bite and down a few beers. They both got a little sloshed, and the battery on Darcy's phone died. Next to the diner, a cheap road hotel beckoned, a place to recharge themselves and the phone. They tore up the sheets on one of the queen-sized beds in a fun, buzzed tangle, but they fell asleep before getting far. They woke early, and they've been on the road for the past two and a half hours.

The dawn becomes bright morning sun, slashing Manhattan's skyscrapers with textured shadows and light.

In the sparse early-morning traffic, the Holland Tunnel delivers Darcy and Jake to a Manhattan neighborhood of stunted brick walk-ups. Scattered people hurry on the sidewalks.

Far off, spindly towers soar above the city. Darcy recognizes them as billionaire condos built on small Midtown plots of land, the only size that open in such a pricey and dense urban area.

The building his great-grandfather owned is just off Fifth Avenue. When they arrive, Darcy stares at the green structure, noting its orderly symmetry, segmented by plain pilasters. *Looks like it was fancier back in the day.*

They find a parking spot down the street, on a block with buildings from a black mirrored rectangle to cheerless midsize office towers and older art deco and Beaux-Art structures.

Darcy grabs the envelope with the legal papers Trevor gave him, and they walk to the green building. A deep entranceway between the closed offices leads to a glass door with wrought-iron grating. Beyond is a lobby with a staircase.

"Now what?" Jake says.

"I guess we'll have to wait until one of these businesses open."

"But you're one of the new owners."

"Not yet. My name isn't on any of the paperwork, so we'll have to make up a story." Darcy checks his phone. "Rockefeller Center is really close. We can get some coffee."

They walk over to the iconic square with the golden Prometheus statue. They lean on railings above a restaurant, which is just beginning to bustle. "He gave fire to men," Darcy says.

"Who?"

He points. "Prometheus. See the flame in his hand? The other gods were angry because fire allowed humans to expand their influence over the world."

"Just like Cooper Tiller."

Darcy laughs. "I guess so. But the other gods punished Prometheus by tying him to a rock where an eagle would eat his liver, which grew back overnight. Every day the eagle would return."

"What's the lesson? Don't make the gods angry?"

"Or don't play with fire."

"Too late," Jake says with a grin. "I've already burnt you." He grabs Darcy at the waist and pulls him close for a kiss.

Darcy pulls back. "Whoa. I can't be sexy before morning coffee." He wishes he could take back his nonsensical words, but Jake has already let him loose.

Why am I driving him away?

The rising sun teases an oily vapor from the streets. They get coffee from a nearby stand and sit at a table. Darcy slips the paperwork from the envelope.

Just above the page, the hand of Prometheus holds the life-giving flame, which Darcy remembers is a metaphor for civilization. The ancient Greeks worshiped this god for giving them business, trade, and a host of other things that kept their cities humming.

All around him is a city with buildings, the smell of the streets, of business.

He sits up. "Buildings require upkeep. They need someone to make sure the plumbing works, broken windows are replaced, things like that. They need a management company."

Understanding, Jake lifts his phone and asks Darcy for the address of the green building. After a moment, Jake says, "TSA Management and Rentals. They're right around the corner."

At a quarter past nine, Darcy and Jake sit side by side in front of a desk in a utilitarian office at TSA Management and Rentals. A young raven-haired woman, seemingly annoyed at having to deal with customers so early, taps her computer to life, looks at the address Darcy has written on a slip of paper, and says, "What are you looking for?"

"Anything," Darcy says. "Retail space, an apartment, or even storage space. We need a toehold in the area for a reason I don't want to get into."

She doesn't care about his reason and types. "There's a storage closet on the first floor. It's only seven by seven, but it's available." She taps some more and says, "I can have an agent show it to you next week."

"We can't wait that long. I can give you a credit card if you let us have the key for a few hours."

She unlocks a thin metal cabinet on the wall, jingling with rows of keys. She flips a ring with two keys from a hook and hands it to Darcy. "Return this directly to me, but I won't be back from lunch until one thirty. The storage locker is on the ground floor, just off the lobby."

He offers his credit card again, but she waves it off and checks her phone. "You guys don't look dangerous."

They walk back to the green building, and the larger key opens the outside door. In the lobby, yellow and green floor tiles form angular mosaics, while in front rises an impressive staircase with three bullnose bottom steps, wider than the rest. The metal balustrade sails up to the landing halfway to the first floor before bending back to climb the split stairs on either side.

It smells musty, blackened cracks spiderweb the tiles, and the paint on the staircase is chipped. Empty squares and archways on the walls look as if they'd once held paintings and sculptures.

Darcy jingles the keys and goes down a short hallway to the left, feeling an absurd responsibility to look at the storage locker. Jake follows, as if he understands. They pass a metal mailbox with four rows of locked slots hanging opposite the stairs.

The smaller key opens the door. Darcy flips on the light, revealing a plain small room with a pile of fancy but old-fashioned brass light fixtures on the floor. Curious, he bends down to investigate. "This building was pretty high-end at one point."

Jake closes the door, and the room goes silent and still. Darcy faces Jake, who wears an unmistakable grin. An erotic charge electrifies the air.

"We didn't get to finish last night," Jake says.

Eager to erase his stupid coffee remark, Darcy grins and they grab each other tight. They shed their clothes and grunt, freezing for nearby footsteps, laughing softly, until they finish with controlled, tight gasps. The room reeks of sex.

They pull on their clothes and sit on the floor, leaning against the wall. Jake says, "So we got inside. Now what?"

Darcy shrugs. "I don't know."

Jake sits up, cocks his head. "I have an idea." He leads Darcy back to the mailboxes, where he finds an overflowing bin of discarded junk mail. Jake kneels on the hard floor in jeans and a T-shirt, his broad shoulders sloping to his waist, the hair on the back of his head mussed. His idea to search the junk mail bin was inspired and clever. It encapsulates everything Darcy finds attractive in a man.

Jake has little concern for fashion and less for pretensions. He's guileless, unstudied, sincere, a hard worker. It's foolish to imbue someone you are only just beginning to know with every desirable quality, but the signs are unmistakable and good.

Quick on the heels of his optimism comes a sickening sense of foreboding, that Jake will soon realize Darcy doesn't know what he's doing and they're in New York for no reason. And Darcy's drug confession still looms.

"Aha!" Jake says, rising, holding a large cardboard store coupon. It's addressed to Charles Greene in apartment seventeen.

CHAPTER TEN

Cleveland, Ohio
1907–1920

July 1907

"And you knew not a single soul when you moved to Cleveland?" said a young British man named George as they walked the plain hallway to Coop's room on the top floor of the Admiral Perry gentlemen's club.

Coop thought of James, the handsome man he'd met at Lower Saranac Lake. "I knew someone. He seems to have moved. But I have my dog, Dolly."

Dolly was waiting at the door, wagging her tail. She was friendly to George, having become used to male visitors.

Coop's single bed was to the immediate left. There was just enough room for a small round table with two chairs, a standing wardrobe, and a tidy desk under a window. An open door revealed his tight water closet.

Coop said, "It's not big, but there's room enough for me and Dolly, isn't that right, my pretty girl?" Dolly panted, circling happily. "I left my mansion behind last year. All in all, I prefer plain living."

George was handsome in a conventional way, with limp blond hair and gray eyes. He sometimes said "rather" in place of "yes."

Coop pulled a bottle of whisky from his desk. "This Kentucky rye costs me dear, for I love smooth whisky." They sat at the table and Coop filled two shot glasses. They toasted each other and knocked it back.

George nodded in surprised agreement that the whisky was

smooth. "Scotch single malt is still superior, but that's a fine dram for America. If you have no friends in Cleveland, what of family?"

"My brother, Kenny, might still be alive, but my parents are gone. It's likely I have unmet cousins and such, but it can be said I have no family."

"No family," George repeated wistfully. "How jolly nice that rings. I'm the second son of a duke. It confers all the obligations of being smart and none of the money to support it."

Coop was confused, and George explained. "Upon my father's death, my older brother became the duke and inherited all the money and the land. And to add another indignity, he married my dear friend Charlotte, who is now his duchess."

Coop poured two more shots. "It doesn't seem fair for only one brother to inherit everything."

"It keeps the family money intact."

"Are you still friendly with Charlotte?"

"We will always care for one another, but the moment their betrothal was announced, I became tongue-tied with her. We would talk for hours before that. I shared the most intimate things, including that only men give me a proper Vlad."

"A what?"

"Vlad the Impaler? A stiffy? She already knew about men like us and was equal parts fascination and worry. Whenever I head off somewhere, her mind drops into cesspools, which I'm sure I exceed in filth. But lack of money keeps me from lingering far afield, and she doesn't rest until I return to the country."

"But you must have some money to afford a membership here at the Admiral Perry Club."

"The family duchy owns the membership. We have investments in American steel as well as the shipping lines on the Great Lakes, and these business trips fall to me. I don't mind. That new steward, Robert, is the most handsome young man I've seen in ages. And the look he gave me earlier was impossible to misread. He's available for a price."

"He gave me the same look," Coop said, remembering the way the shockingly handsome new steward had popped his eyebrows the first time their eyes met. "But you can see the deceit in his eyes."

"Isn't that part of the thrill?"

Coop crinkled his forehead.

"I see we don't agree on the delights of danger, but never mind. You've been mentioned to me several times as the richest member of the Perry Club. You have a coal mine, I'm told."

"Yes. Block bituminous, almost as lucrative as anthracite."

"Block bituminous means most of your coal needs no breaking?" Coop nodded and George helped himself to more whisky. "Once in London, I saw the sorriest slag ever seen. I studied her to remember the face of pure misery. In the end, it was for naught, for the following year I saw breaker boys at a coal mine in Wales."

Coop had seen the same in Pennsylvania, where boys as young as seven years sat on planks nailed over slanted chutes. The coal was dumped at the top and tumbled down the incline to the tipple. The boys snatched away rocks and other impurities as the coal poured into railway carts destined for furnaces, where little fingers, hands, and feet often burned unseen. If a boy lost his balance, the supervisor would order his body removed at the end of the shift.

Coop had tried to imagine such a death, but the horror was too immense. "I would not have breaker boys under any circumstances. At my mine, rotating men can do the job with a crushing machine, a water tank, and a sifter. Half a shift, once a month, that's all any miner must give."

"I've heard of your innovations. Everyone believes you have the most profitable mine in the region."

"So I'm told."

George splashed another shot into their glasses. He held Coop's eyes.

"Would you like me to turn off the lights?" Coop said.

"Rather."

March 1908

"Day's getting colder," Coop said to the front door attendant at the Perry, who gave him a blank smile, his eyes far away. Coop decided to let him be and entered, rubbing his arms to warm up. His eyes caught the striking steward Robert, blond and chiseled, but Robert looked away, knowing Coop wouldn't fall for his devious charms.

Dolly ran to the fireplace in the bar, where employees let her curl up on cold days until four o'clock. She stopped to take in the odd sight of a group at the bar so early in the day, employees and members clustered together. They look petrified and Coop walked up to listen.

"They ought to tear down every one of those masonry buildings," someone said. "Inside, everything's made of wood, but the outside is stone. One spark turns a building into a giant fireplace, all the fire and smoke sucking upward."

Coop sidled up to a young barman who usually worked in the evening. "What's all this, then?"

"An elementary school in Collinwood. First reports of a fire came two hours ago. They say it's as bad as can be. Boris in the kitchen has a little brother who attends, and Andor in the gymnasium has two wee sisters. Neighbors say they heard the fire bell go off, and the whole school was ablaze in no time."

By late afternoon, the outlines of the tragedy in the immigrant community eight miles east of downtown Cleveland came into focus. At nine thirty that morning, a student alerted the janitor to smoke coming from a storage closet under the basement stairs. He rang the fire gong, and students on all three floors lined up for an orderly exit. Teachers calmly opened their classroom doors and gasped when realizing it was not a drill, for flames and smoke had rapidly engulfed the front staircase, blocking one of only two rehearsed exits.

Panicked students rushed down the back stairs, trampling and falling. The stampede bottlenecked in a small vestibule on the ground floor, mere feet from safety, and screaming children piled up the stairs. Within minutes of the alarm, half the students were doomed, with no escape as the flames closed in.

In the following days, the horrific stories gave pause to people across the world: passers-by scrambling to catch children dropped from windows by desperate teachers; would-be rescuers watching helplessly as the flames reached the many students immovably wedged in the vestibule and on the stairs; several families losing all their children. The toll topped more than one hundred and seventy.

Their screams haunted Coop, and yet he nurtured an envy he could never share. Lately, he'd begun to dread the terror of impending death. For all the pain suffered by the Collinwood children, their ordeal was behind them. Many had been too young to know they would die and had spent only their final moments in the dark, ghoulish corridors where Coop increasingly found himself, without a man like Will to lead him to safety.

Days later, Coop joined thousands of people at the famed Lake View Cemetery, where President James Garfield's magnificent tomb commanded the highest spot. Thanks to an outpouring of donations and the beneficence of the cemetery, nineteen children who were burned beyond recognition were buried in a line of white coffins beneath a sprawling, elaborate floral arch.

One glance made clear the poverty of the grieving immigrant families. Not knowing which coffin contained their loved one, they prayed and held rituals at each. They looked ready to buckle, this unendurable grief only the latest for families staggering under the severe economic recession of the past year.

Like many others, Coop made an early but respectful exit. Having never seen anything connected to a president, he wandered over to Garfield's towering memorial building. Hundreds had the same idea and formed a line up the steps. He stood at the bottom and decided his glimpse of the huge statue inside was sufficient.

He walked down the green and gentle slope. A spot to his left looked perfectly situated for a small mausoleum, but who else would lie inside with him? Not Will, not his parents, not Kenny. There was nobody else.

In two years, he would be thirty years old, maybe half of his life already lived.

Strangers, including Coop, had donated to bury the unknown children in this famous cemetery. Who would care where he was buried?

February 1909

Coop and an architect named Richard Everett sat across from each other at a small table in the lounge of the Perry. Everett had appeared with an unkempt bundle of papers bound in a portfolio. On his heels, a waiter carried two gin and tonics, which Coop had never tried.

"You'll love it," Everett said.

Coop took a sip. It carried an unpleasant whiff of perfume.

As Everett settled in to talk, Coop regretted his decision to leave the bar and the library, where the men looked fussy and prim tonight. He'd only meant to be in the lounge long enough to see if an interesting stranger was about, but Everett pounced the moment Coop sat. Only in this room was it permissible to discuss business, and a single man sitting alone was a ripe target, Coop the ripest of them all.

Everett was handsome, and people spoke of his wife as a rare beauty. Sitting next to Coop, he began talking of department stores in London and New York where ladies visited several days a week, spending hours each time.

"Look, Tiller, I know you don't need the money, but you must have something to occupy your day other than the gymnasium. I should think the challenge would get your blood hot, putting all the small pieces together to create a retail brand that will change this city."

"There's Higbee's and Halle's already. And May Company."

"What kind of backwater has just three downtown department stores? Cleveland needs another, more posh, grander. We need Tiller's."

"And you the designer?"

"Who else? I have so many innovative ideas, like moving staircases. And have you heard of revolving doors? They go about in circles. Imagine three or four in a row, delivering ladies of fashion inside, to be seen and, more importantly, to shop." Everett seemed to force his next words. "Tiller, I'd be grateful for the opportunity to invest."

"No," he said without hesitation. "I want nobody looking over my shoulder, questioning my moves."

"I'm asking for ten percent. Nobody of sense can expect such a low investment to give him a voice over the direction of the company."

"I don't need investors."

"And yet, I need an investment." Everett grinned and handed over the folio, a jumble of articles cut from newspapers and magazines. "Read and let your mind fly. But be quick about it because opportunity is fleeting."

Coop read the articles, and, despite himself, he became fascinated by the idea of turning the store into the main product.

Coop kept Dolly tightly leashed as they walked the downtown sidewalks. She seemed to take comfort in being connected to him, and he enjoyed how she frequently looked back to check his whereabouts.

He studied the window displays of the other department stores.

Mannequins of unsmiling, bosomy women posed with lifeless expressions. He noted how the other stores played safe, with similar displays, products, and advertising. He'd been in business long enough to understand that from success grew caution. A bold newcomer might flourish.

As Everett had said, Coop's blood pumped hotter. More significantly, he found himself free of his gloomy thoughts for days at a time.

A department store offered a more useful way to occupy his mind, and he decided in favor of building one.

September 1909

Down the hall from Coop's room at the Perry lived another full-time resident named Edward, a jolly man as thin as a human can be. Once they discovered they shared the same sexual feelings, they became fast friends.

Edward also had a crush on Robert, and Coop said, "My friend George from England comes once a year. He's madly in love with Robert, too. To tell the truth, I don't like the look of that lad. He smiled at me once like he knew how to wrap me about his finger. I gave him a look that left no room for doubt where he stands with me."

Edward had come to Cleveland for a respite from what he called the "crushing crowds" in New York, Chicago, and other major cities. He lived on a trust that sustained him until he came into his inheritance of New England garment factories. One night he announced his intention to move on from Cleveland. Coop was devastated, although he was skilled at hiding his emotions.

They took sips from tumblers of whisky in Coop's room. Edward sprawled on the bed, his legs wide without modesty or invitation, while Coop sat in a chair. Coop wondered again about their lack of desire for one another, which unexpectedly intensified the rarity of their friendship.

"I came here for the calmness, but I miss my friends," Edward said.

Coop had nowhere to go, no friends to meet. He felt his shame scamper across his face. "Can you find another men's club like the Perry, that will look the other way at men who feel as we do?"

"The Perry is permissive, but male environments always attract men who enjoy other men, sexual or not, starting with ancient armies that learned to look the other way."

Coop nodded, his chest filling with cement, his eyes with tears.

Edward looked surprised and moved. "You could come with me."

Coop cleared his throat. "I'm going to build a department store here. I've already purchased the land. And I enjoy living here."

"The Perry is a fine place to live. Especially since the gymnasium has changed the rules after ten o'clock." Coop stared and Edward said, "Didn't you hear about the late-night exercise program?" He drained his tumbler and stood. "I'll be back close to ten and take you down."

At five minutes to ten, Edward knocked on his door, wearing the normal gym attire of a white robe, sandals, with a white unitard underneath. They rode the back elevator to the basement gymnasium. The white tiles of the exercise room came into view, along with a handful of men using the machines, hefting weights, walking about, all stark naked.

"A naked gymnasium?" Coop said.

Edward pulled off his robe. He was naked underneath and his penis emerged from his thin frame like a hose. "It's quite liberating, really. And there's no need to guard against the unexpected stiffy. Here is a world for men to be men, but don't do anything too obvious. Exchange room numbers if another gentleman is interested. The attendants can only look away from so many things."

Coop's heart pounded as he slipped off his unitard. No farm boy ever learned to be bashful, yet it was a funny feeling to walk naked to the exercise equipment. He quite enjoyed it.

October 1910

"And there's the foundation done," Everett said, sweeping his hand along. "I can see it on your face, Tiller. You're thinking it looks much too small. You can't judge a slab of cement. Let me tell you, construction is one illusion after the next. Mostly, you fool yourself into thinking you're near to completion when you've barely begun. Tiller's Department Store will be huge. And thank you again for allowing me to invest."

"It's a favor, you understand, for I need no investors."

Everett nodded. "I'm the envy of everyone I know. Even at ten percent, I think it the best decision of my life."

Coop watched the construction foreman walk his way, with massive arms and a full upper chest, his legs tight inside dungarees. He wore a trim beard and shaved his head. Coop imagined surrendering to his dark eyes. Lately, it seemed the man had taken note of his interest. They exchanged smiles and nods from afar, setting off surges in Coop's chest that left him rattled and shaky.

The man headed straight for him with an intense gaze, a slight part to his lips. He flicked a glance at Everett and walked on, passing closer to Coop than they'd ever been.

Knowing nods. Was that lust in the man's eyes? Did it show in his own?

Everett looked away. "Tiller, everyone wonders if you are rehearsing as a monk. The average young man of thirty years without a wife is ignored. But society gossip never stops about a man as well favored as you."

"There's a girl by the name of Emma in Cadiz."

Any name would have done, yet he'd started with Emma years ago, and stuck with it. He felt she would understand.

"Everyone has heard of Emma and yet no one has seen her."

"She is real. I love her."

Everett nodded. "Others say your love is sincere, and I agree. And yet they ask, where is she? Why are you both content to wait?"

"That is between us." Coop snapped. "I owe nobody an explanation, including you."

Everett gave him a look of admiration. "Don't mistake me for one of those people, for I only want to enlighten you. Families have sent men to Cadiz looking for Emma, did you know?"

Coop drew back. "She is not their concern."

"They want you to marry their daughters."

"I don't care what they want."

Everett threw his head back and laughed. "How I wish I had that spirit when I was your age. My God, how besotted I was with my wife. And even still, I would watch for the hookers and imagine what I could get up to. I never lost the hunger for the dark side, and it feels stronger than ever." He looked angry. "Everyone lies about marriage, especially religions. How dull sex becomes with the same person, even a ravishing beauty. Remain single for as long as you can, or as long as Emma allows."

May 1911

The handsome construction crew chief worked up the courage to approach Coop and introduce himself as Simon. Coop could barely breathe, overwhelmed by such a brazen approach from a man he lusted over.

Simon waved his hand across the construction site teeming with workers. "Let's make like I'm telling you something about the building, so look to where I'm pointing." Seeing the sense of his plan, Coop followed his instructions as Simon said, "I'm a single man, and I enjoy the company of other handsome men."

Simon's casual understanding of his looks and desires started a pounding in Coop's chest. "I live at the Perry, and nobody will suspect anything if you arrive with papers for us to examine in my room."

Coop felt giddy discussing such things in the bright day. They dared a blazing look any onlooker would recognize, and it brought to Coop's mind the time he kissed Will at the Lightning, in a spot visible for miles. He couldn't recall the last time he'd felt such happiness.

Over the next two years, Simon came to the Perry several times a week, but they never set routines. Sometimes they would have drinks in the bar while going over schematics, and Simon would leave within the hour without visiting Coop's room. Or they had lunch or dinner, followed by hours in the gymnasium. By never establishing a pattern, they avoided suspicion.

Coop loved the sight of Simon naked on his bed, his legs spread, and his arms hooked under his head. Little curly hairs covered him from top to bottom, concentrating into black splashes in his armpits and crotch. Achingly handsome, rough-spoken but intelligent, and rugged as a mountain man, he inspired awe and other major emotions in every man and woman who passed.

"Right, that's the bum's rush for me," Simon would say when it was time to leave. Simon's departures became agonizing when Coop recalled the buoyant freedom he and Will had taken for granted.

Hesitantly, Coop began sharing his life with Simon. He told him about repairing the cabin, building the new dock, checking the traps, catching the morning catfish. Jammed together on the single bed naked, Coop would rub Simon's chest hair, or run his hands along his hairy flanks.

"In the summer, sometimes we'd be naked as jaybirds all the livelong day, except if the neighbor girl came visiting. Nobody thought a thing of two boys living in a cabin."

"And what happened to Will?"

"We got rich, that's what happened. We thought we had to move into a mansion, the stupidest house you ever saw for two men like us."

"Why didn't you go back to cabin life?"

Coop remembered Will begging him to sell the mine and live on Lower Saranac Lake for their rest of their lives. "I wasn't thinking clearly." He closed his eyes, feeling his face burn.

Simon ran his hand over Coop's head, cupping it in back. "Now, if I saw clearly when I was a nipper, there's a sailor or two who'd have left North America in fear of my dad's rifle."

They shared a soft laugh, Simon kissed his forehead, and they held each other tight.

August 1911

Coop didn't recognize the woman at the front door of the Perry. "Can I help you?"

"I'm Vic Baylor," she said. "I'm here about the position for a writer of advertisements."

She wore a plain green dress, falling like a rectangle, holding her handbag in front with both hands. Her hair was tidy and neat under a simple hat. With a stoic face and little makeup, she reminded him a bit of his boyhood teacher Miss Everson.

Coop chuckled with amazement. "I was expecting a man named Victor."

"I'm Vic for Victoria."

"I invited you to lunch thinking you were a man. Women are not permitted inside the Perry."

"There are other places to eat lunch. And I do not need to eat just now."

He looked her over, so plain and dour. "I'm not sure you understand what I'm looking for in an advertising writer. I have some innovative plans."

"I mean no disrespect, but I understand it better than you do, Mr. Tiller. I am not a glamorous woman, nor romantic. What I am is rational, with a head for data. What's more, I am a very good writer of advertising copy. Very good indeed."

She had a slight, nervous tremble and out of pity Coop took her to lunch at a white cloth restaurant nearby, filled with executives.

"You did not bring a portfolio," Coop said. "I asked specifically for examples of your work."

"Yes, but I also knew you were expecting a man, and I wouldn't be allowed inside the Admiral Perry Club. It's not appropriate to spread papers on the table of such a fine restaurant as this, so I left it in my room at the boarding house."

"You put that all together before you came?"

"As I said, I'm rational. Now, perhaps you can explain what innovations you have in mind?"

She was the first to ask and he was eager to explain. "It's quite unique. I've seen the research and most stores overlook a huge customer base in men. We must bring men to Tiller's, and one part of my plan is full-page Sunday ads. Each week we show men how they can solve everyday problems by shopping at Tiller's." She listened without expression. "We see a man walking his dog and the leash snaps. He must run after the dog, and it happens again and again. Until he goes to Tiller's and buys a stronger leash. I have a dog myself and I believe such an ad would appeal to me as a man in need of a quality product."

"Does the leash often snap while walking your dog?"

"Well, it was only a possible example."

"I think a pets department is an excellent plan. And stories that solve problems are powerful. But if a man needs a leash, he'll ask a woman to buy one."

"What if he has no woman to ask?"

"There are exceptions in all things, but we must be mindful of widespread behavior. Men shop for things they need immediately. A tie. A belt. A last-minute gift for a sweetheart. When it comes to homewares, women do almost all the shopping. Most of the money spent in stores is spent by women. Women control retail."

The restaurant lighting revealed two old, faint stains on her dress, inside wide lighter patches where she'd scrubbed.

"I see your point," he said. "What can you offer in terms of innovations?"

"Seasonal characters, for a start. Imagine a Snow Queen for Christmas. Mrs. Easter Bunny. I can write backstories, and the characters can appear in the store during the holiday in question. Employees in costumes, of course."

He enjoyed watching her mind at work. "Can you think of a plan for full-page ads?"

She looked away, folding her fingers together, which still trembled. "We can have a weekly feature and call it 'Tiller's Tales.' We'll need talented artists to capture mood and atmosphere. And the stories will be about loss, misunderstandings, unrequited love, but always, always redeemed with a happy ending courtesy of Tiller's. Exotic settings should feature regularly, garden parties with royalty, ski lodges with lumberjacks, ocean liners with men of mystery and pencil mustaches."

"Always so pie-in-the-sky?"

"Of course not. We'll have stories of average homes and motherhood, with dutiful husbands and children who outshine the others."

A silver-domed cart of prime rib rattled past. Her eyes clamped to it, and she took deep breaths, swallowing several times. Her shakes increased, and Coop suddenly realized she wasn't nervous. She was famished.

"I can heartily recommend the prime rib here."

"I do enjoy it."

Coop reached back to stop the cart. "We'll both have the prime rib. Bring the potatoes and all the rest when you can, but serve the meat now."

Vic's eyes watered as the carver set a hunk of prime rib in front of her. She gripped her knife and fork. "Please don't wait until I'm served," Coop said.

A quick nod, glints on flatware, and she was chewing a piece with her eyes closed.

Coop looked down, pretending to be absorbed with cutting his slice while she ate several more pieces. He waited until she seemed less frantic.

"Why did you leave New York and come to Cleveland?"

She flushed. "I don't wish to lie to you. If you insist on an answer, I will be forced to lie."

Possible answers bounced around his mind. "And how many people are needed to run an advertising department for a store of my size?"

"Eight. Ten. But that's for much more than just the Sunday ads. Internal signage, catalogues, ads for special items, and more still. But you need to have the Sunday ad strategy in place first. You should start running ads months before the grand opening."

"How many people will that require?"

"Two writers, two artists."

"And a director to lead them?"

"Of course."

"How does one go about hiring two writers and two artists?"

She looked apprehensive. "I'd counted myself as one of the writers."

"I'm appointing you the director of the department."

Her lips parted slightly. "Mr. Tiller, it would be cruel to mock me."

"Miss Baylor, I am not a cruel man."

June 1912

Everett's architectural office showcased his sophisticated style in white walls, clear glass, and dark stone. His only nod to tradition was a wooden desk.

Coop sat in a barrel-shaped chair in front, which was surprisingly comfortable.

"Six months behind schedule," Coop said. "I must rent offices for my management staff, who are searching for ways to stay busy until we can move into the store."

"The problems with the moving stairs were not of my making," Everett said. "You could read in the papers for yourself how the merger of the manufacturers caused delay after delay. If you want Tiller's to have all the latest conveniences, you must be patient."

"Money is flowing through my fingers like water."

"It's my money, too, remember? Ten percent?"

"That doesn't give you the right to be cavalier about expenses. And it was not just the merger that held our plans in check. I've learned how poor electrical planning added to the delays, that much of the store had inadequate lighting and a new grid was needed, something you kept from me."

With a soft sneer, Everett said, "How did you learn about that, Tiller? Perhaps, oh, *Simon* says?"

Coop felt his face drain and his shoulder twitch.

Satisfied with Coop's reaction, Everett said, "In truth, I see nothing wrong with anything sexual, as long as it doesn't involve children and nobody is forced. Of course, boys get up to all sorts with other boys, but I tried it once as an adult, with a curious fraternity brother. It felt serious in the moment, but we laughed to wake the dead afterward."

"Why are you telling me this?"

He continued as if Coop hadn't spoken. "I paid a visit to Simon last night. He told me you've appointed him head of maintenance. I approve of your choice. He'll make a nice living indeed, and he'll need it for his new family."

Coop's throat went dry.

"My wife is as tenderhearted as she is beautiful. When she learned our housekeeper's daughter was in desperate need of a husband as soon as may be, she asked if I knew anyone on the construction crew. I thought of a way to solve multiple problems at once."

"What did he say?"

Everett raised his voice. "He jumped at the chance. I've done both of you a favor by resolving an untenable situation. A handsome bachelor may be considered a rake until the age of thirty-five, but no more. You are thirty-two and Simon a year older. Gossip about both of you was rampant, and it was eating Simon alive."

Coop couldn't speak. Everett looked sympathetic even as he said, "As an investor, it was a shock when you recklessly hired a woman to direct advertising and marketing. The laughter hasn't subsided in months. You must marry, Tiller, don't you see? It is not unknown for unscrupulous stewards at a place like the Perry to blackmail wealthy men. A scandal will destroy the store before it opens."

He found the courage to say, "I would rather have Simon than the store."

"I'm thankful that Simon has more sense than you, for I must protect my investment."

After a few beats, Coop said, "You are, what, ten years older than I am? And yet you're still making the same mistakes that have kept you unhappy all these years. You think only sexual desire matters, but intimacy is far more important."

Everett scoffed. "A rich man can buy whatever intimacy he needs."

"How stupid you are. People sell sex, not intimacy. It's impossible to buy or sell intimacy."

Everett looked unsettled as Coop left.

December 1912

Coop woke at four in the morning and took a confused but compliant Dolly for a chilly walk. He rushed through a shower before getting dressed and hurrying to the store, where he entered in back by five thirty. He was pleased to see the busy preparations in the backroom and storage areas.

He pushed through a swinging door and stopped to take in the magical view. The store was a Christmas wonderland of glittery cotton snow and boughs of holly, evergreen, and pinecones. The overnight transformation was remarkable, and when he spotted Simon, he stopped to congratulate him.

Simon gave a smile that gripped Coop's heart. "It was a big job, but we all know how important this holiday will be for Tiller's."

"Thank you again," Coop said with a smile. They'd never talked about anything but the store since Everett had forced them apart.

In the middle, just behind the column of moving stairs, a hallway leading to a functional storeroom had been transformed into Candy Cane Lane on the way to the Snow Queen's palace, where Vic was hanging ornaments on display towers along velvet rope lines, enticing baubles for waiting families. Among them were glass and paper depictions of the Snow Queen, which Vic had designed and ordered in June, even before she'd written the Snow Queen's tale. She predicted they would be the biggest sellers of the season.

Two weeks before, workers had hammered the queen's palace together. All who saw it agreed it was a disappointing flat pastel and looked as thrilling as alphabet blocks. Vic insisted on a complete re-do with brown paint and white foam that made it a gingerbread fantasy.

High up, the day's first Snow Queen promenaded on her royal balcony, with a crown of crystal droplets reflecting rainbows. She rehearsed turning gracefully in the awkward, enormous skirt and tested moving the wand for maximum sparkle.

Vic saw him and instantly set about listing improvements for next year.

He gripped her shoulders. "It's a triumph."

She blushed. "Let's hope the public shows up." She checked a watch hanging from her collar. "One hour to go. I know how important this is, Mr. Tiller. After all those delays, this season is vital. This day is vital."

"I think all will go well. You wrote an enticing story for the Snow Queen. The newspaper said they were getting requests for the whole story at once, instead of installments."

"I won't be calm until we see at least a few people waiting for us to open."

In the end, they unlocked the doors fifteen minutes early because so many families were waiting in the cold.

July 1914

Coop looked forward to George's annual visits from England. Even Dolly recognized him and wagged her tail.

The younger brother of the duke was face-down on Coop's bed, his buttocks on display. Coop slapped the exposed skin, slick with sweat. "Would this be one of those ducal coronets you can't stop talking about?"

George sat up, smiling. "You wouldn't want one. They look like someone got bored and stopped making a crown halfway through.

My brother hates wearing his, but his wife has a tiara of exceptional beauty."

"Is that your old friend Charlotte? Are you still close friends?"

"Thank God, yes. I told her all about you. She's most anxious to meet you, and I promised to make you visit England, but now I fear all will be delayed."

"Do you think it's going to get that bad?" Coop said, turning the electronic fan on his desk to the highest speed for some relief from the muggy July night.

"Europe is a mishmash of treaties and alliances that make no sense. Why must the United Kingdom take a side because the heir to the Austro-Hungarian empire was assassinated by a Serb? I can't predict the future any better than I can piss champagne, but if the United States wants influence in Europe, you'll be involved before long."

"I can't see how."

"Well, I'll be going off to war. My family must take a spot, and I'm the second son, so my role is clear."

"But your brother inherited everything when your father died, isn't that right? Then how are you obliged to save the family name? Isn't that his responsibility?"

"Coop, you would never survive in England."

October 1917

All the young men at the Perry were at war, replaced by men in middle-age. Coop became friendly with a gymnasium attendant named Paul who worked evenings, and who advanced the late-night nude rule by stripping himself.

Paul was attractive, but it didn't matter, for Coop and Paul formed the sort of non-sexual friendship he'd enjoyed with the rail-thin Edward.

Paul frequently spent evenings in Coop's room, where they lounged, chatted, and sipped whisky.

"Where did you work before you came to the Perry?" Coop said.

"I was a manager at the Tyrolean Room."

"That's quite a fancy restaurant. Why leave?"

"The war has put a pin in the restaurant business. The Perry pays more, and I work naked, with other naked men. Why complain?"

Coop laughed. "Who would?"

"There are men who object. Only a few, but they are very loud about it."

"Then don't come to the gymnasium at those hours. And what is the harm in seeing another man naked?"

"They don't object to male nudity. They object to male intimacy."

Coop flushed. He was not always as discreet as he knew he should be. "That sort of thing is not going on all the time."

Paul dropped his voice. "You should be more careful. Do you remember a steward named Robert?"

Coop nodded, recalling the handsome steward he'd always distrusted.

"Robert stopped in England on his way to the battlefield. There was some fuss with a duke's family. Talk of blackmail and such. Telegrams were flying across the ocean."

Coop inhaled sharply, drawing a searching look from Paul. Old thoughts he'd long forgotten sprang to life. "Paul, do you remember the Collinwood fire?"

"Who doesn't?"

"It's a strange thing, but I think those children were fortunate in a way. Their most terrifying moment is behind them, that last slip from the light."

"They died horrible deaths."

"I don't fear pain, nor oblivion." He cleared his throat, uncertain about continuing, but he plowed ahead. "But will I know what to do as I sink into death? Will I sense the moment, or simply vanish?"

"You won't have a choice."

"That is the very issue. It terrifies me to imagine fighting to hang on when I can't."

Paul scrunched his face and Coop went quiet. Maybe he could never explain it properly to anyone.

November 1918

Almost the entire staff of Tiller's stood outside, happily watching the celebrations a few blocks away on Public Square. They were burning to experience the joy of Armistice Day, with bands and parades, speeches, and impromptu sing-alongs.

Standing back from the others, Vic looked on happily with folded arms. Coop pushed through the nearest revolving door.

"Not to worry," she said. "We haven't had a customer in twenty minutes, and it'll be hours before we do."

Coop clapped and raised his voice. "Listen, everyone. This day will come only once, so Tiller's is closed until tomorrow, at full pay. Grab your belongings and enjoy yourselves."

With amazed looks, they rushed inside to grab coats, scarves, and handbags. They thanked him profusely as they hurried off.

Linda, an assistant manager on the second floor, came out buttoning a long coat. "I believe no one is behind me, except for the security guards. Thanks so much, Mr. Tiller and Miss Baylor."

Coop waited to speak until Linda was out of earshot. "Why is she thanking you? You'd make them stay late to serve the crowds downtown tonight."

Vic laughed and knocked him with an elbow. "It *is* a happy day, isn't it?"

"Ah, well," Coop said. He could put on a show for everyone but Vic, and his melancholy of recent days rose again in his throat. "To say what I truly think, it's that a war began and has come to an end, and I've done nothing in between."

"Yes, you've done nothing," she said, her voice rich with sarcasm. "You've only built your second successful business and are richer than most people can ever dream. As you say, nothing."

Coop struggled for words.

"I apologize," Vic said softly. "I understand your meaning. But Coop, you are nearly forty years old. If they'd needed you, you would have answered the call."

"Yes, but there's more still. Why did I build this store? What does it matter?"

She took his hands. "Saint John of the Cross had a name for when we are troubled with doubts. He called it a dark night of the soul, and everyone has them. I was having one when you hired me." She gazed up at the storefront. "You built this store, and it saved my life. I hope that's reason enough."

An unexpected sob escaped him, which would have mortified him in front of anyone else. "We share so little with each other, but I think of you as such a close friend."

Tears glinted in her eyes as she placed a hand on his cheek. "Only true soul mates understand one another so well without words."

He pulled her close, and she hugged back tightly.

October 1919

Coop stepped out of the elevator on the main level of the Perry, wearing a tuxedo. He expected a reaction but not the thunderous scale as members and employees cheered his formal look. At the front doors, he bowed and waved to the crowd on the staircase and landing.

The banqueting house was nearby. He'd only just entered when a woman rushed up, wearing a gown he recognized from Tiller's new collection.

She introduced herself as Mabel, wife of a councilman who everyone expected to be the next mayor. "I'm so pleased to see you at a social function, especially one with such a special guest of honor. The duchess asked for you specifically to be seated next to her."

"Her brother-in-law was a friend of mine. He died in the war."

"I see," she said in a singsong voice, greeting others as they passed. "Are you much entwined with the British aristocracy?"

He thought of holding George naked. "I suspect my days of entwining are over."

"I've told the duchess how the entire city has her to thank for dragging you from your men's club at last." The duchess was just ahead, in a gown of silk, satin, and lace that was too dear to offer even at Tiller's. Her diamond tiara glinted across the room. She looked younger than he expected.

The duchess offered emotionless conversation and a placid expression to people standing around the small sweetheart table for two, until Mabel pushed someone aside to introduce him.

The duchess looked thrilled, and the others drifted away.

"What do I call you?" Coop said.

"Call me Charlotte. George admired you so. He said his annual trips to America were only enjoyable after he met you."

He felt a warm glow. "I liked George a great deal, and I was sorry to get your letter. I hope he didn't suffer."

"If I could, I'd repeat the lie they told all the families, that he died without pain. But as you know, he survived the battlefield and died in his old room at the family estate. No matter what you've read about the horrors of mustard gas, you can never be prepared for the truth. And that's all I will say about that."

"He spoke very highly of you."

She smiled sadly. "We were friends long before I met his brother. He asked me to give you a message, and since I knew I'd be traveling to meet the duke in Chicago, I decided to tell you in person. I'm so grateful that dreadful Spanish flu seems to have ended, and I could travel."

"Excuse me, everyone," said the mayor, introducing the duchess and Coop to the crowd. They stood momentarily to wave, and the duchess swished her hand as if scooping air.

"I just used the royal wave," she said after they sat. "It happened without any thought at all. Isn't that remarkable?"

Waiters set down platters of artfully arranged food until their little table groaned. Charlotte said, "Why is everyone else being served on regular china, and we're given enough for a cart horse?"

"It's an acknowledgment of your status. You can have whatever you desire the moment you desire it, because you're special."

"Well, special me desires the contre-filet just there."

"What?"

"Oh, what's the name? Oh, yes, sirloin."

"There's cowboy ribeye or New York strip."

"The narrow one, the New York cut. The bone makes the other a cowboy cut. I must remember that."

"You'd think a duchess would be more familiar with banquet dining, even if it is American."

"The way people talk of you, I expected a man beating his chest and wearing but a loincloth, like the noble savage."

"George talked about me that way?"

"Oh, no, not George. I mean the people hereabout." She dropped her voice. "And yet George was quite taken with your physique. I can see why he was so impressed, even with the tuxedo concealing the best details."

Coop didn't expect such openness and couldn't remember when he'd enjoyed himself so much.

As waiters began clearing away dinner, she put a hand on his arm. "I'm having a lovely time, and I don't mean to spoil the evening, but let me speak while we still have a bit of privacy. George wanted you to know he was planning to marry after the war. He had a streak of the mountebank, for he said he would have his pick of widows. He begged me to encourage you to marry as well."

Coop took a sip of wine.

"No one here said anything impolitic to me, but the gossip about you has surely begun, and you must realize it."

"Charlotte, I sincerely appreciate your concern—"

"No, Coop, no." She shook her head. "I won't be condescended to in such an important matter. You can be jailed. You can lose everything. In many places your life will be at risk. You don't know what happened to George with that wretched man, the former steward at the Perry."

"I heard a little about it."

"It was wrenching. Accusations piled up until you'd think George purely evil when, in fact, he was a kind man."

Coop remembered George asking if he employed breaker boys.

She leaned in. "That steward told George you were the primary target, and that after the war he and his father would find a way to accuse of you of meddling with underage boys. Have you heard from those scoundrels?"

His heart pounding, Coop said, "No. He must have died in battle. And I would never with underage—"

"I know. The world will not. And another vicious liar will no doubt make accusations one day. George urgently wanted you to marry, and I agree. You must marry soon, for it is your greatest defense. Your *only* defense."

October 1919

Vic went slack jawed when Coop proposed. They were in her office, Coop sitting in front of her desk.

"I know we are not meant for romantic marriage," he said. "You have your ways, I have mine. But we love each other, and we can both leave the spotlight of scrutiny."

"Marrying you will put me directly in the spotlight. How will the city react to see us side by side, a bride with a husband ten times more beautiful than she is? Our intentions will be clear in an instant."

"We have a better chance than most to fake true love."

"Coop, I have true love that prevents faking one with you."

"I will never stand in your way with...with her." They'd never discussed the obvious about either of them.

"It's far too risky."

"Do you have any friends, women such as yourself, who will understand and appreciate my proposal?"

She rested her chin on her clasped hands. "Why the sudden rush to the altar?"

He told her about the duchess's warning, his dread of waiting to hear the snap of the trap just before it crushed him.

He didn't tell her how he avoided even going to the gymnasium lately, where he'd never paid a price for his rare, lust-fueled bravado about being seen, but without a doubt he had been seen. Most patrons and employees had. The stewards at the Perry were starting to ask him if he was feeling well, for he spent so much time in his room lately. He trusted none of them. As usual, only Dolly was a true friend.

"I'm sorry, Coop. This may be a rare example of how we women have an easier time of it. It is remarkably easy to escape unwanted attention after a certain age."

"Tell one of your friends she can have all the money and freedom she likes in exchange for marriage. You must know someone."

"I cannot recommend this to anyone I know. It will end in grief."

"It's my only defense."

Impatiently, she said, "You can find a woman who will accept your proposal within the hour. I'm only saying I can't provide her."

Coop left her office feeling somewhat more confident. He rode the moving stairs to the third level and strolled about, casually examining the salesgirls and cashiers. Many met his eyes and smiled with surprise and encouragement. Several approached and asked if he needed anything. It made him anxious to realize how many times they'd noticed his disinterest.

In a quiet corner of the third floor, in the waiting area outside the dressing rooms, a beautiful young woman sat reading a book. Coop had seen her many times, shopping with her mother. He memorized the names of regular customers. She was Elena, and her mother was Blanche.

Elena's soft brown hair surrounded her face like a halo. Her expression radiated serenity, and her skin glowed with youth and health.

She brightened at his approach. "Why, Mr. Tiller," she said, her voice lyrical and sweet.

He felt a stab of guilt at her youth, but the happiness in her eyes kept him from leaving. He asked what she was reading, and he laughed when she held up *Pride and Prejudice*. He sat on a red velvet stool, trying to remember the story. Suddenly, he recalled a detail he'd pondered for years. "Do you think Lizzy was truly angry at Charlotte for marrying Mr. Collins, or did she come to understand how her friend had a good reason?"

Amazed, Elena eagerly discussed the issue until her mother emerged and took in the situation with a glance. With undisguised calculation, Blanche said a waiting room was no place to discuss literature, and would he accept an invitation for luncheon tomorrow at their home?

"My daughter, Elena, is a master chef. I'm sure she'll be thrilled to make something special."

Coop said he'd be delighted, drawing a blush and a smile from Elena.

March 1920

He proposed at Christmastime. Elena wept with happiness. Her parents and four brothers went mad to show off Elena's fantastically wealthy fiancé. Elena's father owned a restaurant considered one of the finest in the country, and the entire family lived in a house with enough servants to attend to all of them.

Yet Coop could buy and sell their father one hundred times over, Elena's brothers were fond of saying.

Coop found himself in a social swirl he never imagined. They settled on a wedding in mid-March, when spring promises summer.

Preparations for the day reached a frenzy but came to a sudden halt forty-eight hours before, when Elena's superstitious mother barred them from seeing each other until they met at the altar. With only two more nights, Coop left the store, nodding and smiling as his employees offered their congratulations.

"Best of luck, Mr. Tiller," said Simon from behind.

Coop stopped, turning his head halfway. Quietly, Simon said, "I wish with all my heart things were different."

For months, Coop had seen Simon across the store and longed to learn what he had experienced on his wedding night. Coop couldn't think of anybody else to ask.

"Can you come to my room at the Perry after work tonight?"

Simon hesitated before saying, "I'll be there in an hour and a half."

It was growing dark as he left the store. With his head filling with questions for Simon, he barely took note of a shabby man leaning against a streetlamp until he said, "Coop."

Coop froze at the familiar timbre of the voice. The man's hands were in his pockets, his head tilted nervously. His skin was rough, like a lump of clay rolled in a gravel pit, with thin gray hair smeared back from his forehead.

His eyes were jaundiced but unmistakable. "Oh, my God," Coop whispered. He flashed on the weeds snapping back as he left the farm. "Kenny."

His brother's smile showed a few slanted yellow teeth. "I been telling people about my rich little brother for years. I saw your name in the paper, and it said you owned a coal mine, but it wasn't till I saw your engagement photo a few weeks back that I knew it was you. You have yourself a mighty pretty girl, the jammiest bits of the jam. And you look like a million bucks. You got some time for this old bum?"

"Are you here for money?"

"I'd ask the exact same thing if I was you. I been poor my whole life. I won't deny it'd be nice to hear some jingle-jangling in my pocket for once, but I came to ask about my kids."

Coop respected his honesty. "I live just over by the square. You can walk beside me, if you like."

Kenny shuffled along, every step an effort. "I never sailed the seven seas. Never crossed the ocean or been to California. You were smart to stay at the farm. I guess Mom and Dad are long gone?"

Red canyons. Flayed faces. He could still smell the metallic blood, slick as ice. From the darkest place in his mind bolted a steely fury to make Kenny feel even the smallest pain of that night. "Soon after you left, Dad shot Mom in the face and then stuck the rifle in his own mouth. Their brains were splattered everywhere."

Kenny gasped and sank to a knee, holding his stomach. "That's a gut punch," he spluttered. "I'm sorry I was a no-account older brother, Coop. I shoulda been there."

Coop looked at his stricken brother with a satisfyingly cold detachment. "I hated you for years." Until he said it, he hadn't even realized it. "You have no right to expect pity from me." And yet, Coop felt his pity stir.

"I know," Kenny said, his voice constricted to a soft whistle. He struggled to stand until Coop had no choice but to hook his arm and lift.

When Kenny was reasonably balanced, Coop said, "Dad said I'd be a millionaire someday." He wondered why he'd shared that, of all things.

"You got every right to rub my face in my mistakes. If it helps, I've never felt more ashamed than I do right now."

"I wasn't trying to make you feel ashamed, Kenny. I don't know why I said that."

"It's because 'I told you so' feels so good to say. I'm used to hearing it from friends, women, my own kids. Maybe someday I'll get the chance to see how it feels for myself."

Kenny plodded like he was shackled, moving in a vaporous cloud of boozy sorrow. Coop wondered if a man could look more broken. He remembered his father shoving Kenny away from the open well into the weeds, and the humiliation on Kenny's face. Coop somehow felt it was the moment Kenny's life went off course. Dad was only trying to keep Kenny safe, but he'd mishandled it.

Kenny gulped. "About what Dad said. I read somewheres you have more than ten million dollars. Can that be right, Coop?"

"That article ran all over the country. I have more, but I keep the amount close to my vest."

"I gotta tell you how strange it feels to have a brother with so much money. Specially that scrawny kid feeding the chickens. Most men would kill for the secret."

"Preparation and luck, but mostly luck. I didn't make the coal. I didn't invent stores. I came along at the right time for both."

"This is hard to say, Coop, but I was kind of hoping you could share your luck with my kids. I have five, and I'd be grateful if you could remember them in your last will and testament. Or even sooner." He pulled a piece of paper from his pocket. "Can I leave their names and addresses with you?"

The paper had the strangely significant texture of heavy crumpling that had been carefully smoothed. There wasn't enough light to read, so he slipped it into his pocket. "I'll do something for them."

"I know I got no right to ask, but you gotta promise me, Coop. I wanna tell them to expect something from you someday. If you keep your promise, they'll have reason to think well of me after I'm gone. If you don't, it'll just be another of my broken promises."

"I promise." The sweeping relief on Kenny's face was unsettling. Until that moment, Kenny was the older brother with a small but unmistakable higher status. In a flash Coop saw it from Kenny's view, straining to see the lofty, incomprehensible heights Coop inhabited.

They reached the Perry. "This is where I live."

Bewildered, Kenny said, "It looks like one-a them new office buildings. Don't you got a big fancy house?"

"It's a gentlemen's club. Like a hotel for men."

"A boardinghouse?"

"I suppose. What are your plans? Are you here for my wedding?"

Kenny kicked the cement. "I never took to church, and I don't have proper wedding clothes. I'm taking the overnight train to Detroit to see an old...well, an old cellmate."

Of course. Coop removed all the bills in his money clip, nearly six hundred dollars. "Take this."

The money shattered Kenny's respectable regret. Wide-eyed, he grabbed the bills, folding and sliding them into a secret pocket. "I sure do appreciate this." Kenny's smile was infused with all the emotions from every smile of his life. Coop saw greed, tenderness, lust, joy, cunning, euphoria, even contentment.

It enraged him.

Coop had worked every waking moment for years. He kept factories running with both coal from his mine and orders from his store. Because of him, ships sailed the oceans, people looked elegant at parties, families stayed warm. He provided direct employment to nearly one thousand people, and supplemental support to tens of thousands more.

Kenny had undoubtedly spent countless hours drunk, many more whooping it up and fucking, and how much time doing things that end in prison? And yet the world gives men like Kenny peace of mind before their weddings and looks with favor on their desires, while demanding men like Coop keep their true feelings hidden.

"I was a bit worried about coming to see ya," Kenny said in good cheer. "But you're just the same as always, Coop. The money ain't changed you a bit. I'm right proud to be your brother, and that's for sure."

The urge to send Kenny sprawling took over. "Just now, you looked like you'd never seen so much money all at once. I could burn six hundred dollars and never miss a penny."

Uncertain, Kenny said, "Yeah, I'll bet."

"What is it with men like you?" Coop growled. "Fucking and breeding like rats. You think your dick is the center of the world."

"Coop, I thought we was good."

In a rage, Coop stalked to the Perry's entrance. He reached into his pocket, feeling Kenny's list of children, next to a crisp page of suggestions from the kitchen wares buyer.

Coop grabbed the buyer's list, and with his back to Kenny, he ripped it several times with great drama. He turned, clutching the torn pieces in his fist. Kenny looked on with anguish and disbelief.

"A man provides for his children. A peckerwood asks his brother."

It was a vicious taunt, for Coop thought there was no shame in a man suffering misfortune and having his rich brother help, but he was too angry to care. As he went inside, he knew he'd never see Kenny again.

He had stopped shaking by the time he reached his room, where Dolly tried to greet him. She could no longer see through her cloudy eyes, but they lit up nonetheless whenever he came home.

He paid a steward named Peter to walk her four times a day, so she didn't need to go outside. Coop scratched her head and told her to remain in her bed, and she flopped with a grateful grunt and soon fell asleep.

He knocked back a shot of whisky, remembering a story about a rich old lady who died and left everything to her cat. It made sense to him now.

He looked at the list of Kenny's children, two girls, three boys. One lived in Boston, the other four in New York City. He folded the paper carefully and placed it in the desk drawer where he stored his most important documents.

He stripped to his flannels and stretched on his bed, his mind adrift until Simon knocked. His blood pumped as he opened the door. Simon's face went surprised but appreciative to see him almost naked.

Dolly woke, concerned until she smelled Simon as he petted her. She remembered him and wagged a few times.

"Poor girl's getting old," Simon said.

Coop took a swig of whisky right from the bottle and handed it to Simon, who did the same.

"Should I shuck to my flannels, too?"

"Make yourself at home," Coop said, lying back on his elbows to watch.

Simon slipped off his shirt and pants. As he lay next to Coop, his flannels bulged at his crotch. Coop gripped it. "Here's what I'm wondering. On your wedding night, how did you get the little man to rise to the challenge?"

"Sally was ten weeks along by then, so I had no pressure. It was almost a year before she asked if anything was wrong."

"And what then?"

"I came up with a plan. She must be silent and still. I close my eyes and think of you or other men. I work myself to almost the point of no return and that's when I act. But everything goes cold immediately, and I finish only half the time."

Coop felt a surge of hope. "And is she content with that?"

Simon gave him a sharp look. "Of course not. But what can she do? What can any of us do?"

Coop lay back. "Do you wish you'd never married Sally?"

"She is mild, and somehow I managed to make another baby inside of her. She doesn't yet know I feel my duty is done and will never touch her again."

"But would you marry her again?"

"No. I thought only of myself, and how unfair the world was to men like us. Just before our wedding, it started to needle me that as unjust as the world is, it was my problem to manage, not hers."

"But she used you, too. She needed a husband."

"If I'd been honest with her from the start, it would be different. But she is all confusion and misery." He wiped his face. "She is kind and doesn't deserve it. I have many regrets, but the issue is bigger than my marriage. Men like us should start our own country."

Lower Saranac Lake felt like a new country. "Will you tell Sally the truth about you?"

He laughed. "She'd believe in Peter Pan before she'd believe creatures like us exist. Most people are the same way. They can't imagine us."

"Maybe we should tell more of them. It's the only way to come into the light."

Simon laid back and hooked his hands behind his head. "Does Elena Parks know the truth about you?"

Coop shook his head. "Perhaps I can keep her happy with a baby or two for a while. Maybe she won't desire physical relations."

Simon rubbed Coop's back. "I do."

They tossed aside their flannels.

The next day, Simon left early, and after he shut the door, Coop sat up at the thought he might never spend another night in bed with a man.

By the time he reached the store, Coop was snappish and brusque with his employees. In the lobby of the management offices, he ignored happy greetings and questions about how he was feeling with his special day so close. He barreled into his office and shouted, "I must concentrate, and I need total silence!" He slammed his door so hard he winced, expecting the frosted glass to shatter.

In a little while, his message had been forgotten, or perhaps they'd misunderstood, for while they kept respectfully quiet, he could hear them.

"Silence!" The world beyond his door went hushed. He heard whispers, and he bellowed, "I can hear you whispering!"

Cheerful voices making deliveries and arriving for meetings were frantically shushed, and when a maintenance worker came to move a painting according to Coop's instructions, he started banging until a chorus of angry hisses sent him away.

Coop filled his mind with jumbled memories dredged up at random, to bury the only memory shining bright. He saw Will's dark hair flying as he ran naked across the dock, heard his laughter, felt his rough kiss on his lips. Coop closed his eyes and clenched his fists to control his tears.

Just past his door, one of the secretaries squeaked a horrified, "Oh!" just before something crashed to the floor.

He slammed both fists on his desk. The sound thundered, and the secretary gave a terrified cry. "Silence!"

"That is enough!" Vic said from her office next door "Everybody go. No, leave all of that. I don't know for how long, just clear out. Ted and Irv, you, too. This instant."

People shuffled, the outer door closed, and the lock clicked. A shadow appeared on the other side of his frosted glass.

Vic said, "I'm worried there's a wild beast in there ready to attack." She waited but he said nothing. "I'm coming in now. No need to make yourself decent, for I can't wait that long."

She pushed the door open while she remained at the threshold. She wore a blue dress with a colorful scarf of teal and pink stripes tied about her neck. He glowered.

"I see how it is," she said, approaching and untying her scarf, which she handed to him. "Wipe your face and blow your nose. I don't like this scarf anyway. The colors aren't evenly saturated."

As he wiped his eyes, she said, "You still have time to call it off."

"Did I tell you the governor is coming? Elena's parents know him."

"The governor will find something else to do if the wedding is canceled."

"There are so many people depending on me. Her family and friends all tell me she has never looked more radiant."

"Elena may smile for everyone, but surely she detects your mood."

"I think she does." He closed his eyes, ashamed he'd hoped Elena would have the courage to call off such a misbegotten plan. It was his responsibility. "At every turn, I see only bad options."

"Sometimes people mistake a good option as one that satisfies everybody. But a good option only solves the problem quickly. People can still be hurt."

"Do you ever wonder why the world hates people like us?"

"They can't comprehend our feelings and desires, just as we can't comprehend theirs."

"So far, it's an even draw."

"But they outnumber us. Hating someone as inferior makes people feel better about themselves, especially if they are the majority."

"It's so stupid. It's a natural fact and all. Just a bit different."

"If we start discussing the irrational state of the world, we'll never stop."

He returned to the Perry much earlier than usual. A steward greeted him with a sack of personal mail, more than he'd received in the past five years. In his room, he tossed it next to other sacks filled with unwanted congratulations.

Dolly thumped her tail and bobbed her head happily, looking in his general direction. Coop remembered her flying leaps over the steps of his mansion in Cadiz as he came into view, and now she couldn't even stand to greet him. "My sweet girl," he said, scratching her cheeks. She groaned and lay back for a belly rub, which he happily gave until she fell asleep.

He sat on his bed watching her snore and groan, remembering her pure gray fur when she was a puppy shivering in Mudlane near the cathouse. Over the last year, the black and white spots that appeared as she grew had become diffuse, and what looked like a splash of whitewash had emerged on her face.

On his desk was a stack of invitations to lunch, dinner, and parties. He looked at the sacks of congratulatory mail. He thought of projects at the store that needed his attention, and he hadn't visited the coal mine in several years. He could face none of it and took a deep breath of frustration.

Always on high alert for him, Dolly heard his voice in the exhale. She opened her eyes and lifted her head, thumping her tail on the floor.

"My sweet girl," he said kneeling to scratch her cheeks, and her tail wagged faster for a bit. Her love and devotion pierced the clouds in her eyes.

Her body clenched and she whined, as if hit by a spasm of pain. It passed, and she rested her head on his hand, giving his arm a lick, taking an enormous breath of contentment for his nearness.

Coop wasn't expected anywhere for the rest of the day and could think of nothing more important than to comfort Dolly. He lay next to her, speaking softly, kissing her face and head, and telling her how grateful he felt for her years of friendship. She took naps, and every time she woke, she had the happiness of finding him beside her.

The steward Peter arrived to take her outside. "Oh, beg your pardon, Mr. Tiller." Dolly thumped her tail once, for she knew and trusted Peter. "Looks like the old girl's not doing so good today," Peter said, stooping next to Coop to stroke her fur.

"Peter, tomorrow is my wedding. I believe Dolly is near the end, and I don't want her to be alone for too long. I'm going to ask my friend Vic to come here after the ceremony to look after her."

"Of course, Mr. Tiller. Just tell him to ask for me, and I'll let him inside."

"Vic is a woman, one of my employees. Dolly knows her well from all the times I took her to the store. She loves Vic almost as much as she loves me. There is no one better."

"I don't know," Peter said nervously. "It's my neck on the line."

"I'll give you a tip of one hundred dollars to meet Vic at the alleyway entrance and bring her up the back elevator. If you get into trouble with your supervisor, I will intervene. I can even have you hired at my store if it comes that."

"I'd take a lot of risks for one hundred dollars. But we need a signal, so I know she's out back." Peter removed a brass button from his pocket. "We all have to carry around an extra button in case one pops off. Just slip it in an envelope and have her send it to me inside."

Dolly gave a long groan, and Coop stroked her head and made soothing sounds.

"She thinks the sun rises to hear you crow, Mr. Tiller."

"She once saved my life from a murderer who nearly got away."

"Holy smokes! You're a stout-hearted heroine, Dolly!"

She wagged rapidly for a bit.

Coop stayed with her into the night. Memories jumbled, breaking into smaller fragments when he tried to put them in order. He looked at Everett's design for his new home, a brick mansion overlooking the lake, in an exclusive and secluded neighborhood. Coop had gently told Elena he'd been unhappy in a mansion, with unused rooms and so much empty space, and she replied that they'd fill it with children who would make joyous noise.

As Coop watched, the electronic lights of an office in a nearby tower snapped off. The world had changed so much since he was a boy, when immediate lights at all hours would have seemed like magic.

He felt a stirring in his soul, his desires still alive, still moving. It seemed they'd grown more powerful in hibernation.

It was impossible to sort his thoughts, given how he measured the phases of his life. The most important began in Elmer's buggy in the Appalachian foothills, at the start of all happiness with Will.

And yet the day Harold arrived with his family in the cart wouldn't leave his mind, and he surrendered to those memories, returning to life in the rural outskirts of Asheville until he fell asleep.

❖

He woke at his desk after dawn on his wedding day.

All morning, Dolly groaned and snored, but she was always comforted to find Coop at her side. He hated to leave her, but she was dying on the only day he could remember when it wasn't possible to cancel his other plans.

At two thirty in the afternoon, Coop left the Perry in a new formal afternoon suit, under a hail of congratulations.

The wedding was at the Old Stone Church, on the north side of Public Square. From there, the newlyweds would ride to Elena's family restaurant not five blocks away in an open-air, horse-drawn carriage, with a quick stop at a photography studio on the way. After dinner and the reception, Coop and Elena would ride back to Public Square, but on the south side where the luxurious Hotel Cleveland had reopened two years before.

All were within walking distance of the Perry.

He reached the church and greeted people as he made his way to the nave, where dark gothic and Romanesque designs provided a bold contrast against pale yellow walls. As he looked for Vic in the pews, people he didn't know waved and nodded and he smiled back.

At long last, Vic entered with a companion who smiled nervously.

He kissed Vic on the cheek. She introduced Elizabeth, who was fair-haired and sharp-eyed and gave him a smile that told of all the good things she'd heard about him. "I can't believe we've never met,"

Coop said, and Elizabeth seconded the feeling. Coop asked for a private moment with Vic, and Elizabeth left to find a spot.

"She seems lovely," Coop said, and Vic looked pleased. "Are you and Elizabeth planning to attend the dinner and reception?"

"I hope you don't mind, but no. Neither of us are comfortable being treated as single women at a wedding reception, and we're not quite ready for the old maids' table."

He explained about Dolly. Vic nodded. "Of course I'll stay with her. She is such a sweet dog." Coop gave her a small envelope with Peter's button and told her the plan.

"If things look like they're at the end..."

"Leave the worry to me. Simply get on with your day." She kissed his cheek and walked off. He watched, filled with gratitude.

The governor created a fuss when he arrived with his wife, and he broke off to introduce himself to Coop with a promise to talk later. By then it was time for the wedding, and Coop surrendered to the romantic mood as Elena approached in her gown. He gave her a tender smile. She looked beautiful and happy throughout. They left the church in the carriage and Coop felt silly when their cheering guests were behind them and the passers-by either squinted in confusion or waved to be polite.

At the photographer's studio, he smiled when told, stood where they wanted him, and posed as they suggested. After another mortifying but mercifully brief ride in the carriage, they arrived at Elena's family restaurant.

The festive roar was deafening. After half an hour, Coop stopped trying to remember names, businesses, or the multiple discussions people insisted they must have over lunch or dinner. Elena's brothers introduced their friends and associates, and strutted about now that the deal was sealed and their sister had safely married a multimillionaire.

Coop's mind would flash on Dolly momentarily before his attention was drawn to something else.

After dinner, speeches began. "Am I expected to speak?" he whispered to Elena.

She shook her head. "Nobody wants to hear from the bridegroom on the wedding day." They shared a happy laugh. They cut cake, drank champagne, and waltzed.

After many hours, the energy in the room started to deflate. Conversations went soft, fewer people danced, and the governor and his wife left to a smattering of applause.

"It's soon time for us to leave," Elena said.

"Must we take the carriage?"

"I think it's foolish, too, but my father was so excited, and we can't seem ungrateful. Now excuse me, I must touch up in the ladies' room. We'll leave when I return."

Momentarily sentimental, Coop kissed her hand. She laughed in gratitude and kissed him on the lips before sweeping off in her gown.

Vic appeared in her wake, smiling as she approached. "All seems to be going well."

"Is Dolly…"

"It won't be long now. I came to tell you that if you wish to see her again, you have little time. She will be gone by morning. Peter said he would spend the night with her, so she won't be alone, but he has to visit his aunt and won't be there until later."

"She is alone now?"

"I dared not wait too long to tell you, in case you'd left."

Coop thought of Dolly waking, confused and in pain, wondering where her friends were. It ripped his heart. "I must go to her. I have to tell Elena."

"I suggest you wait until you are in your hotel room. She will not want anyone to know she spent her wedding night alone."

Only minutes after they arrived at the presidential suite on the top floor of the Hotel Cleveland, Coop told Elena about Dolly. She looked disappointed but agreed. "Yes, you must say goodbye. She hardly knows me, but perhaps I should come with you?"

"She's at the Perry."

"Ah, yes. The famous place forbidden to women."

"I'm sorry. Truly, but Dolly is a part of me. She was with me every step of the way as I built a new life."

Elena gave a tender smile and blushed. "I'm glad you told me before I put on my lingerie. It will be a surprise still."

Grateful she was so understanding but sick with dread at the mention of lingerie, he took the short walk across Public Square. As he stepped off the elevator on his floor, he heard an anguished whine. He raced to his room and was unlocking the door when he heard a thump.

"Dolly!" he said, opening the door carefully in case it might strike her.

He saw her just as she slipped into a puddle of urine. She'd dragged herself a few feet from her bed, knowing that she must go outside to relieve herself. She knew how far it was and she could barely walk, yet she had bravely tried.

She heard him but was too confused and mortified for breaking the rules to feel relieved. "My sweetest girl," he said, gathering her in his arms as she let go of an uncontrollable stream of urine. She wriggled, issuing an anguished apology for making such a terrible mistake.

"It's all right, my pretty girl." His voice broke. He kissed the top of her head and scratched her cheeks. "Just rest."

She understood and slumped in his arm. He used the woven bedspread to dry her before wiping the floor. He could just reach his pillow and he propped it under her rump. When she looked as comfortable as he could make her, he rocked her gently, petting and kissing her, speaking softly. She gave a feeble wag now and then, and every so often she'd lift her head to lick his face or arm.

A dark chasm of grief opened before him. Exhausted from his wedding day, he dozed against the wall until the early hours when suddenly she whined and lifted her head, frantic for him. "I'm here with you, my sweetest girl."

She groaned with relief, dropped her head, and died.

A wave of disbelief took his breath. It was too shocking to be possible. The grief breached his defenses and burst. He cried into her fur, kissing her again and again and, through the fog, wishing to go with her.

CHAPTER ELEVEN

New York, New York
Present day

Darcy faces Jake in front of the mailboxes in the building Cooper Tiller had owned. "Charles Greene has fallen right into my lap. He's upstairs in apartment seventeen."

"What will you say to him?"

"I don't know, but I have to confront him no matter what my lawyer says."

Darcy hops up the stairs and Jake follows. After four floors with four apartments each, they reach the top floor with only two apartments. Seventeen is to the left.

"You saw the size of this building," Jake says. "These units must be huge."

Darcy strikes a note of false bravado, hiding his sudden jitters about making a terrible legal mistake. "Let's find out."

He raps sharply on the door. After a minute, a young man in a dingy T-shirt and shorts appears. Darcy asks for Charles Greene. The kid says he's the cleaner and doesn't know when Charles Greene will return. He closes and locks the door.

"We could get something to eat," Darcy says.

"Why don't we just wait here?"

Darcy sits on the top step. "How long before you have to get back to your gardening clients?"

"Let me worry about that."

"I really appreciate the way you dropped everything to help me. I wouldn't have made it this far without you."

Jake blushes. "It's no trouble."

"It is trouble," Darcy says, suddenly consumed with an impulse to get his worst out there. "I was a bartender when I lived in San Francisco, and I got into the habit of using coke daily. It wasn't much, but I'd snort my first line to wake up in the morning."

Jake's chin drops.

"I wasn't an addict. After my parents died of COVID and my grandmother asked me to move in to help, I gave it up and hardly missed it. I wouldn't blame you for not believing me, but it's the truth."

"I've heard that all before," Jake says, cold and flat. "I told you my sister died of a heroin overdose. I miss her, but she was trouble. Stealing, lying, everyone running around in circles to help, all for nothing. I swore I'd never get involved with anyone who used drugs." He shakes his head and stands, throwing his head back with a deep sigh. "I need to go for a walk."

Darcy reaches into his pocket. "Take the keys." They dangle from his fingers. "So you can get back inside the building."

Jake looks at them but doesn't move. "I have your number. I'll call if I need to get back inside."

If.

Darcy nods, and Jake trudges down the stairs.

Darcy fights the urge to follow, grimacing at the stupid way he'd revealed the truth, but he had to get it out of the way. *If Jake doesn't believe me, I can't do anything about that, but I told the truth.*

The urges ended completely after several months of not using. Maybe he didn't use enough to become seriously addicted, or his supply grew less potent. He didn't consider himself morally superior to someone who got hooked; he just wasn't one of them.

Darcy sinks into himself. Jake has probably already driven off, gone forever.

In a little while, the young cleaner emerges from the apartment. He gives Darcy a blank look, locks the door, and leaves.

Hours seem to pass before Darcy hears the echoes of two men arguing downstairs. He recognizes Jake's voice and stands, hardly daring to believe it.

Jake rounds the corner, next to a man with dark curly hair salted with gray. He has a fine physique with dark skin, Italian or Latino. They see Darcy and stop.

"And who is this?" the man barks.

Darcy ignores him and trots down the stairs to stare into Jake's eyes. "Thank you for coming back."

Jake flushes. "I still have some questions about what you told me, but I waited outside until he arrived," he nods to the man, "and I asked if he was Charles Greene."

The tenderness between them seems to disarm Charles, who looks closely at Darcy. "You're related to Cooper Tiller. I can see it on your face. You're here about his will. You should have responded to my offer through my lawyer instead of just showing up at my door."

"I didn't know until a little while ago that you live here."

He slaps his chest. "You expect me to believe that?"

"I don't care what you believe. That's what happened."

Charles stomps upstairs. "I'm not playing games. I'm calling the lawyer right now, and you'll be sorry you decided to disturb me."

Jake says, "We're not here to cause trouble."

"Too late," he says in a musical tone. He gets to his door and turns. "Look, I don't want to cause trouble for a gay couple. We have enough as it is. But that money is going to fund a huge project to serve queer people all over New York. If you knew my plans, you'd support them."

"My great-grandfather wanted us to share."

"How do you know what Cooper Tiller wanted? He died in 1960."

The door to apartment eighteen creaks open. Charles slaps his thigh and shouts, "Now look what you've done. You've disturbed an old man who needs his rest."

"I'm not disturbed," says the man who rolls out in an electric wheelchair. He's frail and wispy, but he gives a wicked smile. "At least I'm not any more disturbed than I've been my whole life."

"You need to rest."

"Charles," the man says with authority, "you need to release this need to order me about. Why don't you go to your own place and return when you have your anger under control?"

With a fierce look, Charles starts to object before he thinks better of it and charges into his apartment, slamming the door behind him.

"Sorry about that," the man in the wheelchair says. He looks at Darcy and gasps, then he shakes his head, laughing. "I'm so sorry. For a split second, I thought you were my father."

CHAPTER TWELVE

Cleveland, Ohio; New York, New York; and Lower Saranac Lake
1922–1954

May 1922

"Oh, no," Coop said, seeing an unexpected welcoming committee on their lawn as he pulled up to their new brick mansion on the lake. A brass band struck up a peppy marching tune, the suburban mayor and councilmen grinned, and schoolchildren unfurled a banner reading *Welcome to Bay Village!*

Elena clapped happily. "Isn't it spiffy?"

"Did you know your family was planning this?"

"No, and don't be a wet blanket again, Coop. Let's enjoy ourselves for once." Elena got out of the car, and the nanny handed over their new infant from the back seat. Elena carefully arranged the baby blanket to cascade with lace and rushed around to take Coop's hand with a radiant smile, as if they were the picture of familial bliss.

Coop had been looking forward to his first peaceful night in his new home, but he forced a smile when the politicians descended on him with ravenous eyes and handshakes.

In her flowing, bright yellow outfit, Elena looked like a daffodil being bundled into a bright bouquet of flowers as the other women surrounded her to coo at the baby, Mildred.

On the porch, a long row of maids all dressed in the same blue and white uniforms waited to be of service. In back, well out of the way, maintenance workers and groundsmen formed a ragged, impatient line, wearing trousers, shirts, and suspenders.

Coop longed to be among the working men.

❖

September–October 1929

While Elena's spacious bedroom faced the front yard, Coop's smaller room across the hall overlooked the green slope to the lake. From an alcove next to his bed, Coop also had the house's only unrestricted view of two rectangular recesses built into the side of the brick garage. One held a cold water outdoor shower used by male workers on hot days, like today.

The second recess was only visible from the very corner of his window, forcing Coop to jostle a bedside table holding framed photos of Elena and his daughter Millie. He turned the pictures face down before checking if Jason the gardener had left him a signal.

Coop's heart burst into a gallop at seeing Jason's shears stuck into the ground in the brick alcove, meaning the coast was clear. He hurried to the hallway, only to realize he'd left the photos down and the table askew. Ever on the alert for clues about him, Elena would notice. But he didn't want to keep Jason waiting, so he closed his door.

He found Jason planting bulbs at the side of the house. Glazed in sweat, the gardener had stripped to his tank top and pants. He saw Coop and stood, taking off his cap to wipe his forehead, and they shared a quick nod of acknowledgment.

Coop set off for the alcove and slipped inside, confident he was only visible from that corner of the window. Jason arrived and Coop pulled him tight. Jason didn't resist, but he took no initiative and only responded to instructions.

After they finished, Coop gave Jason fifty dollars and rinsed off under the shower. He returned to the house and went upstairs, going still when seeing Elena waiting in the open door of his room.

"I will not try to find a new gardener before winter, but I will dismiss Jason at the first snow." With a blank stare, she lifted her chin and swept into her room, slamming the door.

He looked inside his room. Elena had set the framed photos properly upright and straightened the table.

Without a doubt, Elena had watched his tryst with Jason.

Amazingly he felt hope, for here was a chance to confront all the truths they'd learned to avoid. Coop considered the once-unthinkable possibility of being frank with Elena about his true feelings. He could apologize and even offer favorable divorce terms.

Elena refused to speak to him for weeks, leaving the room when he entered. He was careful to only approach if she was alone, knowing how much she'd hate anyone overhearing.

Coop grew more frustrated until one day he walked into the afternoon salon while a housemaid dusted, and Elena was teaching Millie, now seven years old, a complicated embroidery stitch.

"If you don't speak to me at last, I'll contact a divorce lawyer to discuss matters with you."

Elena icily asked the maid to take Millie. After they left, she glared. "If you were hoping to humiliate me by mentioning divorce in front of others, remember I have heavier humiliations to drop on you."

"Why should we fight? Simply tell me what you want."

"Certainly not a *divorce*," she hissed. "It would only force me and my family to share in your disgrace. You must stew in your own immoral muck."

"Divorce is not uncommon these days. Wouldn't you be happier?"

Hope flashed on her face, a chance for release. She wiped it away. "I would rather die than to be known as a divorcée. To be refused communion, to lose respectable friends, to see my family's disappointment."

"Perhaps I can move away? You know I will always support you."

Again, a glimmer of hope soon squashed. "How will it help if you abandon us? We are married, and everything proceeds from there."

"Only we can take control of our lives. It is up to us."

"You know where I stand."

The next day was Sunday, and Coop drove his wife and daughter to Our Lady of Miracles for Mass. Little Millie, riding in the back seat, hummed happily and Coop soon joined her.

"Shush!" Elena snapped, Millie shrinking back in fear. "Sunday morning isn't playtime."

"That's right, Millie." Coop smiled broadly at his daughter in the rearview mirror. "Remember, you must go to church like this." He made a grotesquely distorted face.

Millie pealed with laughter, while Elena shot him a look of hatred.

The following Friday, a top-heavy stock market started to creak out of balance, and a week later, the dramatic losses prompted banks and investment firms to buy up huge blocks of shares. The market rallied for a day, but on the following Monday, the slide began anew, and on Tuesday, October 29, the market collapsed, wiping out billions of dollars in wealth.

Ashen and trembling, Elena came into his office that night. He was at his desk, and she started her first conversation with him in weeks. "How much have we lost?"

"Not much. I invest mostly in real estate, not stocks. My finances are sound, but I may buy some shares at these prices."

"And what of the store?"

"Vic has kept a sharp eye on things since I made her general manager. I can speak to her tomorrow, but we've been through downturns before. We simply cut back on the luxury items. If I am forced to sell Tiller's tomorrow at a complete loss, it would be little problem for us."

She went soft with relief. "My father and brothers were not so foresighted. They've lost everything, apparently."

"They have nothing to fear as long as I am solvent."

"Do you mean it, Coop?"

"Of course. I will keep all of us afloat."

She struggled with her words.

"Let me have it," he said softly. "No matter how indebted you feel in the moment, you must have such rage for me. It is the least I can do to stand silently while you unleash your anger."

The instantaneous fury in her eyes showed how constantly she felt his betrayal. "When we met, were you looking for a woman you could hide behind? Was your need for disguise greater than my need for a true husband?"

"I didn't think about any of that. I only thought of my own protection."

"And my feelings, my life, were just useful tools for your purpose? You didn't see how I had the desires and fondest hopes of a woman? A person with a heartbeat and such love to share?"

Shame burned his face. "You deserved so much better than me. I wish I had done things differently. I can only promise you'll never want for money, nor your family."

She exhaled a deep breath. "No one can dispute you've been a faithful provider. I have no complaints on that score. And in that spirit, I will not dismiss Jason. He has a family and has only done what you asked. But he doesn't share your loyalty, Coop. You must know that."

"I do."

"No man ever will."

"With all honesty, I can say you are wrong about that."

"Did you know you felt no passion for women when we married?"

"Yes. It was selfish, and yet the whole world was pushing me."

She smiled with melancholic sympathy. "The whole world pushed me into your arms, too."

"It's hard to believe the whole world is wrong, even when you know it in your heart."

"It seems everyone learns that too late. Oh, Coop, we might have been the best of married couples. If I've been angry, it's because it's difficult to watch your dreams die."

He took her hands. "Are you certain you won't consider a divorce? You are still beautiful, with many charms to attract a man who will appreciate them. And you will never want for money."

"I will not consider a divorce. It's too public. Yet," she took a steadying breath, "perhaps I could find a man…"

"An affair?"

"Nothing so tawdry as an affair. A long-term relationship, perhaps. Something discreet and built on mutual respect. I don't know if it's possible, but I must try."

"I'm in no position to forbid it. Nor do I wish to. After my conduct, I'll help you in any way I can and tell any story you ask me to tell."

He kissed her cheek and she leaned into his chest. He wrapped her in his arms and felt a sweet bond, like siblings might share.

1930–1932

One spring day, while Millie had piano lessons in the music room, Coop slipped out to the beach behind the house. As he walked across the lawn, he felt the fossil he'd purchased that morning in his jacket pocket.

The previous year, he'd had a small wooden staircase installed leading to the narrow, rocky shore. When he reached the top landing, he was surprised to see Elena at the bottom, looking out over the water. She looked up and smiled.

Elena wore loose linen trousers and a ruffled top. She'd taken to the daring new fashion for women's slacks, wearing them for everything but church and the most formal occasions. Often, she was the first stylish woman in pants many people had seen, and they gaped like she was a Hollywood movie queen.

The small waves splashed and burbled between the rocks.

"I'm glad you had the staircase built," she said. "It's so exciting to enjoy the water up close."

He too had come to appreciate Lake Erie's theatrical flair, mirroring the sky with colors and textures, creating illusions of jeweled tiles, crackled slate, or expanses of velvet.

He pulled the rock from his pocket, smooth gray and stamped with two half impressions of what looked like big bugs.

Delighted, Elena snatched it from his hand. "I've seen drawings of these, but I can't remember their name."

"Trilobites. They're hundreds of millions of years old. Millie will be ecstatic." He took the rock and placed it upside down in a sandy spot among other water-smoothed stones. It stood out just enough to be noticeable but not obvious.

"I'm glad you've given her such an interesting hobby, Coop."

"It was her idea. She found that first shell fossil, and there was no stopping her."

"Is it fair to plant one?"

"Of course. I bought this from a dealer in Westlake. It's from Lake Erie, so who says she couldn't have found it herself?"

"You are a good father. Millie is a daddy's girl, through and through."

His daughter was his life's unexpected joy. His heart soared when she arrived home from school, and she spontaneously smiled and ran into his arms. They hunted fossils, took long walks along the shore, ate ice cream on the porch, and read books about ancient empires, dinosaurs, and adventures. He was thrilled when she declared *Robinson Crusoe* her favorite novel.

Elena cleared her throat. "I've been waiting for a good time to say this, so while it's just the two of us, I would like another child."

His mind went blank until he recalled Simon's rules for attempting copulation with his wife. He described the procedure for Elena. She laughed. Coop blushed. "I would only insult you if I tried to fake passion."

Serene, she nodded. She'd be surprised to know how much he knew about her relationship with Philip Davenport, a New York real estate magnate who'd inherited a fortune from his father. His unhappy marriage to his wife was widely understood to rest on an inability to conceive.

Elena often left for long weekends in New York.

A handful of people seeking Coop's favor had told him Elena had been seen in New York in Davenport's company. "They are only friends," Coop assured them.

Davenport had restored Elena's verve. In ladies' pants, she moved through the world with spirited confidence, heightening Coop's understanding of the happiness he'd denied her.

A thought struck Coop. "How will I know if the child is mine?"

"You are my husband. Who else?"

He started to speak, but her eyes stopped him. "Yes, I understand. Who else?"

"Daddy!" Millie called from the top of the steps. "And Mommy's here, too!"

She pounded to the beach. Elena gave her a kiss. "Mommy will leave you two to find fossils. I'll just get in the way." She left, and Coop asked Millie about her piano lesson.

"It was good, except Mozart plays tricks with notes and scales."

"He does?" Coop feigned comic anger. "I've always heard he was a sneak. Now, you search that side of the beach, and I'll look over here. Who knows what the waves have delivered for us today?"

She skipped happily and started examining rocks. Coop found a beautiful leaf fossil that he slipped inside his pocket for another day.

Soon, Millie shrieked with amazement, holding the trilobite fossils. Her mouth moved silently, unable to voice her wonder. Coop whooped and hollered, and they raced back to the house to read about trilobites.

Over the next year, Coop and Elena made several attempts for another child with no results. In April of 1932, Elena left for a lengthy stint in New York to help a friend catalogue the contents of a Fifth

Avenue mansion owned by a branch of the friend's family that had recently died out.

She didn't need to add that she'd be spending time with her lover, saying only, "It's a huge task, and I'll be gone for a while. I'll take Millie with me."

"She has six more weeks of school."

"At her age, it's little trouble to miss the final six weeks of classes. I'll send her back if we're not done by September. Or I'll find a school in New York."

Horrified, he said, "If you find a school, you'll never bring her back." He dropped his voice. "Who will leave fossils for her to find?"

She smiled faintly. "Yes. She loves finding fossils with her father. And yet, what kind of mother would leave her child for so long?"

His heart pounded. "Take her for half the summer. In July, I'll fetch her and take her on a trip. Maybe Millie and I can steam to Europe."

"No." She shook her head firmly. "I will send her back when I'm ready."

"Please. No longer than mid-July."

"Do not put demands on me. It is my decision. She will return, that I promise."

He could only trust Elena to be true to her word.

Millie cried at the train station as they departed. Coop choked back his terror and smiled. "Remember to help Mommy as much you can."

"I'll miss you, Daddy," Millie said, grief sharpening her voice like a knife that pierced his spirit. He watched them board the train and turned away before his daughter saw his desolation. He ran Millie's parting words through his mind so often he memorized the tone of every syllable, her sharp intakes of breath.

The weeks creaked by at an agonizing pace. Exactly five weeks after they'd left, he sent a telegram to the Fifth Avenue address, where Elena was staying as she helped her friend.

Elena responded the next day. He ripped open the telegram right on the porch. To his elated surprise, she gave Millie's arrival time and train number the following week. "The work is wearying and I'm exhausted most of the time, so she's better off at home. A nanny will accompany her."

Coop threw himself into the preparations and arrived at the station an hour early. As the train chugged into the terminal, he paced anxiously until Millie emerged in a pink dress with white polka dots and puffy sleeves. Her light brown hair bounced with tight, hairstylist curls. She spotted him and squealed with joy, running into his arms. Coop gave Millie's nanny a generous tip and sent her back to New York.

The next day, from the deck of a steamer Coop and Millie laughed and pointed while their lakefront house slid past. Hours later, they docked at the ornate pier of Cedar Point, the pleasure resort in Sandusky. Coop had reserved a room just off the Grand Pavilion, and they spent a week at the bathing beach, as well as enjoying rides like the Sea Waves, the water toboggan, bicycle boats, and the thrilling Cyclone coaster.

They ate every night at a fine restaurant, watching elegant couples sail across a huge dance floor. Millie squealed with delight when Coop promised to teach her the waltz when she was older.

"Did Mommy take you to ballroom restaurants in New York?"

She shook her head. "Mommy took me to matinee plays and for buggy rides in Central Park. We even rode a boat to see the Statue of Liberty. It was ever so much fun until Mommy started feeling unwell."

His breath caught. "Is Mommy sick?"

"She's tired all the time." She stuffed another bite of macaroni and cheese into her mouth, enraptured by the women's swirling dresses and the men in evening wear.

The summer passed with visits to the zoo and museums and afternoon concerts. The joy of having Millie all to himself soon became weighted with concern for Elena. He sent a telegram asking if all was well and when she expected to return. Without delay, she responded that she felt sluggish, which had slowed their work. "I simply can't travel, but I will keep you updated."

Coop folded the telegram, worried. Summer was nearly over, and Millie would begin school soon. His daughter was becoming suspicious, too. "Daddy, what if we went to New York and helped Mommy finish her work sooner?"

"Darling, we'll just get in her way. She'll have to teach us how to catalog antiques and old books, and we'll make everything slower. Besides, school starts soon, and we'll be rushing around like headless chickens."

She giggled. "Have you ever seen a headless chicken?"

"I have." The blood squirting from their necks flashed in his mind. "And I never want to look like one."

Millie grew more insistent for answers, so Coop sent a telegram demanding Elena set a firm return date. She replied they shouldn't expect her before Halloween. Enraged, Coop wrote: *Your daughter is beside herself with worry, and I admit that so am I. You must assure me you are in good health and have every intention of returning home.*

In return, a single line: *I have every intention of returning home.*

Coop's plan to keep Millie too busy to miss her mother was faltering, so he added swimming lessons, gymnastics, and, with a burst of inspiration, hired a tutor for ballroom dancing. His daughter enjoyed them but wasn't fooled. "When is Mommy coming home?" she asked nearly every day and his answers grew thinner.

School started and one afternoon in mid-September, Millie walked in and ignored his welcome. He watched his daughter's back as she went to the music room for her piano lesson. They were so much alike.

He sent the piano teacher away. "Just this once. I need to talk to my daughter."

After the teacher left, Millie remained on the piano bench, picking at keys, pretending he wasn't there.

"Your mother wrote to say she hopes to be back by Halloween. I didn't tell you because I was trying to persuade her to return earlier."

Millie gave him a pained look. "Does she hate me?"

"No, my darling, no." He knelt and encircled her shoulder. "Nobody could ever hate you, least of all your mother. It is possible she hates me, however."

"Why?"

"Life sometimes becomes so complicated for adults, Millie. When you're older, I promise to tell you everything if you want. But it's a very painful topic for me and your mother."

Defiant, she said, "Maybe I'll ask Mommy."

"I think she'll give the same answer. Believe me, darling, I know exactly how you feel. I remember thinking my parents didn't respect me and how angry it made me. I won't lie to you, but the truth must wait."

She sniffled. "Did your parents tell you the truth?"

The shots exploded in his head, as loud as cannons, followed by the gunsmoke curling in the light of the oil lamps. "They died before they had the chance, which made me even angrier. It was easier to forgive them when I grew up and understood how helpless they felt. I hope it doesn't take you that long to forgive me because I love you so much. I wouldn't be able to live if I thought you hated me."

Her eyes filled with tears. "I don't hate you. I just miss Mommy."

He swept her into a tight hug, rocking and kissing her head. "I know, my darling. I promise she'll be home by Halloween." He hoped Elena wouldn't make a liar of him.

Elena returned without warning early one evening a week before Halloween. Coop and Millie came in from the afternoon salon in disbelief as she paid a cab driver, her bags piled in the hallway. "Oh, there's my little family," she said with strained cheer. She was gaunt and pale, her glorious hair a limp, raggedy mop. Her clothes looked both too tight and too loose.

"Elena," he said. "Have you been seriously ill?"

"I had a touch of something that everyone in New York had as well. I'm feeling better, but I *do* need to rest after that train journey." She pinched off her gloves and smiled at Millie. "Isn't my daughter happy to see me?"

Millie scrunched her face and broke into tears of sadness, rage, and betrayal. She raced out the back door.

As soon as she and Coop were alone, Elena abandoned pretense. "I'm exhausted beyond belief." She took a wobbly step. Coop rushed keep her upright. "Please help me to bed."

The next morning, she looked even worse, and Coop called a doctor. Elena tried to protest but gave up quickly. "But I will speak to him alone."

Coop was waiting at the foot of the stairs when the doctor descended, looking tired and grumpy. He was an older man with little hair and less charm. "She asked me not to say anything to you about her condition, but man-to-man, I think she's being hysterical."

"Say no more," Coop ordered. "You must respect her wishes. Just tell me if she is seriously ill."

"Yes, she's seriously ill, but I don't think she's dying, if that's what you mean. I've left her with some medicines." He handed him a list. "Make sure she takes these vitamins every morning and evening. Send someone to the drugstore right away because she's vitamin deficient. Are you sure you don't want to know the details? As a husband, it's your right."

"If she wants me to know, she'll tell me."

The doctor shook his head. "Can't say I approve of modern marriage."

"Luckily, our marriage is not your concern."

The doctor left, grumbling.

Coop hired nurses who watched over Elena around the clock, administering the medicines and vitamins according to the doctor's schedule.

Once Millie understood how ill her mother was, all was forgiven, and she sat beside her bed, telling Elena about school and showing off gymnastic moves and ballroom techniques.

"That's so wonderful, sweetie," Elena would say feebly. "You'll be the belle of the ball."

Coop checked on his wife several times a day, but only long enough for her to say she felt better and wanted to rest. He didn't believe her, and on her third night home she looked so sick he refused to leave.

"I must talk frankly to my wife for a few minutes," Coop said to the nurse, who nodded and left.

Up close, Elena's pale face had taken on a disturbing shadowy cast, almost gray.

"Dear God, you look very ill." He pulled up a chair and took her hand. It was cool to the touch, and he instinctively warmed it between his.

"I'm sure that horrible doctor ignored my wishes and told you everything."

"I wouldn't let him. He only told me he didn't think you were dying."

Elena's mouth dropped. "Coop, you would have made the most desirable husband if not for…"

He nodded. "But I am very worried about you."

"I know. Millie said you told her I hate you."

"You know children. They don't hear the nuance in words. I said only you might hate me. She was worried she was responsible for your long absence, and I had to reassure her."

"I understood immediately. I told her I don't hate you. She asked why you thought so, and I said I couldn't explain it for many years. I'm glad you were honest with her, for she was so relieved we both gave her the same answer. But she will ask some day." She closed her eyes. "The warmth from your hands feels so nice."

"Would you like me to do the other?"

"The other doesn't feel cold."

What could that mean? "Elena, perhaps we should get you to the hospital."

"If I'm not better in the morning, I'll raise no objections."

"Will you tell me anything about what ails you?"

"Please don't ask questions," she said in a voice filled with unfathomable pain. "I need to rest. Fetch the nurse."

He took a deep breath and promised to check back soon. The nurse was waiting outside, and he said, "Why is she only cold on one side?"

Her eyes flew open. "She wasn't an hour ago. Oh, my God! Call an ambulance this instant!" She rushed into the room. "Mrs. Tiller." Elena could barely raise her head. The nurse pushed back her forehead and held up two fingers. "How many fingers do you see?"

Elena blinked, trying to focus. The nurse ran to the medicine table and saw Coop frozen in place. "Call the ambulance! Now!"

Two hours later, Coop held a sobbing and terrified Millie in a waiting room when a young doctor arrived. The doctor gave Millie a glance and called down the hall for a nurse, who came scurrying and swept Millie away.

"I'll come for you in a minute," Coop promised. He turned to the doctor. "My wife must have the best care. I can afford whatever is required."

"We know who you are, Mr. Tiller, and she is in the best hands you can find in hundreds of miles."

"How is she?"

"She's resting. We'll keep her sedated for at least a week. No visitors. She needs the calm and relaxation."

"What's wrong with her?"

"She had a stroke. Luckily, we caught it early, and there's every expectation she'll recover. But not without some paralysis. I'd advise getting some canes and wheelchairs. I'm sorry to be so blunt."

Coop sank to a chair facing the only wall decoration in the room, a large and ornate crucifix.

The doctor sat beside him. "I have a few questions."

"Of course."

"How long was she in labor?"

The pieces fell into place ruthlessly. Six months in New York.

Sending Millie home before her pregnancy became unmistakable. A maddening refusal to answer the most basic questions.

Thunderstruck, Coop was silent until he realized his reaction could reveal everything. "I don't know," he stammered. "She was in New York."

"She's badly damaged, so it must have been a terrible struggle. She had some internal bleeding, and that's what caused the blood clot that led to the stroke. I assume the child didn't survive?"

Coop turned away. "I don't think so."

"What?"

"Yes, of course the child died," he snapped.

"There's one more piece of bad news. I'm afraid she'll never give birth again. There's nothing else you can do here, so I suggest you return home and get some rest." He scribbled out a prescription. "Here's a little something for you to relax, too."

Coop found Millie in the nurse's station. As they left, he ripped up the prescription and threw it in the trash.

1941–1952

In December of 1941, the Japanese bombed the US naval fleet at Pearl Harbor. The next day, young men lined up by the thousands at military recruiting offices, intent on revenge. Young women volunteered to learn nursing and life-saving skills, and Millie, a nineteen-year-old beauty whose eyes had gone a striking deep violet, was at the head of the line.

Coop donated to the same causes he supported during the last world war, but he declined appointments to rationing boards or fundraising committees, pleading his duties to his invalid wife.

In April of 1942, he headed to the top floor of his department store to see Vic. Riding the metal escalators that had replaced the original wooden moving stairs, he noted how the new fashions looked out of place among the ornate wrought iron fixings, flouncy wall sconces, and flocked wallpaper.

He walked into Vic's office and tossed his hat on her desk. "Sorry I didn't warn you I was coming." She wore a gray blazer and matching skirt over a black blouse. A string of white pearls stood out crisply. "You look very nice," he said, sitting.

She rolled her eyes. "I look like I'm one hundred and fifty years old. I feel so tired all the time."

"I know exactly what you mean. You know what else looks old? This store. Fashionable women wear snappy outfits these days, like yours. We look like fuddy-duddies with all these swoops and curls."

"I've submitted two plans for redesigns and fresh concepts. You've nixed both. I don't have the energy for a third. And that leads us to another subject..." She poured two shots of his favorite whisky, pushing a glass to him.

They knocked back the shots, and she went scarlet as she slammed hers down. In a raspy voice, she said, "It's time for me to retire, Coop. I can suggest several candidates to replace me, but you should do it soon, before holiday planning begins."

Coop's heart sank. He stood at the window to hide his tears.

"Elizabeth and I have found a women's art colony on the Gulf Coast. We'll buy it outright and live in the main house. We've had endless discussions about creating a nurturing environment for established artists, as well as offering scholarships to the most promising young women in the country." She stood, hugging him from behind with her cheek pressed to his back. "This is best for you, too. I don't have the strength to freshen this store and keep it steady through another war."

"Maybe I should sell."

"Will it hurt to let it go?"

"No."

"Then you should. It's an excellent location, and downtown is still growing, so the future is bright. And Tiller's reputation still stands tall. Give it to fresh minds with new ideas."

Simon had died two years before, and now Vic was leaving. *Why hold on?*

She turned him about. "You can't fool me, Coop. You're holding back tears. You're worried about losing the store."

"Losing your friendship, not the store. You deserve a gentle life with Elizabeth, but I have no other friends."

She pulled back. "That's not true."

"It's true for most men my age. Instead of friends, we have wives, children, and grandchildren. If I'd been true to my feelings like you were, things might be different." He pinched and rubbed his forehead. "I didn't mean to ask for your pity."

"You are still close to Millie. That's something."

"She's growing up, and she's undeniably fetching. She'll find a young man soon, as she should, and then where will I be?"

"Elena needs your care and attention, Coop. You owe her."

"I know. I will never abandon her."

Vic returned to her desk and held up the bottle. "One more?"

He nodded. They downed the shot, and Vic spluttered again. She found her voice and said, "Have you ever fantasized about an escape?"

"Well, yes. But I'm not sure where he is. Or if he's still alive."

"If something happens to Elena, and you have the opportunity, don't hesitate to seek him out."

Vic would never advise him to do something disreputable and so he left in a swoon, daring to imagine a reunion with Will, if it ever became possible.

The lost decades loomed, casting the darkest shadows on his dreams, every minute gone for eternity. Coop and Will could never recover the past, and if the regret was too deep, on what lonely, windswept road would Coop perish?

Coop and Will had been robust and virile the last time they were together. Would they even recognize each other as hobbling old men?

Vic retired, and Coop sold Tiller's department store. He told Elena but, as with most things, he wasn't sure she really understood. She never fully recovered her speech, and she avoided talking when possible. She often managed shambling along with a cane, but Coop and Millie took turns pushing her in a wheelchair when the walk was too long. To keep her in the bedroom on the second floor, Coop had a tiny elevator installed.

In June of 1944, Allied forces landed on the northern coast of France. The initial D-Day jubilation cooled as the outcome of the war seesawed. Commanding victories were followed by crushing defeats. When Germany let loose with the V-2 bombs late in the year, the agony of such destructive missiles created widespread dread. It wasn't until February of 1945 and the crippling of Germany's rail infrastructure with the massive bombing campaign in Dresden that the outcome felt certain again. The Nazis fell back inside their own borders. People wondered when Germany would surrender, but Coop knew the war would end only when Hitler was dead.

Once again, his mind drifted to the Collinwood children. He found an old book about the fire at the library, a tattered copy falling to pieces. He was shocked to realize nearly forty years had passed. It felt like no time at all.

The book featured rough schematics of all three floors of the school, as well as the basement. He imagined what everyone in the school saw, heard, and felt, from the moment the alarm rang. He memorized the paths of the students and teachers on every floor, picturing their journeys to safety or to death.

One afternoon, Coop and Elena were on the back porch quietly watching the lake when Maria, his wife's latest full-time helper, came outside and excitedly said, "The wireless just announced that Hitler has killed himself." Coop and Elena shared an ecstatic look, and he was pleased she immediately grasped the enormity of the moment.

Over the next week, German cities and armies capitulated piecemeal, but the full, unconditional surrender came on May 7. Millie ran off with a pack of joyful friends to celebrate with a huge crowd downtown. Coop, Elena, and Maria listened to the celebrations from the wireless on the porch.

The next year, Millie went to university to take classes in paleontology, and in her second year met a graduate student teacher named Bob Kohl. Coop wasn't surprised when after a two-year romance, they got engaged. Millie marrying a scientist suddenly seemed inevitable.

They planned an outdoor wedding on the back lawn, but Elena insisted Millie take her to New York to shop for wedding outfits. "We'll have so many more choices."

"Would you like me to come and help?" Coop said.

"No. Only me and my daughter, a true girls' getaway."

They returned after a week, with a mountain of boxes and bags. Millie bubbled with excitement, but Elena had a serious setback, losing her concentration and slumping to the side almost as much as those first months after the stroke.

They were on the back porch in their usual spot when he dared raise the topic of her health. "I felt my energy slipping away months ago, but I'm glad I forced myself to go. Coop, you must have learned I gave birth in 1932. Yes?"

He nodded. "Before you had the stroke."

"Have you never wondered what happened to the baby?"

Coop sat up. "Surely, the baby died. The doctor said you were seriously injured."

"My son is still alive. That's why I needed to go to New York."

"What?"

"He was Phillip's child. Phillip begged me to give the baby to him and his wife, who was barren. He argued I'd already given you a child, so it was only fair I let him keep his. His wife wanted the baby as well."

"His wife knew about you?"

"Yes, just as you did. The pregnancy was a nightmare. I was sick the whole summer, and I didn't have the strength to resist Philip's demands. I resolved to fight for my child after I returned home and could regain my health. After my stroke, I realized the boy was better off with a healthy mother."

"My God, Elena how you must have suffered."

"Not as much as Philip did. Only recently, I learned he lost all his money and shot himself just before the war. Two years ago, his wife died, impoverished. I had to see my son in the flesh. His name is Vander."

"Did you see Vander last week in New York?"

"I wanted to offer him some financial aid. He doesn't know who I am, but I know where he lives, and I made Millie take me to the same café every day in case I spotted him. I was sure I would recognize him, and I did, the instant I saw him walk by. He is nearly seventeen."

"Did you introduce yourself?"

"I didn't dare. I was so wrong, Coop."

"You did what felt sensible at the time."

"I don't mean that. Vander is your spitting image. We tried to conceive that one time early in 1932, remember? It was so clumsy and sloppy it never crossed my mind he might be yours. One look will confirm it." She reached into a pocket with agonizing care and removed a folded slip of paper. "Here is where you can find…our son."

He remembered Kenny giving him a list of his children, whom Coop had anonymously gifted ten thousand dollars each several years before to fulfill his promise to his brother.

Yet this was his child. He held the paper, speechless, wondering what his obligations were, whether he should rage or cry or simply walk into the lake until he sank beneath the waves.

"Please don't hate me," Elena said.

"I don't know how I feel, but I will never hate you. Does Millie know?"

She shook her head, tears in her eyes. "I would have told her if I'd had the courage to introduce myself, but I was too shocked."

Millie and Bob had a lavish wedding on the back lawn, and the next day left on an airplane for a honeymoon in Hawaii. When they returned, they moved into the family home. Coop was glad Bob didn't let pointless male pride keep Millie from living in the only home she'd ever known.

About two months after the wedding, Elena began a noticeable decline. Their discussion about Vander was their longest talk in years, and Coop was beginning to realize they'd never have another of any length.

By early 1950, Bob was deep into his PhD program and Millie wanted to finish her undergraduate degree before having children. As their first anniversary approached, Elena went into a rapid downward spiral, and she was soon slipping away. Her skin grew so frail Coop feared ripping it with a touch. She rarely spoke more than a word at a time, and she gave wispy smiles to familiar faces.

One morning, a nurse woke him with a knock on his door. He knew Elena had died before he saw the nurse, crying and shaking.

When Elena had had her stroke, Coop had ordered a mausoleum built down the hill from President Garfield's memorial building at Lake View Cemetery, at the very spot that had struck him as a good location when he'd attended the mass funeral for the Collinwood children. He'd shown it to Elena and Millie after it was finished, and they made approving noises when seeing the building that looked like a little Greek temple, with the name "Tiller" carved in deep beveled letters on the pediment.

After Elena's interment, Coop and Millie sent everyone away until they were alone, watching the cemetery workers lock the copper-plated doors. Millie leaned into him, weeping softly as Coop rubbed her arm.

Coop sniffled. "She deserved better than me."

She squeezed him tightly. "Whatever problems you had, you

redeemed yourself." He sensed the question coming. "Daddy, remember you said you'd be honest with me when I became an adult and asked about your problems with Mommy?"

"Yes." His heart raced. He'd rehearsed his response long ago. "I married your mother with a lie in my heart. I never loved her as a husband should. She sensed it from the start, but you were already a little girl when she confronted me. She didn't want a divorce, so she took her freedom back in the only way she could, and with my full blessing."

"What do you mean?" She wiped her nose with a hankie. "You loved each other."

"But not as husband and wife. You see," he took a deep breath. "I felt no passion for her. I felt no passion for any woman. I used her to hide from the world, and it's my life's biggest shame."

Millie's tears had stopped. "You never felt passion?"

"Only for other men."

Millie took a step back.

He plowed ahead. "When I finally admitted the truth to her, she found release with another man, who was unhappily married himself." He thought of Simon and many others. "It happens more than people realize. If I hadn't promised to be honest with you, I'd have carried the secret until I was in there, next to your mother."

Millie tottered, and Coop gripped her arm. She yanked free. It felt like she was ripping his heart in two, yet he was glad to unburden himself. "Darling, if you want the full story, I will tell you. Maybe not now, but after you've had time to consider."

"You think I'll be content after I consider this sordid story for a while?"

"It isn't sordid. Your mother and I were tossed into this world with no plan, no maps, no way to navigate except to feel our way about. I love you more than I love anything, but with your mother gone, I owe no apologies to a living soul. I did my best."

With a gasp, she ran off. He followed slowly but Millie had already driven off in his car. He went to the office and called a cab. While he waited, he examined the red granite memorial for the unidentified children of Collinwood, reading the names again and again.

He returned to his empty home, walking to his room, where he found a note taped to his door in his son-in-law's writing: *We're taking the ferry to Kelly's Island and will stay at one of the inns for a bit.*

He wondered how much she'd revealed to her husband, but it didn't matter. Coop's false world had collided with his true feelings at last. When the picture focused, it was the fake world in rubble, while his true life stood unharmed.

Inside his room, he opened a dresser drawer and removed a hidden stack of snapshots of him and Will in those first years of the coal mine, as well as of their trip to Lower Saranac Lake. A rush of excitement he hadn't felt in years surprised him with its clarity and filled him with resolve. Even his darling daughter's disgust didn't tarnish the only genuine life and love he'd ever known.

How brief that time was.

The very next morning, an early call woke Coop. It was the first shift manager at the coal mine, and he described a shattered access road, as well as months of tremors and minor cave-ins. Coop closed the mine until he could arrange for safety inspectors.

The next day, Coop was still trying to find a full inspector's team when news came of the mine's implosion. A supervisor over the phone said, "All that remains is to seal it up."

He started planning a trip for Cadiz when a thought stopped him. He grabbed his camera and drove east. Traffic around downtown was busy, but he didn't mind creeping along. It gave him a chance to think.

After the stock market collapsed in 1929, Coop had snapped up shares for next to nothing. His accounts grew until he divested almost all his real estate in favor of stocks. With a fortune of more than fifty million dollars, he needed to make some decisions soon.

With downtown behind him, he got off the freeway and reached his destination a few minutes later. A low, ornamental fence threaded with vines surrounded what, at first glance, looked like an elegant and well-kept garden. Only when Coop entered through the elaborate brick and wrought-iron gate did the reality come into focus. The memorial garden on the site of the Collinwood fire was overgrown and unkempt.

A path surrounded a central area thick with wildflowers and cattails. An older woman sat on a bench to the right, seemingly deep in thought. Coop went left to avoid disturbing her. In the middle of the square, tiny green and white blooms floated in a pond.

He sat on a bench, dimly remembering how the gardens were designed with a lily pond in the exact spot of the back stairs, where most of the children had perished. All about, weeds and native plants burst from flower beds. He could just make out the barest remains of small hedges, the dead branches trimmed into shape.

It reminded him of the beautiful, wild meadows around Lightning Mountain, and it seemed more suitable somehow than a fancy garden.

Something tiny splashed, and the little flowers undulated with the ripples. The movement was hypnotic, as if the children had noticed him and were reaching for help.

"May I join you?"

The lady who'd been sitting on the bench smiled warmly while clutching a patent leather handbag. She wore a blue skirt and a blazer with a white blouse. A small hat trimmed with netting sat atop her dark hair, streaked with gray.

"Of course," Coop said. She sat, and what could have felt cramped and awkward was natural, even comforting. They could be the best of friends, he thought.

"My name is Ingrid. Were you a student here?"

"No, but I've never been able to forget the fire."

"I hope you're not shocked by the state of the memorial gardens. They tidy up every so often, but it requires so much upkeep. I think I prefer when nature roughens the edges this way. It feels more appropriate than all that fussiness. We were mostly poor immigrants. My parents always felt they had to get dressy to visit, and it prevented them from coming many times."

"Did your family know someone who died?"

"My older sister, Maddy. She was in fourth grade, on the second floor. Today is her birthday. She died on the back stairs." She nodded to the pond. "Right there."

"I'm sorry."

"I was in the third grade, on the first floor. Very few of my classmates survived. Not even my teacher." Her smile faltered. "I can still hear the sounds, but I've gotten used to them. It's the things I've never talked about that still keep me awake at night." She paused. "Perhaps telling a stranger will come more easily. May I share a story about that day?"

"Of course."

"When the fire gong rang, we lined up to march down the back stairs. But the moment our teacher opened the door and the smoke poured in, all order dissolved. Realizing there was an actual fire was a shock. There was a central open area and neither staircase was enclosed. I saw the fire swallow the front one like it was ravenous from hunger. For years, people have wondered why the students panicked. I've never heard anyone give the real reason, which is that the fire looked and sounded like a beast rising from hell. You can't imagine the terror. I remember the heat on my skin and smelling my hair singe. It wasn't until the next morning that I saw how the front of my dress was browned. Like toast."

He felt a chill to be a pair of eyes away from the long-ago horror.

"I heard a teacher say, 'To the windows.' I ran back to my classroom, where a window was already open. It was a good eight or ten feet to the ground and not a little daunting, but what choice did I have? I saw people running from every direction to help, but I couldn't wait for them to catch me. I jumped."

"Were you injured?"

"Not a scratch or a sprain. When I realized I was safe, I was exhilarated until I remembered my sister and my friends. And also... well, this is the main thing I've never told anyone. Just before I returned to my classroom, I saw my teacher on the back stairs, throwing children from her path, the way men throw sacks of mail from train cars. The newspapers said she died trying to rescue students, but it didn't look that way to me."

"You think she was swept up in the panic?"

"I go around and around. At the bottom of the back stairs was a vestibule with double doors. The back doors were open but one of the vestibule doors had fallen back into place and tripped the spring latch. It blocked half the escape route. Maybe she was trying to unlatch the door and free the backup, but isn't it more likely she was trying to escape a fiery death? She was twenty-six years old and still had a lifetime to live."

They went quiet for a long time. "Did you feel guilty that your sister died?"

"My mother always said Maddy would have wanted me to live. But even more, I wanted to live. From the moment I saw the flames until I landed on the ground outside, my only thought was to save myself. That's how it should be, don't you think? There's no hope for anything if you don't survive. There's no redemption, no forgiveness, no love. If at all possible, you must survive. Caring for others doesn't mean you should surrender your life. That's what the fire taught me."

Coop thought he could hear dozens of whispered assents in the air.

A young man was taking a shortcut through the gardens, and Coop asked him to snap several photos of him and Ingrid. When he was done, the young man said, "Why do they call these the memorial gardens?"

Coop was shocked, but Ingrid said pleasantly, "There's a plaque just there that explains." He thanked her and left.

"I can't believe he didn't know," Coop said. "More than one hundred and seventy children died."

"So many people have forgotten."

"But it changed all the school fire laws in the country. All over the world. Schools in London and Paris closed for inspections."

She patted his hand. "I'm glad you remember, Coop. I'm so pleased to have met you. I feel we have a strange bond. I can't explain it."

Coop remembered his immediate sense of connection to her. "Me, too," he said.

He drove home, his mind full of Ingrid's story about her teacher's desperate scramble to live. He also thought about Ingrid jumping from the window. Her only thought was to save herself, and she'd felt no guilt afterward. "That's how it should be," she'd said.

Back home in his office, he began a letter to his daughter. His story poured from his pen, beginning with his life on the farm. He stopped only when his arm grew too tired, and he slept for a while before waking early to finish.

He left out the news about her brother Vander. It felt too brutal to add that to the mix of what he was asking her to understand. It could wait.

His missive to his daughter ran more than twenty pages, and he realized it might come in handy for the son he'd never met. He copied them in a letter that started with *Dear Vander*.

His arm was cramped when he set aside Vander's letter and

slipped the original pages into a manila envelope and wrote *Millie* on the cover.

Ingrid jumped, he told his himself as he dropped it on a table in the front hall.

He packed nothing but his letter for Vander, legal and banking ledgers, and some clothes. He also took a small pack of photos of his life with Elena and Millie, as well as his secret photos with Will. It all fit in a small bag with a carrying strap.

As the train left Cleveland for Cadiz, Coop felt the spirit of adventure rise in him again, as resolute as ever.

1950–1955

After two weeks of setting things in motion to close and seal the mine, Coop left Cadiz for New York City.

He found his son's address in Greenwich Village, a brownstone walk-up on Christopher Street. Elena had helpfully written down the name of the café where she'd seen Vander walk by. Coop took an outside table for a late dinner.

Anticipating a long wait, he ordered appetizers and a huge meal. The waiter had no sooner set down a small dish of something in a yellow sauce than a younger version of himself walked past with a male friend.

It seemed as if his son had stepped out of one of his snapshots from the coal mine, except Vander was trimmer, neater, more compact and fashionable than Coop had ever been. His longish, light hair was Hollywood-style contoured, and he wore an open-necked shirt under a sweater vest. He cut a fine figure in high-waisted, pleated slacks. His friend was equally stylish, but much taller with dark hair.

Coop jumped up, clutching his bag, watching Vander melt into the evening crowds. Frantic, he used the silverware to weigh down a one hundred dollar bill on the table and rushed after them.

What could he say to Vander? Did his son know he was adopted? How would he feel to have a strange man introduce himself as his father?

The crowd had swallowed Vander, but his tall friend provided an easy beacon. They rounded a corner and almost immediately stepped down, below the sidewalk. Coop arrived a moment later, at the top of a cement staircase that led to a bar, the door propped open to the temperate night.

Inside, a mini grand piano took up precious space in the small, dark-paneled room. A handful of customers sat at the bar or tiny tables, but others were already coming in behind him, and it would fill up quickly.

Vander and his friend slid onto stools at the edge of the bar, and Coop hurried to take a spot close enough to hear his son order two beers. The bartender, a man with an old-fashioned handlebar mustache, grinned lustily at his son. "Coming right up, blue eyes."

Vander and his friend laughed, and Coop dropped his face to hide his shock. He peeked out into the room and saw two men holding hands below the surface of a table, not blatant but not hidden.

With a start, he realized all the customers were men.

A life-affirming thrill burned through him that took all his strength to contain. Coop ordered his favorite whisky with a beer chaser, listening to his son complain about his landlord.

"He wants another five dollars a week!" Vander said indignantly. "I told him that's not a fair price for a studio with a shared bath."

In a richly inflected voice, his friend said, "Unless you're sharing with that dreamboat Ralph who lives downstairs. Then it's worth ten dollars more each week."

They burst out laughing, and Coop left, exultant, knowing what to do.

Two nights later in the early evening, Coop went to the same café, where the waiter recognized him and seated him at the same table with extreme solicitousness.

"You left a hefty tip last time," the waiter said, clearly worried about a mistake.

"Don't expect a repeat. I had to run off rather unexpectedly."

He ordered another huge meal and had just started on the salad when Vander walked past, this time alone.

"Vander," he said, taking another one hundred dollar bill from his wallet and slipping it under a plate.

His son stopped, casting a bewildered look back.

Coop approached him with a smile, pulling a large, thick envelope from his bag. Vander gave it a glance. "May we talk?" Coop said. "It's about your parents."

"My parents are dead."

Coop gestured to a park across the street. "I promise it will take only as long as you want."

A small marker announced the tiny, triangular park as Sheridan Square, and Coop and Vander sat on a bench. Coop held up the envelope. "Inside you'll find a key as well as a note of ownership in your name to a loft apartment near Fifth Avenue. You'll also find a few snapshots along with a letter that explains my life and where you came from. Did your parents ever explain you were adopted?"

Vander looked stunned but intrigued. "Yes, but I never gave it any mind. My father went broke and died, and my mom struggled to raise me. It eventually killed her. She sacrificed to give me the best life she could. I don't care who gave birth to me."

"I understand," Coop said sympathetically, rummaging through the envelope until he removed an old photo of him and Will on the shores of Lower Saranac Lake, shirtless, Coop resting on Will's chest. "Look at this."

As Coop had hoped, Vander's eyes went wide. He pointed to Coop in the photo. "Who is this man?"

"That's me, and the other man is the greatest love of my life. My resemblance to you must tell you something."

"Are you saying you're my real father?"

Coop handed him the envelope and took the photo back. "This photo is precious to me, and I'll keep it. I wrote a letter that explains myself as best as I can." He stood. "I'll write when I settle. Maybe you'll decide to visit me someday. I hope so."

Coop left, deciding at that moment to include Vander in his will. He thought of George and the way his brother the duke inherited everything. To avoid such monumental unfairness, he would carve out amounts for his descendants, to pass around his fortune to as many people as possible.

He also decided that nobody would inherit his complete estate upon his death. At his age, it might come too soon, and dumping fortunes onto Millie and Vander's backs might crush them. Since he gave the apartment to Vander, it seemed only fair to give Millie the house she loved.

It would be better for them both if he forbade inheritance of his full estate until one of them died, with a trust of three million dollars each to tide them over. By then, the survivor would be responsible enough to manage so much money.

He'd heard other wealthy men gripe about wills and inheritance and greedy offspring. Coop thought his plan settled things nicely.

❖

Coop stepped from the car at Lower Saranac Lake just as the leading wind of a thunderstorm blew a mingled scent of thick pine and peppery sweet poplar. It revived his memories of the summer he spent with Will at the lake house. He saw the promontory through the trees, but the large house where George and Phil hosted wealthy gay men was gone, replaced with a cabin fronting the lake. A shed and an elevated rainwater tank sat off to the side, just like on the Lightning.

He walked down the gravel drive. His heart felt like it would pump out of his chest. A soothing ruffle of cool air brushed up from the lake as the storm clouds rolled in from the west.

Curled in a fading sun shaft next to the cabin, an alert, mid-sized black mutt lifted its head and barked uncertainly, almost as if Coop looked like he belonged. A large blond Lab came padding and stiffened with alarm, issuing a more threatening bark.

"What's all the racket?"

The voice paralyzed Coop. From around the side of the cabin came a man wearing baggy work clothes. His long gray hair blew about his face, and Coop felt a tingle at the memory of moonlight riding Will's dark, teenage waves. Even from a good twenty feet away, Will's eyes revealed his familiar soul. The years ran off like quicksilver.

Will recognized Coop at first glance. "I always wondered if I'd see you standing there someday."

"Do I look like you expected?"

Will cocked his head. "I never conjured an image. But it's good to see you, Coop."

"You live alone?"

"No. I live with Runty and Sandy." Hearing their names, the dogs looked up. "You wanna come inside for a bit?"

"I'd like to stay longer than a bit."

Will hesitated. "You better come in. Supposed to be a hell of a storm later."

Will led him inside to a roomy space with a kitchen with all the latest appliances, a beautiful living room, and two large bedrooms.

Will said, "It's not our mansion in Cadiz, but it's home."

Coop snorted. "I have another mansion, in Cleveland. This suits me better."

Will motioned for him to sit on the sofa. "I have some venison, if you're hungry."

"I'm not hungry for venison."

Will sat in a chair that creaked. "Why are you here, Coop?"

"My wife died. My daughter is married. I have another child, but that's a longer story. Right now, I only want to hear about you."

Will leaned back. "After I left, I lived in Pittsburgh for ten years. I decided to explore Los Angeles. The movie industry. It was all egos, deadlines, investment after investment. I thought I could handle anything, but I didn't know which way to turn without you. While I still had some money left, I came here, tore down the old house, and built this cabin. How did you know where to find me?"

"It seemed the most logical place. Did you ever meet someone else?"

Will looked away. "I thought so a few times. An actor whose name you would recognize. A producer. But not like you."

"I never found anyone like you, either."

"I saw your wedding announcement in the paper. She seemed a beautiful young lady."

"I ruined her life."

Will blew a huge breath. "You saved mine. For a while."

"We can save each other again, for whatever time we have left."

"Can we?"

"Yes. If we want. It might take some time, but as long as we can try, we should."

A brilliant flicker of lightning filled the room with a pulsating dance, followed by an instantaneous crash of thunder. The lights went out.

"The electricity always goes out in a storm," Will said, standing. "I have a generator."

Coop shot to his feet and pulled him tight, cupping the back of his head. "I've never feared the dark, nor the lightning."

Will smiled. "The Lightning gave us life."
They leaned in for a kiss.

❖

After five years, Coop thought spring mornings on Lower Saranac Lake rivaled the Lightning for beautiful calm. He sat at a small table on the porch with a cup of coffee.

The smooth water revealed a perfect, upside-down world until a gentle wind stirred impressionist ripples. A blizzard of thistledown tumbled on the breeze. A duck stepped into the lake followed by her chirping chicks.

Vander had left the day before after one of his short visits, excited about a handsome new coworker at the Frick Museum who was whip smart but unpretentious and shy.

"How do you know when you love someone?" Vander had asked Coop yesterday morning while they sipped coffee in this spot.

"It's like you've been hit by a brick, like you can't imagine how you got through life before you met him."

Vander smiled. "That's exactly how it feels, but how do I know if he feels the same way?"

"Remember what I told you? Ingrid jumped? Give it a try. You'll know soon enough if he feels the same way, and if he does, don't ever let him go. Nothing you do in life will feel worth it without him."

Vander went silent for a long time. "I wish I'd met Elena. I know you didn't have a great marriage, but all the same she gave birth to me. Maybe someday I can meet Millie. She's my full sister, and it's weird I've never laid eyes on her."

"She's busy with the new baby, but she promised to visit again. I'll let you know and maybe you can coordinate trips. I'd like that."

"You're sure it won't be awkward?"

"At my age, being surrounded by people I love is life itself."

Vander had given Coop and Will tight hugs before he left.

The breeze picked up just as Will stepped out to the porch with a mug of coffee. Coop gave him a smile and squeezed his hand when he sat in the other chair.

Will laughed. "You always get maudlin and romantic after your son leaves."

"I'm glad I have a son who asks for and appreciates my honest opinions. We're an important example for him."

Will burped. "A couple of old farts living in a lakeside cabin. He can aspire to higher things."

"I never did. This is what I wanted since we were teenagers. Remember what Elmer said?"

"Elmer? You mean that old hillbilly?"

"Remember what he told you?"

Will scrunched his face. "What?"

"He said, 'This is where you belong.' It's been true our whole lives."

They smiled and gripped hands.

CHAPTER THIRTEEN

New York, New York; Saranac Lake; and Cleveland, Ohio
Present day

Darcy and his great-uncle Vander sit alone in the building just off Fifth Avenue. Sagging groups of frayed furniture create small pods in the massive apartment. Darcy sits among a group of couches and chairs, with Vander alongside in his wheelchair.

Vander let Darcy read the letter Cooper Tiller gave him in Sheridan Square, and afterward, he told Darcy everything he'd learned about his father's life in the years he visited Coop and Will at Lower Saranac Lake before they died.

Darcy's thrilled by his great-grandfather's triumph in finding his boyhood love, sharing their final ten years together as unapologetic gay pioneers. Even the bittersweet ache of the lost decades shrinks in the brilliant sheen of the same confidence that founded a coal mine and a department store.

Yet fear sours Darcy's happiness, the heavy knowledge about his own miserable romantic relationships with other men. He thinks of Jake, who left Vander's apartment hours ago to give them privacy, and regrets squeeze his heart.

"Are you thinking of that handsome young man you arrived with?" Vander says.

Startled, Darcy nods.

"Remember what I told you about my father's advice?"

"Ingrid jumped."

Vander smiles. "If you love him, jump. The decades will fly past either way. Better to have him by your side."

Haltingly, Darcy tells him about Jake's sister, dead of an overdose, and how he'd admitted his own drug use but hasn't had time to learn how Jake feels about it.

Vander remains serene. "He didn't leave."

Maybe he did. He's been gone a while.

At the end of the cavernous room is the dining area with several tables and chairs that lead to the kitchen on a diagonal. Blocking a straight route is a massive pile of ornate metal pilasters, statues, and framed paintings, which Darcy knows were the decorative elements stripped from the building, leaving it bare. Darcy recognizes the dog with crossed scars on his head from the glass panels at the family mansion, here painted in oil, and clearly an animal dear to Cooper Tiller's heart.

Darcy says, "Why are you claiming all of Cooper Tiller's estate?"

"It was Charles's idea. He has a grand plan to build an LGBT center, with senior housing, a shelter for kids thrown out of their homes, even a high school. It's why I married him, to give him some money to work with in case I died before Millie."

"It isn't fair to my family," Darcy says, surprised to be so calm.

"I told him to respect my father's wishes, but he's so driven. I also told him I don't think he has any hope of getting the entire estate."

At realizing Charles's major mistake, Darcy sits up and laughs. "He stripped away all these decorative elements and piled them up in here so this building can be demolished. The local arts council won't be any the wiser."

Vander gives a loud laugh. "He told me he was going to have them restored, but by God, I think you're right. This land is far more valuable without the building. He is devious, but in a generous way. I'm certain he meant only to raise as much money for the center as he could. But either way, I'm far too old to move, and nothing's happening to this building until I'm gone. You'll have to fight it out after that."

"There won't be any fighting. I'm not opposed to selling this land." He grins. "Don't tell Charles."

Vander says, "I'll persuade him to drop his legal challenges. It's my inheritance, after all. You really do look so much like my father."

"Grandma Millie always told me the same thing."

"I never met my sister Millie. We exchanged sporadic letters, but we never quite managed to get together. Her daughter was your mother, is that right?"

"Yes." Darcy tells him about this family, and how they grew up in middle-class, suburban Cleveland. "We assumed there was no money left from Cooper Tiller's estate."

Vander tells Darcy to pull a stack of thick photo albums from a low shelving unit. They huddle at a coffee table, and Darcy flips through the pages slowly. The photos begin with Vander's young life as the adopted child of the Davenports. They pose in beautiful rooms, at seaside resorts, in fancy clothes and stylish hairstyles. Halfway through the first album, Darcy flips a page, and the rich surroundings vanish, along with the father. Vander and his mother pose in front of a brick wall, in a stairwell with chipped paint.

"These photos come after my father lost everything and committed suicide. Even if you knew nothing about us, it's all visible."

In the later photos, Mrs. Davenport wears simple dresses, her hair cut short and sensible. She gives brave smiles, but her natural vivacity has faded to a thin glisten. Vander goes to great lengths to defend the Davenports, and Darcy listens respectfully but after a while can only think about how long Jake has been away.

Soon, Jake returns. Vander gives Darcy a wink as Jakes steps into the room with their overnight bags and groceries. He says, "Don't mind me, I'm going to make us dinner."

Darcy locks his eyes with Jake's but the glance is fleeting and unreadable as Jake heads to the kitchen.

Over the sound of Jake chopping, Darcy flips to a page with photos of Coop and Will as rugged young men. "My father gave me these photos from their youth," Vander says. "I took the later ones when I visited their cabin on Lower Saranac Lake." As older men, Coop and Will smile on the cabin porch, wave from a rowboat, and pose with two dogs.

Darcy points to a couple of photos of an older Coop standing next to a woman with gray-streaked hair, in a raggedy but formal garden.

"Let me see those," Vander says. After Darcy carefully removes the pictures, Vander peers at them and says, "I have no idea who that lady is or where this was taken." He puts them on the coffee table.

Darcy gasps at a photo at the bottom of the page. "That's my Grandma Millie and Grandpa Bob! And there's my mom!" His grandparents stand next to Coop and Will in front of Lower Saranac

Lake. Coop holds the toddler who would grow up to marry the sailor and give birth to Darcy and his sisters.

Vander says, "Millie was upset after our father told her about Will, but she got over it, apparently with the encouragement of her husband."

"She accepted me right away when I told her I was gay." Darcy blinks away tears. "I wish she'd told me her own father was gay."

"It was a different time," Vander says. "Some things were unspoken. I'm glad those days are behind us."

Jake calls them to the table, which is set with a bowl of pasta and veggies, breadsticks, and two open bottles of red wine.

On the first bite, Darcy says, "This is really good."

Vander seconds the sentiment.

They finish dinner, drink wine, and talk until it grows dark. The mood grows languid with yawns.

Jake starts to clean up dinner, but Darcy says, "I'll take care of that. Why don't you lie down?"

Jake looks relieved and sinks away into the couch. Almost immediately, soft snores rise.

Vander covers a yawn and says it's time for him to go to bed.

"First, can you tell me something? All my life I thought Cooper Tiller was interred in the family mausoleum in Cleveland, but he wasn't. Do you know where he's buried?"

"He's with Will in a tiny cemetery twenty minutes from Lake Saranac Village. I can't remember the name. It's a little mountain hamlet." Darcy takes out his phone, does a quick search for nearby cemeteries, and finds one a bit north. Vander squints at the map. "That must be it, but it's been so long."

"Thank you for everything," Darcy says, giving Vander a hug as Vander pats his back.

"Thank you, Darcy, for coming to visit. I haven't had such a good time in years."

Vander rolls off in his wheelchair, and after washing the dishes, Darcy sits on the couch opposite a sleeping Jake, the coffee table between them scattered with photo albums. Darcy picks up the two pictures of Coop and the mystery lady in the formal gardens. He leans back, wondering if he can rest after everything he's learned.

In the darkened hush of two thirty in the morning, he's wide awake with excitement and wonder. Learning the true story of his great-grandfather, concealed for more than a century, is likely the richest reward he'll ever have, but he's seized with sudden doubts. Intellectually, he knows it's real, but he must see something, touch something, to make it three-dimensional truth.

In a flash, he knows what to do. He finds Jake's keys and slips into the night.

❖

Hours later, near the end of the mountain cemetery's third row, Darcy finds a double grave carved with two names. On the right it reads: *Cooper Clayton Tiller.*

Overcome, Darcy sinks to his knees. He runs his fingers along the deep letters of his great-grandfather's name. Tears blind him until he wipes them away and reads the name to the left: *Rex William Herrington.*

He places one hand on each name, feeling he's ushering Coop and Will into the family memory where they'll live in the open at last.

He takes a picture of the headstone and thinks for a moment before sending it to his sisters with the message *I have so much to tell you.*

He ignores the many texts, presumably from Jake who woke up to find Darcy gone with his truck, until he feels the sun radiating on his back and sweating trickling from his armpits.

He pats the granite, which is cool to the touch even in the heat. "Thank you," he says aloud.

❖

The next day as they return from New York, Jake exits the highway before they reach downtown Cleveland. In a few minutes, they find a spot to park.

When Darcy returned to Manhattan yesterday after his jaunt to the Adirondacks, he was prepared for Jake's rage for taking his truck. Jake might regret the time he'd spent wooing him, wary about daily drug use and the irrational stunt with the truck. He might take his keys and leave Darcy in New York.

Instead, Jake had held up the photos of Cooper Tiller with the old lady in the garden and said, "This is a photo of Cooper Tiller with my great-great-grandma Ingrid. I know exactly where this picture was taken."

The next day, back in Cleveland at the site of the Collinwood school fire, they walk up a path to a rectangular, raised garden. In the top planter area, a small tree towers above trimmed bushes and flowers. Cascading down the sloped sides, tiles bear the names of the victims.

"They tore out those formal gardens a long time ago," Jake says. "This memorial is in the exact spot of the lily pond, which means this is the spot of the back stairs where most of the children died. Where Aunt Maddy died."

The greenery draws Darcy in, his vision unfocused. Wind blows the branches and leaves, as if the children are still reaching for help from the pile wedged in the vestibule. He aches with grief. Have these souls been swirling here for more than a century, clinging to this spot, unable to leave?

No, we are not stranded, comes the answer in too many voices to count. Darcy hears children, adults, parents, those who tried to save them, and those who never forgot. He hears a male voice above all, his great grandfather, he knows: *A soul is unbounded and timeless. If the living come here in pain, we comfort them.*

In barely a whisper, Jake says, "Every time I come here, I feel like I can almost hear them."

Jake, his face patinated by years of emotion about the fire, trudges to a bench facing the memorial. Darcy sits next to him and takes his hand. "I swear I'm not lying about the coke. I used it every day, but it wasn't hard to kick. I'm not saying I'm better than people who get hooked, but I promise I don't use drugs anymore."

Jake works their fingers together. "I believe you. You don't have to keep explaining. I'm sorry if I made it seem like you did."

A soft smile grows on Jake's face. If this were a movie, Darcy thinks, the music would become stirring, with strings and soaring voices. The hush around the memorial feels much more natural, the way even the greatest love stories from history started, with gripped hands and hearts pounding, and leaves pattering in the wind. Darcy stands, breaks off a leafy twig, and hands it to Jake. Jake twirls it in his fingers before brushing it across his lips, giving Darcy a shy smile.

About the Author

Bud Gundy is a Lambda Literary Award finalist and has won two Emmy Awards. He works as an executive producer at KQED, the PBS and NPR affiliate in San Francisco. He was raised in North Olmsted, Ohio, as the youngest of ten children.

Books Available From Bold Strokes Books

Inherit the Lightning by Bud Gundy. Darcy O'Brien and his sisters learn they are about to inherit an immense fortune, but a family mystery about to unravel after seventy years threatens to destroy everything. (978-1-63679-199-9)

Pursued: Lillian's Story by Felice Picano. Fleeing a disastrous marriage to the Lord Exchequer of England, Lillian of Ravenglass reveals an incident-filled, often bizarre, tale of great wealth and power, perfidy, and betrayal. (978-1-63679-197-5)

Murder on Monte Vista by David S. Pederson. Private Detective Mason Adler's angst at turning fifty is forgotten when his "birthday present," the handsome, young Henry Bowtrickle, turns up dead, and it's up to Mason to figure out who did it, and why. (978-1-63679-124-1)

Three Left Turns to Nowhere by Jeffrey Ricker, J. Marshall Freeman & 'Nathan Burgoine. Three strangers heading to a convention in Toronto are stranded in rural Ontario, where a small town with a subtle kind of magic leads each to discover what he's been searching for. (978-1-63679-050-3)

One Verse Multi by Sander Santiago. Life was good: promotion, friends, falling in love, discovering that the multi-verse is on a fast track to collision—wait, what? Good thing Martin King works for a company that can fix the problem, right...um...right? (978-1-63679-069-5)

Fresh Grave in Grand Canyon by Lee Patton. The age-old Grand Canyon becomes more and more ominous as a group of volunteers fight to survive alone in nature and uncover a murderer among them. (978-1-63679-047-3)

Loyalty, Love & Vermouth by Eric Peterson. A comic valentine to a gay man's family of choice, including the ones with cold noses and four paws. (978-1-63555-997-2)

Bury Me in Shadows by Greg Herren. College student Jake Chapman is forced to spend the summer at his dying grandmother's home and soon finds danger from long-buried family secrets. (978-1-63555-993-4)

A Different Man by Andrew L. Huerta. This diverse collection of stories chronicling the challenges of gay life at various ages shines a light on the progress made and the progress still to come. (978-1-63555-977-4)

Busy Ain't the Half of It by Frederick Smith and Chaz Lamar Cruz. Elijah and Justin seek happily-ever-afters in LA, but are they too busy to notice happiness when it's there? (978-1-63555-944-6)

Pursuit: A Victorian Entertainment by Felice Picano. An intelligent, handsome, ruthlessly ambitious young man who rose from the slums to become the right-hand man of the Lord Exchequer of England will stop at nothing as he pursues his Lord's vanished wife across Continental Europe. (978-1-63555-870-8)

Best of the Wrong Reasons by Sander Santiago. For Fin Ness and Orion Starr, it takes a funeral to remind them that love is worth living for. (978-1-63555-867-8)

Coming to Life on South High by Lee Patton. Twenty-one-year-old gay virgin Gabe Rafferty's first adult decade unfolds as an unpredictable journey into sex, love, and livelihood. (978-1-63555-906-4)

His Brother's Viscount by Stephanie Lake. Hector Somerville wants to rekindle his illicit love affair with Viscount Wentworth, but he must overcome one problem: Wentworth still loves Hector's brother. (978-1-63555-805-0)

Quake City by St John Karp. Can Andre find his best friend Amy before the night devolves into a nightmare of broken hearts, malevolent drag queens, and spontaneous human combustion? Or has it always happened this way, every night, at Aunty Bob's Quake City Club? (978-1-63555-723-7)

Accidental Prophet by Bud Gundy. Days after his grandmother dies, Drew Morten learns his true identity and finds himself racing against time to save civilization from the apocalypse. (978-1-63555-452-6)

Somewhere Over Lorain Road by Bud Gundy. Over forty years after murder allegations shattered the Esker family, can Don Esker find the true killer and clear his dying father's name? (978-1-63555-124-2)